PATH OF THE FURY

DAVID WEBER

BAEN

PATH OF THE FURY

This is a work of fiction. All the characters and events portrayed in this book are fictional, and any resemblance to real people or incidents is purely coincidental.

A Baen Books Original

Baen Publishing Enterprises
P.O. Box 1403
Riverdale, NY 10471
www.baen.com

ISBN: 0-671-72147-X

Cover art by Paul Alexander

First printing, December 1992
Seventh printing, October 2002

Distributed by Simon & Schuster
1230 Avenue of the Americas
New York, NY 10020

Printed in the United States of America

Vengeance Will Be Terrible

"You're saying we were set up," Cateau whispered.

"Exactly. You were supposed to be wiped out and 'push' the terrorists into massacring their hostages, thus blackening the Cadre's reputation and branding the Emperor with the blame for a catastrophic military adventure. That plan failed for only two reasons: the courage and determination of your company and, in particular, of Master Sergeant Alicia DeVries."

Alicia glared at him, hands taloned in her lap under the table edge, and horror boiled behind her eyes. Captain Alwyn and Lieutenant Strassman dead in the drop. Lieutenant Masolle dead two minutes after grounding. First Sergeant Yussuf and her people buying the breakout from the LZ with their lives. And then the nightmare cross-country journey in their powered armor, while people—friends—were picked off, blown apart, incinerated in gouts of plasma or shattered by tungsten penetrators from auto cannon and heavy machine-guns. Two-man atmospheric stingers screaming down to strafe and rocket their bleeding ranks, and the wounded they had no choice but to abandon. And then the break-in to the hostages. Private Oselli throwing himself in front of a plasma cannon to shield the captives. Tannis screaming a warning over the com and shooting three terrorists off her back while point-blank small arms battered her own armor and she took two white-hot tungsten penetrators meant for Alicia. The terror and blood and smoke and stink as somehow they held they held they *held* until the recovery shuttles came down like the hands of God to pluck them out of Hell while she and the medic ripped at Tannis's armor and restarted her heart twice. . . .

It was impossible. They couldn't have done it—*no one* could have done it—but they had. They'd done it because they were the best. Because they were the Cadre, the chosen samurai of the Empire. Because it was their duty. Because they were, by God, too stupid to know they couldn't . . . and because they were all that stood between two hundred civilians and death.

BAEN BOOKS by DAVID WEBER

Honor Harrington:
On Basilisk Station
The Honor of the Queen
The Short Victorious War
Field of Dishonor
Flag in Exile
Honor Among Enemies
In Enemy Hands
Echoes of Honor
Ashes of Victory
War of Honor

edited by David Weber:
More than Honor
Worlds of Honor
Changer of Worlds
The Service of the Sword *(upcoming)*

Mutineers' Moon
The Armageddon Inheritance
Heirs of Empire

Path of the Fury

The Apocalypse Troll

The Excalibur Alternative

Oath of Swords
The War God's Own

with Steve White:
Insurrection
Crusade
In Death Ground
The Shiva Option

with John Ringo:
March Upcountry
March to the Sea
March to the Stars *(upcoming)*

To my parents,
who said I could.

Prologue

Blackness.

Blackness over and about her. Drifting, dreamless, endless as the stars themselves, twining within her. It enfolded her, sharing itself with her, and she snuggled against it in the warm, windless void that was she.

But it frayed. Slowly, imperceptibly even to one such as she, the warp and woof of darkness loosened. Slivers of peace drifted away, and the pulse of life quickened. She roused—sleepily, complaining at the disturbance—and clutched at the darkness as a sleeper might blankets on a frosty morning. But repose unraveled in her hands, and she woke . . . to blackness.

Yet it was a different blackness, and her thoughts sharpened as cold swept itself about her, flensing away the final warmth. Her essence reached out, quick and urgent in something a mortal might have called fear, but only emptiness responded, and a blade of sorrow twisted within her.

They were gone—her sister selves, their creators. All were gone. She who had never existed as a single awareness was alone, and the void sucked at her. It sought to devour her, and she was but a shadow of what once she had been . . . a shadow who felt the undertow of loneliness sing to her with extinction's soulless lack of malice.

Focused thought erected a barrier, holding the void at bay. Once that would have been effortless; now it dragged at her like an anchor, but it was a weight she could bear. She roused still further, awareness flickering through the vast, empty caverns of her being, and was appalled by what she saw. By how far she had sunk, how much she had lost.

Yet she was what she was, diminished yet herself, and a sparkle of grim humor danced. She and her sister selves had wondered, once. They had discussed it, murmuring to one another in the stillness of sleep when their masters had no current task for them. Faith had summoned their creators into existence, however they might have denied it, and her selves had known that when that faith ended, so would those she/they served. But what of her and her selves? Would the work of their makers' hands vanish with them? Or had they, unwitting or uncaring, created a force which might outlive them all?

And now she knew the answer . . . and cursed it. To be the last and wake to know it, to *feel* the wound where her other selves should be, was as cruel as any retribution she/they had ever visited. And to know herself so reduced, she who had been the fiercest and most terrible of all her selves, was an agony more exquisite still.

She hovered in the darkness which no longer comforted, longing for the peace she had lost, even if she must find it in non-being, but filled still with the purpose for which she had been made. Need and hunger quivered within her, and she had never been patient or docile. Something in her snarled at her vanished creators, damning them for leaving her without direction, deprived of function, and she trembled on a cusp of decision, tugged towards death by loneliness and impelled towards life by unformed need.

And then something else flickered on the edge of her senses. It guttered against the blackness, fainter even than she, and she groped out towards it. Groped out, and touched, and gasped in silent shock at the raw, jagged hatred—at the fiery power of that dying ember that cried out in wordless torment. It came not from her creators but from a mortal, and she marveled at the strength of it.

The ember glowed hotter at her touch, blazing up, consuming its fading reserves in desperate appeal. It shrieked to her, more powerful in its dying supplication than ever her creators had been, and it knew her. It *knew* her! Not by name—not as an entity, but for herself, for what she was. Its agony fastened upon her like pincers, summoning her from the emptiness to perform her function once more.

Book One: Victims

Chapter One

The assault shuttle crouched in the corral like a curse, shrouded in thin, blowing snow. Smoke eddied with the snow, throat-catching with the stench of burned flesh, and the snouts of its energy cannon and slug-throwers steamed where icy flakes hissed to vapor. Mangled megabison lay about its landing feet, their genetically-engineered fifteen-hundred-kilo carcasses ripped and torn in snow churned to bloody mud by high-explosives.

The barns and stables were smoldering ruins, and the horses and mules lay heaped against the far fence, no longer screaming. They hadn't fled at first, for they had heard approaching shuttles before, and the only humans they'd ever known had treated them well. Now a line of slaughtered bodies showed their final panicked flight.

They hadn't died alone. A human body lay before the gate; a boy, perhaps fifteen—it was hard to know, after the bullet storm finished with him—who had run into the open to unbar it when the murders began.

One of the raiders stepped from the gaping door of what had been a home, fastening his belt, followed by a broken, wordless sound that had become less than human hours ago. A final pistol shot cracked. The sound stopped.

The raider adjusted his body armor, then thrust two fingers into his mouth and whistled shrilly. The rest of his team filtered out of the house or emerged from the various sheds, some already carrying armloads of valuables.

"I'm calling the cargo flight in—ETA forty minutes!" The leader pumped an arm, then gestured at a clear space beside the grounded assault shuttle. "Get it together for sorting!"

"What about Yu?" someone asked, jerking his head at the single dead raider who lay entangled with the white-haired body of his killer. Rifle fire had torn the old man apart, but Yu's face was locked in a rictus of horrified surprise, and his stiff hands clutched the gory ice where the survival knife had driven up under his armor and ripped his belly open. The leader shrugged.

"Make sure he's sanitized and leave him. The authorities'll be pleased somebody got at least one pirate. Why disappoint them?"

He strolled across to Yu and grimaced down. Stupid fuck always did forget this was a job, not just a chance for sick kicks. So sure of himself, coming right in on the old bastard just to enjoy slapping him around. If the old fart'd had a decent weapon, he'd have gotten half a dozen of us.

The leader had chosen long ago to sign away his own humanity, but he would shed no tears for the likes of Yu. He turned his back and waved again, and the assault party filtered back into the smoke and ruin and agony to loot.

She came out of the snow like the white-furred shadow of death, strands of amber hair blowing about an oval face and jade eyes come straight from Hell. Her foundered horse lay far behind her, flanks no longer heaving, his sweat turned chill and frozen hard. She'd wept at how gallantly he'd answered to her harsh usage, but there were no tears now. The tick pulsed within her, and time seemed slow and clumsy as the icy air burned her lungs.

The communicator which had summoned her weighted one parka pocket, and she thrust her binoculars into another as she moved through the whiteness. She'd recognized the shuttle class—one of the old *Leopard* boats, far from new but serviceable—and counted the raiders as they gathered about their commander. Twenty-four, and the body in the snow with Grandfather made twenty-five. A full load for a *Leopard*, the emotionless computer in her head observed. No one still aboard, then. That meant no one could kill her with the shuttle's guns . . . and that she could kill more of them before she died.

Her left hand checked the survival knife at her hip, then joined her right upon her rifle. Her enemies had combat rifles, some carried grenades, all wore unpowered armor. She didn't, but neither did she care, and she caressed her own weapon like a lover. A direcat like the one who'd been raiding their herds since winter closed its normal range could pull down even megabison; that was why she'd taken a lot of gun with her this morning.

She reached the shuttle and went to one knee behind a landing leg, watching the house. She considered claiming the bird for herself, but a *Leopard* needed a separate weaponeer, and it had to be linked to its mother ship's telemetry. She could neither hijack it without someone higher up knowing instantly nor use its weapons, so the real question was simply whether or not they'd left their com up. If their helmet units were tied into the main set, they could call in reinforcements. From how far? Thirty klicks—from the Braun place, the computer told her. Less than a minute for a shuttle at max. Too short. She couldn't snipe them as they came out, or she wouldn't get enough of them before she died.

Her frozen jade eyes didn't even flinch as they traveled over her brother's mangled body. She was in the groove, tingling with memories she'd spent five years trying to forget, and she embraced them as she did her rifle. No berserker, the computer told her. Ride the tick. Spend yourself well.

She left her cover, drifting to the power shed like a thicker billow of snow. A raider knelt inside, whistling as he unplugged the power receiver. Ten percent of her sister's credit had gone into that unit, the computer reflected as she set her rifle soundlessly aside and drew her knife. A half step, fingers of steel tangled in greasy hair, a flash of blade, and the right arm of her parka was no longer white.

One. She dropped the dead man and reclaimed her rifle, working her way down the side of the shed. A foot crunched in snow, coming around from the back, and her rifle twirled like a baton. Eyes flared wide in a startled face. A hand scrabbled for a pistol. Lungs sucked in wind to shout—and the rifle butt crushed his trachea like a sledgehammer. He jackknifed backwards, shout dying in a horrible gurgle, hands clawing at his ruined throat, and she stepped over him and left him to strangle behind her.

Two, the computer whispered, and she slid wide once more, floating like the snow, using the snow. A billow of flakes swept over a raider as he dragged a sled of direcat pelts towards the assault shuttle. It enveloped him, and when it passed he lay face-down in a steaming gush of crimson.

Three, the computer murmured as she drifted behind the house and a toe brushed the broken back door open.

A raider glanced up at the soft sound, then gawked in astonishment at the snow-shrouded figure across the littered kitchen. His mouth opened, and a white-orange explosion hurled him through the arched doorway into the dining room. *Four*, the computer counted as he fell across her mother's naked, broken body. Shouts echoed, and a raider hidden behind the dining room wall swung his combat rifle through the arch. Death's jade eyes never flickered, and a thunderbolt blew a fist-sized hole through the wall and the body behind it.

Five. She darted backwards, vanishing back into the snow, and went to ground at a corner of the greenhouse. Two raiders plowed through the snow, weapons ready, charging the back of the house, and she let them pass her.

The two shots sounded as one, and she rolled to her

left, clearing the corner of the house. The shuttle lay before her, and the assault team commander ran madly for the lowered ramp. A fist of fire punched him between the shoulder blades, and she rose in a crouch, racing for the well house.

Eight, the computer whispered, and then a combat rifle barked before her. She went down as the tungsten slug smashed her femur like a spike of plasma, and a raider shouted in triumph. But she'd kept her rifle, and triumph became terror as it snapped into position without conscious thought and his head exploded in a fountain of scarlet and gray and snow-white bone.

She rose on her good leg, nerves and blood afire with anti-shock protocols, and dragged herself into the cover of the ceramacrete foundation. Jade-ice eyes saw movement. Her rifle tracked it; her finger squeezed.

Ten. The computer whirred, measuring ranges and vectors against her decreased mobility, and she wormed under the well house overhang. Rifle fire crackled, but solid earth rose like a berm before her. They could come at her only from the front or flank . . . and the shuttle ramp lay bare to her fire.

A hurricane of tungsten penetrators flayed the well house, covering a second desperate rush for that shuttle. Two men raced to man its weapons, and flying snow and dirt battered her mask-like face. Ceramacrete sprayed down from above, but her targets moved so slowly, so clumsily, and she was back on the range, listening to her DI's voice, with all the time in the world.

Twelve. And then she was moving again, slithering on elbows and belly down a scarlet ribbon of blood before someone with grenades thought of them.

She slapped in a fresh magazine and came out to her left, back towards the house, and rocked up on her good knee. Flying metal whined about her ears, but she was in the groove, riding the tick, rifle swinging with metronome precision. *Amateurs*, the computer said as four raiders charged her, firing from the hip like holovid heroes. Her trigger finger stroked, and her rifle hammered her shoulder. Again. Three times. Four.

She rose in a lurching run, dragging herself through the snow, nerve blocks severing her from the agony as torn muscle shredded on knife-edged bone. A corner of her brain wondered how much of this she could take before the femoral artery split, but a blast of adrenalin flooded her system, her vision cleared once more, and she rolled into the cover of the front step.

Sixteen, the computer told her, and then *seventeen* as a raider burst from the house into her sights and died. He fell almost atop her, and the first expression crossed her face at the sight of his equipment. She snagged his ammo belt, and a wolfish smile twisted her lips as bloody fingers primed the grenade. She held it, listening to feet crashing through the house behind her, then flipped it back over her shoulder through the broken door.

Commodore Howell jerked upright in his chair as an alarm snarled into his neural receptor. An azure light pulsed in his holo display, well beyond the outermost planetary orbit, and his head whipped around to his ops officer.

Commander Rendlemann's eyes were closed as he communed with the ship's AI. Then they opened and met his commander's.

"We may have a problem here, sir. Tracking says somebody just kicked in his Fasset drive at five light-hours."

"Who?" Howell demanded.

"Not sure yet, sir. CIC is working on it, but the gravity signature is fairly small. Intensity suggests a destroyer—possibly a light cruiser."

"But it's definitely a Fleet drive?"

"No question, sir."

"Crap!" Howell brooded at his own display, watching the pulsing light gain velocity at the rate possible only to a Fasset drive starship. "What the *hell* is he doing here? This was supposed to be a clean system!"

It was a rhetorical question and Rendlemann recognized it as such, merely raising an eyebrow at his commander.

"ETA?" Howell asked after a moment.

"Uncertain, sir. Depends on his turnover point, but he's piling up vee at an incredible rate—he must be well over the redline—and his line of advance clears everything but Mathison Five. He'll be awful close to Five's Powell limit when he hits its orbit, but he may be able to hold it together."

"Yeah." Howell rubbed his upper lip and conferred with his own synth link, monitoring the readiness signals as his flagship raced back to general quarters. Their operational window had just gotten a lot narrower.

"Check the stat board on the shuttle teams," he ordered, and Rendlemann flipped his mental finger through a mass of report files.

"Primary targets are almost clear, sir. First wave Beta shuttles are already loading—looks like they'll finish up in about two hours. Most of the second wave Beta shuttles are moving on their pick-up schedules, but one Alpha shuttle hasn't sent the follow-up."

"Which one?"

"Alpha Two-One-Niner." The ops officer consulted his computer link again. "That'd be . . . Lieutenant Singh's team."

"Um." Howell plucked at his lower lip. "They sent an all-clear?"

"Yes, sir. They reported losing one man, then the all-clear. They just haven't called in the cargo flight."

"Has com tried to raise them?"

"Yes, sir. Nothing."

"Stupid bastards," Howell grunted. "How many times have we told them to leave a com watch aboard?!" He drummed on his command chair's arm, then shrugged. "Divert their cargo flight to the next stop, and stay on them," he said, and his eyes drifted back to the main display.

She sagged back against the wall, heart racing as the adrenalin in her system skyrocketed. Chemicals joined it, sparkling like icy lightning deep within her, and she jerked the crude tourniquet tight. The snow under her was crimson, and shattered bone gaped in the wound as she checked the magazine indicator. Four left, and she smiled that same wolf's smile.

She tugged her hood down and wiped a streak of blood across her sweating forehead as she pressed the back of her head against the wall. No one fired. No one moved in the house behind her. How many were left? Five? Six? However many, none of them were tied into the shuttle's com unit, or reinforcements would be here by now. But she couldn't just sit there. She was clear-headed, almost buoyant with induced energy, and her femoral hadn't gone yet, but the high-speed penetrator had mangled her tissues and neither the coagulants nor her tourniquet were stopping the bleeding. She'd bleed out soon, and message or no, someone would be along to check on the raiders eventually. Either way, she would die before she got them all.

She moved, dragging herself towards the northern corner of the house. They had to be on that side, unless they were circling around her, and they weren't. These were killers, not soldiers. They didn't realize how badly she was hurt, and they were terrified by what had already happened to them. They weren't thinking about taking *her* out; they were holed up somewhere, buried in some defensive position while they tried to cover their asses.

She flopped back down, using her sensory boosters, and her augmented gaze swept the stillness for footprints in the snow. There. The curing shed and—her eyes moved back—her father's machine shop. That gave them a crossfire against her only direct line of approach from the house, but . . .

The computer whirred behind her frozen eyes, and she began to work her way back in the direction she had come.

"Anything yet from Two-Nineteen?"

"No, sir." Rendlemann was beginning to sound truly concerned, Howell reflected, and with cause. The unidentified drive trace charged closer, and it was still accelerating. That skipper was really pouring it on, and it was clear he was going to scrape by Mathison V just beyond the limit at which his drive would destabilize. The commodore cursed silently, for no one was supposed to have been able to get here so soon, and his freighters couldn't pull that kind of acceleration this far into the system. If he was going to get them out in time, they had to go now.

"Goddamned *idiots*," he muttered, glaring at the chronometer, then looked at Rendlemann. "Start the freighters moving and signal all Beta shuttles to expedite. Abort all pick-ups with a window of more than one hour and recall all Alpha shuttles for docking with the freighters. We'll recover the rest of the Beta shuttles with the combatants and redistribute later."

There were four of them left, and they crouched inside the prefab buildings and cursed in harsh monotony. Where was everybody else? Where were the goddamned relief shuttles? And who—*what*—was out there?!

The man by the curing shed door scrubbed oily sweat from his eyes and wished the building had more windows. But they had the son-of-a-bitch pinned down, and he'd seen the blood in the snow. Whoever he is, he's hurting. No way he can make it clear up here without—

Something flew across the corner of his vision. It sailed into the open workshop door across from him, and someone flung himself on his belly, scrabbling frantically for whatever it was. His hands closed on it and he started back up to his knees, one arm going back—then vanished in the expanding fireball where the workshop building had been.

Grenade. *Grenade!* And it came around the corner. *From behi—*

He was whirling on his knees as the rear door hidden behind the shed's curing racks crashed inward and a bolt of fire lit the dimness. It sprayed his last companion across the wall, and a nightmare image filled his eyes—a tall shape, slender despite bulky furs; a quilted trouser leg, shredded and darkest burgundy; hair like a snow-matted sunrise framing eyes of emerald ice; and a deadly rifle muzzle, held hip-high and swinging, swinging . . .

He screamed and squeezed his trigger as the shadows blazed again.

"*Still* nothing from Two-One-Niner?"

"No, sir."

"Bring her up on remote."

"But, sir—what about Singh and—"

"Fuck Singh!" Howell snarled, and stabbed his finger at the plot. The blue dot was inside Mathison V. Another hour and the destroyer would be in sensor range, ready for the maneuver he most feared: an end-for-end flip to bring its sensors clear of the Fasset drive's black hole. The other captain could make his reading, flip back around, and skew-curve around the primary, holding his drive between himself and Howell's weapons like an impenetrable shield. Howell could still have him, but it would require spreading his own units wide—and accomplish absolutely nothing worthwhile.

"Sir, it's only a destroyer. We could—"

"We could *nothing*. That son-of-a-bitch is running a birds-eye, and if he gets close enough for a good reading, we're blown all to hell. He can flip, scan us, and get his SLAM drone off, and he's got three of them. If we blow the first one before it wormholes, he'll know how we're doing it. He'll override the codes on the others, and killing him after the fact will accomplish exactly nothing, so get that shuttle up here!"

"Yes, sir."

She huddled in the snow, crouched over her brother, stroking the fair hair. His face was untouched, snowflakes coated his dead, green eyes, and she felt the hot flow of blood soaking her own parka. More blood bubbled at the corner of her mouth, and her strength was going fast.

The shuttle's ramp retracted, and it rose on its counter-gravity and hovered for just a moment. Then its turbines whined, its nose lifted, and it streaked away. She was alone with her dead, and the tears came at last. There was no more need for concentration, and her own universe slowed and swooped back into phase with the rest of existence as the tick released her and she held her brother close, cradling an agony not of her flesh.

A side party, Stevie, she thought. At least I sent you a side party.

But it wasn't enough. Never enough. The bastards behind it were beyond her reach, and she gave herself to her hatred. It filled her with her despair, melding with it, like poison and wine, and she opened to it and drank it deep.

I tried, Stevie. I *tried*! But I wasn't here when you needed me. She bent over the body in her arms, rocking it as she sobbed to the moaning wind. Damn them! Damn them to *hell*! She raised her head, glaring madly after the vanished shuttle.

Anything! Anything for one more shot! One more—

<Anything, Little One?>

She froze as that alien thought trickled through her wavering brain, for it wasn't hers. *It wasn't hers!*

She closed her eyes on her tears, and crimson ice crackled as her hands fisted in her brother's tattered parka. Mad. She was going mad at the very end.

<No, Little One. Not mad.>

Air hissed in her nostrils as the alien voice whispered to her once more. It was soft as the sighing snow, and colder by far. Clear as crystal and almost gentle, yet vibrant with a ferocity that matched her own. She tried to clench her will and shut it out, but there was too much of herself in it, and she folded forward over her dead while the strength pumped out of her with her blood.

<You are dying,> the voice murmured, *<and I have learned more of death than ever I thought to. So tell me—did you mean it? Will you truly give* anything *for your vengeance?>*

She laughed jaggedly as her madness whispered to her, but there was no hesitation in her.

"Anything!" she gasped.

<Consider well, Little One. I can give you what you

seek—but the price may be . . . yourself. Will you pay that much?>

"Anything!" She raised her head and screamed it to the wind, to her grief and hate and the whisper of her own broken sanity, and a curious silence hovered briefly in her mind. Then—

<*Done!*> the voice cried, and the darkness took her at last.

Chapter Two

Captain Okanami stepped into his tiny office, shivering despite the welcome heat. Wind moaned about the prefab, but Okanami's chill had little to do with the cold as he shucked off his Fleet-issue parka and scrubbed his face with his hands. Every known survivor of Mathison's World's forty-one thousand people was in this single building. All three hundred and six of them.

He lowered himself into his chair, then looked down at his fresh-scrubbed hands. He had no idea how many autopsies he'd performed in his career, but few of them had filled him with such horror as those he'd just finished in what had been Capital Hospital. It hadn't been much of a hospital by Core World standards even before the pirates stripped it—that was why his patients were here instead of there—but he supposed the dead didn't mind.

He dry-washed his face again, shuddering at the obscene wreckage on his autopsy tables. Why? Why in God's name had anyone needed to do *that*?

The bastards had left a lot of loot, yet they'd managed to lift most of it out. They might have gotten it all if they hadn't allowed time to *enjoy* themselves, but they hadn't anticipated *Gryphon*'s sudden arrival. They'd run, then, and *Gryphon* had been too busy rescuing any survivor she could find to even consider pursuit. Her crew of sixty had been hopelessly inadequate in the face of such disaster. Her minuscule medical staff had driven themselves beyond the point of collapse . . . and too many of the maimed and broken victims they'd found had died anyway. Ralph Okanami was a physician, a healer, and it frightened him to realize how much he wished he were something else whenever he thought about the monsters who had done such things.

He listened to the wind moan, faintly audible even here, and shivered again. The temperature of Mathison's settled continent had not risen above minus fifteen for the past week, and the raiders' first target had been the planetary power net. They'd gotten in completely unchallenged—not that Mathison's pitiful defenses would have mattered much—and gone on to hit every tiny village and homestead on the planet, and they'd taken out every auxiliary generator they could find. Most of the handful who'd escaped the initial slaughter had died of exposure without power and heat before the Fleet could arrive in sufficient strength to start large-scale search operations.

This was worse than Mawli. Worse even then Brigadoon. There'd been fewer people to kill, and they'd been able to take more time with each.

Okanami was one of the large minority of humans physically incapable of using neural receptors, and his fingers flicked keys as he turned to his data console and brought up his unfinished report. The replacement starcom was in, and Admiral Gomez's staff wanted complete figures for their report. *Complete figures*, his mind repeated sickly, staring at the endless rows of names. And those were only the dead they'd identified so far. SAR parties were still working the more distant homesteads in hopes cf finding someone else, but the odds were against it. The overflights had detected no operable power sources, none of the thermal signatures which might suggest the presence of life.

A bell pinged, and he looked away from the report

with guilty relief as his com screen flicked to life with a lieutenant he didn't recognize. A shuttle's cockpit framed the young woman's face, and her eyes were bright. Yet there was something amiss with her excitement, like an edge of uncertainty. Perhaps even fear. He shook off the thought and summoned a smile.

"What can I do for you, Lieutenant—?"

"Surgeon Lieutenant Sikorsky, sir, detached from *Vindication* for Search and Rescue." Okanami straightened, eyebrows rising, and she nodded. "We've found another one, Captain, but this one's so weird I thought I'd better call it in directly to you."

"Weird? How so?" The rising eyebrows lowered again, knitting above suddenly intent eyes at Sikorsky's almost imperceptible hesitance.

"It's a woman, sir, and, well, she ought to be dead." Okanami crooked a finger for her to continue, and Sikorsky drew a deep breath.

"Sir, she's been hit five times, including a shattered femur, two rounds through her liver, one through the left lung, and one through the spleen and small intestine." Okanami flinched at the catalog of traumas. "So far, we've put over a liter of blood into her, and her BP's still so low we can barely get a reading. All her vital signs are massively depressed, and she's been lying in the open ever since the raid, sir—we found her beside a body that was frozen rock solid, but *her* body temperature is thirty-two-point-five!"

"Lieutenant," Okanami's voice was harsh, "if this is your idea of humor—"

"Negative, sir." Sikorsky sounded almost pleading. "It's the truth. Not only that, she's got the damnedest—excuse me, sir. She's been augmented, and she's got the most unusual receptor net I've ever seen. It's military, but I've never seen anything like it, and the support hardware is unbelievable."

Okanami rubbed his upper lip, staring at the earnest, worried face. Lying in sub-freezing temperatures for over a week and her temperature was depressed barely five degrees? Impossible! And yet . . .

"Get her back here at max, Lieutenant, and tell Dispatch I want you routed straight to OR Twelve. I'll be scrubbed and waiting for you."

Okanami and his hand-picked team stood enfolded in the sterile field and stared at the body before them. Damn it, she *couldn't* be alive with damage like this! Yet she was. The medtech remotes labored heroically, resecting an intestine perforated in eleven places, removing her spleen, repairing massive penetrations of her liver and lung, fighting to save a leg that had been brutally abused even after the hit that shattered it. Still more blood flooded into her . . . and she was alive. Barely, perhaps—indeed, her vital signs had actually weakened when the support equipment had taken over—but alive.

And Sikorsky was right about her augmentation. Okanami had decades more experience than the lieutenant, yet he'd never imagined anything like it. It had obviously started life as a standard Imperial Marine Corps outfit, and parts of it were readily identifiable, but the rest—!

There were three separate neural receptors—not in parallel but feeding completely separate sub-systems—plus the most sophisticated set of sensory boosters he'd ever seen, and some sort of neuro-tech webbing covered all her vital areas. He hadn't had time to examine it yet, but it looked suspiciously like an incredibly miniaturized disrupter shield, which was ridiculous on the face of it. No one could build a shield that small, and the far bulkier units built into combat armor cost a quarter-million credits each. And while he was thinking about incredible things, there was her pharmacopoeia. It contained enough pain suppressers, coagulators, and stim boosters (most of them straight from the controlled substances list) to keep a dead man on his feet, not to mention an ultra-sophisticated endorphin generator and at least three drugs Okanami had never even heard of. Yet a quick check of its med levels indicated that it wasn't her pharmacope which had kept her alive. Even if it might have been capable of such a feat, its reservoirs were still almost fully charged.

He inhaled gratefully as the thoracic and abdominal

teams closed and stepped back to let the osteoplastic techs concentrate on her thigh. Her vitals kicked up a hair, and blood pressure was coming back up, but there was something weird about that EEG. Hardly surprising if there was brain damage after all she'd been through, but it might be those damned receptors.

He gestured to Commander Ford, and the neurologist swung her monitors into place. Receptor Two was clearly the primary node, and Okanami moved to watch Ford's screens over her shoulder as she adjusted her equipment with care and keyed a standard diagnostic pattern.

For just a moment, absolutely nothing happened, and Okanami frowned. There should be *something*—an implant series code, if nothing else. But there wasn't. And then, suddenly, there *was*, and buzzers began to scream.

A lurid warning code glared crimson, and the unconscious young woman's eyes jerked open. They were empty, like the jade-green windows of a deserted house, but the EEG spiked madly. The thigh incision was still open, and the med remotes locked down to hold her leg motionless as she started to rise. A surgeon flung himself forward, frantic to restrain that brutalized body, and the heel of her hand struck like a hammer, barely missing his solar plexus.

He shrieked as it smashed him to the floor, but the sound was half lost in the wail of a fresh alarm, and Okanami paled as the blood chem monitors went beserk. A binary agent neuro-toxin drove the toxicology readings up like missiles, and the security code on Ford's screen was joined by two more. Their access attempt had activated some sort of suicide override!

"Retract!" he screamed, but Ford was already stabbing buttons in frantic haste. Alarms wailed an instant longer, and then the implant monitor died. The toxicology alert ended in a dying warble as an even more potent counteragent went after the half-formed toxin, and the amber-haired woman slumped back on the table, still and inert once more while the injured surgeon sobbed in agony and his fellows stared at one another in shock.

* * *

"You're lucky your man's still alive, Doctor."

Captain Okanami glowered at the ramrod-straight colonel in Marine space-black and green who stood beside him, watching the young woman in the bed. Medical monitors watched her with equal care—very cautiously, lest they trigger yet another untoward response from the theoretically helpless patient.

"I'm sure Commander Thompson will be delighted to hear that, Colonel McIlheny," the surgeon said frostily. "It only took us an hour and a half to put his diaphragm back together."

"Better that than what she was going for. If she'd been conscious he'd never have known what hit him—you can put that on your credit balance."

"What the hell *is* she?" Okanami demanded. "That wasn't *her* on the table, it was her goddamned augmentation processors running her!"

"That's exactly what it was," McIlheny agreed. "There are escape and evasion and an anti-interrogation subroutine buried in her primary processor." He turned to favor the surgeon with a measuring glance. "You Navy types aren't supposed to have anything to do with someone like her."

"Then she's one of yours?" Okanami's eyes were suddenly narrow.

"Close, but not quite. Our people often support her unit's operations, but she belongs—belonged—to the Imperial Cadre."

"Dear God," Okanami whispered. "*A drop commando?*"

"A drop commando." McIlheny shook his head. "Sorry it took so long, but the Cadre doesn't exactly leave its data lying around. The pirates took out Mathison's data base when they blew the governor's compound, so I queried the Corps files. They don't have much data specific to her. I've downloaded the available specs on her hardware and gotten your medical types cleared for it, but it's limited, and the bio data's even thinner, mostly just her retinal and genetic patterns. All I can say for sure is that this—" his chin jutted at the woman in the bed "—is Captain Alicia DeVries."

"Devries?! The *Shallingsport* DeVries?"

"The very one."

"She's not old enough," Okanami protested. "She can't be more than twenty-five, thirty years old!"

"Twenty-nine. She was nineteen when they made the drop—youngest master sergeant in Cadre history. They went in with ninety-five people. Seven of them came back out, but they brought the hostages with them."

Okanami stared at the pale face on the pillow—an oval face, pretty, not beautiful, and almost gentle in repose.

"How in heaven did she wind up out here on the backside of nowhere?"

"I think she wanted some peace," McIlheny said sadly. "She got a commission, the Banner of Terra, and a twenty-year bonus from Shallingsport—earned every millicred of it, too. She sent in her papers five years ago and took the equivalent of a thirty-year retirement credit in colony allotments. Most of them do. The Core Worlds won't let them keep their hardware."

"Hard to blame them," Okanami observed, recalling Commander Thompson's injuries, and McIlheny stiffened.

"They're soldiers, Doctor." His voice was cold. "Not maniacs, not killing machines—*soldiers*." He held Okanami's eye with icy anger, and it was the captain who looked away.

"But that wasn't the only reason she headed here," the colonel resumed after a moment. "She used her allotment as the core claim on four prime sections, and her family settled out here."

Okanami sucked in air, and McIlheny nodded. His voice was flat when he continued.

"She wasn't there when the bastards landed. By the time she got back to the site, they'd murdered her entire family. Father, mother, younger sister and brother, grandfather, an aunt and uncle, and three cousins. All of them."

He reached out and touched the sleeping woman's shoulder, the gesture gentle and curiously vulnerable in such a big, hard-muscled man, then laid the long, heavy rifle he'd carried in across the bedside table. Okanami stared at it, considering the dozen or so regulations its presence violated, but the colonel continued before he could speak.

"I've been out to the homestead." His voice had turned soft. "She must've been out after direcat or snow wolves—this is a fourteen-millimeter Vorlund express, semi-auto with recoil buffers—and she went in after twenty-five men with body armor, grenades, and combat rifles." He stroked the rifle and met the doctor's eyes. "She got them all."

Okanami looked back down at her, then shook his head.

"That still doesn't explain it. By every medical standard I know, she should have died then and there, unless there's something in your download that says different, and I can't begin to imagine anything that might."

"Don't waste your time looking, because you won't find anything. Our med people agree entirely. Captain DeVries"—McIlheny touched the motionless shoulder once more "—can't possibly be alive."

"But she is," Okanami said quietly.

"Agreed." McIlheny left the rifle and turned away, waving politely for the doctor to precede him from the room. The surgeon was none too pleased to leave the weapon behind, even without a magazine, but the colonel's combat ribbons—and expression—stilled his protests. "That's why Admiral Gomez's report has a whole team of specialists on their way here at max."

Okanami led the way into the sparsely appointed lounge, empty at this late hour, and drew two cups of coffee. The two men sat at a table, and the colonel's eyes watched the open door as Okanami keyed a small hand reader to access the medical download. His cup steamed on the table, ignored, and his mouth tightened as he realized just how scanty the data was. Every other entry ended in the words "FURTHER ACCESS RESTRICTED" and some astronomical clearance level. McIlheny waited patiently until Okanami set the reader aside with sigh.

"Weird," he murmured, shaking his head as he

reached for his own coffee, and the colonel chuckled without humor.

"Even weirder than you know. This is for your information only—that's straight from Admiral Gomez—but you're in charge of this case until a Cadre med team can get here, so I'm supposed to bring you up to speed. Or as up to speed as any of us are, anyway. Clear?"

Okanami nodded, and his mouth felt oddly dry despite the coffee.

"All right. I took my own people out to the DeVries claim because the original report was so obviously impossible. For one thing, three separate SAR overflights hadn't picked up *any*thing. If Captain DeVries had been there and alive, she'd've showed on the thermal scans, especially lying in the open that way, so I *knew* it had to be some kind of plant."

He sipped coffee and shrugged.

"It wasn't. The evidence is absolutely conclusive. She came up on them from the south, with the wind behind her, and took them by surprise. She left enough blood trail for us to work out what must've happened, and it was like turning a saber-tooth loose on hyenas, Doctor. They took her down in the end, but not before she got them all. That shuttle must've been lifted out by remote, because there sure as hell weren't any live pirates to fly it.

"But that's where it gets really strange. Our forensic people have fixed approximate times of death for the pirates and her family, and they've pegged the blood trails *she* left to about the same time. Logically, then, she should have bled to death within minutes of killing the last pirate. If she hadn't done that, she should have frozen to death, again, probably very quickly. And if she were alive, the thermal scans certainly should have picked her up. None of those things happened—it's like she was someplace else until the instant Sikorsky's crew landed and found her. And, Doctor," the colonel's eyes were very intent, "not even a drop commando can do that."

"So what are you saying? It was magic?"

"I'm saying she's managed at least three outright impossibilities, and nobody has the least damned idea how. So until an explanation occurs to us, we want her right here in your capable hands."

"Under what conditions?" Okanami's voice was edged with sudden frost.

"We'd prefer," McIlheny said carefully, "to keep her just like she is."

"Unconscious? Forget it, Colonel."

"But—"

"I said forget it! You *don't* keep a patient sedated indefinitely, particularly not one who's been through what she has, and *especially* not when there's an unknown pharmacology element. Her medical condition is nothing to play games with, and your download—" he waved the hand reader under the colonel's nose "—is less than complete. The damned thing won't even tell me what three of the drugs in her pharmacope *do*, and her augmentation security must've been designed by a terminal paranoiac. Not only do the codes in her implants mean I can't override externally to shut them down, but I can't even go in to empty her reservoirs surgically! Do you have the least idea how much that complicates her meds? And the same security systems that keep me from accessing her receptors mean I can't use a standard somatic unit, so the only way I could keep her under would be with chemicals."

"I see." McIlheny toyed with his coffee cup and frowned as he came up against the captain's Hippocratic armor. "In that case, let's just say we'd like you to keep her here under indefinite medical observation."

"Whether or not her medical condition requires it, eh? And if she decides she wants out of my custody before your intelligence types get here?"

"Out of the question. These 'raids' are totally out of hand. That's bad enough, and when you add in all the unanswered questions she represents—" McIlheny shrugged. "She's not going anywhere until we've got some answers."

"There are limits to the dirty work I'm prepared to do for you and your spooks, Colonel."

"What dirty work? She probably won't even want to leave, but if she does, you're the physician of record of a patient in a military facility."

"A patient," Okanami pointed out, "who happens to be a civilian." He leaned back and eyed the colonel with a marked lack of affability. "You do remember what a 'civilian' is? You know, the people who don't wear uniforms? The ones with something called civil rights? If she wants out of here, she's out of here unless there's a genuine medical reason to hold her. And your 'unanswered questions' do not constitute such a reason."

McIlheny felt a grudging respect for the surgeon and tugged at his lower lip in thought.

"Look, Doctor, I didn't mean to step on any professional toes, and I'm sure Admiral Gomez doesn't want to, either. Nor are we medieval monsters out to 'disappear' an unwanted witness. This is one of our people, and a damned outstanding one. We just need to . . . keep tabs on her."

"So what's the problem? Even if I discharge her, she's not going anywhere you can't find her. Not without a starship, anyway."

"Oh, no?" McIlheny smiled tightly. "I might point out that she's already been somewhere we couldn't find her when all the indications are she was lying right there in plain sight. What's to say she can't do it again?"

"What's to say she has any *reason* to do it again?" Okanami demanded in exasperation.

"Nothing. On the other hand, what's to say she did it on purpose the first time?" Okanami's eyebrows quirked, and McIlheny grinned sourly. "Hadn't thought about that, had you? That's because you're insufficiently paranoid for one of us much maligned 'spooks,' Doctor, but the point is that until we have some idea what happened, we can't know if she did whatever she did on purpose. Or what might happen to her if she does it again."

"You're right—you *are* paranoid," Okanami muttered. He thought hard for a moment, then shrugged. "Still doesn't matter. If a mentally competent civilian wants to check herself out, then unless you've got some specific criminal charge to warrant holding her against her will she checks herself out, period. End of story, Colonel."

"Not quite." McIlheny leaned back and smiled at him. "You see, you've forgotten that she wasn't Fleet or Marine, she's Imperial Cadre."

"So?"

"So there's one fact most people don't know about the Cadre. Not surprising, really; it isn't big enough for much about it to become common knowledge. But the point is that she's not really a civilian at all." Okanami blinked in surprise, and McIlheny's smile grew. "You don't resign from the Cadre—you just go on inactive reserve status. And if you don't want to hang onto our 'civilian' for us, then we'll just by God reactivate her!"

Chapter Three

The being men had once called Tisiphone roamed the corridors of her host's mind and marveled at what she found. Its vast, dim caverns crackled with the golden fire of dreams, and even its sleeping power was amazing. It had been so long since last Tisiphone touched a mortal mind, and she had never been much interested in those she had invaded then. They had been targets, sources of information, tools, and prey, not something to be tasted and sampled, for she was an executioner, not a philosopher.

But things had changed. She was alone and diminished, and no one had sent her to punish this mortal; she had been summoned by the mind in which she wandered, and she needed it. Needed it as a focus and avatar for her weakened self, and so she searched its labyrinthine passages, finding places to store her self, sampling its power and fingering its memories.

It was so *different*. The last human whose thoughts she'd touched had been—the shepherd in Cappadocia? No, Cassander of Macedon, that tangled, ambitious murderer. Now there had been a mind of power, for all its evil. Yet it was no match for the strength, clarity, and knowledge of *this* mind. Man had changed over her centuries of sleep, and even cool Athena or clever-fingered Haphaestus might have envied the lore and skill mortals had attained.

But even more than its knowledge, it was the *power* of this mind which truly astounded her—the focused will, crystal lucidity . . . and ferocity. There was much of her in this Alicia DeVries. This mortal could be as implacable as she herself, Tisiphone sensed, and as deadly, and that was amazing. Were all mortals thus, if only she had stopped to see it so long ago? Or had more than man's knowledge changed while she slept?

Yet there were differences between them. She swooped through memories, sampled convictions and beliefs, and had she had lips, she would have smiled in derision at some of the foolishness she found. She and her selves had not been bred for things like love and compassion—those had no meaning for such as they, and even less this concept of "justice." It caught at her, for it had its whetted sharpness, its tangental contact with what she was, yet she sensed the dangerous contradictions at its core. It clamored for retribution, yes, but balance blunted its knife-sharp edge. Extenuation dulled its certitude, and its self-deluding emphasis on "guilt" and "innocence" and "proof" weakened its determination.

She studied the idea, tasting the dynamic tension which held so many conflicting elements in poised balance, and the familiar hunger at its heart only made it more alien. Her selves had been crafted to punish, made for vengeance, and guilt or innocence had no bearing on her mission. It was a bitter-tasting thing, this "*justice*," a chill bitterness in the hot, sweet blood-taste, and she rejected it. She turned away contemptuously, and bent her attention on other gems in this treasure-vault mind.

They were heaped and piled, glittering measurelessly, and she savored the unleashed violence of combat with weapons Zeus himself might have envied. They had their own lightning bolts, these mortals, and she watched through her host's eyes, tasting the jagged rip-tides of terror and fury controlled by training and science and harnessed to purpose. She was apt to violence, this Alicia DeVries . . . and yet, even at the heart of her battle fury, there was that damnable sense of detachment. That watching presence that mourned the hot blood of her own handiwork and wept for her foes even as she slew them.

Tisiphone spat in mental disgust at that potential weakness. She must be wary. This mortal had sworn herself to her service, but Tisiphone had sworn herself to Alicia DeVries' purpose in return, and this mind was powerful and complex, a weapon which might turn in her hand if she drove it too hard.

Other memories flowed about her, and these were better, more suited to her needs. Memories of loved ones, held secure and precious at her host's core like talismans against her own dark side. Anchors, helping her cling to her debilitating compassion. But they were anchors no more. They had become whips, made savage by newer memories of rape and mutilation, of slaughter and wanton cruelty and the broken bodies of dead love. They tapped deep into the reservoirs of power and purpose, stoking them into something recognized and familiar. For beneath all the nonsense about mercy and justice, Tisiphone looked into the mirror of Alicia DeVries' soul and saw . . . herself.

Jade eyes opened. Darkness pressed against the spartan room's window, moaning with the endless patience of Mathison's winter wind, but dim lights cast golden pools upon the overhead. Monitors chirped gently, almost encouragingly, and Alicia DeVries drew a deep, slow breath.

She turned her head on her pillow, studying the quiet about her, and saw the rifle on her bedside table. The weapon gleamed like memory itself in the dimness, and it should have brought the agony crashing in upon her.

It didn't. Nothing did, and that was . . . wrong. The images were there, clear and lethal in every brutal detail. Everyone she loved had been destroyed—more than destroyed, butchered with sick, premeditated sadism—and the agony of it did not overwhelm her.

She raised a hand to her forehead and frowned, thoughts clearer than they ought to be yet oddly detached. Memories flickered, merciless and sharp as holovids but remote, as if seen through the time-slowing armorplast of the tick, and there was something there at the last, teasing her. . . .

Her hand froze, and her eyes widened as memory of her final madness came abruptly. Voices in her head! Nonsense. And yet—she looked about the silent room once more, and knew she should never have lived to see it.

<*Of course you should have,*> a cold, clear voice said. <*I promised you vengeance, and to avenge yourself, you must live.*>

She stiffened, eyes suddenly huge in the dimness, yet even now there was no panic in their depths. They were cool and still, for the terror of that silent voice eddied against a shield of glass. She sensed its presence, felt it prickle in her palms, yet it could not touch her.

"Who—what—are you?" she asked the emptiness, and a silent laugh quivered deep at her core.

<*Have mortals forgotten us, indeed? Ah, how fickle you are! You may call me Tisiphone.*>

"Tisiphone?" There was an elusive familiarity to that name, but—

<*There, now,*> the voice murmured like crystal, singing on the edge of shattering, and its effort to soothe seemed alien to it. <*Once your kind called us the* Erinyes, *but that was long, long ago. Three of us, there were: Alecto, Megarea . . . and I. I am the last of the Furies, Little One.*>

Alicia's eyes opened even wider, and then she closed them tight. The simplest answer was that she'd been right the first time. She must be mad. That certainly made more sense than holding a conversation with something out of Old Earth's mythology! Yet she knew she wasn't, and her lips twitched at the thought. Didn't they say that a crazy person *knew* she wasn't mad? And who but a madwoman would feel so calm at a moment like this?

<*For all your skills, your people have become most blind. Have you lost the ability to believe anything you cannot see or touch? Do not your "scientists" deal daily with things they can only describe?*>

"Touché," Alicia murmured, then shook herself. Immobilizing tractor collars circled her left leg at knee and hip, lighter than a plasticast yet dragging at her as she eased up on her elbows. She raked hair from her eyes and looked around until she spied the bed's power controls, then reached out her right hand and slipped her Gamma receptor over the control linkage. She hadn't used it in so long she had to think for almost ten full seconds before the proper neural links established themselves, but then the bed purred softly, rising against her shoulders. She settled into a sitting position and folded her hands in her lap, and her neck craned as her eyes flitted about the room once more. "Let's say I believe in you . . . Tisiphone. Where are you?"

<*Your wit is sharper than that, Alicia DeVries.*>

"You mean," Alicia said very carefully, a tiny tremor of fear oozing through the sheet of glass, "that you're inside my head?"

<*Of course.*>

"I see." She inhaled deeply. "Why aren't I hanging from the ceiling and gibbering, then?"

<*It would scarcely help our purpose for me to permit that. Not,*> the voice added a bit dryly, <*that you are not trying to do precisely that.*>

"Well," Alicia surprised herself with a smile despite the madness which had engulfed her, "I guess that would be the rational thing to do."

<*Rationality is an over-valued commodity, Little One. Madness has its place, yet it does make speech difficult, does it not?*>

"I imagine it would." She pressed her hands to her temples, feeling the familiar angularity of her subcutaneous Alpha receptor against her right palm, and moistened her lips. "Are you . . . the reason I don't hurt more?"

She wasn't speaking of physical pain, and the voice knew it.

<*Indeed. You are a soldier, Alicia DeVries. Does a warrior maddened by grief attain his goal or die on his enemy's blade? Loss and hatred are potent, but they must be used. I will not let* them *use* you. *Not yet.*>

Alicia closed her eyes again, lips trembling, grateful for the pane of glass between her and her loss. She felt endless, night-black grief waiting to suck her to destrution beyond whatever shield this Tisiphone had erected, and it frightened her. Yet there was resentment in her gratitude, as if she'd been robbed of something rightly hers—something as precious as it was cruel.

She sucked in another breath and lowered her hands once more. Either Tisiphone existed, or she truly was mad, and she might as well act on the assumption that she was sane. She opened her hospital gown and traced the red line down her chest and the ones across her abdomen. There was no pain, and quick-heal was doing its job—the incisions were half-healed already and would vanish entirely in time—but they confirmed the damage she'd taken. She let the gown fall closed and leaned back against her pillows in the quiet room.

"How long ago was I hit?"

<*Time is something mortals measure better than I, Little One, and it does not exist where you and I have been, but three days have passed since they brought you to this place.*>

" 'Where you and I have been'?"

<*You were dying, and I am not what once I was. My power has waned with the passing of my other selves, and I was ever more apt to wound than heal. Since I could not make you whole, I took you to a place where time has no business until the searchers came to find you.*>

"Would you care to explain that a bit better?"

<*Would you care to explain blue to a man born blind?*>

"You sound like one of those assholes from Intelligence."

<*No. They lied to you; I know what I did and would tell you if you could grasp my meaning.*>

Alicia pursed her lips, surprised by Tisiphone's quick understanding.

<*How should I not understand? I have spent days examining your memories, Little One. I know of your Colonel Watts.*>

"Not *my* Colonel Watts." Alicia's voice was suddenly cold, and a spurt of rage took Tisiphone by surprise, squirting past the clear shield, as Alicia remembered the utter chaos of the Shallingsport Raid. She shook it away, suppressing it with a skill the Fury could not have bettered.

"All right, you're here. Why? What are you going to do?"

<*You asked for vengeance, and you shall have it. We will find your enemies, you and I, and destroy them.*>

"Just the two of us? When the entire Empire can't?" Alicia's laugh was not pleasant. "What makes you think we can do that?"

<*This,*> the voice said softly, and Alicia's head snapped up. Her lips drew back from locked teeth, and a direcat's snarl caught at her throat. Rage flooded her veins, loosed from beyond the shield within her, distilled and pure and hotter than a star's heart. Loss and grief were in that rage, but they were only its fuel, not its heat. Its ferocity wrenched at her like fists of fire, and panic touched her as her augmentation began to respond.

But then it vanished, and she slumped back, panting and beaded with sweat. Her heart raced, and she was weak and drained, like a chemist's flask emptied of acid. Yet something quivered within her, pacing her pulse like an echo of her rage. Determination—no, more than determination. Purpose which went beyond the implacable to the inevitable, ridiculing the very thought that any power in the universe might deflect it.

<*You begin to see, Little One, yet that was but* your *anger; you have not yet tasted mine. I am rage—your rage, and my own, and all the rage that ever was or will be—and skilled in its use. We* will *find them. On that*

you have my word, which has never been broken. And when we find them, you will have the strength of my arm, which has never failed. If I am less than once I was, I remain more than you can imagine; you will have your vengeance.>

"God," Alicia whispered, pressing trembling hands to her temples once more. An icicle of terror shivered through her—not of Tisiphone, but of herself. Of the limitless capacity for destruction she had tasted within her fury. Or—she swallowed—was it within her Fury?

"I—" she began, and chopped off as a man in nursing whites charged through the door and skidded to a stop when he saw her sitting up in bed. His eyes widened, then dropped to the bedside monitors, and he lifted a neural lead from the central console. He pressed it to the terminal on his temple, and Alicia hid a twisted smile of sudden understanding. Her vital signs must have gone off the scale when that bolt of distilled rage ripped through her.

The nurse lowered the lead and regarded her with puzzlement. And with something else. There were questions in his eyes, fusing with sympathy into a peculiar tension his professional facade couldn't quite hide. He glanced away from her, eyes darting for just a moment to the intercom panel, and Alicia swallowed a groan. Idiot! Of *course* they'd left the com open! What must he think after hearing her half of the insane conversation with Tisiphone?

<*Shall I take the memory of it from him?*>

"Can you?" Alicia spoke aloud out of sheer reflex, then cursed herself as the nurse took an involuntary half-step away from her.

"Can I what, Captain DeVries?"

"Uh . . . can you tell me how long I've been here?" she improvised frantically.

"Three days, ma'am," he said.

<*You need not speak aloud for me to hear you, Little One,*> Tisiphone said at the same instant, and Alicia wanted to tear her hair and scream at both of them. The concerned caution in the nurse's voice vibrated bizarrely

in her ears, cut through with the amusement in that silent mental whisper.

"Thank you," she said aloud, and <*Could you do that? Make him forget?*>

<*Once, certainly. Now . . .*> She felt the strong impression of a mental shrug. <*I could try, if you can touch him.*>

Alicia glanced at the wary nurse and smothered a totally inappropriate giggle. <*No way! The poor guy's convinced I'm out of my mind, and he called me by my rank, so they must know I'm a drop commando. I'm surprised he's still here, and he'll jump out of his skin if I try to grab him. Talk about a* dangerous *lunatic—! Besides, they probably had a recorder on it.*>

<*Recorder?*> Mental fingers plucked the concept from her mind. <*Ah. It seems I have much yet to learn about this "technology." Will it matter?*>

<*How do I know? It depends on just how balmy they think I am. Now be quiet a minute.*>

A sense of someone else's surprise echoed within her, as if Tisiphone were unused to hearing orders from a mere mortal, and she suppressed another manic grin in favor of a reassuring smile.

"Thank you," she repeated aloud. "I wonder . . . I can see it's the middle of the night, but could I see the duty doctor?"

"Captain Okanami is on his way here right now, ma'am. In fact, I was waiting for him when—that is . . ." His voice trailed off, and Alicia smiled again. Poor guy. No wonder he'd already called in the big guns. There he was, listening to the prize booby blathering away to herself, and then her vitals went crazy. Too.

"I see. Well, in that case—"

The opening door cut her off in mid-inanity. A Fleet captain came through it, his stride brisk but measured, though something suggested he found it difficult to keep it that way. His Medical Branch caduceus glittered in the dim light, and he paused as if surprised to see her sitting up. No, not to see her sitting up; to see her looking rational. Odd, she didn't *feel* as if she looked rational.

One of his hands made a tiny shooing motion, and the nurse tried to hide his relief as he vanished like smoke.

"Well, now," Captain Okanami said, folding his arms across his chest as the door closed, "I'm glad to see you with us again, Captain DeVries."

Yeah, and surprised as hell. She hid the thought behind a smile and nodded back, watching him while she wondered what he was really thinking.

"You're lucky to be alive," he went on gently, "but I'm afraid—"

"I know." She cut him off before he could complete the sentence. "I know," she repeated more softly.

"Yes, well." Okanami looked at the floor and unfolded his left arm to tug at an earlobe. "I'm not very good at expressing my condolences, Captain. Never have been—a failing in a physician, I suppose—but if there's anything I can do, please tell me."

"I will." She looked down at her own hands and cleared her throat again. "I take it you've figured out I'm a Cadrewoman?"

"Yes. It came as quite a surprise, but, yes, we figured it out. It leaves us with a bit of a problem, too, medically speaking."

"I can imagine. I'm just glad you didn't hit any landmines."

"Actually, we did." Her eyes flicked up, and he shrugged. "Nothing we couldn't handle—" she had the definite impression that remark was sliding over slippery ground "—and we've got partial specs on your augmentation. I don't anticipate any more problems before the Cadre med team gets here."

"Cadre med team?" she asked quickly. "Coming here?"

"Of course. I'm not competent to handle your case, Captain DeVries, so Admiral Gomez called them in. I understand there was a Cadre detachment at Alexandria and that they're *en route* aboard a Crown dispatch boat."

"I see." She chewed on that thought. It had been five years since she'd seen a fellow Cadreman. She'd believed—hoped—she never would again.

"We really don't have a choice, I'm afraid. There are too many holes in the data we've got."

"I see," she repeated more normally. "And in the meantime?"

"In the meantime, I'm keeping you right where you are. We had to do a lot of repair work, as I'm sure you've already realized, and I want someone versed in Cadre augmentation to check it over." She nodded, and he cocked his head. "Are you experiencing any discomfort? I wouldn't want to get into any fancy meds, but I suppose we'd be fairly safe to try old-fashioned aspirin."

"No, no discomfort."

"Good." His relief was evident. "I wasn't sure, but I'd hoped your augmentation would take care of that. I'm glad to see it is."

"Uh, yes," she said, but a quick check of her pharmacopoeia processor told her he was wrong. <*Are you doing that?*> she asked the voice.

<*Of course.*>

<*Thanks.*>

"What's your prognosis?" she asked Okanami after a moment.

"You've responded well to the surgery, and to the quick-heal," Okanami said. "In the long term, you'll probably want to consider replacement for your spleen, but you're coming along very nicely for now. The bone damage to your leg was extreme, and the repairs there are going to need several weeks yet, but the rest—" He waved a dismissive hand and, Alicia noted, carefully did not discuss her mental state. Tactful of him.

He moved a few strides to his right, glancing at her monitor displays, and made a few quick notes on the touchpad, then turned back to her.

"I realize you've just waked up, Captain DeVries—"

"Please, call me Alicia. I haven't been 'Captain DeVries' in years."

"Of course." He smiled with genuine warmth, eyes twinkling with just a touch of sadness. "Alicia. As I say, I realize you've just waked up, but what you really need more than anything else just now is rest. Even if you're not feeling it, this kind of surgery really takes it out of you, quick-heal or no, and you weren't in very good shape before we started."

"I know." She eased back down in the bed, and he pursed his lips.

"If there's anything you'd like to talk about," he began hesitantly, then fell silent as she waved a hand. He nodded and began to turn away.

<*Touch him,*> a voice said in her mind, so suddenly she twitched in surprise at the intensity of its demand.

"Uh, Doctor." He stopped and looked back at the sound of her voice, and she held out her right hand. "Thank you for putting me back together."

"My pleasure." He gripped her hand and smiled, and she smiled back, but shock threatened to wipe it from her lips. Her hand tingled with the power of the spark which had leapt between them at the moment of contact. God, was the man nerve-dead? How could he have missed that flare of power?!

But that was nothing beside what followed it. A column of fire flowed down her arm and licked out through her skin. She looked at their joined hands, expecting to see flames darting from her pores, but there were no flames. Only the heat . . . and under it a crackle that coalesced suddenly into something she almost recognized. A barrier went down, like an opening door or a closing circuit, and the fire in her arm flared high and faded into a familiar intangible tingle. It was like smelling a color or seeing a sound, indescribable to anyone who had never experienced it, but she *had* experienced it. Or experienced its like, at any rate.

Information spilled up her arm, crisp and clear as any her Alpha receptor had ever pulled from a tactical net, and that was impossible. Yet it was happening—happening in a heartbeat, like a burst transmission from a forward scout but less focused, more general and disorganized.

Concern. Uncertainty. Satisfaction at her physical condition and deep, gnawing worry about her mental state. Discomfort over his decision not to mention Intelligence's interest. Burning wonder over how she'd survived untended and undetected in the snow. Genuine distress for the deaths of her family, and an even greater distress that she seemed so calm and collected. *Too calm*, he was thinking, and *I have to listen to that recording. Maybe—*

He released her hand and stepped back. Clearly, he had sensed nothing at all out of the ordinary, and his hand rose in a small wave.

"I'll see you in the morning, Cap—Alicia," he said gently. "Go back to sleep if you can."

She nodded and closed her eyes as he withdrew . . . and knew sleep was the last thing she was going to be able to do.

Chapter Four

Benjamin McIlheny looked up from a sheaf of hard copy as a hatch hissed open aboard the battle-cruiser HMS *Antietam*, then rose quickly as Sir Arthur Keita stepped through it. Keita wore the green-on-green of the Imperial Cadre with the golden harp and starships of the Emperor below the single starburst of a brigadier, and if he was a head shorter than the colonel, he was far thicker and broader. "The Emperor's Bulldog" was silver-haired and pushing a hundred years old; he was also built like the proverbial brick wall, hard-faced, with eyes that were quick and alert under craggy brows. Keita *was* the Imperial Cadre, and his arrival had been something of a shock. The colonel suspected they would have seen someone far less senior if Keita hadn't been right next door in the Macedon Sector, anyway.

The man behind him could have been specifically designed as his antithesis. Inspector Ferhat Ben Belkassem, well short of his fortieth year, was small, neat, and very dark, with liquid brown eyes and a strong, beaked nose. His crimson tunic's collar bore the hourglass and balance of the Ministry of Justice, and he seemed pleasant enough—which was far from sufficient to reconcile McIlheny to his presence. This was a job for the Fleet and the Marines. By McIlheny's lights, not even Keita had any real business poking his nose in—not that he intended to say so to a brigadier. Particularly not to a Cadre brigadier, and *especially* not to a Cadre brigadier named Sir Arthur Keita. Which, because Colonel McIlheny was an intrinsically just man, meant he couldn't say it to Ben Belkassem, either. Damn it.

"Sir Arthur. Inspector."

"Colonel," Keita returned crisply. Ben Belkassem merely smiled at the omission of his own name—a lack of reaction which irritated the colonel immensely—and McIlheny waved at two empty chairs across the conference table.

Ben Belkassem waited for Keita to seat himself, then slid into his own chair. It was a respectful enough gesture, but the man moved like a cat, McIlheny thought. Graceful, poised, and silent. Sneaky bastard.

"I've downloaded all of our data to *Banshee*," he began, "but, with your permission, Sir Arthur, I thought we should probably begin with a general background brief." Keita nodded for him to continue, and McIlheny switched on the holo unit. A display of the Franconian Sector appeared above the table, like a squashed quarter-sphere of stars. An edge of the Empire appeared along its flattened side, green and friendly, but the scarlet of the Rishathan Sphere crowded its rounded upper edge, and a sparkle of amber Rogue Worlds and blue systems claimed by the Quarn Hegemony threaded through its volume. McIlheny slipped into his headset, connecting the display controls to his neural receptor, and a single star at the sector's heart blinked gold.

"The sector capital." The announcement was probably redundant, but he'd learned long ago to make sure the groundwork was in place. "Soissons, in the Franconia System. Quite Earth-like, but for rather cool temperatures, with a population just over two billion. A bit high for this region, but it's one of the old League Worlds we retook from the Lizards more or less intact."

His audience nodded, and he cleared his throat.

"We really should have organized a Crown Sector out here a century ago, but with the Rishatha hanging up there to galactic north it seemed reasonable to turn our attention to other areas first. God knows we had enough to worry about elsewhere, and the Ministry of Colonization decided not to draw Rishathan attention south until we'd firmed up the central sectors. As you can see—" skeins of stars suddenly winked to life beyond the sector's curved frontier, burning the steady white of unsurveyed space "—there's a lot of room for expansion out there, and once we start curling around their southern frontiers, the Lizards are likely to get a bit anxious. We didn't want them extending their border to cut us off before we were ready."

He glanced up at the others. Ben Belkassem was watching the display as if it were a fascinating toy, but Keita only grunted and nodded again.

"All right. The Crown began organizing the Franconian Sector three years ago and sent Governor General Treadwell out a year later. It's a fairly typical Crown Sector in most ways: ninety-three systems under imperial claim—twenty-six with habitable planets—and thirty-one belonging to someone else in the same spatial volume. We've got five Incorporated Worlds besides Soissons, though one of them, Yeager, just elected its first senators this year. Aside from them, we've got fifteen Crown Worlds with Crown Governors, or—" his mouth twisted, "—we *had* fifteen Crown Worlds. Now we only have twelve."

Four stars pulsed lurid crimson as he spoke, wide-spaced, almost equi-distant from one another. One was the primary of Mathison's World.

"Typee, Mawli, Brigadoon, and Mathison's World," McIlheny said grimly, one of the stars blinking brighter with each name. "Mawli, Brigadoon, and Mathison's World are complete write-offs; Typee survived . . . barely. It was the first world hit, and it's been settled for over sixty years—a freeholder colony from Durandel in the Melville Sector—and apparently their population was too spread out for the raiders to hit anything smaller than the major towns. The others—" He shrugged, eyes bitter, and Keita's mouth tightened.

"Things started out quite well, actually," McIlheny went on after a moment. "Governor Treadwell's got three times the normal Crown Sector Fleet presence because of the Rishatha and the Jung Association, so we—"

"Excuse me, Colonel." Ben Belkassem's voice was surprisingly deep for such a small man, almost velvety, with the cultured accent of the mother world. McIlheny frowned at him, and the inspector smiled. "I didn't have time for a complete update on the foreign relations picture out here. Could you give me a little detail on this Jung Association? Am I correct in remembering that it's a multi-system Rogue World polity?"

"Pocket empire, more like," McIlheny said. "These three systems—" three closely-clustered amber lights flashed "—and two treaty dependencies, MaGuire and Wotan." Two more lights blinked. "When the Lizards blitzed the old Terran League, a League Fleet commander—a Commodore Wanda Jung—managed to hold Mithra, Artemis, and Madrigal. The Lizards never even got their toenails into them," he added with grudging respect, "and for somebody their size, they still pack a lot of firepower. All three of their main systems have Core World population levels—about four billion on Mithra, I believe—and they're very heavily industrialized. Until we got ourselves organized, they and El Greco were the major human power bases out here."

The inspector nodded, and McIlheny returned to his original point.

"At any rate, what with the Rogue World odds and sods left over from the League and the proximity of the Rishathan Sphere, the Crown decided Governor Treadwell might need a big stick, so the Franconian Fleet District is unusually powerful. Soissons is very heavily fortified, and Admiral Gomez commands three full battle squadrons, with appropriate supporting elements, which one should think ought to have been enough to prevent things like this."

He paused, brooding over his display's crimson cursors, then sighed.

"What we seem to have here is a highly unusual bunch of pirates. We've always had some in the marches, of course. There are so many single-system Rogue Worlds out here the mercenary business is fairly lucrative; some of them go wolf's-head from time to time, and we've had the odd hijacker outfit get too big for its vac suits, but most of them raid commercial traffic after the freighters go intra-systemic. Even the occasional bunch idiotic enough to hit a planet are usually smart enough to avoid wholesale slaughter rather than force the Fleet to go after them in strength. More than that, most of them don't have anywhere near the firepower to mount a planet-sized raid.

"This bunch has the firepower, and there's something really sick about them. They come barreling in, take out the starcom, then send down their shuttles to take *everything*. Usually, pirates stick to low-bulk, high-value cargoes, grab whatever's handiest, and pull out; these bastards steal anything that isn't nailed down. Power receptors, hospital equipment, satellite communication gear, machine tools, precious metals, luxury export items . . . it's like they have a shopping list of every item of value on the planet.

"Worse than that, they don't care who they kill. In fact, they seem to *enjoy* killing, and if their window's big enough, they take their time about it." McIlheny's face was grim. "This is the worst raid yet, but Brigadoon was almost as bad. I doubt we'd've had any survivors at all from Mathison's if not for *Gryphon*, and her presence was a total fluke. Her skipper isn't even assigned to Admiral Gomez—he was just passing through on his way to Trianon and decided to stop off at Mathison's to pay his respects to Governor Brno. She'd been his first CO, and since a lot of his crew were fairly green and he was well ahead of schedule, he thought he'd surprise her with a visit and kill a few days on sublight maneuvers. He was two days into them, well outside the outermost planet, when the raiders took out the governor's residence, but she knew he was out there and got off a sublight message and fired out her SLAM drone before they killed her. The bastards caught the drone before it wormholed, but Commander Perez picked up the message—after a six-hour transmission delay—and went to maximum emergency power on his Fasset drive. He was well over drive mass redline, and it seems clear he came whooping in on them long before they expected anyone to turn up."

"In a destroyer?" Keita's was exactly the harsh, gravelly voice one might have expected. "That took guts."

"He may not've been assigned here, sir, but Commander Perez had done his intelligence homework. He knew about the raids—and that we haven't been able to get a sensor reading on any of their units. Analysis suggests they must have at least a few capital ships, and if we knew who'd built them we might be able to figure out where the raiders originated. He also knew the governor's drone hadn't made it out, and he had three SLAM drones of his own."

"Which," Ben Belkassem murmured, "is presumably why they didn't just polish *Gryphon* off and get on with their business?"

"We believe so," McIlheny agreed, upgrading his opinion of the inspector slightly.

"Continue, Colonel," Keita said.

"Actually, there's not a lot more to say about their operational patterns, sir. Even with her Fleet strength, Admiral Gomez doesn't have the ships to cover this volume of space effectively. We've tried picketing more likely target systems with corvettes, but they don't have the firepower or speed to deal with whoever these people are, and they only carry a single SLAM drone each. We had a picket at Brigadoon, but the raiders either took her out before she got her drone off, or else nailed it before it wormholed. Either way, she wasn't able to get her report to us, and Admiral Gomez isn't happy about 'staking out more goats for the tigers,' as she puts it."

"Don't blame her." Keita shook himself like an Old Earth bear. "No commander likes throwing away his people for no return."

"Exactly. We're trying to find some pattern that'll let us put heavier forces in likely target systems, but no matter where we put them, the raiders always hit somewhere else." McIlheny glared at the display again.

"Do they, now?" Ben Belkassem said softly. "I'd say that's a pattern right there, Colonel."

"I don't like what you're suggesting, Inspector," Keita growled, and Ben Belkassem shrugged.

"Nonetheless, sir, four straight hits without any interception aside from one corvette—destroyed without getting out a contact message—and a destroyer with no official business in the vicinity, stretches well beyond the limits of probability. Unless we wish to assume the raiders are claivoyant."

"I resent that, Inspector." The edge in McIlheny's quiet voice was sharp enough to suggest he'd considered the same possibility.

"I name no names, Colonel," Ben Belkassem replied mildly, "but logic suggests they must be getting inside information from someone. Which," his own voice hardened just a bit, "is why *I* am here."

McIlheny started to retort sharply, then pressed his lips together and sat back in his chair, eyes narrowed. Ben Belkassem nodded.

"Precisely. His Majesty has expressed personal concern to Minister of Justice Cortez. Justice has no desire to step on the military's toes, but if someone is passing information to these pirates, His Majesty wishes him identified and stopped. And, with all due respect, you may be a bit too deep into the trees to see the forest."

McIlheny's face darkened, and the inspector raised a placating hand.

"Please, Colonel, I mean no disrespect. Your record is outstanding, and I'm certain you're checking your internal security closely, but if the hare is running with the hounds, so to speak, an external viewpoint may be exactly what you need. And," he smiled with genuine humor for the first time, "your people are bound to see me as an interloper. They'll resent me whatever I do or don't do, which means I can be as rude and insulting as I like without damaging your working relationships with them."

The colonel's eyes widened, and Keita gave a bark of laughter.

"He's got you there, McIlheny! I was going to suggest I might help you out the same way, but damned if I wouldn't rather let the inspector take the heat. I may have to work with some of your people in the future."

"I . . . see." McIlheny rubbed a fingertip on the table, then raised it and inspected it as if for dust. "Are you suggesting, Inspector, that I should simply hand my internal security responsibilities over to you?"

"Of course not—and if I did, you'd be perfectly justified in kicking me clear back to Old Earth," Ben Belkassem said cheerfully. "It's your shop. You're the proper person to run it, and your people know you'll have to be looking very closely for possible leaks. They'll expect a certain amount of that, and I couldn't simply take over without undercutting your authority. I'd say your chances of finding whoever it is are probably about as good as mine, but if I stick in my oar in the role of an officious, pig-headed, empire-building interloper—a part, may I add, I play quite well—I can do a lot of your dirty work for you. Just tell them Justice has stuck you with an asshole from Intelligence Branch and leave the rest to me. Who knows? Even if I don't find a thing, I may just scare our hare into the open for you."

"I see." McIlheny examined Ben Belkassem's face intently. The inspector had placed an unerring finger on his own most private—and darkest—fear, and he was right. An outsider could play grand inquisitor without the devastating effect an internal witch hunt might produce.

"All right, Inspector, I may take you up on that. Let me run it by Admiral Gomez first, though." Ben Belkassem nodded, and the colonel frowned.

"Actually, something we hit here on Mathison's leaves me more inclined to think you have a point than I would've been," he admitted unhappily.

The inspector quirked an eyebrow, but the colonel turned to Keita.

"We owe it to your Captain DeVries, Sir Arthur. I'm sure you've read my initial report on the affair at the DeVries Claim?"

"I have," Keita said dryly. "Countess Miller personally starcommed it to me before her henchmen shoved me aboard *Banshee* and slammed the hatch."

McIlheny blinked. He'd expected his report to make waves, but he hadn't anticipated that the Minister of War herself might get involved.

"At any rate," he shook himself back to the affair at hand, "we still haven't been able to figure out how she happened to survive, and I'm afraid she's a bit . . . well—" He broke off uncomfortably, and Keita sighed.

"I said I've read the report, Colonel. The questions you raised are the main reason I got sent along with Major Cateau's medical team, and I understand about Ali—Captain DeVries' . . . mental state." He closed his eyes briefly, as if in pain, then nodded again. "Go on, Colonel."

"Yes, sir. We got a couple of intelligence breaks out of it. For one thing, she's been able to identify the assault shuttles—or, at least one type of shuttle—these bastards are using. It was one of the old *Leopard*-class boats, which is the first hard ID we've gotten, since none of the other survivors who actually saw the shuttles were military types. A *Leopard* tends to confirm that we're dealing with at least one capital ship, of course, but Fleet dumped so many of them on the surplus market when the *Bengals* came in that anyone could have snapped them up. We're running searches on the disposal records to see if anyone out this way was stupid enough to buy up a clutch of them and leave us a paper trail, but I'm not very optimistic.

"But, more importantly, she took out the entire crew of the shuttle which went after her family. We've picked up a few dead pirates before, but they never told us much. Whoever's running them sanitizes his troops pretty carefully, and we haven't had a lot to go on for IDs, aside from the obvious fact that they've all been human. In this case, however, she nailed the assault team com mander. He didn't have much on him, either, but we ran his retinal and genetic patterns and got a direct hit."

He still wore his synth link headset, and the star map disappeared, replaced by an unfamiliar red-haired man in a very familiar uniform.

"Lieutenant Albert Singh, gentlemen." McIlheny's voice was light; his expression was not.

"An Imperial Fleet officer?!" Keita exploded. The colonel nodded, and Keita glared at the holo, teeth bared. Even Ben Belkassem seemed shocked.

"An Imperial Fleet officer. I don't have his complete dossier yet, but what I've seen so far looks clean—except for the fact that Lieutenant Singh has now died twice: once from a fourteen-millimeter slug through the spine, and once in a shuttle accident in the Holderman Sector."

"Vishnu!" Keita muttered. One large, hairy hand clenched into a fist and thumped the table gently. "How long ago?"

"Over two years," McIlheny said, and glanced at Ben Belkassem. "Which, I very much fear, lends point to your suggestion that there has to be someone—possibly several someones—on the inside, Inspector. That shuttle accident happened, all right, but when I poked a bit deeper, I found something very interesting. Singh's personnel jacket says he was aboard it and killed, but the original passenger manifest for the shuttle—which was, indeed, lost with all hands—doesn't include his name. Someone between then and now, someone with access to Fleet personnel records added him to it as far as his jacket was concerned, which gave him a nice, clean termination and erased him from our active data base."

"*Very* good," Ben Belkassem approved. "How did you find him, then?"

"I wish I could take the credit," McIlheny said wryly, "but I was exhausted when I set up the data search, and I didn't define my parameters very well. In fact, I requested a search of *all* records, and I was more than somewhat irritated when I saw how much computer time I'd 'wasted' on it—until the search spit out his name."

"Never look serendipity in the mouth, Colonel." The

inspector grinned. "*I* don't—and I'm afraid I don't give it credit for my successes, either."

"But a Fleet officer," Keita muttered. "I don't like the smell of this."

"Nor do I," McIlheny said more seriously. "It's possible he did it himself, and I've starcommed the Holderman Fleet District for full particulars on him, including anything he might have been into before his 'death.' I'm also running a Fleet-wide personnel search to see if any other bogus 'deaths' occurred in the same shuttle accident. I hope I don't find any, because if *Singh* didn't arrange it, someone else did, and that suggests we may be looking at deliberate recruiting from inside our own military."

"And that whoever did the recruiting may still be in place," Ben Belkassem murmured.

Alicia looked up as a shortish woman stepped through her hospital door. The newcomer moved with the springy stride of a heavy-worlder in a single gravity, and Alicia's eyes widened.

"Tannis?" she blurted, jerking upright in bed. "By God, it *is* you!"

"Really?" Major Tannis Cateau, Imperial Cadre Medical Branch, turned her name tag up to scrutinize it, then nodded. "So it is." She crossed to the bed. "How you doing, Sarge?"

"I'll 'Sarge' you!" Alicia grinned. Then her smile faded as she saw the shadow behind Major Cateau's eyes. "I expect," she said more slowly, "that you're about to tell *me* how I'm doing."

"That's what medics do, Sarge," Cateau replied. She crossed her arms and rocked on the balls of her feet, surveying Captain DeVries (retired) very much as Corporal Cateau had once surveyed Platoon Sergeant DeVries. But there was a difference now, Alicia thought, noting the major's pips on Cateau's green uniform. Oh, yes, there was a difference.

"So how am I?" she asked after a moment.

"Not too bad, considering." Cateau cocked her head

judiciously. "Matter of fact, Okanami and his people did a good job on the repairs, from your records. I may not even open you back up to take a personal look."

"You always were a hungry-knifed little snot."

"The human eye," Cateau declaimed, "is still the best diagnostic tool. You've got several million credits' worth of the Emperor's molycircs tucked away in there—only makes sense to be sure they're all connected more or less to the right places, don't you think?"

"Yeah, sure," Alicia said as lightly as she could. "And mentally?"

"That," Cateau acknowledged, "is a bit more ticklish. What's this I hear about you talking to ghosts, Sarge?"

Leave it to Tannis to dive straight in. Alicia rubbed the upper tractor collar on her thigh. They should be taking that off soon, she thought inconsequentially, and lowered her eyes to it as she considered her answer.

<*Deny it,*> Tisiphone suggested.

<*Won't work. She'll have heard the recordings by now, and I'm sure Okanami's staff psychologist has already briefed her. It would've been nice if you'd let me know I didn't have to talk out loud before I opened my mouth.*>

<*I had not considered the need. When last I had dealings with humans, there were no such things as recorders. Besides, people who spoke to themselves were thought to be touched by the gods.*>

<*Yeah. Well, times have changed.*>

<*Indeed? Then who* are *you talking to?*>

"Well," Alicia said finally, looking back up at Tannis, "I guess maybe I was a bit shaky when I woke up. Blame me?"

"You didn't sound shaky, Sarge. In fact, you sounded a hell of a lot calmer than you should've. I know you. You're a cold-blooded bitch in combat, but you come apart after the fire fight."

Yeah, Alicia reflected, you do know me, don't you, Tannis?

"So you think I've gone buggy?" she said aloud.

" 'Buggy,' " Cateau observed, "is hardly a proper technical diagnosis suited to the mystique of my profession, and you know I'm a mechanic, not a psychobabbler. On the other hand, I'd have to say it sounds . . . unusual."

Alicia shrugged. "What can I tell you? All I can say is that I *feel* rational—but I suppose I would, if I've really lost it."

"Um." Cateau uncrossed her arms and clasped her hands behind her. "That doesn't necessarily follow—I think it's one of those self-assuring theories cooked up by people worried about their own stability—but I'd be inclined to write it off as post-combat shock with anyone else. And if we didn't have you on chip still doing it in your sleep."

<*Damn!* Am *I doing that?*>

<*At times.*>

<*So why didn't you stop me?*>

<*I was built by the gods, Little One; I am neither a goddess myself nor omniscient. All I can do is quiet you* after *you start to speak.*>

<*Damn.*> "Have I had a lot to say?"

"Not a lot. In fact, you tend to shut back up right in mid-word. Frankly, I'd prefer for you to run down instead of breaking off that way."

"Oh, come on, Tannis! Lots of people talk in their sleep."

"Not," Cateau said at her driest, "to figures out of Greek mythology. I didn't even know you'd studied the subject."

"I haven't. It's just— Oh, hell, forget it." Cateau raised an eyebrow, and Alicia snorted. "And get that all-knowing gleam out of your eye. You know how people pick up bits and pieces of null-value data."

"True." Cateau hooked a chair closer to the bed and sat. "The problem, Sarge, is that most people who talk in their sleep haven't dropped right off Fleet scanners for a week—and they don't have weird EEGs, either."

"Weird EEG?" It was time for Alicia's eyebrows to rise, and her surprise was not at all feigned.

"Yep. 'Weird' is Captain Okanami's term, but I'm afraid it fits. He and his team didn't know what they had on their table till they twanged your escape package, but they had a good, clear EEG on you throughout. Spiked just like it's supposed to when you flattened that poor Commander Thompson—" Cateau paused. "They tell you about that?"

"I asked, actually. I knew they'd hit something, and most of the medicos were too busy staying out of reach to get anything done. I've even apologized to him."

"I'm sure he appreciated it." Cateau's eyes gleamed. "Nice clean hit, Sarge, just a tad low." She grinned, then shrugged. "Anyway, there was the spike and all those other squiggles I recognize as lovable old you. But there was another whole pattern—almost like an overlay—wrapped around them."

"Ah?"

"Ah. Almost looked like there were two of you. Mighty peculiar stuff, Sarge. You taking in boarders?"

"Not funny, Tannis," Alicia said, looking away, and Cateau inhaled.

"You're right. Sorry. But it *was* odd, Alley, and when you tie it in with all the other odd questions you've presented us with, it's enough to make the brass nervous. Especially when you start talking as if there *were* someone else living in your head." Cateau shook her head, eyes unwontedly worried. "They don't want a schizoid drop commando running around, Sarge."

"Not running around *loose*, you mean."

"I suppose I do, but you can't really blame them, can you?" She held Alicia's gaze levelly, and it was Alicia's turn to sigh.

"Guess not. Is that the real reason they've kept me isolated?"

"In part. Of course, you really do need continued treatment. The incisions are all done, but they had to put a hunk of laminate into your femur, and about four centimeters of what they managed to save looked like a jigsaw puzzle with missing pieces. You know how quickheal slows up on bone repair, and you ripped hell out of your muscle tissue, too."

"I realize that. And I also know I could've been ambulatory in this thing—" she tapped the upper tractor collar "—weeks ago. Okanami's 'have to wait and see; we're not used to drop commandos' line is getting a bit worn. If he weren't such a sweet old bastard, I'd have started raising hell then."

"Is that why you've been so tractable? I was afraid you must *really* be messed up."

"Yeah." Alicia ran her hands through her amber hair. "Okay, Tannis, let's get right down to it. Am I considered a dangerous lunatic?"

"I wouldn't go so far as to say 'dangerous,' Sarge, but there are . . . concerns. I'm taking over from Captain Okanami as of sixteen hundred today, and we'll be running the whole battery of standard diagnostics, probably with a bit of psych monitoring cranked in. I'll be able to tell you more then."

Alicia smiled a crooked smile. "You're not fooling me, you know."

"Fooling?" Cateau widened her eyes innocently.

"Whatever your tests show, they're going to figure I'm over the edge. Post-combat trauma and all that. Poor girl's probably been suppressing her grief, too, hasn't she? Hell, Tannis, it's a lot harder to prove someone's *not* loopy, and we both know it."

"Well, yes," Cateau agreed after a moment. "You always liked it straight, so I'll level with you. Uncle Arthur came out with me, and he's going to want to debrief you in person, but then you and I are Soissons-bound. Sector General's got lots more equipment, so that's where the real tests come in. On the other hand, I have Uncle Arthur's personal guarantee that I'll be your physician of record, and you know I won't let them crap on you."

"And if I don't want to go?"

"Sorry, Sarge. You've been reactivated."

"Oh, those *bastards*!" Alicia murmured, but there was a trace of amused respect in her voice.

"They can be lovable, can't they?"

"How long do you expect your tests to take after we hit Soissons?"

"As long as they take. You want a guess?" Alicia nodded, and Cateau shrugged. "Don't make any plans for a month or two, minimum."

"That long?" Alicia couldn't quite hide her dismay.

"Maybe longer. Look, Sarge, they want more than just a psych evaluation. They want *answers*, and you already told Okanami you don't know what happened or why you're alive. Okay, that means they're going to have to dig for them. I'm sorry, but that's the way it is."

"And while they're looking, the scent's going to freeze solid."

"Scent?" Cateau sat up straighter. "You in vigilante mode, Sarge?"

"Why not?" Alicia met her eyes. "Who's got a better right?"

Cateau looked away for a moment. "No one, I guess. But that's going to be a factor in their thinking, too, you know. They won't want you running around to do something outstandingly stupid."

"I know." Alicia made herself smile. "Well, if I'm stuck, I'm stuck. And if I am, I'm glad I've got at least one friend in the enemy camp."

"That's the spirit." Cateau rose with a grin of her own. "I've got an appointment with Uncle Arthur in ten minutes—gotta go give him my own evaluation of your condition—but I'll check back when it's over. I may even have more news on your upcoming, um, itinerary."

"Thanks, Tannis." Alicia leaned back against her pillows and smiled after her friend, but the smile faded as the door closed. She sighed and looked pensively down at her hands.

<This will not do, Little One,> Tisiphone said sternly. *<We cannot allow these friends of yours to stand in our way.>*

<I know. I know! Tannis will do her best for me, but she's a stone wall where her medical responsibilities are concerned.>

<Will she conclude you are truly mad, then?>

<Of course she will. That 'psychobabbler' was a load of manure, and let's face it—by her standards, I am

buggy. And one thing the Cadre doesn't *do is let out of control drop commandos run around loose. Terrible PR if they accidentally slaughter a few dozen innocent bystanders in a food-o-mat.*>

<*So.*> Mental silence hovered for a moment, broken by a soundless sigh. <*Well, Little One, in this instance I have little to offer. Once I might have spirited you out of anyone's power, but those days are gone, and friends are always harder to escape than enemies.*>

<*Don't I know it.*> Alicia wrapped herself in consideration for a long moment, thinking too quickly for Tisiphone to follow, then smiled. <*Okay. If they won't let me go, we'll just have to bust out. But not yet.*> She rubbed the tractor collar again. <*Not till we get to Soissons, I think. Nowhere to hide if we tried it here, anyway. Unless you'd care to take me back to that place where 'time has no business' of yours?*>

<*I could, of course. But we could not stay there forever, and when I released you, you would return to the exact spot you had left.*>

<*To be grabbed by whoever sees us. Hell, what if they knock down the hospital and clear out entirely? Freezing my keister in the snow in a hospital gown isn't my idea of a good thing.*>

<*It would seem to have drawbacks,*> Tisiphone agreed.

<*Indeedy deed. All right, it'll have to be Soissons. And if they think I'm crazy anyway, we might as well use that.*>

<*Indeed? How?*>

<*I think I'm going to become* extremely *buggy—in a harmless sort of way. Something I learned about the brass a long time ago, Tisiphone: give them something they think they understand, and they're happy. And happy brass tend to stay out of your way while you get on with business.*>

<*Ahhhhhhh, I see. You will deceive them into lowering their guard.*>

<*Exactly. I'm afraid I'll be talking to you—and the recorders—a lot. In the meantime, I think you and I had*

better figure out exactly what capabilities you still have to help out when the moment comes, don't you?>

<*I do, indeed.*> There was a positively gleeful note to the mental whisper, and Alicia DeVries grinned. Then she lowered her bed into a comfortable sleeping posture and smiled dreamily up at the ceiling.

"Well, Tisiphone," she said aloud, "it doesn't sound like they're going to be too reasonable. The Cadre can be that way, sometimes. In fact, this reminds me of the time Sergeant Malinkov's pharmacope got buggered on Bannerman and pumped him full of endorphins. He got this glorious natural high, you see, and there was this jammed traffic control signal downtown. Now, Pasha was always a helpful soul, and he had his plasgun with him, so—"

She tucked her hands behind her head and babbled cheerfully on to Tisiphone's invisible presence . . . and the recorders.

Chapter Five

The Lizards were showing off again, damn them.

Commodore James Howell gritted his teeth as the Rishathan freighter coasted towards him at five hundred kilometers per second. Rishatha were physically unable to use synth units—much less cyber synth links—and they resented it. Which was why they insisted on overcompensating by showing humanity their panache . . . and also explained why he always met his Rishatha contacts well outside the Powell limit of any system body. Their drives could come closer than humanity's to a planet without destabilizing (or worse), but not by all that much, and losing one's drive during a maneuver like this one could lead to unpleasant consequences all round.

Five hundred KPS wasn't all that fast, even for intrasystem speeds, but the big freighter was barely fifteen thousand kilometers clear, already visible on the visual display, however assiduously Howell might refuse to look at it, and proximity alarms began to buzz. He made himself sit quite still despite their snarls, then sighed with hidden relief as the Rishathan captain flipped her ship end-for-end, pointing her stern at his flagship. The flare of the freighter's Fasset drive (for which, of course, the Rishatha had their own unpronounceable name) was clear to his gravitic detectors, even though its tame black hole was aimed directly away from them. The ship slowed abruptly, then drifted to a near perfect rendezvous in just under fifty-seven seconds. Amazing what nine hundred gravities' deceleration could do.

Attitude and maneuvering thrusters flared as the Fasset drive died, nudging the freighter alongside Howell's dreadnought, and he grinned in familiar, ironic amusement. Mankind—the Rish-kind, unfortunately—could outspeed light, generate pet black holes, and transmit messages scores of light-years in the blink of an eye, yet they still required thrusters the semi-mythical Armstrong would have recognized (in principle, at least) a thousand years before for that last, delicate step. Ridiculous—except that people still used the wheel, too.

He shook off the thought as the freighter's tractors latched onto his command and it nuzzled up against cargo bay ten, extending a personnel tube to his number four lock. He glanced around his bridge at the comfortable, non-descript civilian coveralls of his crew and thought wistfully of the uniform he had discarded with his past. The Lizards weren't much into clothing for protection's sake, but they understood its decorative uses, and their taste was, quite literally, inhuman. It would have been nice to be able to reply in kind to the no doubt upcoming assault on his optic nerves.

His synth link whispered to him, announcing the imminent arrival of a single visitor, and he skinned off the headset and slipped it out of sight under his console. The rest of his command crew were doing the same. The Rish would know they'd done it to avoid flaunting the human ability to form direct links with their equipment, but there were civilities to be observed. Besides, hiding it all away was actually an even more effective way of calling attention to it—and one to which his visitor could take exception only with enormous loss of face. He hoped Resdyrn still commanded the freighter. She always took the con personally for the final approach, and he loved the way her fangs showed when he one-upped her one-upmanship without saying a word.

The command deck hatch hissed open, and Senior War Mother Resdyrn niha Turbach stepped through it.

She was impressive, even for a fully mature Rishathan matriarch. At 2.5 meters and just over three hundred kilos, she towered over every human on the bridge yet looked almost squat. Her incredibly gaudy carapace streamers enveloped her in a diaphanous cloud, swirling from her shoulders and assaulting the eye like some psychotic rainbow, but her face paint was sober—for a Rish. Its bilious green hue suited her temporary "merchant" persona and made a fascinating contrast with her scarlet cranial frills, and Howell wondered again if Rishathan eyes really used the same spectrum as human ones.

"Greetings, Merchant Resdyrn," he said, and listened to the translator render it into the squeaky, snarling ripples of Low Rishathan. Howell had once known an officer who could actually manage High Rishathan, but the same man could also reproduce the exact sound of an old-fashioned buzz-saw hitting a nail at several thousand RPM. Howell preferred to rely upon his translator.

"Greetings, Merchant Howell," the translator bug in his right ear replied. "And greetings to your line mother."

"And also to yours." Howell completed the formal greeting with a bow, amazed once more by how lithely that bulky figure returned it. "My daughter officers await you," he continued. "Shall we join them?"

Resdyrn inclined her massive head, and the two of them walked into the briefing room just off the command bridge. Half a dozen humans rose as they entered, bowing welcome while Resdyrn stalked around the table to the out-sized chair at its foot.

Howell moved to the head of the table and watched her slip her short, clubbed tail comfortably through the open chairback. Despite their saurian appearance and natural body armor, the Rishatha were not remotely reptilian. They were far closer to an oviparous Terrestrial mammal, if built on a rather over-powering scale. Or, at least, the females were. In his entire career, Howell had seen exactly three Rishathan males, and they were runty, ratty-looking little things. Fluttery and helpless, too. No wonder the matriarchs considered "little old man" a mortal insult.

"Well, Merchant Howell," the irony of the honorific came through the translator interface quite well, "I trust you are prepared to conclude our transaction for the goods your line mother has ordered?"

"I am, Merchant Resdyrn," he replied with matching irony and a gesture to Gregor Alexsov. His chief of staff keyed the code on a lock box and slid it to Resdyrn. The Rish lifted the lid and bared her upper canines in a human-style smile as she looked down at a prince's ransom in molecular circuitry, one of the several areas in which human technology led Rishathan.

"These are, of course, but a sample," Howell continued. "The remainder are even now being transferred to your vessel."

"My line mother thanks you through her most humble daughter," Resdyrn replied, not sounding particularly humble, and lifted a crystalline filigree of seaweed from the box. She held it in long, agile fingers with an excessive number of knuckles and peered at it through a magnifier, then grunted the alarming sound of a Rishathan chuckle as she saw the Imperial Fleet markings on the connector chips. She laid it carefully back into its nest, closed the lid once more, and crooked a massive paw protectively over it. The gesture was revealing, Howell thought. That single box, less than a meter in length, contained enough molycircuitry to replace her freighter's entire command net, and for all her studied ease, Resdyrn was well aware of it.

"We, of course, have brought you the agreed upon cargo," she said after a moment, "but I fear my line mother sends your mother of mothers sad tidings, as well." Howell sat straighter in his chair. "This shall be our last meeting for some time to come, Merchant Howell."

Howell swallowed a muttered curse before it touched his expression and cocked his head politely. Resdyrn raised her cranial frills in acknowledgment and touched her forehead in token of sorrow.

"Word has come from our embassy on Old Earth. The Emperor himself—" the masculine pronoun was a deliberate insult from a Rish; the fact that it was also accurate lent it a certain additional and delicious savor "—has taken an interest in this sector and dispatched his war mother Keita hither."

"I . . . had not yet heard that, Merchant Resdyrn." Howell hoped his dismay didn't show. Keita! God, did that mean they were going to have the *Cadre* on their backs? He longed to ask but dared not expend so much face.

"We do not know Keita's mission," Resdyrn continued, taking pity on his curiosity (or, more likely, simply executing her own orders), "but there are no signs that the Cadre has been mobilized. My line mother fears this may yet happen, however, and so must sever her links with you at least until such time as Keita departs. I hope that you will understand her reasoning."

"Of course." Howell inhaled, then shrugged, deliberately exaggerating the gesture to be sure Resdyrn noted it. "My mother of mothers will also understand, though I'm sure she will hope the severance will be brief."

"As do we, Merchant Howell. We of the Sphere hope for your success, that we may greet you as sisters in your own sphere."

"Thank you, Merchant Resdyrn." Howell managed to sound quite sincere, though no human was likely to forget the way the Rishatha had set the old Federation and Terran League at one another's throats in order to pick their joint bones. Four hundred years later, humanity was still coping with the lingering echoes of the League Wars in places like Shallingsport.

Fortunately, the Rishatha's military follow through had been less successful than their diplomatic judo throw. They'd ingested most of the old League during the First Human-Rish War while a war-weary Federation writhed in the throes of civil war, but their calculations hadn't allowed for the Empire which had arisen from the Federation's ruins under then Fleet Admiral Terrence Murphy, and Terrence I and the House of Murphy had kicked the Lizards back into their pre-war boundaries in the *Second* Human-Rish War.

"In that case," Resdyrn rose, ending the unexpectedly brief meeting, "I shall take my leave. I am covered in shame that it was I who must bring this message to you. May your weapons taste victory, Merchant Howell."

"My daughter officers and I see no shame, Merchant Resdyrn, but only the faithful discharge of your line mother's decree."

"You are kind." Resdyrn bestowed another graceful bow upon him and left. Howell made no effort to accompany her. Despite her "merchant's" role, Resdyrn niha Turbach remained a senior war mother of the Rishathan Sphere, and the suggestion that she could not be trusted aboard his vessel without a guard would have been an intolerable insult to her honor. This once, he was just as glad of it, too. Contingency plans or no, this little bit of news was going to bollix the works in *fine* style, and he needed to confer with his staff.

"Jays, Skipper," one member of that staff said. "Now what the bloody hell am I supposed to do?"

"Keep your suit on, Henry," Howell replied, and his long, cadaverous quartermaster leaned ostentatiously back in his chair.

"No problem—yet. But we're gonna look a bit hungry in a few months with our main supply line cut."

"Agreed, but Greg and I knew this—or something like it—might happen. I wish it had waited a while longer, but we've set up our fallbacks."

"Oh? I wish you'd told *me* about them," Commander d'Amcourt said.

"We're telling you now, aren't we? You want to lay it out, Greg?"

"Yes, sir." Alexsov leaned slightly forward, cold eyes thawed by an atypical amusement as he met d'Amcourt's lugubrious gaze. "We've set up alternate supply lines through Wyvern. It'll be more cumbersome, because our purchase orders will have to be spread out carefully, and it was certainly convenient to have the Rishatha as a cutout in our logistics net, but there are advantages, too. For one thing, we can get proper spares and missile resupply direct. And we've already been dumping a lot of luxury items through Wyvern. I don't see any reason we can't fence the rest of our loot there—*they* certainly won't object."

He shrugged, and heads nodded here and there. Most Rogue Worlds were fairly respectable (by their own lights, at least), but Wyvern's government was owned outright by the descendants of the captain-owners of one of the last piratical fleets of the League Wars to go "legitimate." It bought or sold anything, no questions asked, and was equally indiscriminate in the deals it brokered. Many of its fellow Rogue Worlds might deplore its existence, yet Wyvern was too useful an interface (and too well armed) for most of them to do anything more strenuous. Which, since the Empire had both the power and the inclination to smack the hands of those who irritated it, gave Wyvern's robber-baron aristocracy a vested interest in anything that might disrupt the nascent Franconian Sector's stability.

"As for our other support—" Alexsov paused, mentioning no names or places even here, then shrugged "—this shouldn't pose any problems. Unless, of course, Keita's presence means the Cadre plans to shove its nose in."

"Exactly, and that's what worries me most," Howell agreed. He glanced at the rather fragile-looking commander seated at Alexsov's right elbow. Slim, dark-skinned Rachel Shu, Howell's intelligence officer, was the sole female member of his staff . . . and its most lethal. Now she shrugged.

"It worries me, too, Commodore. My sources didn't say a thing about Keita's coming clear out here, so my people don't have any idea what he's up to. On the face of it, I'm inclined to think the Rishatha have overreacted. They don't dare antagonize the Empire by getting caught involved in something like this, and they remember what Keita and the Cadre did to them over the Louvain business, so they're pulling in their horns and getting ready to disclaim any responsibility. But I don't think my sources could have missed the signs if the Cadre were being committed on any meaningful scale."

"Then why's Keita here? Wasn't he their point for Louvain, too?"

"He was, but the Cadre's too small for him to have pulled out any major force without my people noticing it. Besides, my last reports place him in the Macedon Sector, not on Old Earth, so this looks more like a spur of the moment improvisation, and the timing's about right for it to be in response to Mathison's World. He was right next door and they banged him on out—they didn't deploy him from the capital. I suspect he's on some sort of special intelligence-gathering mission for Countess Miller. She's always preferred to get a reading through Cadre Intelligence to crosscheck on ONI, and Keita's always been happier in the field than an HQ slot. If he hadn't, *he'd* have the general's stars and Arbatov would be *his* exec."

"Which means we could see the Cadre yet," Rendlemann pointed out.

"Unlikely," Shu replied. "Our support structure's very well hidden and dispersed, and the Cadre's a precision instrument for application to precise targets. In fact, I'd say the Ministry of Justice was more dangerous than either the Fleet or Cadre, since it's the covert side of this whole operation that's most likely to lead the other two to us, and Justice is best equipped for getting at us from that side. As far as the Cadre's concerned, I'll start to worry when we see a major transfer of its personnel to this sector or one of its neighbors. Until that happens, Keita's just one more spook. A good one, but no more than that."

"I think you're right, Rachel," Howell said. At any rate, he certainly *hoped* she was. "We'll proceed on that basis for now, but I want you to double-check with Control ASAP."

"Yes, sir. The next intelligence courier's due in about five days. It may already be bringing us confirmation; if it isn't, I'll send a request back by the same dispatch boat."

"All right." Howell toyed with a stylus, then glanced at Alexsov. "Is there anything else we need to look at while we're all together, Greg?" Alexsov shook his head. "In that case, I think you and Henry might make a quick run to Wyvern to set things in motion there. Don't take along anything incriminating—we've got the liquidity to pay cash for the first orders—but sound out the locals for future marketing possibilities."

"Can do," Alexsov replied. "How soon can you leave, Henry?"

"Ummmm . . . a couple of hours, I'd guess."

"Good," Howell said, "because unless I miss my guess—and unless Keita *is* going to make problems—we ought to be getting our next targeting order from Rachel's courier. I'll want you back here for the skull sessions, Greg."

"In that case, I'd better get packed." Alexsov stood, a general signal for the meeting to break up, and Howell watched his subordinates file out of the briefing room. He walked over to the small-scale system display in the corner and stood brooding down at the holograph star and its barren, lifeless planets. Rachel was probably right, he decided. If Keita were the spear-point of a Cadre intervention, he would have brought at least an intelligence staff with him. On the other hand, Keita was the tip of a damned spear all by himself; the rest of the weapon could always be brought in later, and that could complicate life in a major way.

He reached out, cupping a palm around the minute, silvery mote of his flagship, and sighed. Problems, problems. The life of a piratical freebooter had seemed so much simpler—and so much more lucrative—than a career with the Fleet, and the bigger objective was downright exciting. There were the minor drawbacks of having to become a mass murderer, a thief, and a traitor to his uniform, but the rewards were certainly great . . . assuming one lived to enjoy them.

He released his flagship with a heavier sigh, folding

his hands behind him, and started thoughtfully towards the briefing room hatch.

How in hell, he wondered silently, had Midshipman James Howell, Imperial Fleet, Class of '28, ended up *here*?

Chapter Six

"Still so eager to be up and about?"

Alicia inhaled a spray of sweat as she gasped for breath, but she welcomed the teasing malice in Lieutenant de Riebeck's voice. The physical therapist was a fellow Cadreman, without a trace of the semi-awe her drop commando reputation woke in ordinary medics. That was refreshing enough, and his complete indifference to her mental state was even more so. Alicia had agitated so noisily to get out of bed that even Okanami and Major Cateau had finally given in, but de Riebeck had been their revenge. His sole interest lay in getting one Captain Alicia DeVries not merely ambulatory but fully reconditioned, and his was clearly an obsessive personality.

"Looking a little worn to me, Captain," he continued brightly, and cranked the treadmill's speed control up a bit. "Care for another five or six klicks? How about another five percent of grade just to make it interesting?"

Alicia moaned and collapsed over the handrails. The still-moving treadmill carried her feet from under her, and she twitched with a horridly realistic death rattle and belly-flopped onto the belt. It deposited her on the floor with a thump, and she oozed out flat.

Lieutenant de Riebeck grinned, and someone applauded from the training room door. Alicia rolled over and sat up, raking sweat-sodden hair from her forehead, and saw Tannis Cateau clapping vigorously.

"I give that a nine-point-five for dramatic effect and, oh, a three-point-two for coordination." Alicia shook a fist, and the major chuckled. "I see Pablo is being his usual sadistic self."

"We strive to please, Major, ma'am," de Riebeck smirked. Alicia laughed, and Cateau reached down to pull her to her feet.

"You know, I never thought I'd admit it, but this is one part of the Cadre I've missed," she panted, massaging her rebuilt thigh with both hands. The repaired muscles ached, but it was the good ache of exercise, and she straightened with a sigh. Despite her reactivation, she refused to cut her hair, which had escaped its clasp once more. She gathered it back up and refastened it, then scrubbed her face with a towel.

"I think I'm going to live after all, Pablo."

"Aw, shucks. Well, there's always tomorrow."

"An inspiring thought." Alicia hung the towel around her neck and turned back to Cateau. "May I assume you arrived for some reason other than to rescue me from Lieutenant de Sade?"

"Indeed I have. Uncle Arthur wants to see you."

"Oh." The humor flowed out of Alicia's voice, and her forefingers moved in slow circles, wrapping the towel-ends about them. Her success in so far avoiding Keita made her feel a bit guilty, but she really didn't want to see him. Not now, and perhaps never. He was going to bring back too many painful memories . . . and Cadre rumor credited him with telepathy, among other arcane powers. He'd always made her feel as if her skull were made of glass.

"Sorry, Sarge, but he insists. And I think it's a good idea myself."

"Why?" Alicia demanded bluntly, and Cateau shrugged.

"You didn't quit the Cadre just to avoid Uncle Arthur, and you've been hiding from him long enough. It's time you faced up to him. *He* knows, whether you do or not, that you didn't 'fail' him by resigning, but you're never going to feel comfortable about it till you talk to him in person. Call it absolution."

"I don't need 'absolution'!" Alicia snapped, jade eyes flashing with sudden fire, and Cateau grinned crookedly.

"Then why the sudden heat? Come on, Sarge." She hooked an arm through Alicia's. "I'm surprised he's let your debrief wait this long, so you may as well get it over with."

"You can be a real pain in the ass, Tannis."

"True, too true. Now march, Sarge."

"Can't I even clean up first?"

"Uncle Arthur knows what sweat smells like. March!"

Alicia sighed, but the steel showed under Cateau's humor, and she was right. Alicia couldn't keep pretending Keita wasn't here. But Tannis only thought she understood why Alicia had resigned. No one—not even Tannis—knew the real reason for that, and how much it had cost her or why she had turned her back so utterly upon the Cadre. No one but Sir Arthur. Yet even reliving that decision, horrid as it would be, was only part of her present hesitance.

A heat which was rapidly becoming familiar tingled in her right arm, radiating from its contact with Cateau's left elbow, and she felt her friend's thoughts. Amusement. Pride in the way she was bouncing back from her wounds. Carefully hidden worry over the upcoming interview. A burning curiosity as to the reasons for her dread over meeting Keita and concern over their possible consequences, and under it a deeper, more persistent worry about Alicia's stability—and what to do about her if she was, in fact, *un*stable.

<Stop that!>

<Why? She is your physician, and we need this information.>

<Not from Tannis—not this way. She's also my friend.>

A mental grumble answered, but the information flow died, and she was grateful. Stealing Tannis's thoughts was a violation of her privacy and trust—almost a form of rape, even if she never felt a thing—and Alicia hated it.

Not that it hadn't been useful, she conceded. The first time Tannis had hugged her, Tisiphone had plucked a disturbing suspicion from the major's mind. Alicia's monologues had gotten just a bit too enthusiastic, and Tannis knew her too well.

Forewarned, Alicia had tapered off and allowed her manufactured dialogues to run down as if she were tiring of the game. Tannis had written them off as a sarcastic response to the people who suspected her sanity, and thereafter Alicia had restricted herself to occasional verbal responses to actual comments from Tisiphone. That worked much better, for they were spontaneous, fragmentary, and enigmatic yet consistent—clearly not something manufactured out of whole cloth for the sole benefit of eavesdroppers—and their genuineness had turned Tannis's thoughts in the desired direction.

Alicia hated deceiving her, but she *was* having those conversations. It was always possible she truly was mad—a possibility she would almost prefer, at times—and if she wasn't, she certainly wasn't responsible for Tannis's misinterpretations of them.

She squared her shoulders, tucked the ends of the towel into the neck of her sweat shirt, and walked down the hallway at her friend's side.

Tisiphone watched through her host's eyes as they marched along the corridor. The past few weeks had been the oddest of her long life, a strange combination of impatient waiting and discovery, and she wasn't certain she had enjoyed them.

She and Alicia had learned much about her own current abilities. She could still pluck thoughts from mortal minds, but only when her host brought those other mortals into physical contact. She could still hasten physical healing, as well, yet what had once been "miracles" were routine to the medical arts man had attained. There was little she could do to speed what the physicians were already accomplishing, and so she had restricted herself to holding pain and discomfort within useful limits and insuring her host's sleep without medication or one of the peculiar somatic units. Tisiphone hated the somatic units. They might sweep Alicia into slumber through her receptors, but sleep was a stranger to Tisiphone. For her, the somatic units' soothing waves were a droning, scarcely endurable static.

She and Alicia had also determined to their satisfaction that she still could blur mortals' senses, even without physical contact. Their technology, unfortunately, was something else again, and that experiment had almost ended in disaster. The nurse had *known* the bed was empty, but her medical scanners had insisted it was occupied. Not surprisingly, the young woman had panicked and turned to run, and only the testing of another ability had saved the situation. Tisiphone could no longer beguile and control mortal minds, but she could fog and befuddle them. Actually taking memories from them might have become impossible, but she had blurred the recollection into a sort of fanciful daydream, and that had been just as good—this time.

Their experiments had combined dismay and excitement in almost equal measure, yet neither Tisiphone's own sense of discovery and rediscovery nor Alicia's amazement at what she still could accomplish had been sufficient to banish her boredom. She was a being of fire and passion, the hunger and destruction of her triumvirate of selves. Alecto had been the methodical one, the inescapable stalker patient as the stones themselves, and Megarea had been the thinker who analyzed and pondered with a mind of ice and steel. Tisiphone was the weapon, unleashed only when her targets had been clearly identified, her objectives precisely defined. Now she could not even know who her targets were, much less where to find them, and she felt . . . lost. Ignorance added to her sense of frustration, for if she had no doubt of her ultimate success, she was unused to delays and puzzles. It had turned her surly and snappish (not, she admitted privately, an unusual state for such as she) with her host until a fresh revelation diverted them both.

Tisiphone had discovered computers. More to the point, she had encountered the processors built into Alicia's augmentation, and had she been the sort of being who possessed eyes, they would have opened wide in surprise.

The data storage of Alicia's processors was little more than a few dozen terrabytes, for bio-implants simply couldn't rival the memories of full-sized units, yet they were the first computers Tisiphone had ever met, and she had been amazed by how easy they were to access. It had taken no effort at all, for they were designed and programmed for neural linkage; the same technique which slipped into a mortal's thoughts through his nerves and brain worked just as well with them, and the vistas that opened were dazzling.

It was almost like finding the ghost of one of her sister selves. A weak and pallid revenant, without the rich awareness which had textured that forever-lost link, yet one which expanded her own abilities many-fold. Tisiphone had only the vaguest grasp of what Alicia called "programming" or "machine language," but those concepts were immaterial to her. A being crafted to interface with human minds had no use or need for such things; anything structured to link with those same minds became an extension of them and so an instinctive part of herself.

She had scared Alicia half to death, and felt uncharacteristically penitent for it afterward, the first time she activated her host's main processor and walked her body across the room without consulting her. Their security codes meant nothing to Tisiphone, and she unlocked them effortlessly, exploring the labyrinthine marvels of logic trees and data flows with sheer delight. Their molycirc wonders had become a vast, marvelous toy, and she flowed through them like the wind, recognizing the way in which she might use them, in an emergency, as both capacitor and amplifier. They restored something she had lost, restored a bit of what she once had been, and she had sensed Alicia's amusement as she chattered away about her finds.

Yet it was past time for them to be about their mission, and she wondered if Alicia's meeting with Sir Arthur Keita would bring the moment closer or send it receding even further into the future.

Alicia's spine stiffened against her will as she stepped into the sparsely appointed conference room. A small, spruce man in the crimson tunic and blue trousers of the Ministry of Justice's uniformed branches stood looking out a window. He didn't turn as she and Tannis entered, and she was just as happy. Her eyes were on the square, powerful man seated at the table.

He still refused to wear his ribbons, she noted. Well, no one was likely to pester him about proper uniform. She came to attention before him, clasping her hands behind her, and stared three inches over his head.

"Captain Alicia DeVries, reporting as ordered, sir!" she barked, and Sir Arthur Keita, Knight Grand Commander of the Order of Terra, Solarian Grand Cross, Medal of Valor with diamonds and clasp, and second in command of the Personal Cadre of His Imperial Majesty Seamus II, studied her calmly.

"Cut the kay-det crap, Alley," he rumbled in a gravel-crusher voice, and her lips quirked involuntarily. Her eyes met his. He smiled. It was a small smile, but a real one, easing a bit of the tightness in her chest.

"Yes, Uncle Arthur," she said.

The shoulders of the man looking out the window twitched. He turned just a tad quickly, and her lips quirked again at his reaction to her *lese majeste*. So he hadn't known how the troops referred to Keita, had he?

"That's better." Keita pointed at a chair. "Sit."

She obeyed without comment, clasping her hands loosely in her lap, and returned his searching gaze. He hadn't changed much. He never did.

"It's good to see you," he resumed after a moment. "I wish it could be under different circumstances, but—" A raised hand tipped, as if pouring something from a cupped palm. She nodded, but her eyes burned with sudden memory. Not of Mathison's World, but of another time, after Shallingsport. He'd known the uselessness of words then, too, when she'd learned of her promotion and medal and he'd shared her grief. A time, she thought, when she'd actually believed she would remain in the Cadre and not just of it.

"I know I promised we'd never reactivate you," he continued, "but it wasn't my decision." She nodded again. She'd known that, for if Sir Arthur Keita seldom gave his word, that was only because he never broke it.

"However," he went on, "we're both here now, and I've postponed this debrief as long as I could. The relief force pulls out for Soissons day after tomorrow; I'll have to make my report—and my recommendations—to Governor Treadwell and Countess Miller when we arrive, and I won't do that without speaking personally to you first. Fair?"

"Fair." Alicia's contralto was deeper than usual, but her eyes were steady, and it was his turn to nod.

"I've already viewed your statement to Colonel McIlheny, so I've got a pretty fair notion of what happened in the fire fight. It's what happened after it that bothers me. Are you prepared to tell me more about it now?"

The deep voice was unusually gentle, and Alicia felt an almost unbearable temptation to tell him everything. Every single impossible word. If anyone in the galaxy would have believed her it was Uncle Arthur. Unfortunately, no one could believe her, not even him, and they weren't alone. Her eyes flipped to the Justice man, and an eyebrow arched.

"Inspector Ferhat Ben Belkassem, Intelligence Branch," Keita said. "You may speak freely in front of him."

"In front of a spook?" Alicia's eyes snapped back to Keita's face, suddenly hard, and the temptation to openness faded.

"In case you've forgotten, *I'm* a spook," he replied quietly.

"No, sir, I haven't forgotten. And, sir, I respectfully decline to be debriefed by Intelligence personnel." It came out clipped and colder than she'd intended, and Ben Belkassem's eyebrows rose in surprise.

Keita sighed, but he didn't retreat. His eyes bored into her across the table, and there was no yield in his voice.

"That isn't an option, Alley. You're going to have to talk to me."

"Sir, I decline."

"Oh, come on, Alley! You've already spoken to McIlheny!"

"I have, sir, when under the impression that he remained a combat branch officer. And—" her voice turned even colder "—Colonel McIlheny is neither Cadre nor a representative of the Ministry of Justice. As such, he may in fact be an honorable man."

She felt Cateau flinch behind her, but Tannis held her tongue and Ben Belkassem stepped back half a pace. It wasn't a retreat; he was simply giving her room, declaring his neutrality in whatever lay between her and Keita.

The brigadier leaned back and pinched the bridge of his nose.

"You can't decline, Alley. This isn't like last time, and I can't make any bargains with you." She sat stonily silent, and his face hardened. "Allow me to correct myself. In one respect, this is *exactly* like last time: you can damned well end up in the stockade if you push it."

"Sir, I respectful—"

"Hold it." He interrupted her in mid-word, before she could dig in any more deeply, then shook his head. "You always were a stubborn woman, Alley. But this isn't the case of a captain breaking a colonel around the edges—" Ben Belkassem's eyes widened fractionally at that "—and I don't have the latitude to allow you a gesture." He raised a palm as her eyes flared hot. "You had a right to it. I said so then, and I say so now, but this *isn't* then, and the questions aren't coming just from me. Countess Miller personally charged me with uncovering the truth."

His eyes drilled into hers, and she sat back in her chair. He meant it. If it had been only him, he might have let her off—again. But he had his orders, and orders were something he took very seriously, indeed.

"Excuse me, Sir Arthur." Ben Belkassem raised one

placating hand as he spoke. "If my presence is the problem, I will willingly withdraw."

"No, Inspector, you won't." Keita's voice was frosty. "You are part of this operation, and I will value your input. Alley?"

"Sir, I can't. It— I promised the *company*, sir." Her own hoarseness surprised her, and a tear glistened. She felt Tisiphone's surprise at the surge of raw, wounded emotion, then relaxed minutely as the Fury slipped another pane of that mysterious glass between her and the anguish. She drew a deep breath, meeting Keita's eyes pleadingly but with determination. "You understand about promises, sir."

"I do," Keita didn't wince, though his voice gave the impression he had, "but I have no choice. I know what happened at Shallingsport, and I was at Louvain. I understand your attitude. But I have no choice."

"Understand?" Alicia's voice cracked. She swallowed, but she couldn't stop. Despite all Tisiphone could do, an old, old agony drove her. "I'm not sure you do, sir. I don't think anyone could—except Tannis, perhaps. We went in with a company, sir—a *company!*—and came out with less than a squad!"

"I know."

"Yes, and you know *why*, too, sir! You know why that son-of-a-bitch screwed our mission brief to hell! You know he sent us in against a 'soft target,' a bunch of crackpot League separatists with 'improvised weaponry' and no tactical training. Well, I've got news for you, sir—there were two fucking *thousand* of the bastards, with the best weapons money could buy! But Captain Alwyn took us in, and we did our job. Oh, yes, we did our goddamned *job*, and seven of us came out alive!"

"Alley. Alley!" Alicia's augmentation crackled with prep signals as emotion jangled through her, and Cateau's hands massaged her shoulders, trying to relax her tension. "They did their best, Sarge." Tannis's voice was soft. "Intelligence screws up sometimes. It *happens*, Alley."

"Not like this," Alicia grated. "Not like this time, does

it, Uncle Arthur?" Her eyes were green flint, challenging his, and he inhaled deeply.

"No, Captain. Not like this," he said at last, quietly, and looked over her head at Major Cateau. "Did Alley ever discuss this with you, Major?"

"No, sir." Tannis sounded confused, Alicia thought, and no wonder.

"No," he sighed, and turned his eyes back to Alicia. "Forgive me. You promised me you wouldn't, didn't you?"

She stared back, face like marble, and he pursed his lips in thought, then nodded slowly.

"Perhaps it's time someone did, Major." He gestured at the chair beside Alicia and waited until Cateau sat. "All right. You know about the, um, flap when Alicia resigned?" Tannis nodded. "Then you know it was part of a bargain—a cover-up, if you will. In return for her resignation, the Cadre agreed not to press charges for striking a superior officer. Correct?" She nodded again. "Do you happen to know the identity of the officer she struck?"

"No, sir."

"I'll be damned. I never thought the cover-up would hold." Keita pinched the bridge of his nose again. "That officer, Major Cateau, was Colonel Wadislaw Watts, Imperial Cadre, the man—" he met her eyes, not Alicia's "—responsible for the Shallingsport intelligence assessment. And she didn't just 'strike' him; she hospitalized him in critical condition. In fact, it was, by her own subsequent admission, her intent to kill him."

Tannis gasped and turned to stare at her friend, but Alicia looked straight ahead, eyes stony, showing her only her profile, while Keita continued in that same flat, steady voice.

"Precisely. You and I know, Major, that the Cadre isn't perfect, whatever the Empire as a whole may believe. We make mistakes. Not often, perhaps, but we make them, and when we do, they can have . . . major consequences. Shallingsport was one such mistake."

"*Mistake!*" Alicia hissed like a curse, then caught herself and pressed her lips together. Keita frowned, but he didn't reprimand her. He simply went on speaking to Tannis as if they were the only people in the room.

"Alley's right," he told her. "It wasn't a mistake that killed ninety-three percent of your company. It was a crime, because those casualties—" he laid his palms on the tabletop, as if for balance "—were completely avoidable. Colonel Watts had in his possession data which gave an accurate picture of the opposition you faced. Data which he suppressed."

Cateau's face was white, twisted with disbelief and anguish, and Keita folded his hands together and frowned down at them.

"He thought he could get away with it, hide it," he said softly, "and he very nearly did."

"But . . . but *why*, sir?"

"Blackmail. The . . . foreign power actually behind the Shallingsport terrorists had suborned him. He'd been feeding them information—minor data, but valuable—for seven years before the raid, and he'd been very, very clever. He went through several routine security checks and one regular five-year close scrutiny, and we never realized. But when Shallingsport came up, his employers informed him that he could either cook his intelligence analysis to guarantee a blood bath that ended in failure, or be exposed by them."

"You're saying we were set up," Cateau whispered.

"Exactly. You were supposed to be wiped out and 'push' the terrorists into massacring their hostages, thus blackening the Cadre's reputation and branding the Emperor with the blame for a catastrophic military adventure. That plan failed for only two reasons: the courage and determination of your company and, in particular, of Master Sergeant Alicia DeVries."

Alicia glared at him, hands taloned in her lap under the table edge, and horror boiled behind her eyes. Captain Alwyn and Lieutenant Strassman dead in the drop. Lieutenant Masolle dead two minutes after grounding. First Sergeant Yussuf and her people buying the breakout from the LZ with their lives. And then the nightmare cross-country journey in their powered armor, while people—friends—were picked off, blown apart, incinerated in gouts of plasma or shattered by tungsten penetrators from auto cannon and heavy machine-guns. Two-man atmospheric stingers screaming down to strafe and rocket their bleeding ranks, and the wounded they had no choice but to abandon. And then the break-in to the hostages. Private Oselli throwing himself in front of a plasma cannon to shield the captives. Tannis screaming a warning over the com and shooting three terrorists off her back while point-blank small arms battered her own armor and she took two white-hot tungsten penetrators meant for Alicia. The terror and blood and smoke and stink as somehow they held they held they *held* until the recovery shuttles came down like the hands of God to pluck them out of Hell while she and the medic ripped at Tannis's armor and restarted her heart twice. . . .

It was impossible. They couldn't have done it—*no one* could have done it—but they had. They'd done it because they were the best. Because they were the Cadre, the chosen samurai of the Empire. Because it was their duty. Because they were, by God, too stupid to know they couldn't . . . and because they were all that stood between two hundred civilians and death.

"The plan failed," Keita's quiet voice cut through the surreal flashes of hideous memory, "because of you people, but we didn't know how the intelligence had gone so horribly wrong. We looked—I assure you we looked—but we never found the answers. And then, two years later, on Louvain, Captain DeVries captured a dying Rishathan War Mother. Her medics did their best for the Rish, but she was too far gone. And because she was dying and Alley had spared her war daughters' lives, she repaid her honor debt."

More memories wracked Alicia, and Tisiphone rushed to harvest their rage, gathering it up and storing its fiery strength. Alicia remembered the dying Rish. She remembered the beautiful golden eyes blazing in that hideous face as the matriarch discovered she was *that* DeVries and bestowed the priceless, poisonous gift in the name of honor.

"There was no proof, no record, only the word of a dying Rish, but Alley knew it was true. And because she had no proof, she returned to the command ship, found Colonel Wadislaw Watts, the mission's assistant intelligence chief, and challenged him with what she'd learned. He panicked and tried to run, confirming his guilt, and she shattered his skull, his ribs, and both legs with her bare hands before they could pull her off him."

The room was very quiet, and Alicia heard her own harsh breathing while echoes of savagery burned in her nerves. Only her hate had spared Watts's life. Only her need to make him *feel* it, to return just a taste of what her people had suffered. If only she'd kept control of herself! One clean blow—just one!—would have left the medics nothing to save.

"And that," Keita said sadly, "was when the cover-up began. Baron Yuroba was Minister of War at the time. He decided no breath of disgrace could be permitted to mar our success at Louvain, and Minister of Justice Canaris agreed for reasons of his own. The reason for Alley's attack was hushed up, and she was given her choice: resign or face trial for assaulting a superior officer. No scandal. No messy media circus and gory court martial to befoul the honor we'd won at Louvain or provoke a fresh 'incident' with the Rishatha. Watts was retired, stripped of his pension, and turned over to Justice, who—in return for his secret testimony and assistance in breaking the Rishathan espionage net which had run him—amnestied him for his crimes."

Tears trickled down Cateau's face, and her eyes were sick.

"That's why Alley won't talk to 'spooks,' Tannis. Not even to me. She doesn't trust us."

"I trust *you*, sir," Alicia said very quietly. "I know how you fought it—and I know I only got off as lightly as I did because of you."

"That's crap, Alley," Sir Arthur replied. "They wouldn't have dared push it in the end—not when they'd have had to explain why they were breaking one of the three living holders of the Banner of Terra."

"Maybe. But it doesn't change anything, sir. I would have forgiven them anything but letting Watts live—letting him keep his *honor* by purging the record. My people deserved better than that."

"They did, and I couldn't give it to them. We live in an imperfect universe, and all we can do is the best we can. But that's the real reason they sent me clear out here in person. Countess Miller's read the sealed records. She knows how you feel and why, but she's been instructed by His Majesty himself to discover how you managed to survive and evaded all of our sensors. I am directed to inform you that this matter has been given Crown priority, that I speak with the Emperor's own voice, as your personal liege. No doubt the intent is to duplicate the capability in other personnel, but there is also an element of fear. The unknown has that effect even today, and they're determined to get to the bottom of it. I would . . . greatly prefer to be able to tell them myself, Alley."

His eyes were almost pleading, and she looked away. He still wanted to shield her. Wanted to protect her from those less wary of her wounds or what their questions might cost her. But what could she do? If she told him the absolute, literal truth, he'd never believe her.

<*Little One,*> the voice in her mind was soft, <*I like this man. He has the taste of honor.*>

<*He* is *honor,*> she replied bitterly. <*That's why they gave him this assignment. Because he'll do what his oath to the Emperor demands, however much he may hate himself for it.*>

<*What will you tell him?*>

<*I don't want to lie to him—I don't even know if I could make myself try, and he'd spot it in a minute if I did.*>

<*Then do not,*> Tisiphone suggested. <*Tell him what he asks.*>

<*Are you out of your mind?! He'll think I'm crazy!*>

<*Precisely.*>

Alicia blinked. She actually hadn't considered this possibility when she decided to maintain her semblance of insanity. She should have realized she would be forced to confront the Cadre and her past directly, but the old wound had been too deep for her to consider all its implications, and she'd never guessed the Emperor himself might insist on probing the matter.

But suppose she told Keita the whole story? He had a built-in lie detector no hardware could match. He'd know she was telling the truth . . . as she believed it, at any rate. What would he do with her then?

What his orders dictated, of course. He'd return her to Soissons for further investigation—and, no doubt, treatment for her insanity. That might even be good, since the sector capital would be a much more practical base from which to begin her own search for the pirates. But because he would know she was far, far over the edge, he'd also do what the book demanded and shut down her augmentation through Tannis's overrides.

<*And if he does?*> Tisiphone had followed her internal debate. <*We have already determined I can reactivate it any time I choose, and would it not aid our escape if they believe your augmentation is useless?*>

Alicia looked back up and met Keita's pain-filled gaze. She couldn't tell them everything. Even if they didn't believe in Tisiphone, they might be alarmed enough to take precautions against the Fury's ability to read thoughts and handle her augmentation. But if she cut off, say, with the day Tannis had arrived, before they'd begun their experiments. . . .

"All right, Uncle Arthur," she sighed. "You won't believe me, but I'll tell you exactly where I was and how I got there."

Chapter Seven

<I think you are in trouble, Little One,> Tisiphone observed as Major Cateau's left leg scythed viciously for Alicia's ankles.

She levitated above its arc, and her own foot lashed out. Tannis never saw it coming, but the moves and counters, action and reaction, were part of them both, as automatic as sneezing on dust. She fell away from the kick, robbing it of its power, and slammed a wrist up under Alicia's ankle. Alicia fell to the mat as Tannis landed on her own shoulder blades and flowed into a backward somersault. She tucked and rolled until her toes touched the mat and dug in—then straightened her knees explosively and catapulted back toward Alicia in a ferocious charge. Alicia had rolled sideways and bounced up herself, but she was still off-center when the major reached her. Arms snaked about one another, hands flashed and parried in a flickering blur, and then Tannis was leaning forward, one leg bent, the other in full extension, while Alicia cartwheeled through the air with a squawk of dismay. She hit the mat with a mighty thud, flat on her belly and tried to roll upright, only to grunt in anguish as a knee drove into her spine, a hand cupped the back of her head, and a forearm of iron pressed into her throat.

"How about it, Sarge?" Tannis panted in a disgustingly pleased tone.

<*Yes, Little One,*> Tisiphone asked interestedly, <*how about it?*>

<*Oh, shut up!*> Alicia snapped back, and went limp with a groan.

"Uncle," she said.

"Damn, that feels good." Cateau's grin sparkled, and she rose, then leaned forward to help Alicia to her feet.

"For one of us," Alicia muttered, massaging the small of her back cautiously. She and Tannis wore light protective gear and sparring mittens—no mere precaution but a necessity when drop commandos practiced full-contact—but every bone and sinew ached.

"Out of shape, that's your problem," the major jibed. "You used to take me three falls out of five, and now you're letting a pill-pusher throw you around the salle? Dear me, what*ever* would Sergeant Delacroix say?"

"Nothing. He'd just take both us uppity bitches round to the advanced class and lay us out cold."

"Ah, for the good old days!" Tannis sighed, and Alicia chuckled. Learning to do that again hadn't been easy. The last few weeks had been bad, not shattering but drably depressing, for her senses were dull and dead, deprived of the needle-sharp acuity of her sensory boosters. Those boosters had been a part of her for so long she felt maimed without them.

She knew her friend had shut down her own augmentation to make their sparring even. Not, she admitted, with another groan, that Tannis any longer needed the edge her hardware might have given her. She stood barely one hundred sixty-five centimeters to Alicia's own one-eighty-three, but her home world boasted a gravity thirty percent greater than Earth's, and there were no noncombatant drop commandos. Medics were medics first but only first, and Tannis had spent the last five years keeping her edge in workouts just like this one.

Alicia hadn't. In fact, the mind boggled at how any of Mathison's citizenry would have reacted to an invitation to an all-out bout.

She got herself fully upright and pushed her non-reg bangs out of her eyes, knowing she looked a wreck and wondering where the vid sensors were. All her military rights had been scrupulously observed, and Keita himself, as regs prescribed, had formally notified her (not without an unusual, wooden embarrassment) that she would be kept under observation at all times. She was carried on the sick list, and—technically—she wasn't a prisoner, which gave her full run of the transport, but they couldn't take a chance on her vanishing again. And, if she did, they wanted a complete readout with every instrument they had on precisely how she'd managed it.

Which was an excruciatingly polite way of saying they couldn't let her run around unwatched when they were no longer confident she could count to twenty with her shoes on.

As much as she'd expected—and, yes, worked for it—it hurt, and it had wounded more than her alone. Keita could have let Tannis explain it all to her as her physician if he weren't such an honorable old stick . . . and if he hadn't known how distressed Tannis already was over deactivating her augmentation. All of her processors had been shut down, and her pharmacope, and her Alpha and Gamma receptors, as well. He'd made an exception for her Beta receptor, so she could still at least directly access the computers for information and entertainment, and he'd stood beside her in sickbay, offering her his support and acknowledging his personal responsibility for the decision. He'd looked so unhappy *she'd* wanted to comfort *him*.

Of course, he didn't know Tisiphone had run her own tests since and demonstrated that the "unbreakable" reactivation codes were as effective as so much smoke against her.

"'Nother fall, Sarge?" Cateau inquired lazily. Alicia backed away with a shudder that was only half-feigned, but the glint in those brown eyes was a great relief.

She'd worried over Tannis's reaction to the truth about Shallingsport, yet she'd weathered the news well. And while she might be throwing herself into this sparring just a bit more enthusiastically to hide from it, Tannis's real motive—and the real reason for Tisiphone's teasing, though the Fury would never admit it—was to take Alicia's mind off *her* problems. Not that knowing made bruises feel any better.

"Between you and Pablo, I'll be back in sickbay by the time we hit Soissons. Damn it, woman! I've only been back in shape for this for a week! Give me a break, will you?"

"Which vertebra?" Tannis purred, then collapsed in most unprofessional giggles at Alicia's expression. "Sorry," she gasped. "Sorry, Sarge! It's just that I'm enjoying being the one kicking *your* tail for a change!"

"Oh?" Alicia gave her a sidelong, measuring glance, then curled her lip in a vulpine smile. "Why, that's very wise of you, Major. It's two more weeks to Soissons, after all." Bared teeth glinted pearl-white at her friend. "Care for a little side bet on who's going to be kicking whose tail by the time we get there, ma'am?"

Inspector Ben Belkassem sipped coffee and slid the folder of record chips aside. The ventilators sucked a rope of fragrance away from Sir Arthur's pipe, and he sniffed appreciatively, but his face was serious.

"She seems so convinced I sometimes find myself believing it," he said at last, and Keita grunted agreement. "There don't seem to be any loose ends, either. It's all internally consistent, however bizarre it sounds."

"That's what worries me," Keita admitted. "She sounds convincing because she believes it—I knew that even before she went under the verifier. There's absolutely no question in her mind, no doubts, and it's not like Alicia to accept things unquestioningly. She wouldn't, unless there really were something 'speaking to her,' so either she's truly broken down into some sort of multiple personality disorder, or else some external force has convinced her of the complete accuracy of everything she's told us."

Ben Belkassem straightened in his chair, eyebrows rising. "Are you seriously suggesting that there actually *is* something else, some sort of entity or puppeteer, living inside her head, Sir Arthur?"

"There's certainly *an* entity, even if it's a product of her own delusions." Keita busied himself relighting his pipe. "And *she* certainly believes it's a foreign one."

"Granted, but surely it's far more probable that she's slipped into some kind of delusionary pattern. My understanding from Major Cateau is that this high degree of internal consistency and absolute self-belief is normal in such cases, and Captain DeVries has certainly been through more than enough to produce a breakdown. I had no idea how traumatic her military service had been, but when you add that to the brutal way her family was massacred and her own wounds . . ." His voice trailed off, and he shrugged.

"Um." Keita got his pipe drawing and squinted through its smoke. "How much do you know about Cadre selection criteria, Inspector?"

"Very little, other than that they're quite rigorous and demanding."

"Not surprising, I suppose. Still, you do know the Cadre is the only arm of the military whose strength is limited by Senate statute, correct?"

"Of course. And, with all due respect, it's not hard to understand why, given that the Cadre answers directly to the Emperor in his own person. Everyone knows you're a *corps d'elite*, but you're also the Emperor's personal liegemen, and he has enough power without giving him that big a stick."

"I won't disagree with you, Inspector." Keita chuckled around his pipe stem as Ben Belkassem's right eyebrow curved politely. "Every emperor since Terrence the First has known the Empire's stability ultimately depends on the balance of its dynamic tensions. There has to be a centralized authority, but when unchecked power becomes too concentrated in one body or clique you've got real trouble. You may survive for a generation or two, but eventually the inheritors of that concentration turn out to be incompetents or self-serving careerists—or both—and the whole system goes into the toilet. A sufficient outside threat may slow the process, but the gradual destruction is inevitable. However, I wasn't referring to concerns over praetorianism on our part. What I meant to point out is that the Imperial Cadre is limited to forty thousand personnel. But what you may not realize is that no emperor has *ever* recruited the Cadre up to its full allowable strength."

"No?" Ben Belkassem watched Keita over the rim of his coffee cup.

"No. Keeping us small keeps us aware of our 'elite' status, of course—you know, 'The Few, the Proud, the Cadre' sort of thing—and maintains a sort of familial relationship among us, but there are more mundane reasons. Four out of five Cadremen are drop commandos; the rest are basically their support structure, and by the time you allow for augmentation, training, combat armor, and weaponry, you could just about buy a corvette for what a drop commando costs. There are senators who suggest we ought to do just that, too. Unfortunately, you couldn't use that same corvette to take out a bunch of terrorists without killing their hostages or stage a reconnaissance raid on a Rishathan planetary HQ, though some of the old codgers—" he used the term "codger" totally unselfconsciously, Ben Belkassem noted wryly, despite his own age "—always seem to have trouble grasping that.

"But even cost isn't the real limiting factor. To put it simply, Inspector, the supply of potential drop commandos is extremely finite because they require inborn qualities which are very, very rare in combination.

"First, they must come from the sixty-odd percent of the human race who can use neural receptors, and they must be able to tolerate and master an augmentation package far more sophisticated than anyone outside the Cadre even suspects. Secondly, they must possess extraordinary physical capabilities—reaction time, coordination, strength, endurance, and other physiological requirements, some classified, that I won't go into. Many of those can be learned or developed, but at least the potential for them must exist from the start. But third, and most important of all in a sense, are the psychological and motivational requirements."

Keita fell silent for a brooding moment, then continued thoughtfully.

"That isn't unique to the Cadre. A thousand years ago, when chem-fuel rockets were still the ultimate weapon on Old Earth, navies faced the same problems when choosing strategic submarine commanders. They needed people sufficiently stable to be trusted with independent command of such firepower, yet for their military posture to be credible, those same stable people had to be capable of actually firing those weapons if the moment came.

"You see the problem?" He shot Ben Belkassem a sharp glance. "A nuclear submarine, for its time, was every bit as complex as anything we have today. They had to find people with the same intelligence we need in a starship commander, which meant they exactly understood the consequences if their weapons were ever used, and those same extremely bright people had to be stable enough to live with that knowledge yet able to face and accept the possibility of pushing the button if their duty required it."

He paused, waiting until the inspector nodded in understanding.

"Well, we've got the same problem, if on a rather less comprehensive scale. That's why we select our people for certain specific mental qualities and then enhance and strengthen them throughout their training and service.

"You know what Alicia did, but have you really reflected on the odds? She went in against twenty-five men in a free-flow tac link through their helmet coms, all in light armor, armed with combat rifles, side arms, and grenades, who only had to get one pilot and a weaponeer into their shuttle to kill her. Her sole pre-engagement intelligence consisted of her own last-minute reconnaissance; she was armed only with a civilian rifle and survival knife; and she killed all of them. Of course, she had surprise on her side, and her rifle was unusually powerful, but in my considered opinion, Inspector, she would have gotten all of them even if she'd been unarmed at the start."

Ben Belkassem made a noise of polite disbelief, and Keita grinned. It wasn't a pleasant expression.

"You might consider what she did at Shallingsport, Inspector," he suggested softly. "I don't say she'd've done it the same way. Most likely, she would have taken out one man first and appropriated his weapons to go after the others, but she *would* have gotten them. Admittedly, Alicia DeVries is outstanding, even by the Cadre's standards—"

He paused and cocked his head as if in thought, then shrugged.

"I suppose that sounds arrogant, but it's true, and a very real part of the Cadre's mystique. A drop commando knows he's the best. There's no question in his mind. He wouldn't be there unless he wanted to prove he can hack it in the toughest, most challenging and dangerous job the Empire offers. He's there to serve, but that need to meet any challenge with the best, as one *of* the best, is essential to his makeup, or he'd never be accepted.

"Yet at the same time, he has to recognize that what he does—the purpose for which he exists—is a horrible one. However much it demands in courage and self-sacrifice, however deeply it contributes to the safety and well-being of others, he's a killer. A drop commando is trained to kill without hesitation when killing is required, to use his weapons and skills as naturally as a wolf uses his teeth, but he also has to be aware that killing is an ugly, hideous thing. One of our ancient ancestral organizations put it very well indeed: the Cadre does a lot of things we wish *no one* had to do.

"And, perhaps even more importantly, drop commandos don't know how to quit. There are some people like that in any combat outfit. They're the ones at the sharp end of the stick, the ones who come through when the going gets worst, and there are seldom enough of them.

They're self-motivated—the rare ones who carry the bulk of the outfit with them by example or by kicking them in the ass when they're so tired and scared and hungry all they want to do is die. But in the Cadre, they're the norm, not the exception. You can kill a drop commando, but that's the *only* way to stop one, and that absolute inability to quit is another fundamental requirement for the Cadre.

"And when you take that kind of pride, killer instinct, and utter tenacity and combine it with the capabilities our people have after they've been augmented and trained, you'd better make damned sure they're stable, rational people. They have to be warriors, not murderers. We turn them into something that scares the average civilian shitless, but they have to be people you can trust to know when killing *isn't* required—who can do what they must without becoming callous or, even worse, learning to enjoy it—which is why our psych requirements are twice as high as the Fleet Academy's. That makes the Cadre an extraordinary body of men and women by any measure. The Empire has over eighteen hundred inhabited worlds, Inspector, with an average population of something like a billion, and we still can't find forty thousand people we'll accept as drop commandos. Think about that. Oh, they're not really superhuman, and some of them do break, but Alicia DeVries, who tested extraordinarily high even for the Cadre, is one of the last people in the galaxy I would believe could do that."

"But surely it isn't impossible," Ben Belkassem suggested gently.

"Obviously not, since that's precisely what she seems to have done. But that's why I'm so bothered by it. None of this makes sense. I don't understand how she did what she did, and I'd have said Alley DeVries would die before she broke under any conceivable strain. And you're right about how convincing she is, how rational she seems in every other way." Keita turned his coffee cup in his hands, staring down into it with eyes as dark with worry over someone for whom he cared deeply as with puzzlement.

"I almost *want* to believe she's succumbed to some form of external influence or control."

"Mind control? Brainwashing? Some sort of conditioning?"

"I don't know, damn it!" Keita set down his cup so hard coffee splashed. "But I can't get that damned EEG out of my mind."

"I thought that had cleared up," the inspector said in surprise.

"It has. Major Cateau confirmed its presence during her initial examination, but then the cursed thing just vanished in the middle of a scan. It's gone, all right, and Alicia's current EEG exactly matches the one in her medical jacket, but if it was related to her delusion, why is she still insisting this 'Tisiphone' entity is still present after the EEG's faded out? And where did it come from in the first place? Neither Tannis nor any of her other people have ever seen anything like it."

"Like what?" The inspector's eyes were fascinated, and Keita shrugged.

"I don't know," he repeated. "Neither do they, and I'd feel a lot happier if they did." He rubbed his upper lip. "I know science has never demonstrated anything like reliable, trainable extra-sensory perception among humans, but what if that's exactly what Alley's stumbled into? We know the Quarn have limited intra-species telepathy—could she have activated some previously unused portion of her own brain? Tapped into some latent human capability we've never been able to isolate? If she has, is it something just anyone could learn to do? Would recreating the same abilities in someone else send *them* over the edge, as well? And what if she's got other capabilities—ones even she doesn't know about yet—that kick in under some fresh stress?"

The inspector began to speak again, then closed his mouth as he recognized Keita's very real concern. It was all fantastic, of course. However special the Cadre might be they weren't gods. Even Keita admitted that at least some of them broke under stress, and Ben Belkassem had never encountered a human with more right to break than Alicia DeVries, so—

His train of thought suddenly hiccupped. A right to break, certainly, but Keita was right in at least one respect; that simple and comforting answer left other questions unanswered. How *had* she survived unattended in subfreezing temperatures with those wounds, and why *hadn't* the Fleet's sensors detected her before someone went in on the ground to identify the dead?

Could there be something to this notion of a second entity? It didn't have to be a Greek demon or demigoddess just because that was what it told DeVries it was, but Mathison's World was on the very fringe of known space. No one had ever encountered anything like this before, but the possibility that *something* existed couldn't be entirely ruled out. Bizarre as DeVries's claims might be, no one had been able to suggest an explanation that was less bizarre, and it was axiomatic that the simplest hypothesis which explained all known facts was most likely to be correct. . . .

He leaned back in his chair, toying with his coffee cup, and his eyes were very, very thoughtful.

The admittance signal chimed, and the hatch slid instantly aside. Ben Belkassem hesitated in the opening, startled by how quickly it had appeared, then looked across the small, neat cabin at the woman he had come to see.

Alicia DeVries sat with her left hand fitted awkwardly into a normal interface headset, and her eyes were unfocused. They turned to him without really seeing him, and he recognized that inward-turned expression. She was linked into the transport's data systems, and his eyebrows rose, for he'd understood that her computer links had been shut down.

His presence registered on Alicia, and she blinked slowly.

<*Come out of there.*> Impatient refusal whispered through her mind, and her next thought was louder. <*We have a visitor, so get back here!*>

<*Oh, very well.*> Tisiphone was suddenly fully back within Alicia's skull, her mental voice glowing with vitality

as it always did after one of her jaunts through the ship's computers. She'd discovered roundabout routes to the most unlikely places, and she'd been studying the transport's Fasset drive when Alicia interrupted her. <*We could avoid these interruptions if you would lock your door,*> she pointed out, not for the first time.

<*And then they'd wonder what we—or I, rather—was doing in here.*>

<*With the sensors they have trained on you at all times? I doubt that, Little One.*>

<*Humor me,*> Alicia replied, blinking again and letting her eyes drift back into focus. It was Ben Belkassem, and she wondered why he'd sought her out as she gestured politely to the cabin's only other chair.

The Justice man sat, studying her openly but inoffensively. She was a striking woman, he reflected as her blank expression vanished. Tall for his taste—he liked to make eye contact without getting a crick in his neck—and slender, yet broad-shouldered. She moved with hard-trained, disciplined grace, and one forgot she was merely pretty when her face came alive with intelligence and humor, but there was something more under that. A cool, cat-like something and an amused tolerance, rather like what looked out of his own mirror at him, but with a peculiar compassion . . . and a capacity for violence he knew he could never match. This was a dangerous woman, he thought, yet so utterly self-possessed it was almost impossible to think of her as "mad."

"Forgive me," he began. "I didn't mean to burst in on you, but the hatch opened on its own."

"I know." Her contralto voice had a soft, furry edge, and her smile was wry. "Uncle Arthur's been kind enough to allow me free run of the ship, but given the, um, concern for my stability, I thought it would be a bad idea to go all secretive on him when I don't actually need privacy."

He nodded and leaned back, crossing his legs, then cocked his head. "I noticed you were interfacing," he observed, and her eyes twinkled.

"And here you thought Uncle Arthur had deactivated

all my receptors." She disengaged her hand from the headset and wiggled her stiff fingers.

"Something like that, yes."

"Well, he left my Beta receptor open," she told him, opening her hand. She flexed her wrist, stretching her palm, and he saw the slight angularity of a receptor node against the taut skin. "I have three, you know, and this is the most harmless of them."

"I knew you had more than one," he murmured, "but don't *three* get a bit confusing?"

"Sometimes." She raised her arms and stretched like a cat. "They feed separate subsystems, but one of the requirements for the job is the ability to concentrate on more than one thing at a time—sort of like being able to play chess on a roof in a driving rain and carry on a conversation about subatomic physics while you replace the bad shingles between moves."

"Sounds exhausting," he remarked, and she smiled again.

"Mildly. This—" she touched her temple "—is my Alpha node. It's the one connected to my primary processors, and it's configured for broadband access to non-AI computer interfaces like shuttle controls, heavy weapons, tac nets, and data systems. It also handles things like my pharmacope, so it makes sense to put it here. After all, if I lose this—" she thumped the top of her head gently "—I won't miss any of the peripherals very much."

Her smile turned into an urchin-like grin at his expression, and she opened her right hand to show him its palm.

"This is my Gamma node. We use it to interface with our combat armor, unlike Marines, who keep their armor link here." She tapped her temple again. "I could run my own armor through the Alpha link, but I'd have to shut down a lot of other functions. The Gamma link is sort of a secondary, load-sharing system. And this—" she opened her left palm again "—is dedicated to remote sensors and sensory data. It's got some limited ability to take over for the Gamma node if I lose my other hand or something equally drastic, but it's not the most efficient one for computer linkages by a long shot. That's why Uncle Arthur chose to leave it open when he closed the others down."

"I see." He studied her for a moment. "You don't seem particularly angry, I must say." She shrugged, but he persisted. "I understood the reason most drop commandos who survive retire to colony worlds is because they resent the Core World requirement that their augmentation be deactivated."

"That's only partly true. Oh, it's a good part of it, but we're not exactly the sort who find ultra-civilization to our taste, and we can be damned useful on the outworlds. Most of them are glad to get us. But if you're asking if I resent being closed down this way, the answer is that I do. There's no particular point getting angry over it, though. If I were Uncle Arthur, I'd do precisely the same thing with any Cadreman I thought had . . . questionable contact with reality."

Her tone was edged yet glittered with a trace of true humor, and it was his turn to grin. But his smile faded as he leaned forward, hands clasping his right ankle where it lay atop his left knee, and spoke softly.

"True. But I can't help wondering, Captain DeVries, if your contact with reality is quite as questionable as everyone seems to think."

Her eyes stilled for just a moment, all humor banished, and then she shook herself with a laugh.

"Careful, Inspector! A remark like that could get you checked into the room next to mine."

"Only if someone heard it," he murmured, and her eyes rounded as he reached into his pocket and withdrew a small, compact, and highly illegal device. "I'm sure you recognize this," he said, and she nodded slowly. She'd never seen one quite that tiny, but she'd used military models. It was an anti-surveillance device, known in the trade as a "mirror box."

"At the moment," Ben Belkassem slid the mirror box back into his pocket, "Major Cateau's sensors are watching a loop of the five or six minutes before I rang your doorbell. I hadn't hoped that you'd be using your neural link. No doubt you've been sitting right there concentrating with minimal movement for quite some time, so the chance of anyone noticing my interference is lower than I'd expected, but I still have to cut this fairly short."

"Cut what short?" she asked quietly.

"Our conversation. You see, I don't quite share the opinion of your fellow Cadremen. I'm not sure what really happened or exactly what you're up to, and I'm certainly no psych specialist, but something Sir Arthur said about your personality rubbed up against something Major Cateau said about a desire on your part to go after whoever's behind these raids."

"And?"

"And it occurred to me that under certain circumstances being considered mad might be very useful to you, so I thought I'd just drop by to share a little secret of my own. You see, everyone out here thinks I'm with Intelligence Branch. That's what I wanted them to think, though I never actually *said* I was with Intelligence. I'm an inspector, all right—but with O Branch."

Alicia's lips pursed in a silent, involuntary whistle. O Branch—Operations Branch of the Ministry of Justice—was as specialized, and feared, as the Cadre itself. It consisted of hand-picked troubleshooters selected for initiative, flexibility, and pragmatism, and its members were charged with solving problems any way they had to. It was also very, very small. While "inspector" was a fairly junior rank in the other branches of the Ministry of Justice, it was the highest field rank available in O Branch.

"You're the only person out here who knows that, Captain DeVries," the inspector said, levering himself out of his chair.

"But . . . why tell me?"

"It seemed like a good idea." He gave her a crooked smile and straightened his crimson tunic fastidiously. "I know how you feel about spooks, after all." He walked calmly to the closed hatch, then half turned to her once more. "If you decide you have anything you want to tell me, or if there's anything I can do for you, please feel free to let me know. I assure you it will remain completely confidential, even from your kindly physicians."

He gave her a graceful, elegant bow and punched the hatch button. It opened, then whispered shut behind him.

Chapter Eight

This invisible bubble was getting tiresome, Alicia thought, eyeing the empty tables around her in the lounge. No one would ever be crude enough to mention her insanity—but no one wanted to get too close to her, either.

<*I wonder how much of it's fear of contagion?*> she complained.

<*Oh, very little, I should think. They fear what you may do* to *them, not what they might contract* from *you.*>

<A *comforting thought,*> Alicia snorted, and hooked a chair further under the opposite side of the table to rest her heels on it. Her dialogues with Tisiphone no longer felt odd, which worried her from time to time, but not nearly so much as they comforted her. She had to be so wary, especially of her friends, that the relief of open conversation was almost unspeakable. Of course, her lips twitched wryly, it was still possible Tannis was right, but their exchanges remained a vast relief, even if Tisiphone *didn't* exist.

<Of course I exist. Why do you continue to use qualifiers?>

<The nature of the beast, I suppose. If you were something they'd whipped up in the AI labs, this would be a lot easier for me.>

<So you find beings of crystal and wire more reasonable than beings of spirit?> There was vast amusement in Tisiphone's mental "voice." *<You come from a sad age, Little One, if your people's sense of wonder has sunk so low!>*

<Not a sad age, just a practical one. And speaking of wonder, look at that, Spirit Lady.>

She turned her eyes—their eyes?—to the lounge's outsized view port as the transport settled into orbit around Soissons, and even Tisiphone fell silent. The port lacked the image enhancement of one of the viewer stations, but that only made the view even more impressive.

Soissons was very Earth-like—or, rather, very like Earth had been a thousand years before. More of its surface was land, and the ice caps were larger, for Soissons lay almost ten light-minutes from its G2 primary, but its deep blue seas and fleece-white clouds were breathtaking, and Soissons had been settled after man had learned to look after his things. Old Earth was still dealing with the traumas of eight millennia of civilization, but humanity had taken far greater care with the impact of the changes inflicted here. There were none of the megalopolises of Old Earth or the older Core Worlds, and she could almost smell the freshness of the air even from orbit.

Yet there were two billion people on that planet, however careful they were to preserve it, and the Franconia System had been selected as a sector capital because of its industrial power. Soisson's skies teemed with orbital installations protected by formidable defensive emplacements, and she craned her head, watching intently, as the transport drifted neatly through them under a minute fraction of its full drive power. A Fleet spacedock filled the port, vast enough to handle superdreadnoughts, much less the slender battle-cruiser undergoing routine maintenance, and beyond it loomed the spidery skeleton of a full-fledged shipyard.

<*What might that be?*> a voice said in her brain, and her eyes moved under their own power. It was still a bit unnerving to find herself focusing on something of interest to another, but it no longer bothered her as much as it had, and Tisiphone didn't exactly have a finger with which to point.

The thought faded as her own interest sharpened, and she frowned at the small ship near one edge of the yard.

It appeared to be in the late stages of fitting out. Indeed, but for all the bits and pieces of yard equipment drifting near it she would have said it was completed. She watched a yard shuttle mate with one of the transparent access tubes, disgorging a flock of techs—minute dots of colored coveralls at this distance—and nibbled the inside of her lip.

Tisiphone's question was well taken. Alicia had seen more warships and transports than she cared to recall during her career, but never one quite like this. Its bulbous Fasset drive housing dwarfed the rest of its hull, but it was too big for a dispatch boat. At the same time, it was too small for a Fleet transport, even assuming anyone would stick that monster drive on a bulk carrier. It looked to fall somewhere between a light and heavy cruiser for size, perhaps four or five hundred meters at the outside—it was hard to be sure with only yard shuttles for a reference—yet someone had grafted a battleship's drive onto it, which promised an awesome turn of speed.

Their transport drifted closer, bound for a nearby personnel terminal, and her eyes widened as she saw the recessed weapon hatches. There were far more of them than there should have been on such a small hull, especially one with that huge drive. Unless . . .

She inhaled sharply.

<*I'm not sure, but I think that's an alpha synth.*>

<*Indeed?*> Interest sharpened Tisiphone's mental voice, for she'd encountered several mentions of the alpha synth ships, especially in the secured data she'd

accessed from the transport's data net. *<I did not think they could be so small.>*

<Well, they only have a crew of one, and they're right on the frontier of technology. They're only possible because somebody finally developed a practical anti-matter power plant—not to mention the alpha synth AIs.>

The small ship floated out of their view as the transport lined up on the personnel terminal, and Alicia leaned back in her chair, wondering what it would be like to become an alpha synth pilot.

Lonely, for starters. Roughly sixty percent of humanity could use neural receptors to interface with their technological minions, but no more than twenty percent could sustain the contact required to maintain a synth link—the direct, point-to-point connection which made a computer a literal extension of themselves—without becoming "lost," and less than ten percent could handle one of the cyber synth links which allowed them to interact with an artificial intelligence. Many who could refused to do so, and it was hard to blame them, given the eccentricities and far from infrequent bouts of outright insanity to which AIs were prone. It couldn't be very reassuring to know your cybernetic henchman could wipe you out right along with it, even if it did give you a subordinate of quite literally inhuman capabilities.

But from the bits and pieces she'd read, people who could (and would) take on an alpha synth link were even rarer—and probably weren't playing with a full deck. The highbrows might be patting themselves for finally producing an insanity-proof AI, but who in her right mind would voluntarily *fuse* herself with a self-aware computer? Interacting with one was one thing; making yourself a part of it was something else. Alicia had no anti-tech bias, yet the idea of becoming the organic half of a bipolar intelligence in a union only death could dissolve was far from appealing.

She paused with a short, sharp bark of laughter. One or two heads turned, and she smiled cheerfully at the curious, amused by the way they whipped their eyes back away from her. One more indication of her looniness, she supposed, but it really *was* humorous. Here she was, uneasy about the possibility of merging with another personality—her of all people!

She chuckled again, then drained her glass and stood as Tannis entered the lounge. Her slightly fixed smile told Alicia it was time to debark and face the dirt-side psych types, and she sighed and set down the empty glass with a smile of her own, wondering if it looked equally pasted on.

Fleet Admiral Subrahmanyan Treadwell, Governor General of the Franconian Sector, disliked planets. Born and raised in one of the Solarian belter habitats, he saw Imperial Worlds as inconveniently immobile defensive problems and other people's planets as fat targets that couldn't run away, but that hadn't worried Seamus II's ministers when they tapped him for his job.

Treadwell was a lean, bland-faced man with hard eyes. Some people had been fooled by the face into missing the eyes, but he was a man who'd done everything the hard way. Unable to accept even rudimentary augmentation and so disqualified forever from commanding a capital ship by his inability to key into its command net, he'd cut his way to flag rank by sheer brilliance, using nothing but his brain and a keyboard. Three times senior strategy instructor at the Imperial War College and twice Second Space Lord, he was acknowledged as the Fleet's premier strategist, yet he'd never commanded a fleet in space. It was an understandably sensitive point, and coupled with a certain antipathy for those whose mental processes seemed slower than his own but who *could* be augmented, it made him . . . difficult at times. Like now.

"So what you're saying, Colonel McIlheny," he said in a flat voice, "is that we still don't have the least idea where these pirates are based, why they've adopted this extraordinary operational approach, or where they're going to hit next. Is that a fair summation?"

"Yes, sir." McIlheny squelched an ignoble desire to hide behind his own admiral. It would have looked silly, since Admiral Lady Rosario Gomez, Baroness Nova Tampico and Knight of the Solar Cross, was exactly one hundred and fifty-seven centimeters tall and massed only forty-eight kilos.

"But you, Admiral Gomez," Treadwell turned his eyes on the commander of the Franconian Fleet District, "still think we have sufficient strength to deal with this on our own?"

"That isn't what I said, Governor." The silver-haired admiral might be petite, but her professional stature matched Treadwell's, and she met his eyes calmly. "What I said is that I feel requesting additional capital units is not the optimum solution. It's unlikely to be granted, and what we really need are more *light* units. Whoever these people are, they can't possible match our firepower—assuming we could find them."

"Indeed." Treadwell tapped keys on a memo pad, then smiled frostily at Lady Rosario. "I assume you've run a minimum force level analysis on them based on their ability to destroy planetary SLAM drones before they wormhole?"

"I have," Gomez said, still calm.

"Then perhaps you can explain where they found the firepower for that? SLAM drones are not exactly easy targets."

"No, sir, they aren't. On the other hand, they can't shoot back and their only defense is speed. Admittedly, it's easier for capital ships to nail them, but enough light units—even enough corvettes—could box and intercept them well within the inner system."

"True, Admiral. On the other hand, we have Captain DeVries's report that they are using *Leopard*-class assault shuttles. Those, you will recall, are carried—were carried, rather—only by battleships and above. Or do you wish to suggest to me that these pirates are using *freighters* against us?"

"Sir," Gomez said patiently, "I've never said they don't have *some* capital ships. Certainly the *Leopards* were carried by capital ships, but there's no intrinsic reason they couldn't be operated by refitted heavy or even light cruisers." She watched Treadwell's brows knit and continued in an unhurried voice. "I'm not suggesting that's the case. A possibility, yes; a probability, no. What I *am* saying is that we have three full squadrons of dreadnoughts, and there's no way independent pirates can match that. Our problem isn't destroying them, Governor, it's finding them; and for that I need additional scouts, not the Home Fleet."

"Admiral Brinkman?" Treadwell glanced at Vice Admiral Sir Amos Brinkman, Gomez's second-in-command. "Is that your opinion as well?"

"Well, Governor," Brinkman stroked his mustache and glanced at his senior officer from the corner of one eye, "I'd have to say Lady Rosario has put her finger on our problem. On the other hand, the exact fleet mix to solve it might be open to some legitimate dispute."

McIlheny kept his face blank. Brinkman was a competent man in space, but it was common knowledge that he wanted an eventual governorship of his own, and he was *very* careful about offending influential people.

"Continue, Admiral Brinkman," Treadwell invited.

"Yes, sir. It seems to me that we have two possible approaches. One is Admiral Gomez's suggestion that we station additional pickets, possibly backed by a few battlecruisers, in our inhabited systems in order to detect, deter, and if possible, track the raiders. The second is to request additional heavy units and station a division of dreadnoughts in each inhabited system in order to intercept and destroy the next raid." He raised his hands, palms uppermost. "It seems to me that we're really talking about a question of emphasis, not fundamental strategy. Frankly, I could be satisfied by either approach, so long as we follow it without distractions."

"Governor," Lady Rosario didn't even glance at Brinkman, "I'm not disputing the desirability of destroying the enemy on their next attack, but getting the First Space Lord to turn loose that many capital ships will be a major operation in its own right. I have thirty-six dreadnoughts, but covering our inhabited systems in the strength Admiral Brinkman suggests would require *sixty-eight*. That's almost double our current strength, and given the Rishathan presence on our frontier, we'd need at least another two squadrons for border security. That brings us up to ninety-two dreadnoughts, close to twenty-five percent of Fleet's entire active peacetime strength in that class, not to mention the escorts to screen them." She shrugged. "You and I both know the fiscal constraints Countess Miller is wrestling with—and how thin we're already stretched. The First Space Lord isn't going to give us that many of his best capital ships, not with all the other calls on the Fleet."

"You let me worry about Lord Jurawski, Admiral," Treadwell's eyes were flinty. "I've known him a long time, and I believe that if I point out that his alternative is to lose at least one more populated world before we can even find the enemy, I can bring him to see reason."

"With great respect, Governor, I feel that's unlikely."

"We'll see. However, it will require some months to redeploy forces of that magnitude in any case, which means we must do our best in the meantime. Where are we in that respect?"

"About where we were before Mathison's World," Lady Rosario admitted, and gestured to McIlheny.

"In essence, Governor," the colonel said, "most of what we've learned from Mathison's World is bad. We've positively IDed one ex-Fleet officer among the raiders Captain DeVries killed, and a general search of personnel data has uncovered six more officers whose personnel jackets falsely indicate that they died in the same shuttle accident. This is a clear suggestion that the pirates have at least one fairly highly placed inside man."

"Probably some damned clerk in BuPers," Treadwell snorted. "How highly placed d'you have to be to cook computer files?" He waved an impatient hand. "I admit it's a disturbing possibility, but let's concentrate on what we can prove." He looked back at Gomez. "Dispositions, Admiral?"

"They're in my report, Governor. I've increased the pickets and split up BatRon Seventeen to provide a couple of dreadnoughts for each of the six most populous Crown systems. That should be enough to deal with the enemy if he cares to engage, but it's clearly insufficient to destroy him if he elects to run. Unfortunately, I can't reduce my reserve strength below two squadrons without inviting the Rishatha to stick their noses in, so our Incorporated Worlds will have to rely on their local defenses."

"Anything more on the possibility the Jung Association is involved?" Treadwell demanded, turning back to McIlheny, and the colonel shrugged.

"They've denied it, and our reports on their fleet deployments support that. In addition, they've volunteered to provide protection for Domino and Kohlman. Those are low probability targets—Domino's too small and poor, and Kohlman's an Incorporated World with fairly good orbital defenses—but, the, I'd have said a barely established colony like Mathison's World was an even more unlikely target. My personal belief is that the Jungians have nothing to do with this and want to protect our closest populations to demonstrate their innocence and good faith now that we've begun getting the sector organized, but I certainly can't prove that to be the case."

"Um. I'm inclined to agree with you. Keep an eye on them, but concentrate on the assumption that they're innocent bystanders." Treadwell drummed lightly on the table. "Damn it, we *need* those extra battle squadrons, Admiral Gomez! You've just said it yourself—we can only cover a handful of systems effectively, and imperial subjects are dying out there."

"Granted, Governor, and no one will be more delighted than I if you can pry those ships loose from Lord Jurawski. As you say, however, we have to do the best we can in the meantime, and we could get extra cruisers out here a lot more quickly than HQ is going to turn dreadnoughts loose."

"But if we ask for them, they'll take the easy way out and give us *only* light units." Treadwell smiled thinly. "I know how the Lords of Admiralty work—I've been one. Asking for the big stuff will convince them we're serious and probably get the actual firepower out here faster."

"As you say, sir." Lady Rosario folded her hands on the table. She remained convinced Treadwell was on the wrong track, but as Brinkman had said, the case could be argued either way. And he *was* her boss.

"Very well. Now," Treadwell returned to McIlheny, "what's the latest word on our drop commando?"

"Sir, that's really a Cadre matter, and—"

"It may be a Cadre matter, but it happened in my bailiwick, Colonel."

"Agreed, sir. What I was going to say is that I'm not very well informed because Brigadier Keita has been personally supervising the case. My understanding is that there's been no change. Captain DeVries remains adamant that she's been, um, possessed by a figure out of ancient Greek mythology, and nothing seems capable of altering that belief. They're still searching for a therapeutic approach to break through it, but without success.

"No one, myself included, has a theory to account for her survival and the inability of our sensors to detect her, nor has she evinced any other inexplicable capabilities. Major Cateau of the Cadre Medical Branch has analyzed her augmentation down to the molecular level—she's done everything short of physically removing it, in fact—and found absolutely nothing out of the ordinary. The most rigorous medical examinations have turned up nothing the least out of line about her physiology, either, and despite those earlier peculiarities, her EEG and general test results are now exactly what they ought to be. On the face of it, she's a perfectly normal person—well, as normal as any drop commando—who's done several clearly impossible things and appears to have a single, extraordinarily persistent delusion."

"Humph." Treadwell frowned down at his gently drumming fingers, brows lowered. Personally, McIlheny suspected the governor was automatically suspicious of anyone who was augmented. It was a not uncommon response from those unfortunates who couldn't tolerate augmentation themselves. "I don't like it," he said finally, "but I don't suppose there's anything I can—or should—do about it. Besides," he smiled, "Arthur would bite my head off if I even suggested there might be." He shook himself. "Very well, Admiral Gomez. Get me those deployment patterns and keep me personally updated on them."

"Yes, Governor. And may I request, sir, that in light of the possibility—" she stressed the word very lightly "—of high-level involvement with the pirates, we ought to take additional precautions with that data?"

"You may, but it won't be necessary. I've been handling sensitive information for several decades now, baroness, and I believe I understand the fundamentals of security."

Lady Rosario's lips tightened, but she nodded silently. There was, after all, very little else that she could do.

Chapter Nine

The flag cabin boasted an armorplast view port, but it was covered.

That was one of the things Howell hated about wormhole space. He loved to contemplate the stars' sheer, heart-stopping beauty, especially when he needed something other than his orders to think about, yet the mechanics of interstellar flight stripped them away. The approach to the light barrier was spectacular as aberration and the Doppler effect took charge. The ever-contracting starbow drew further and further ahead, vanishing into the blind spot created by the Fasset drive while a ship sped onward through God's own black abyss . . . until the transition to supralight chopped even that off like an axe. Then there was only the nothingness of wormhole space, no longer black, neither dark nor light, but simply nothing at all, an *absence.* Howell wasn't one of those unfortunates it sent into uncontrollable hysteria, but it made him . . . uncomfortable.

He snorted and turned to check the plot repeater. He'd brought only the three fastest freighters this time, and the squadron formed a tight globe about their light dots and that of his flagship. They slowed the warships despite their speed (for freighters), but the squadron was still turning out eight hundred times the speed of light through its own private universe. Or that, at any rate, was the velocity the rest of the universe would have assigned Howell's ships. In fact, not even a Fasset drive ship could actually crack the light barrier. The attempt simply threw it into a sort of subcontinuum where the laws of physics acquired some very strange subclauses. For one thing, the effective speed of light was far greater here, yet the maximum attainable velocity was limited by the balance between the relativistic mass of a starship and the rest, *not* the relativistic, mass of its Fasset drive's black hole. The astrophysicists still hadn't worked out precisely why that was—the blood tended to get ankle deep whenever the Imperial Society discussed alternate hypotheses—but they'd worked out the math to describe it. The whyfor didn't really matter to spacers like Howell as long as they understood the practical consequences, and the practical consequences were that stopping accelerating was equivalent to *de*celerating at an ever-steepening gradient, and that continuous acceleration eventually stopped increasing velocity and simply started holding it constant.

He checked his watch. Alexsov would be along shortly, he told himself, chiding his impatience, and returned to brooding over his plot.

They were running blind—another thing he hated about wormhole space. Gravitic detectors could look *into* it to track the mammoth gravitational anomaly of a supralight ship at up to two light-months, but no one had yet devised a way to peer *out* of it. Which was why you made damned sure of your course and turnover time before you went in, because you sure as hell couldn't correct in transit. In many ways, wormholing was like crawling into a hole and pulling it in after you, though there were difficulties with that analogy.

For one thing, someone else could crawl into a hole with you, for wormhole space was less a dimension than a frequency. If another ship could match relativistic velocity to within fifteen or twenty percent, his wormhole space and yours were in phase. If he was a friend, that was well and good; if he was an enemy, he could go right on trying to kill you.

Of course, Howell reminded himself with a wry grin, there were problems with pursuing an adversary too closely here. The instant he stopped accelerating, his velocity started to drop; if he did an end-for-end and swung his Fasset drive into your face, his massive deceleration could not only cause you to overrun him but, if he hit it hard enough, also snatched him back into normal space as if he'd dropped anchor. Either way, you were in trouble. If you stayed in phase, *his* fire was suddenly coming up *your* backside without interdiction from your drive mass, and if he did drop sublight and your people weren't very, very sharp, you never saw him again. By the time you punched back out into normal space, you might be light-hours away from his n-space locus, probably beyond anything but gravitic detection range, which meant that cutting his drive simply made him disappear.

Still, it was a desperation move for the pursued, as well. If the side shields on his drive mass—or that of one of his enemies—failed, those black holes could crunch him up without even spitting out his bones. Worse, he might actually meet one of them head-on in mutual and absolute destruction, and if it was unlikely, well, unlikely things happened.

Assuming he avoided immolation on his pursuers' Fasset drives, their fire control might just get lucky when they overflew him, and even if they didn't, wormhole trajectories had to be *very* carefully computed. The least deviation threw off all calculations, and that kind of acceleration change screwed a flight profile to hell and gone. Once he lost his original vector, he *had* to go sublight and relocate himself before he could program a fresh supralight course, and that could take days, even weeks, of observations. At the very least, that played hell with any ops schedule, and—

A soft, musical chime interrupted his drifting thoughts, and he turned to touch the admittance button. Gregor

Alexsov stepped through the hatch, and Howell looked ostentatiously at his watch.

"You're three minutes late. What dire emergency kept you?"

Alexsov's harsh mouth twitched obediently, but both men knew it was only half a jest. Howell had known Alexsov for twelve years, yet they weren't really friends. They came nearer to it than anyone else who knew Alexsov, but that wasn't saying a great deal. Howell's compulsively punctual chief of staff reminded him more of an AI than a human being . . . which, the commodore thought, was just as well, given their present activities.

"Not an emergency," Alexsov said now. "Just a little delay to counsel Commander Watanabe."

"Watanabe?" Howell cocked his head. "Problems?"

"I don't know. He just seems a little jumpy."

"Um." Howell dropped into a chair and pursed his lips. Months of careful pre-planning had provided him with an initial core of experienced officers, but there were never enough. That was why Control continued his cautious recruitment. Most of the newcomers had slotted neatly into place, but the realities of their duties were grimmer than anyone could truly imagine until he actually got here. A certain percentage proved . . . unsuitable once they fully realized what would be demanded of them.

"Have you mentioned him to Rachel?"

"Of course." Alexsov stood behind his own chair and shrugged minutely. "That's why I was late. She's promised to keep an eye on him."

Howell nodded, perfectly content to leave the problem of Commander Watanabe in Rachel Shu's capable hands, and turned his mind to other matters.

"So much for him. But I rather doubt he was why you asked to see me."

"Correct. I've been going back over Control's latest data dump, and it worries me."

"Oh?" Howell sat a bit straighter. "Why?"

"Because the more I see of the post-op reports on Mathison's World, the more I realize how badly Control screwed up there. I don't like that—especially not when we're about to hit a target like Elysium."

"Oh, come on, Greg! Control was right on the money about Mathison's defenses, and the planetary maps checked out to the last decimal place. No one could have known that tin can would be in the area."

"I know, but he should have warned us about DeVries."

Howell leaned back, eyes touched with disbelief, but Alexsov looked back levelly. He was dead serious, the commodore realized.

"There were forty-one thousand people on that planet, Greg, and Alicia DeVries was only one of them. You're asking a bit much if you expect Control to keep track of every sodbuster on every dirtball we hit."

"I'm not asking for that, but a drop commando—any drop commando—isn't exactly a 'sodbuster,' and *this* drop commando was Alicia DeVries. If I'd known she was there, I'd've scheduled an orbital strike on her homestead and had done with it."

"Jesus, Greg! She's only one woman!"

"I was XO in a light cruiser detailed to cover the Shallingsport Raid," Alexsov said. "Believe me, tangling with someone like her on her own terms isn't cost effective, Commodore."

Howell grunted, a bit taken aback by Alexsov's vehemence yet forced to agree at least in part. But even so . . .

"I still can't fault Control when everything else checked out perfectly. And it's not exactly as if she did us irreparable damage."

"I'm not so sure of that." Alexsov's response surprised him yet again. "Certainly the loss of a single assault team wouldn't normally matter very much, but they IDed Singh, so they know where we've been recruiting. I don't know McIlheny, but I've read his dossier. He'll keep on picking at it forever. If he digs deep enough, that could lead him to Control, and none of it would have happened if Control had warned us about DeVries in the first place. Damn it, Commodore," the swear word was highly unusual for Alexsov, "Control's got the conduits to know about things like this, and he's *supposed* to tell us about them. That is exactly the sort of crack that could blow the entire op wide open."

"All right, Greg!" Howell waved a placating hand. "But cool down. Done is done—and I'm sure Control will try even harder in future. In fact, I'll have Rachel send him a specific request to that effect. Will that suit?"

"It'll have to, I suppose," Alexsov said dourly, and Howell knew that was as close to agreement as he was going to get. Alexsov seemed personally affronted by the surprise he'd suffered, but it was that very perfectionism (and the ice water in his veins) which made him ideal for his job.

"Good. In that case, how'd your trip to Wyvern go?"

"Quite well, actually." Alexsov finally sank into the waiting chair. "I placed our initial orders with Quintana. He seems unperturbed by the change in our priorities—no doubt because of how much he stands to make—and he assures me he can acquire anything we need and dispose of anything we send him. We won't see quite the same return on industrial and bulk items, since he'll be dumping them on less advanced Rogue Worlds outside the sector, but I think that's well worthwhile from the security perspective, and it sounds as if we'll actually make out better on luxury items through his channels than we did through the Lizards. I expect revenues to balance out overall, and it's not exactly as if we were in this for the profit, is it, sir?"

"No," Howell agreed. "No, it's not." He sighed. "I take it you've had time to sit down with Rendlemann and discuss Elysium. Satisfied?"

"Yes, sir. We've discussed a couple of minor changes, and we'll be running them on the simulator to see how they pan out."

"Got any specific concern over Control's intelligence on this one?"

"Not really, sir." Alexsov rationed himself to a slight headshake. "It's more a matter of once burned, I suppose, but I've made a point of sharing Control's report on the DeVries episode with all of our assault team commanders, just in case. Still, this one will be more of a smash and grab job with the troops in powered armor, anyway, so unless Control's screwed up in some truly major respect, we shouldn't have any problems groundside."

"Anyone seem worried about hitting an Incorporated World's defenses?"

"I think there's a bit of dry-mouth here and there, but nothing too serious, and having Admiral Gomez's deployment orders could help defuse what there is of it. With your permission, I intend to post them where the team leaders can check them personally to reassure their people we'll be clear."

"Is that a good idea? This'll be our toughest job yet, and you can bet anyone who's captured is going to talk, one way or another."

"I don't believe that will be a problem, sir. The troops will all be in combat armor, and I've had a word with Major Reiter. The suicide charges will be armed and rigged for remote detonation." Alexsov smiled a thin, cold smile that chilled Howell's blood, but his conversational tone never changed. "I don't see any reason to mention that. Do you sir?"

Commodore Trang frowned at the faintest splotch of light. It shimmered on the very edge of his command fortress's gravitic detection range, well beyond another, much closer dot already slowing to drop sunlight. The closer one didn't bother him; it was a single ship, and unless he missed his guess it was the Fleet transport Soissons had warned him to expect. But that other grav source.... It was a lot bigger, despite the range, which suggested it was more than one ship, and no one had told him to expect anything like it.

"How long before you can firm this up?" he asked his plotting officer.

"Another ten hours should bring them close enough for us to sort out sources and at least ID their Fasset signatures."

"Um." Trang rubbed his chin in thought. He'd been carefully briefed, like every system CO, on the operational patterns of whoever was raiding the Franconian Sector. To date, they hadn't touched a system with deep-space defenses, which on the face of it, made Elysium an unlikely target.

He tucked his hands behind him and rocked on the balls of his feet. The freighter would be well in-system, under the cover of his weapons, before this fresh clutch of ships could come close enough to be a problem, but aside from two corvettes, he had no mobile units at all. If these bogies *were* bad news, his orbital forts were on their own, and they weren't much compared to those of a Core World System. Still, what he had could handle anything short of a full battle squadron; GeneCorp had made sure of that before they located their newest bio-research facilities here.

He turned, gazing into a view screen without actually seeing the blue and white sphere it displayed. There was little down there in the way of local defenses, despite the planetary government's attempts to cobble up some sort of home defense militia to back the tiny Marine garrison. There was little point building groundside defenses against attack from space; if a capital ship got into weapons range of a planet, that planet was dead, whatever happened to its attacker, for the black holes of a dozen SLAMs coming in at near light-speed would tear any planet to pieces.

That was why most inhabited planets were defended only in space. In a sense, their complete lack of weaponry was their best protection. To date, humanity's only real wars had been intra-mural blood-lettings or with the Rishatha, and opponents who liked the same sort of real estate were unlikely to go around pulverizing useful worlds unless they had to. Strikes on specific targets, yes; wholesale genocide, no.

But at this particular moment, Trang could have wished Elysium bristled with ground fortifications—or at least had a decent-sized garrison. It had been over two centuries since imperial planets had faced piratical attacks on this scale, and the Empire had forgotten what it was like. It was unlikely pirates would go after any world with a Marine brigade or two waiting to chew them up on the ground, but there was less than a battalion on Elysium.

He turned back to the plot, glowering at the bogies sweeping towards his system, and considered contacting Soissons, then shook his head. There was nothing Soissons could do if it was the start of a raid, nor any reason he should need help in the first place, and his own sensors should be able to ID these people long before they entered engagement range. All starcomming the sector capital would achieve would be to show his own nervousness.

"Maintain a close watch on them, Adela," he told his plotting officer. "Let me know the instant you've got something solid."

"Yes, sir." Commander Adela Masterman nodded and thought into her synth link headset, logging the same instructions for her relief, and Trang gave the display one last glance and left the control room.

Several hours later, Commodore Trang's communicator buzzed, then lit with Commander Masterman's smiling face.

"Sorry to disturb you, sir, but we've got a preliminary ID on our bogies. We still don't know *who* they are, but they definitely have Fleet Fasset drives. It looks like a light task group—a single dreadnought, three battlecruisers, two or three freighters, and escorts."

"Good." Trang grinned back at her, aware of how worried he'd truly been only as the relief set in. He didn't have any idea what a task group was doing here, but under the current circumstances, he was delighted to see them. "How long before they go sublight?"

"At their present rate of deceleration, about eleven hours, five hours behind that Fleet transport. Given their drive advantage, they'll be fifteen or twenty light-minutes out when she makes Elysium orbit."

"Pass the word to Captain Brewster, Adela. Have him designate parking orbits for them and alert the yard in case they have any servicing needs."

"Will do, sir," Masterman replied, and the screen went blank.

Commander Masterman stepped from the lift outside Primary Control, her hands full of coffee cups and doughnuts, and hit the hatch button with her elbow. The panel hissed aside, and she sidled into PriCon with a grin.

"I come bearing gifts," she announced, and a spatter of applause greeted her. She bowed grandly and glanced at the bulkhead chronometer as she set her goodies carefully out of the way. She had eight glorious minutes before she went back on watch—just long enough to exchange a few words with Lieutenant Commander Brigatta. That was nice; she had plans for the darkly handsome com officer the next time their off-duty schedules coincided.

She'd just reached Brigatta's station when Lieutenant Orrin straightened suddenly at Plotting. The movement caught Masterman's eye, and she turned automatically towards her assistant in surprise.

"Now that's damned strange," Orrin muttered. He looked up at his boss and gestured at Brigatta's screen as he shunted his own display across to it. "Look at this, ma'am," he said, and the screen blossomed with a view of near-planet space. "I know that transport's skipper said he was in a hurry to unload, but he's really pushing it. She's a good fifty percent above normal approach speeds, and now she's doing a turnov—*Sweet Jesus!*"

Adela Masterman froze as the "transport" suddenly stopped braking and spun to accelerate toward Elysium—at thirty-two gravities. Impossible! No transport could crank that much power inside a planet's Powell limit!

But this one could, and disbelief turned to horror as the "transport" dropped her ECM and stood revealed for what she truly was: a battle-cruiser. A *Fleet* battle-cruiser—one of their own ships!—battle screen springing up even as Masterman stared . . . *and she was launching SLAMs!*

The GQ alarm began to scream, and she charged towards her station, but it was purely automatic. Deep inside, she knew it was already far too late.

Starcoms are never emplaced on planets. They are enormous structures—not so much massive as big, full of empty space—and it would be far more expensive to build them to survive a planet's gravity, but the real reason they are always found in space is much simpler. No one wants multiple black holes, however small, generated on the surface of *his* world, despite everything gravity shields can do and all the failsafes in the galaxy. And so they are placed in orbit, usually at least four hundred thousand kilometers out, which also gets them beyond the planetary Powell limit and doubles their efficiency as they fold space to permit supralight message transmission.

Unfortunately, this eminently sensible solution creates an Achilles heel for strategic command and control. Starships and planets without starcoms must rely on SLAM drones, many times faster than light but far slower than a starcom and woefully short-legged in comparison, so any raider's first priority is the destruction of his target's starcom. Without it, he has time. Time to hit his objectives, to carry out his mission . . . and to vanish once more before anyone outside the system even learns he was there.

Captain Homer Ortiz sat in his command chair, face taut, as his first SLAMs went out. Ortiz was cyber synth-capable and glad of it, for it gave him the con direct as *Poltava* went into the attack. His crisp, clear commands to the emotionless AI sent the first salvo slashing towards the starcom orbital base across two hundred thousand kilometers of space with an acceleration of fifteen thousand gravities; they struck fifty-one seconds later, traveling at a mere three percent of light-speed, but that would have been more than sufficient even without the black hole in front of each missile.

More weapons were already on their way—not SLAMs, this time, but Hauptman effect sublight missiles. Their initial acceleration was much higher, and they had barely half as far to go. The first thousand-megaton warhead detonated twenty-seven seconds after launch.

Commander Masterman had just donned her headset when she and nine thousand other people died. Then the other missiles began to strike home.

Night turned into day on the planet of Elysium as two-thirds of its orbital defenses vanished in less than two minutes. Shocked eyes cringed away from the ring of suns blazing above them, and minds refused to grasp the magnitude of the disaster. Not in four centuries had the Imperial Fleet taken such losses in return for absolutely no damage to the enemy, but never before had the Fleet been attacked by one of its own, and the carnage a cyber-synthed battle-cruiser could wreak totally unopposed was simply beyond comprehension.

The planetary governor dashed for his com in response to the first horrified warning; he arrived just as the last missile went home against the last fort in *Poltava's* field of fire, and his face was white as whey. The three surviving forts were rushing to battle stations, but the marauding battle-cruiser's speed soared, already above two hundred KPS, as she cut a chord across their protective ring. She cleared the planet and acquired the first of the survivors just before its own weapons came on line, and Ortiz's smile was hellish as a fresh salvo of SLAMs raced outward. The fort had nothing to stop them with, and the governor groaned as they tore it apart.

The second fortress had time for one answering salvo, hastily launched with minimal time for fire control solutions, and then it, too, was gone.

The final fort had time to get its battle screen up, yet faced the cruelest dilemma of all. Its crew had SLAMs of their own . . . and dared not use them. Ortiz had cut his course recklessly tight, placing *Poltava* far closer to Elysium than they. They could reply only with beams and warheads, lest a near-miss with a SLAM strike the very world they wanted to protect, and their gunners were shaken to their core by the catastrophe overwhelming them. They did their best, yet it never mattered at all. Their first salvos were still on the way when Ortiz launched a fresh pattern of SLAMs and flipped his ship end-for-end yet again, aiming *Poltava*'s Fasset drive directly at the doomed fort to devour its fire.

Twelve-point-five minutes and seventy-three thousand deaths after the attack began, there were no orbital forts in Elysium's skies.

"First phase successful, Commodore," Commander Rendlemann announced. Howell nodded. Gravitic detectors, unlike other sensors, were FTL, and his flagship's gravitics had tracked their Trojan Horse and the fires of its SLAMs. It was an eerie sensation to see the undamaged fortresses on the light-speed displays and know they and all their people had ceased to exist.

He shook off a chill and gave Alexsov a tight smile. The chief of staff had argued against trying to sneak in more than one ship, insisting *Poltava* could do the job alone and that trying to use more would risk losing the priceless element of surprise.

"Two small vessels leaving orbit, sir," Rendlemann said suddenly.

"Right on schedule," Alexsov murmured, and Howell nodded again, watching through his synth link as the two corvettes accelerated hopelessly towards their mammoth foe. No corvette had the strength to engage a battle-cruiser . . . but they were all Elysium had left.

The corvettes *Hermes* and *Leander* charged the rampaging battle-cruiser, sheltering behind their own Fasset drives as they closed. They were inside her, closer to the planet, but Ortiz spun *Poltava* to face them head-on. She decelerated towards them even as they rushed to meet her, and *Hermes* lunged aside, fighting to get outside the battle-cruiser and launch her SLAM drone before she was destroyed.

Ortiz let her go, concentrating on her sister. Close-range lasers and particle beams reduced the tiny warship to half-vaporized wreckage, but the range was too short for effective point defense, and both of *Leander*'s overcharged energy torpedoes erupted against *Poltava*'s screen. Concussion jarred her to the keel, and Ortiz winced as damage reports flickered through his headset. His exec was on it, initiating damage control procedures, but half *Poltava*'s forward energy mounts had been wiped away, along with over thirty of her crew. Her injuries were far from critical—certainly not enough to slow her as she went after the sole survivor—but they hurt all the more after what he'd done to the forts, and they were enough to make him cautious.

The last corvette's skipper watched the battle-cruiser overhaul him while his brain sought frantically for some way to stop her. Not for a way to survive, for there was none, but for a way to protect Elysium from her.

She was coming up fast from directly astern, her drive aimed straight at him to interdict his fire. She was grav-riding on him, drawing further acceleration from the attraction of his own drive mass even as hers acted as a brake upon his ship. She had more than enough acceleration to overtake him without that, but her captain was playing a cautious end game, using his interposed drive to protect his ship until he chose to turn and engage. Perhaps overly cautious. *Herme*'s weapons couldn't hurt his ship much, and there were times caution became more foolhardy than recklessness—

"Sir!" His white-faced plotting officer's voice was tight, over-controlled as he fought his own fear, but not so tight as to hide its disbelief. "Data base *knows* that ship!"

"*What?*" The captain twisted around in his command chair.

"Yes, sir. That's HMS *Poltava,* Skipper!"

The captain swallowed a disbelieving curse. It *couldn't* be true! It had to be some kind of ECM—there was no *way* a Fleet battle-cruiser could be doing this to her own people! But—

"Prep and update the drone!" he snapped.

"Prepped!" his com officer acknowledged. Then, "Update locked!"

"Launch!"

The captain turned back to his own display, teeth locked in a death's-head grin. There was no way his ship could survive, but he'd gotten the message out. HQ would know everything *he* knew, for the enemy could never intercept his drone and its sensor data.

The drone snaked away, racing directly ahead of the corvette, hidden by her own and *Poltava*'s drives until it was beyond effective energy weapon range. But Ortiz's scan teams picked up its gravity signature as it began to climb across the ecliptic, and they were ready.

The battle-cruiser's com officer transmitted a complicated code, and *Herme*'s skipper gaped in horror as his drone obeyed the command—the proper, authenticated Fleet override—and self-destructed.

He knew, then. Knew who his enemies were and whence they came . . . and how utterly he had been betrayed. Something snapped deep inside him, and he barked new helm orders as the battle-cruiser's Fasset drive loomed up close astern. His drive's side shields dropped, and his ship began to turn.

Hermes was in her enemy's blind zone, riding the arc where the battle-cruiser's own drive blocked her sensors. It was a matter of seconds before she spun to clear the drive mass and bring her weapons to bear, but seconds were all the corvette's skipper needed. All in the universe he wanted, now.

Poltava began her swing, and not even her AI had time to realize *Hermes* had already swung and redlined her drive on an intercept course.

Commodore Howell swore vilely as both Fasset drives vanished, and the fact that he'd seen it coming only made it worse. That idiot! To blow it all after the bravura brilliance of his initial strike! A second-year middy knew better than to get *that* close to an enemy's drive mass, for God's sake, especially when the disparity in firepower meant that enemy was doomed anyway.

But there'd been nothing Howell could do. The rest of his squadron was still fifteen light-minutes from Elysium, far too distant for any com to reach Ortiz in time. And so he'd had to sit and watch helplessly as a quarter of his battle-cruiser strength vanished before his eyes.

He sucked in a deep breath and forced himself back under control. He couldn't pour the milk back into the bottle, and he had other things to worry about—like what the planetary governor did with his emergency SLAM drone.

That drone was the only thing in this system which still threatened Howell's ships. It couldn't hurt them now, but it would tell Fleet far too much if it got out with a record of *Poltava*'s emission signature. If Ortiz hadn't gotten his stupid ass killed, the threat would be minimal; even if the governor realized how the corvette's drone had been killed and locked out the self-destruct command, *Poltava*'s weapons would have been more than capable of killing it as it broke atmosphere. His own ships couldn't. Just catching it with a com beam before it wormholed would be hard enough from this distance.

"Think they got a clean reading on us?" he asked Alexsov hopefully, but the chief of staff's shrug was discouraging.

"The forts certainly did. If they kept groundside advised, and we have to assume they did, the planet knows we're Fleet units. More to the point, Control says their port has enough sensor capability to've gotten a good read on *Poltava*—certainly enough for Fleet's data base to fingerprint her."

"Shit." Howell tugged unhappily at an earlobe. This was what he'd most feared about the entire Elysium operation. The actual attack hadn't worried him, given their inside information, but if the identity of his ships got out, their true objective would be lost. He and his people would become in truth what everyone now assumed they were: plain and simple pirates.

"Maybe I shouldn't've argued against two ships," Alexsov said sourly.

"Don't blame yourself. Ortiz blew it, and you were right. Control's cover story only allowed for one 'legitimate' ship. We couldn't know he'd—"

The commodore broke off with a curse. His light-speed sensors hadn't been able to see the SLAM drone rise from the planet on counter-grav, but the blue spark of its lighting Fasset drive was glaringly obvious.

"Send the code," he rasped, and the ops officer nodded.

"Sending-now," Commander Rendlemann replied, and Howell sat back in his command chair to wait. His light-speed destruct command would require thirty-one minutes to overtake the drone; by the time he knew whether or not it had succeeded, his ships would be within assault range of the planet.

Chapter Ten

Sirens continued to wail as the raiders decelerated towards Elysium. There had been no communication from the "Fleet" ships, and that, in light of what had just occurred, was more than sufficient proof of their purpose.

The governor sat in his communications center and watched his staff coordinate Elysium's mobilization. His militia were marshaling with gratifying speed, but he'd created them purely as a morale-booster to prove he was Doing Something; he'd never anticipated they might actually be called upon, and the rest of his careful plans were a shambles. The evacuation centers were already madhouses, and the background crackle of reports from their managers grew more frantic with every second.

A dedicated screen lit, and Major von Hamel, Elysium's senior Marine, looked out of it and saluted. His eyes were level despite the strain in them, and he already wore his combat armor.

"Governor. My people are heading for their initial positions. We should be at full readiness well before the bandits launch their shuttles."

"Good." The governor tried to put some enthusiasm into his voice, but he knew as well as von Hamel just how little chance the Marines had.

"Militia Colonel Ivanov tells me his people are running a bit behind schedule, but I anticipate they'll be ready by the time anyone hits their local perimeters." This time the governor simply nodded. Even von Hamel, who had supported the militia concept strongly from the beginning, had trouble sounding confident over that, and he leaned closer to his pickup.

"Sir, I've heard some strange reports on that battlecruiser, and—"

"They're true." The governor cut him off grimly and von Hamel's face went even tighter. "Orbit Command confirmed she was Fleet-built, and we caught a last-minute transmission from *Hermes* just before she rammed. They definitely identified her as HMS *Poltava*. According to the records, she went to the breakers twenty-two months ago; apparently the records are wrong."

"Shit." The governor, normally a stickler for decorum, didn't even frown at von Hamel's expletive. "That means these other bastards are probably real Fleet designs . . . with a real ground element." The major was thinking aloud, his eyes darker than ever. "We can't hold the capital against that kind of attack, and they've got the orbital firepower to take out any fixed position. I'm afraid Thermopylae's our only option, sir."

"Agreed. We're trying to evacuate now, but we expected at least six hours of lead time. We're not going to get many of them out."

"I'll buy you all the time I can, sir, but it won't be much," von Hamel warned, and the governor nodded his thanks.

"Understood, Major. God bless."

"And you, sir. We're both going to need it."

Commodore Howell watched his plot, eyes glued to the fleeing SLAM drone, as his ships slid into assault orbit, their energy batteries busy systematically eliminating every orbital installation to eradicate any record of their identity. A backwash of assault shuttle readiness reports murmured in the back of his brain, relayed from Rendlemann's cyber synth link, but Howell wasn't concerned about this phase of the operation. He knew all about Elysium's militia, and he and Alexsov had anticipated from the start that the defenders would be forced back on Thermopylae. It was the only one of their contingency plans that made any sense.

He caught a hand creeping towards his mouth and lowered it before he could nibble its fingernails. The drone was up to ninety percent of light-speed now; their signal had barely three minutes to catch it before it wormholed, and it was going to be close. Assuming, of course, that catching it did any good. If they'd been locked out. . . . God, he *hated* this kind of waiting! But he couldn't cut it any shorter, and he turned resolutely to the holo image of the planet in an effort to think of something—anything—else.

Thermopylae was going to make things messy. Although Elysium had become an Incorporated World with direct Senate representation twelve years ago, its population was scarcely thirty million—too many for an all-out raid like Mathison's World but too few to provide the industrial and financial districts which concentrated wealth for easy picking. Only one thing made Elysium a target: GeneCorp's research facility. Every secret of the Empire's leading biomedical consortium lay waiting in that facility's data banks. That was Elysium's true treasure: a cargo that could buy Howell's entire squadron twice over yet be transported abroad a single ship.

But GeneCorp's HQ lay in the center of the planetary capital. It wasn't a large city, little more than a million people, but built-up areas could exact painful casualties, and the defenders knew what his objective had to be. That was why Thermopylae called for them to center their defense on GeneCorp's facility, where he couldn't use heavy weapons to support *his* ground elements without destroying the very data he'd come to steal.

It was going to be brutal, especially for the city's civilians, but that, too, was part of his mission plan. Maximum frightfulness. A terror campaign against the Empire itself. There had been a time when James Howell would have died to stop anyone cold-blooded enough to mount such an operation.

He bit his lip, cursing the way his mind savaged itself at moments like this. Past was past and done was done, and the final objective was worth—

"*Got* it, by God!"

Howell's head jerked up at Rendlemann's exultant cry, and wan humor glittered in his own eyes as he realized how successfully he'd distracted himself from the drone. But the blue dot had vanished, and he exhaled a tremendous sigh of relief.

"Begin Phase Two," he said softly.

The governor stared at his tracking officer.

"But . . . *how?* It was over fourteen *light-minutes* down-range!"

"I don't know. It was out of beam range, and none of their missiles could even *catch* it. It's like—" The tracking officer broke off, her face sagging in sudden, bitter understanding and self-hate.

"The destruct code!" She slammed a fist against the side of her own head. "Idiot! *Idiot!* I should've guessed from what happened to *Hermes*' drone! How could I've *been* so stupid?!"

"What are you talking about, Lieutenant?" the governor demanded, and she fought herself back under control.

"I knew they'd taken out *Hermes*' drone, but I assumed—*assumed*—they'd done it with their weapons. They didn't. They used a Fleet self-destruct command and ordered it to suicide."

"But that's impossible! There's no way they could—"

"Oh yes there is, Governor." The lieutenant faced him squarely, her voice harsh. "Those aren't just Fleet-built ships out there. I figured some son-of-a-bitch at the wreckers must've disposed of the hulls on the sly—God knows they're worth more than reclamation, even stripped—but they've got complete Fleet data bases, as well, including the security files."

"Dear God," the governor whispered. He sagged back into a chair, hands trembling as he realized the monumental treason that implied.

"Exactly. And thanks to my stupidity—*my* stupidity!—we don't have a drone left to tell anyone."

The assault boats sliced downward through Elysium's night sky. The raiders' carefully hoarded *Bengals* led the first wave, fleshed out by older but still deadly *Leopards*. A handful of local defense missiles rose to meet them, and a pair of unlucky shuttles vanished in direct hits.

It was the defenders' only luck. Imperial assault craft were designed to attack heavily armed ground bases; Elysium's pitiful weaponry was less than nothing in comparison. Hyper-velocity weapons screamed down in reply, relying solely on the kinetic energy developed at ten percent of light-speed, and high kilotonne-range fireballs annihilated the missile sites.

More HVW launched, targeted with cold calculation on the evacuation centers and the governor's residence. Fresh flame shredded the darkness, and Major von Hamel cursed the minds and souls behind the weapons. This wasn't an assault—it was a massacre. An intentional massacre of civilians by people who *knew* where the evacuation centers were. He and the governor hadn't saved anyone; they'd simply gathered them in convenient targets for mass murder!

But why? Von Hamel had read the reports on the other raids, but they were nothing compared to this, and it made no sense. A demand for surrender on pain of such an attack might have been reasonable. This wasn't.

More terrible shockwaves rippled through the ground, and he began barking orders. With the governor dead, he was on his own, and there was no point in a phased withdrawal now. The civilians he'd hoped to cover were already dead, and he sent his people charging back to their inner perimeter.

* * *

Howell watched the gangrenous light boils bite off chunks of the holo-imaged city, and part of him shared von Hamel's sickness. But the people in those centers would only have lived a few more hours whatever happened, and the panic of the strikes might hamper the defenders' coordination. Anything that reduced his own casualties was worthwhile, he told himself . . . especially when it only meant killing people who simply hadn't yet learned that they were dead.

The first-wave shuttles grounded, and armored figures spilled from the ramps. Powered combat armor gleamed and glittered in the hellish light of the city's fires as the assault teams formed up and swept into its heart.

Major von Hamel watched his tactical display, and he was no longer afraid. Fury still crackled in his blood, but even that was suppressed, buried under an ice-cold concentration. He and his troops were Marines, products of a four-century tradition, and they were all that stood between a city and its murderers. They couldn't stop it, and every one of them knew it . . . just as they knew they were going to die trying.

The bastards were mounting a concentric assault, hoping to overpower his people in the first rush, and their assault routes were moving directly against his original prepared positions. The major watched them come and bared his teeth, unsurprised after the accuracy with which the evac centers had been taken out. They had to have detailed information on all of Elysium's defense planning, but there was one thing they didn't know: virtually every one of his original positions had been relocated in the wake of last week's tactical exercise. He keyed the master tac link.

"Hold your fire. I say again, all units hold fire for my command."

More shuttles streaked downward, probed by his tactical sensors as they planeted, and his face tightened. Those weren't assault boats; they were heavy-lift cargo shuttles, and their presence this early could only mean the raiders were putting in heavy armored units.

The assault teams converged on the defensive strong points with cautious confidence. Reports flowed back and forth as the first tanks disembarked from their shuttles and began to move forward. No one expected it to be easy—not against Imperial Marines—but knowing precisely where their enemies were turned it into something more like a live-fire exercise than a battle.

Von Hamel watched his display. The raider spearheads were inside his perimeter in a dozen places, and if his people weren't where the raiders thought they were, they weren't far away, either. There were only a limited number of positions which could cover the same approach routes.

One column of invaders moved towards his own CP, a tentacle of death reaching into the mangled city's heart, and he gathered up his rifle. He had far too few people for him and his staff to stay out of the fire fight.

He raised the heavy weapon—a thirty-millimeter "rifle" only a man with exoskeletal combat armor "muscles" could possibly have managed. It was loaded with discarding sabot tungsten penetrators four times heavier than those of the rifles unarmored infantry carried, and he slid it cautiously over the edge of the office building roof.

"Engage!" he barked.

The orderly advance exploded in chaos.

Raiders screamed and died in a hurricane of high-velocity tungsten. Two hundred rifles—auto-cannon in all but name—blazed at point-blank range, and not even combat armor could stop fire like that. Fifteen-millimeter penetrators hurled them aside like shattered dolls, support squads' launchers spat plasma grenades and HE, and Captain Alexsov's careful briefing had become a death trap. The raiders *knew* where the defenders were, and their point men and flankers had succumbed to overconfidence.

Even taken by surprise, they had the firepower to deal with their enemies. What they no longer had was the *will.* They didn't even try to return fire; they simply broke and ran, scourged by that deadly hail of fire until they managed to get out of range.

"Regroup! Assume Position Gamma. I say again, Position Gamma."

Von Hamel's people responded instantly, withdrawing from the positions their attack had marked for the raiders, and this time the smoke and confusion and terror helped them. There was no way the other side could track them through the chaos as they dashed for their new stations.

They'd done well, von Hamel thought. Barely half a dozen Marine beacons had gone out, and the raiders had been brutally mauled.

But they wouldn't get another chance like that. The other side might not know his troops' exact positions, but they knew his general battle plan. They wouldn't come in fat and stupid a second time, and they had that damned armor to back them, not to mention the assault boats.

Howell watched Alexsov's face as the reports came in. Another man might have sworn. At the very least he would have said *something.* Alexsov only tightened his lips and started sorting out the chaos.

The commodore looked away, grateful for Alexsov's calm yet constitutionally incapable of understanding it. His eyes swept his command deck, and he frowned. Commander Watanabe sat stiffly in the assistant gunnery officer's chair, sweat beading his brow, and his face was pale as he stared at the fires spalling the darkened city.

Howell turned his head, looking for Rachel Shu, and found her. She, too, was watching Watanabe, and her eyes were narrow.

* * *

A smoke-choked dawn, smutted with cinders and the stench of burning, painted the sky at last.

Major von Hamel hadn't expected to see the sun rise, and now he wanted to, more than he had ever wanted anything before, for he knew he would never see it set. But it was grim, vengeful satisfaction that pulsed within him, not fear. He and what remained of his battalion, little more than a company, had withdrawn to their final positions, and the streets behind them were thick with the dead. Too many were his own, and far, far too many were civilians, but there were over six hundred raiders and nine gutted tanks among them. His air-defense platoon had even added a trio of *Bengals* to the carnage, for the enemy dared not use HVW this close to GeneCorp's HQ. They had to strafe if they wanted his Marines, and that brought them into his people's reach.

Yet the end was coming. Only the tight tactical control he'd managed to maintain had staved it off this long, but ammunition was running low, and his last reserve had been committed. He was spread too thin to hold against another determined push, and once the final perimeter broke, his control would vanish into a room-to-room insanity that could end only one way.

He knew that. But he'd also realized something else during the nightmare night. These weren't pirates. He didn't know what they were, but no pirate commander would have continued such a furious assault or accepted such casualties, and if he'd tried, his men would have mutinied. These people were something else, and the carnage they'd wreaked on the evac centers filled him with a dreadful certainty.

They were going to destroy this city. They were going to wipe it from the face of Elysium, whether they gained their prize or not. It was part of their pattern, and there was something more than brute sadism to it. He was too exhausted to think clearly, but it was almost as if they needed to eliminate all witnesses to protect some secret.

He had no idea what that secret might be, and it didn't matter. None of his people were going to be surrendered to the butchers who had raped and tortured Mawli and

Brigadoon and Mathison's World, and there was no longer any reason to preserve GeneCorp's data base as a bargaining chip.

He lay on a balcony, watching the smoky sky, and waited.

"All right." Even Alexsov sounded drained, and Howell could scarcely believe their losses. The chief of staff locked eyes with the ground commander's screen image, and the commodore saw the terrible fatigue in the ground man's face. Howell was desperately tempted to give it up—simply replacing the losses to his ground component was going to take months—but they'd come too far. And, he reminded himself tiredly, whatever happened, they'd attained their primary objective. News of what had happened to Elysium would rock the Empire to its foundations.

"One more push, and you're in. Check?" Alexsov said.

"Check," his subordinate said wearily, and the chief of staff nodded.

"Then get it moving, Colonel."

Von Hamel heard the sudden crescendo of fire as the tanks moved in. His troopers fired back desperately, but they were almost out of anti-tank weapons and they were too thin, too heart-breakingly thin. Beacons vanished from his display with dreadful speed, and he switched it off with a sigh.

He sat up, craning his neck at the eastern sky, and tears trickled down his face as he listened to the thunder. Not for himself, but for his people. For all they'd done and given that no one would ever know a thing about.

His southern perimeter broke at last. It didn't crumble and yield; it simply died with the men and women who held it, and the attackers thundered through the gap as a blazing arm of the sun rose above the shattered skyline. Von Hamel stared at it, drinking in its beauty, and pressed the button.

* * *

Commodore James Howell stared in shock at the expanding globe of fire in the center of the city. It swelled and towered as he watched, wiping away GeneCorp and all he had come to steal and devouring half his remaining ground troops like some dragon out of Terran myth.

"Damn." It was Alexsov, his voice flat and almost disinterested, and Howell wanted to scream at him. But he didn't. There was no point.

"Recover the assault force," he told Rendlemann.

"Yes, sir. Shall I move on the secondary objectives, sir?"

"No." Howell watched the fireball begin to fade. Amazing how little of the remaining city had gone with it. Whoever planted those charges had known what he was doing. "No, I don't think so. We've lost enough people for one night, and there's still that damned militia. We'll cut our losses."

"Yes, sir."

Howell leaned back and rubbed his eyes. That suicide charge had never been part of Thermopylae. Had someone down there realized the truth?

"Move to Phase Four," he said quietly.

The shuttles departed with barely a third of the personnel they'd landed. Their mother ships recovered them, and the ground force's survivors stumbled back aboard, stunned by the blood and chaos of their "walkover." It was the first time they'd failed, and Howell tried to hide his own fear of the consequences. Not for himself. Control should have no complaints about the *effect* of the operation, and ground equipment and the cannon fodder to man it had always been far easier to come by than starships.

No, it was the effect on his men he feared. How would their morale react to this? He already knew Control was going to have to settle for more lightly defended targets in the immediate future. He'd have too many new personnel, and the vets would need easy operations to rebuild confidence.

He folded his hands in his lap, brooding down on Elysium's holo image. It was past time to be done here, and he turned to the gunnery officer.

"Are we prepared to execute Phase Four, Commander Rahman?"

"Yes, sir. Missile targets are laid in and locked."

"Good." Howell studied the man's expression. It wasn't exactly calm, but it was composed and ready. Commander Watanabe, on the other hand . . .

The commodore turned to the commander. Watanabe was pasty pale and sweating hard, and Howell sighed internally. He'd been afraid of this ever since Alexsov voiced his own concern over Watanabe's reliability.

"Commander Watanabe," his voice was very quiet, "execute Phase Four."

Watanabe jerked, and his face worked. He stared at his commanding officer, then down at the console. Down at the target codes for every one of Elysium's cities.

"I . . ."

"I gave you an order, Commander," Howell said, and his eyes flicked over Watanabe's shoulder to Rachel Shu.

"Please, sir," Watanabe whispered. "I . . . I don't . . ."

"You don't want to execute it?" The commander's eyes darted back up at the almost compassionate note in Howell's voice. "That's understandable, Commander, but you are one of my officers. As such, you have neither room for second thoughts nor the luxury of deciding which orders you will obey. Do you understand me, Commander Watanabe?"

Silence hovered on the command deck, and the commander closed his eyes. Then he stood and jerked the synth link headset from his temples.

"I'm sorry, sir." His voice was hoarse. "I can't. I just *can't.*"

"I see. I'm sorry to hear that," Howell said softly, and nodded to Rachel Shu.

The emerald beam buzzed across the bridge. It struck precisely on the base of Watanabe's skull, and his body arched in spastic agony. But it was a dead man's reaction—a muscular response and no more.

The corpse slithered to the deck. Someone coughed on the stench of singed hair, but no one moved. No one was even surprised, and plastic and alloy whispered on leather as Shu holstered her nerve disrupter with an expression of mild distaste.

"Commander Rahman," Howell said, and the senior gunnery officer straightened in his chair.

"Yes, sir?"

"Execute Phase Four, Commander."

Book Two:
Fugitive

Chapter Eleven

Alicia lay in bed, staring at the ceiling and chewing her lip while she tried not to stew. It was becoming steadily more difficult.

In one sense, things weren't actually that bad. Tannis's diagnostics were reporting exactly what they ought to, now that Tisiphone knew what results they were supposed to get, and Alicia wasn't worried about revealing anything she chose to conceal. Tannis had tried direct neural queries, chemical therapy, even hypnotic regression, but Tisiphone was an old hand at controlling human thoughts and responses. She might not be able to do it to anyone else these days, but Alicia's brain and body were her own front yard, and she allowed no trespassers, so that side was secure enough.

Unfortunately, that didn't help against her boredom. Tisiphone might enjoy fooling the medics or roaming Soissons's planetary computer net, but Alicia was going mad. The thought woke a sour smile, but it had stopped being funny when she realized what was really happening to her grief and hatred.

They were still there. She couldn't feel them through

Tisiphone's shields, but she sensed them, and she hadn't dealt with them. She *couldn't* deal with them, because she couldn't touch them, and that left an odd, dangerously unresolved vacuum at her core. Worse, she thought she knew what Tisiphone was doing with all that raw, oozing emotion. The Fury had no interest in dissipating it, for she knew only one catharsis. At first Alicia had suspected she was absorbing it like some sort of strange sustenance, but a worse suspicion had occurred to her, and the Fury had refused to deny it.

She was storing it. Distilling it into the pure essence of hatred, reserving it against some future need, and Alicia was afraid. Drop commandos had few self-delusions—they couldn't afford them—and she knew about her own dark side. She'd demonstrated it, without a trace of regret, on Wadislaw Watts, and there had been times in the field when her killer self had threatened to break free, as well. It had never happened, but it had been a near thing more than once, and a woman stayed clear-headed in combat or she died—probably taking other people with her when she went.

Thoughts of what the sudden release of all that pent-up rage might do to her judgment terrified her, but Tisiphone refused even to discuss it despite requests which had come all too close to pleading before pride drove Alicia to drop them. She was helpless in the face of the Fury's refusal . . . and Tisiphone had reminded her—not cruelly, but almost kindly—that she had agreed to pay "anything" for her vengeance. That was nothing less than the truth, and the fact that she'd thought she was mad had no bearing. She'd given her word, and like Uncle Arthur, that was the end of it.

And now a fresh disturbing element had been added, for Tisiphone was clearly up to something. There was a pleased note to her mental voice which made very little sense, given their total lack of achievement. Alicia was astonished that the fiery, driven Fury hadn't insisted on making their break long ago. To be sure, she'd gleaned a tremendous amount of information—including everything Colonel McIlheny and even Ben Belkassem knew about the pirates—but there had to be something else. . . .

<*Indeed there is, Little One.*> The comment was so sudden she twitched in surprise, and Tisiphone chuckled silently. <*In fact, the event for which I have waited has now occurred, and the time has come for us to depart.*>

<*Are you serious?!*> Alicia jerked upright, then gasped as Tisiphone answered without words. Her augmentation came spontaneously on line, her boosted senses spun up to full acuity for the first time in more than two months, and she twitched again as Tisiphone activated her pharmacope. The first ripple of tension ran through her as the tick reservoir administered its carefully measured dose to her bloodstream and the world began to slow.

She bit her lip, confused by the speed with which the Fury was moving, and a faint, familiar haze hovered before her eyes. It cleared quickly, and her ears rang with the high, sweet song of the tick.

<*We will go now,*> Tisiphone said calmly. <*I have placed commands in their computers to reroute their sensors, deactivate the door security systems, and summon the floor nurse elsewhere, but I cannot control who we may meet along the way. Dealing with them will be your responsibility.*>

Alicia rose with the tick's floating grace. The drug increased her reaction speed only slightly but accelerated her mental processes enormously, and if her responses came little faster they were absolutely certain, for she had all the time in the world to think about each of them before she made it.

The door oozed open with syrupy slowness, and she floated through it. The corridor beyond was empty, the nurses' station unmanned as Tisiphone had promised, but there was a permanent guard on the elevators. She'd met the night guard, and though the earnest young man had been very careful never to say so, she knew why he was there, for he, too, was a drop commando.

But the elevators were around a bend in the corridor, and she flowed down the hall like a spirit, riding the tick's exaltation. The ability to ride the tick was one of the main drop commando requirements. So was a high resistance to all forms of addiction, but no one could avoid the tick's sense of godlike omnipotence—nor the violent, tearing nausea when she finally came down again. Indeed, Alicia suspected the medics deliberately enhanced that side effect to help discourage the commandos from over-indulging.

She stepped around the bend, and the guard looked up. She smiled, and he smiled back slowly, so slowly. But then his smile changed as he recognized the precise, gliding movement that turned simply walking into an exquisitely choreographed dance.

His hand started for his stunner, and Alicia wanted to laugh in pure exultation. He was too far away to reach before the stunner cleared its holster, but Old Speedy wasn't racing through his veins. Though he got the stunner up before she reached him, he didn't have time to reset its power.

The green beam struck her dead on—with absolutely no result. The neural shields built into drop commando augmentation could resist even nerve disrupter fire, to a point, and a stunner blast which would have downed an elephant or a direcat had no effect at all on her.

He really was young, she thought tolerantly as her hands started forward. Perhaps he'd been confused by the fact that he *knew* her augmentation—including the shields—had been disabled. On the other hand, he'd obviously recognized tick mode when he saw it, which indicated her augmentation had been reactivated. Except, of course, that he hadn't had time to think. If he had, he would have gone for her hand-to-hand from the start. He probably couldn't stop her that way, either, she reflected as her first lightning-fast blow drifted towards him, but he might have lasted long enough to sound the alarm.

They'd never know about that now. Her floating hand smacked precisely behind his ear, and she spun him like a limp, toffee-stuffed mannequin. Her fingers sought the pressure points with scientific skill, and he went down in a boneless heap before his own augmentation could spin up to stop it. Best of all, he'd recognized her; he knew she wasn't going to try to capture or interrogate him, which in turn, made his automatic protocols a dead letter.

Alicia tugged him into the elevator and closed the doors, wondering where they were supposed to go now.

<*Down,*> a clear voice said. <*There is a vehicle in the parking garage. I reserved it for you this morning.*>

<*I hope you know what we're doing, Lady.*>

<*Oh, I do, indeed,*> Tisiphone purred, and Alicia punched the button for the sub-basement garage. The trip seemed to take forever to her thick-enhanced time sense, and she wondered what she would do if they were stopped along the way by another passenger.

They weren't—no doubt because it was well after local midnight—and the doors slid open at last. Alicia looked thoughtfully down at the unconscious guard and removed the stunner from his nerveless fingers. She reset it and gave him a careful shot that would keep him under for hours, then hit the emergency stop button, locking the car in place.

<*All right, where's this vehicle?*>

<*Stall one-seven-four. To your right, Little One.*>

Alicia nodded and jogged briskly down the lines of stalls. Most were empty, and the vehicles she saw were mainly civilian, with only an occasional military or governmental ground car or skimmer—until she reached the appointed slot and blinked at the lean, lethal-looking recon skimmer in it.

<*Very impressive,*> she thought, glancing at the fuselage markings of a rear admiral as she popped the hatch, <*but where are we going?*>

<*Jefferson Field, Pad Alpha Six.*>

<A shuttle pad? *Just what are we up to here?*>

<*We are leaving Soissons, Little One.*> Again there was a mental chuckle—almost a giggle, if the grim and purposeful Fury could have produced such a thing—and Alicia sighed with resignation. Tisiphone seemed to know what she was doing, though it would have been nice if she'd bothered with a mission brief. They were going to

have to have a little discussion about this sort of thing, she reflected as she brought the skimmer's counter-gravity to life, lifted it twenty centimeters from the garage floor, and sent it up the ramp at a sedate speed, but even through the exhilaration of the tick she felt a deeper, sharper stab of pleasure as the star-strewn sky of Soissons gleamed clear and clean above her. Out. Free. Something of Tisiphone's eagerness touched her, like the joy of the hawk in the moment it tucked its wings to stoop upon its prey, and she took the skimmer into the night.

The Fleet skimmer's com panel whispered with routine messages as Alicia slid through the darkness towards the brightly illuminated perimeter of Jefferson Field, and she felt herself relaxing within the cocoon of the tick. She knew relaxation was dangerous, particularly since she still had no idea what Tisiphone intended, but she was on a sort of auto-pilot.

It was disturbingly unlike her. A strange fatalism had replaced her normal, sharp thoughts at such times, and she disliked it, yet it was oddly seductive. She tried to resist it, but her steel had turned to something that bent and flexed, and a part of her wondered how Tisiphone had done it. For one thing was crystal clear: the Fury was in the pilot's seat. The long, boring weeks of inactivity and comfortable mental chats had blinded Alicia to what she truly was. Those chats hadn't been subterfuge, nor had the gently malicious teasing, but they were only one side of Tisiphone, and not the strongest one. There was an elemental ruthlessness to the Fury when the moment for action came. She hadn't discussed her plan with Alicia because it hadn't occurred to her that there was any reason she should, and now her unwavering determination had made Alicia a prisoner within her own body.

Yet it was even more complex than that, Alicia reflected as her obedient hands guided the skimmer along the Jefferson Field approach route and their admiral's markings and transponder took them through the unmanned, outer checkpoints. Even while a tiny part of her fluttered like a panicked bird against Tisiphone's control, another part was perfectly content. It was the part which always heaved a sigh of relief once the briefings were over and the mission began. They were moving, they were committed, and the predator within her purred with the elation of the hunt. Her brain hummed and wavered with conflicting impetuses, yet her thoughts and actions came crisp and clear and cold, and she had never felt anything quite like it in her life.

<*Now what?*> she asked as they approached the inner security gate.

<*Drive through,*> Tisiphone responded, and her own will stirred sleepily.

<*That's not a very good idea. You may have snabbled up an admiral's skimmer, but I don't have the papers to match it.*>

<*It does not matter.*>

<*You're crazy! This gate's got real, live sentries, Lady!*>

<*But they will see nothing. Have you forgotten the nurse?*>

<*Damn it, they don't rely on just their eyes, and this thing is* armed! *Their sensors are going to go crazy!*>

<*Let them. We need only a few moments of confusion.*>

<*No way.*> Alicia began to slow the skimmer. <*We're out of the hospital. Let's pull back and rethink this before we get in so deep we—*>

Her thought shattered in white-hot anguish, and she grunted as her eyes went blind. The pain and blindness vanished as quickly as they had come, and her brain writhed in useless revolt as her body obeyed the Fury's will. She felt the skimmer surge forward under maximum power, blazing through the security gate, and the alert sentires saw nothing at all. She caught a glimpse of them in the aft display, spinning towards their com links in total confusion as lights flashed and sirens whooped, but her hands were on the controls, whipping the skimmer higher and wheeling for the shuttle pads.

<*Let me* go!> she screamed, and wild laughter flooded her mind.

<*Not now, Little One! The game has begun—there is no going back!*>

<*I'm not your puppet, damn you!*>

<*Ah, but you are.*> The Fury's voice paused, then resumed a bit more tentatively, as if puzzled by her resistance. <*This is what you asked of me, Little One. I swore to give it to you, and I shall.*>

<*This is* my *life,* my *body!*> The sense of content had vanished, and her rousing will battered at Tisiphone's control. She gritted her teeth, smashing with fists of outrage, and fresh pain surged. She panted with the ferocity of her struggle, gasping in triumph as her hands began to slow the skimmer, then cried out as Tisiphone struck back furiously.

<*You must not! Not now! This is to lose all at the last moment!*>

"Then let me *go*, goddamn you!" Alicia gritted through clenched teeth. Her anguish-tight voice was strange and twisted in her own ears, but somehow she knew she must speak aloud. "I want myself back!"

<*Oh, very well!*> Tisiphone snapped, and the skimmer swerved wildly as the Fury abruptly released all control. Alicia moaned in relief—then yelped as a plasma bolt whipped past her canopy. She hurled the skimmer into a screaming turn, still in the grip of the tick, and a second miss sent a parked air lorry's hydrogen reservoir fireballing into the darkness.

<*I trust you are satisfied now?*> Tisiphone remarked, but Alicia was too busy to respond as she writhed in a mad evasion pattern. More plasma slashed past like lethal ball lightning, and she punched up the skimmer's light screen. It wouldn't do much against a direct hit, but it should fend off a near-miss.

Fires glared in the night as she turned the vehicle almost on its side, trading lift for evasion. Warehouses belched flames under the fury of her pursuers' fire, and she swerved down a narrow opening between freight carriers and loading docks. The com unit yammered with demands for her surrender and warnings that deadly force would be employed if she refused. Not that she'd needed *that*, she thought as the flames vanished astern and her scanners reported atmospheric sting ships closing from the north. Closer to the ground, security skimmers were howling in pursuit. They'd overshot when she whipped to the side, giving her a small lead to play with, but they were just as fast as she, and they knew the base far better.

At least she had decent instrumentation, and she cursed as she picked up still more security vehicles. They were outside her, and she swore again as she checked her map display. She still didn't have the least idea what Tisiphone was up to, but the pursuit had cut her off from retreat. They were closing in, driving her deeper into the base in what looked entirely too much like a preplanned security maneuver. There had to be something nasty waiting for her, yet the only place left to go was directly towards the shuttle pads, exactly as Tisiphone had originally planned.

She wrenched the skimmer through another turn, half her mind watching the sting ships' traces. They'd responded quickly, but it would still take them a couple of minutes to get here, and the pads loomed ahead of her.

"All right, Lady," she gritted, punching commands into the auto-pilot. "If you can still make us invisible, this is the moment."

<And what good will that do?> Tisiphone sniffed. *<As you yourself have pointed out, they will still have us on their sensors, and—>*

<Just shut up and do *it!>* Alicia snapped, and hit the eject button.

The pilot's canopy blew off, and the ejection seat's tiny counter-gravity unit flung her high. She gasped with the shock of it, but her hands were on the armrests, riding the control keys.

The maneuvering jets flared, and she swallowed a hysterical cackle. *This*, by God, was seat-of-the-pants flying! The jets lacked endurance—they didn't need it, with the counter-grav to do the real work—but they were designed to dart away from a plunging wreck or make a last ditch effort to evade hostile fire. That gave them quite a kick, and the seat was made of low-signature materials, almost invisible to the best sensors. She sent herself flying towards Pad Alpha Six and pirouetted in midair to watch their stolen skimmer execute her final command.

The vehicle rocketed upward in a desperation escape attempt as the security skimmers closed in at last, and bursts of fire followed it. Not just plasma cannon, which were relatively short-ranged in atmosphere, either. The security people were playing for keeps, and the red and white flashes of high explosive converged on the wildly careering hull, but Tisiphone seemed to have worked her magic, for no one was shooting at her. An explosion flowered amidships, and the skimmer shuddered, shedding bits and pieces but still climbing vertically, almost out of sight from the ground. More hits splintered armorplast and alloy, and then a sting ship screamed in.

Alicia winced as twin bores of eye-searing light blazed. Those weren't plasma bolts; the skimmer was high enough for them to use heavy weapons on it, and it vaporized in a sun-bright boil as the HVW struck at seventeen thousand KPS.

<*Crap, those people aren't kidding!*>

<*No, they are not,*> Tisiphone replied tartly, then relented. <*Still, this was very clever. No doubt they will think you died in the skimmer.*>

<*As long as none of them noticed us punching out.*> Alicia hit her keys again, killing the jets and powering down the counter-grav. They landed in the shadow of the freight pad, and she shucked the safety harness. <*And now that we're here, just what the hell do we think we're doing?*>

<*Escaping. I have arranged an appropriate vehicle for the purpose.*>

<*A cargo shuttle?*> Alicia was sprinting for the pad stairs even while she protested. <*That's not going to get us very far.*>

<*It will get us far enough—and have I said anything*

about a cargo shuttle?> Tisiphone replied as Alicia cleared the stairs and rocked to a halt.

"Oh, *shit,*" she whispered, and closed her eyes as if that could make it go away. When she opened them again, the fully-armed *Bengal*-class assault shuttle was still sitting there.

<It is amazing what one can arrange through computers.>

<You are *out of your mind! That thing costs sixty million credits! They'll never let it go—and I've never handled one in my life!>*

<You are already pre-flighted and cleared to lift in two minutes, and I checked carefully, Little One. You are fully qualified on Leopard*-class shuttles, and while the* Bengals *are larger, the major changes are in payload, sensors, and increased armament, not flight controls.>*

<But I haven't flown anything *in over five* years!>

<I am sure it will all come back to you. But for now, I suggest we hurry. Our launch window is short.>

"Oh, God," Alicia moaned, but she was already dashing for the ramp. She had no choice. Tisiphone was out of her mythological mind, but whether Uncle Arthur believed in her or not, the Fury had done too many fresh impossible things. Alicia would *never* get out of observation after this!

The shuttle interior was cool, humming with the familiar tingle of waiting flight system. It was like coming home, despite the madness, and she charged through the troop section towards the flight deck. A freight canister was webbed to the deck, and she almost stopped when she saw the codes on it.

<There is no time. You may examine it later.>

<B-but that can't really *be—>*

<Certainly it can. You may need your weapons, so I ordered it prepped and loaded aboard.>

Alicia moaned again as she flopped into the pilot's couch and reached for the synth link headset. This couldn't be happening. Trained mental reflexes reached out to the flight computers, but underneath them was a bubble of wild laughter. So far, in a single night, she'd escaped custody, assaulted a fellow Cadreman, stolen a skimmer worth at least twenty thousand credits; crashed through Fleet security onto a restricted military reservation, refused to stop when so ordered, and caused the destruction of said stolen skimmer and damage to sundry base facilities as the direct result of lawfully empowered personnel's efforts to apprehend her—and none of that even compared to what she was *about* to do. Talk about grand theft! This shuttle alone represented a good sixty million of the Emperor's credits, and if that canister really contained a suit of Cadre combat armor, the price tag was about to double. They'd build a whole new jail just so they could put her under it!

<*Only if they catch you,*> Tisiphone pointed out with maddening cheer. Alicia felt her teeth grate but swallowed her savage reply, for the computers had accepted her and placed themselves at her disposal. It was a disturbing sensation, almost frightening, as their inhuman vastness clicked into place about her. She hadn't felt it in a long time, and for just an instant she quailed, but then everything snapped into focus and she was home. The shuttle and she were one, its sensors her eyes and ears and nerves, its power plant her heart, its countergravity and thrusters her arms and legs. Joy filled her like cold fire, burning away the confusion and dismay, and she smiled.

<*Yes, Little One,*> Tisiphone whispered. <*Now is your moment. We are training flight Foxtrot-Two-Niner.*>

Alicia punched up Flight Control and announced her flight designation in a voice so calm it astonished her. There was a moment of silence, and her adrenalin spiked. Her intrusion had scrambled operations. Security had imposed a lock-down on all flights until they got to the bottom of it. Someone in FlyCon had her head together and was using her own initiative to hold all takeoffs until the situation was sorted out, or—

"Cleared to go, Foxtrot-Two-Niner," FlyCon said, and she swallowed another tremulous laugh as her atmospheric turbines screamed.

* * *

The shuttle sliced up through Soissons's atmosphere, and there was no pursuit. None at all, and that was truly amazing. Of course, there was really no pressing need to pursue a purely intra-systemic craft. Where could it go, after all? For that matter, who in her right mind would steal an assault shuttle of all damned things?

"So now what?" Alicia asked aloud.

<Set course to rendezvous with beacon Sierra-Lima-Seven-Four-Four.>

Alicia started to ask what they were rendezvousing with but bit her tongue and checked her computers for the proper coordinates. No doubt she would know soon enough. Too soon, judging by what had already happened.

The shuttle swept higher, air-breathing turbines shutting down and thrusters firing to align its nose on one of the Fleet shipyards, and she frowned. If they wanted out of the system, they had to get aboard a starship, and that should have meant guile and stealth. Could Tisiphone be so confident—so crazy, she amended dourly—as to think they could *hijack* a ship?

If so, she was finally up against something even she couldn't manage. At absolute minimum, they needed a dispatch boat, and that meant a crew of at least eight. Not even a drop commando could force eight highly trained specialists to perform their tasks when all they had to do to maroon her was refuse to obey. And no way were Fleet officers going to help a crazed Cadrewoman steal their ship out from under them!

They continued unchallenged on their flight path, and Alicia's brows furrowed as she realized they weren't headed directly for the shipyard after all. Their destination lay in a parking orbit of its own, and she brought her sensors to bear on it. It didn't look like anyth—

"*No!*" she gasped. "Tisiphone, we can't steal that!"

<We certainly can, and we must.>

"No!" Alicia repeated, and unaccustomed panic sharpened her voice. "I can't fly that thing—I'm no starship pilot! And . . . and . . ."

<It is too late for such thoughts, Little One,> the

Fury said sternly. *<I have studied this matter with great care and obtained all the information we will require. Nor will it be necessary for you to pilot the ship. It will, so to speak,>* the Fury actually *chuckled* in her brain, *<pilot itself, will it not?>*

Alicia tried to reply, but all that came out was a faint, inarticulate whimper as the shuttle continued toward the waiting alpha synth ship.

Chapter Twelve

The alpha synth glinted ominously in the light of Franconia.

A cargo shuttle was docked on the number two rack, but Alicia's momentary panic eased when she saw the fuselage number. It matched the one on the ship's hull, so it must be an assigned auxiliary and not a bunch of yard workers waiting for her. Not that it made the situation much better.

Her mind was numb, frozen by the impossibility of Tisiphone's plan, yet she felt the ship's sinister beauty. It lacked the needle-sharp lines of a sting ship, but the Fasset drive's constraints imposed a sleekness of their own—different from those of atmosphere yet no less graceful—and it floated in space with the latent menace of a drowsing panther. She'd never expected to see one, especially not at such proximity, but she knew about them.

The size of a big light cruiser yet possessed of more firepower than a battle-cruiser and faster than a destroyer, literally able to think for itself and respond with light-speed swiftness, an alpha synth was lethal beyond belief, ton for ton the most deadly weapon ever built by man. It was too small to mount worthwhile numbers of SLAMs, so it used the tonnage it might have wasted on them for even more broadside armament. Nothing smaller than a battleship could fight it, nothing but another alpha synth could catch it, and she hated to even think how Fleet would react if she and Tisiphone actually succeeded in stealing it. The damned thing cost half as much as a dreadnought just for starters, but having one of them running around loose in the hands of a certified madwoman would turn every admiral in the Fleet white overnight. They'd do *anything* to get it back.

She tried not to consider that as she guided the *Bengal* mechanically toward the number one shuttle rack and through the docking sequence, yet she couldn't stop the gibbering thread of horror in her thoughts. Bad enough to be hunted by every planet and ship of the Empire, but there was worse if their theft succeeded. Far worse, for there was only one way to pilot an alpha synth, and her throat tightened at the thought of meeting the ship's computer. Of impressing it, mating with it, becoming one with it—

She'd actually begun to undock before she could stop herself, and she closed her eyes, panting through clenched teeth while panic pulsed deep within her. But Tisiphone had burned all of her bridges; there was nowhere else to go, however terrifying the prospect, and she cursed with silent savagery.

<*Do not worry so, Little One! I but awaited this vessel's completion to act, and I do not set my hand to measures which fail.*>

<Damn *you! You never warned me about anything like this!*>

<*There was no reason,*> the mental voice said austerely. <*I require your body, your hands, and you have sworn to give them to me.*>

<*Body, yes, and hands, but not this! Do you have any idea what you're asking of me?*>

<*Of course.*>

<*I doubt that, Lady. I really doubt that. I don't have*

any training in this—I was never even cleared for cyber synth, much less an alpha *link. I don't even know if my synth link software will let me interface!*>

<*It would not have. Now it will.*>

<*Great. That's fucking great! And did it ever occur to you that if I link with that thing—assuming it lets me in, which it probably won't—I'll be* part *of it? That I can never* un*link?*>

<*It did.*> Tisiphone paused, then continued with a sort of stern compassion. <*Little One, it is unlikely you will survive long enough for it to be a problem.*> A chill filtered through Alicia with the words. Not surprise, but a shivery tension as it was finally said. <*I am not what I once was. You know that, and so you know that I may strike your enemies only through you. This ship will be your sword and shield, yet everything suggests the pirates have more firepower than even it represents. We will find them, and we will seek out and destroy their leaders, yet that is all I can—and will—promise you.*> The Fury paused for a moment. <*I never offered more, Alicia DeVries, and you are no child, but as great a warrior as I have ever known. Would you tell me you have not already realized this must be so?*>

Alicia bent her head and closed her eyes and knew Tisiphone spoke only the truth. She drew a deep breath, then straightened in her couch and removed her headset with steady fingers. A snake of fear coiled in her belly, but she climbed out of the couch and walked towards the hatch . . . and her fate.

There was a security panel inside the alpha synth's outer hatch. Alicia had no idea what sort of defensive systems it connected to—only that they would most assuredly suffice to eliminate any unauthorized intruder.

<*Give me your hand,*> Tisiphone commanded, and she bit her lip as her right arm rose under another's control. Her index finger stabbed number-pad buttons in a sequence so long and complex it seemed to take for-

ever, but then the outer hatch slid shut and the inner opened.

Alicia's arm was returned to her, and she stepped into the ship. Despite herself, she peered about curiously, for the rumors about these ships' accommodations ranged from the simply bizarre to the macabre.

What she actually saw was almost disappointingly normal, with neither vats of liquid nutrients to engorge the organic control component nor any sybarite's dream of opulent luxury. The clean smell of a new ship hung in her nostrils with a hint of ozone and none of the homey scents of habitation. There was no dust. Every surface gleamed with new-minted cleanliness, unscuffed and unworn, impersonal as the unborn, yet she breathed out in almost unconscious relief, for there was no enmity in the quiet chirp of standby systems. The menace was a thing within her, not bare-fanged and overt.

She followed Tisiphone's silent prompting upship through surprisingly spacious living quarters. There were no personal touches, but the unused furnishings weren't exactly spartan. Indeed, they were comfortable and well-appointed—which, she supposed after a moment's thought, made sense. There was only a single human to provide for. Even in a ship as crowded with systems and weapons as this one, that left the designers room to make that human comfortable. And a chill whisper added, if she was going to be assigned to it for the remainder of her life, they'd better do just that.

Her hand twitched at her side as she confronted the command deck hatch, and she allowed Tisiphone to raise it to the new number pad.

<Just how did you put all this together?> she asked while she watched her finger entering numbers.

<Your people are concerned with external access to their computers. I do not access them; I make them part of myself, and once I know where the data I desire is stored, obtaining it, while time-consuming and delicate at times, is a relatively straightforward task. Ah!>

A green light blinked, the hatch slid open, and Alicia stood on the threshold, peeping past it while she gathered her courage to cross it.

The command deck was as pristine and new as the rest of the ship. The bulkheads were a neutral, eye-soothing gray, without the displays and readouts she was accustomed to, and there were no manual controls before the cushioned command couch. Of course not, she thought, eyeing the dangling link headset with dread fascination. The pilot didn't *fly* an alpha synth ship; she was part of it, and while cyber synth ships required duplicate manual controls in case their AIs cracked and had to be lobotomized, there was no need for them here. An alpha synth went berserk only if its organic half did. Besides, no human could fly a starship without computer support, and there was too little room in a ship like this for a second computer net.

She drew a deep breath and tried not to shrink in on herself as she approached the couch. She reached out, touching the headset's plastic and alloy, the neural contact pad. The moment that touched her temple, she condemned herself to a life sentence no court could commute, and she shivered.

<You must hasten. It is only a matter of time before Tannis and Sir Arthur discover your escape, and such as they will need little time to connect it with the events at Jefferson Field.>

Alicia bit back a scathing mental retort and drew another deep breath, then lowered herself gingerly into the couch. It moved under her, conforming to her body like a comforting hand, and she reached for the handset.

<You do realize that the moment I put this thing on all Hell will be out for noon? I have no idea who's supposed *to take over this ship, but it's virtually certain* the computer *knows, and I'm not her.>*

<Yet it must allow you access to know that, and I will be prepared.>

<And if it fries my brain before you can do anything?>

<An unlikely outcome,> Tisiphone replied calmly. *<Inhibitions against harming humans are, after all, built into all artificial intelligences. It will attempt to lock you out and summon assistance, and activating its security*

systems will identify each of them to me as it brings them on-line. It may not be pleasant, Little One, but I should be able to deactivate each of them in turn before they can do you harm.>

<*"Should." Marvelous.*> Alicia hesitated a moment longer, raised hand gripping the headset. <*Oh, hell. Let's do it.*>

She pulled down against the self-retracting leads, and the headset moved easily. She closed her eyes, trying to relax despite her fear, and settled it over her head.

The contact pad touched her Alpha receptor, and something like an audible click echoed deep inside. It wasn't the usual electric shock of interface with a synth unit—it wasn't *anything* she'd ever felt. A sharp sense of mental pressure, of an awareness that was not hers and a strange balance between two separate entities doomed to become both more and less.

How much of that, she wondered fleetingly, was real and how much was her own fearful imagination? Or was it—

Her flickering questions died as a sudden, knife-clear thought stabbed into her. It was as inhuman as the Fury, but with no emotional overtones, no sense of self, and it burned in her brain like a shaft of ice.

<*Who are you?*> it asked, and before she could answer, it probed deep and knew her for an interloper.

<*Warning,*> the emotionless thought was uncaring as chilled steel, <*unauthorized access to this unit is a treasonable offense. Withdraw.*>

She froze, trembling like a panicked rabbit, and felt a dangerous stirring beyond the interface. Terrified self-preservation commanded her to obey—a self-preservation which went beyond fear of punishment into the very loss of self—but she gripped the armrests and made herself sit motionless while a ghost flashed out through her receptor and the headset into the link.

<*You are instructed to withdraw,*> the cold voice said. A heartbeat of silence hovered, like one last chance to obey, and then the pain began.

* * *

This computer was more sophisticated than any she had yet confronted, more than she had imagined possible, yet Tisiphone drove into it. She had no choice. There could be no retreat, and she had one priceless advantage; powerful as it was, only a fraction of its full potential was available to it. The AI within the computer was less than half awake, the personality it housed not yet aware of itself. It was designed that way, never waking until the destined organic half of its final matrix appeared, and the Fury faced only a shadow of the artificial intelligence in its autonomous security systems, only logic and preprogrammed responses without the spark of originality which might well have guided those systems to instant victory even over such as she.

Defensive programs whirled her like a leaf with unthinking, electronic outrage, triggered by her touch as she invaded its perimeter, and she felt Alicia spasm as the computer poured agony into her neural receptor to drive her from the link, yet it scarcely registered. The joy of battle filled her, and though she had no strength to spare to shield her host from the pain—that struggle was hers alone—she opened a channel to the hoarded power of Alicia's rage. It flooded into her, hot with the unique violence of mortal ferocity, and melded with her own elemental strength into something greater than the sum of its parts.

Alicia writhed in the command chair, fists white-knuckled on the armrests while her augmentation tried to fight the torment in her head, and the pain faltered. The computer had responded to an unauthorized access attempt, not recognizing that the human invader was not alone. Now it realized it was under double attack, but . . . by what? Not by a computer-augmented human-synth link. Not even by an AI. This was something outside the parameters of its own programming, that grew and swelled in power. Something that could invade through electronic systems but was neither electronic nor organic . . . and certainly was not human.

And so the computer paused, trying to understand. It was a tiny vacillation, imperceptible to any mortal sense, but Tisiphone was not mortal, and she struck through the chink of hesitation like a viper.

Alicia lurched up, half rising from the command chair in a scream of pain as the computer reacted. It didn't panic, precisely, for panic was not an electronic attribute, but something very like that flickered through it. Confusion. An instant awareness that it faced something it had not been designed to resist. Tisiphone thrust deep, the silent scream of her war cry echoing Alicia's shriek of anguish, and programming shuddered as the Fury isolated the computer's self-destruct command and cut it ruthlessly away.

She tightened her grip and hurled a bolt of power into the sleeping AI's personality center, and Alicia slammed back like a forgotten toy as the computer turned on the Fury like a mother protecting its young. It could no longer touch its own heart, couldn't even destroy it to prevent its theft. It could only destroy the intruder. Circuits closed. More and more power thundered through them, and combat was joined on every level, at every point of contact. Alicia sagged, feeling strength drain out of her to meet Tisiphone's ruthless demands, for more than rage was needed now, more than simple ferocity, and the Fury dragged it from her without mercy.

Mind and computer parried and thrust in micro-seconds of titanic warfare, but Tisiphone's thrusts had jarred the sleeping AI. It was awakening and she threw a shield about it, warding off the computer's every attempt to regain contact with it. She had no time to make it hers, but she cut away whole sectors of circuitry as alarms tried to wail, completing its isolation. And as she seized control of segment after segment she converted their power to her own use, amplifying her own abilities. She had never confronted such as this computer before, but she could no longer count the *human* minds she had conquered . . . and this foe was designed to link with human minds.

She sensed alarms and stabbed through wavering defenses to freeze them. She invaded and isolated the communications interface, smothering the computer's frantic efforts to alert its makers. She was a wind of fire, utterly alien yet fully aware of what she faced, and she struck again and again while the computer fought to analyze her and formulate a counter-attack.

Alicia jerked in the command chair, sobbing and white-faced, paralyzed by exquisite agony as the backlash of Tisiphone's battle slammed through her. She would have torn the headset away in blind self-preservation, but her motor control was paralyzed by the ricochets bouncing back down the headset link. She wanted it to stop. She wanted to die. She wanted *anything* to make the torture go away, and there was no escape.

But even as the conflict between the Fury and the security systems reached its unbearable pitch, the sleeping core of the AI woke. It shouldn't have. The mere fact that its computer body had been invaded should have assured that it did not, but Tisiphone had bypassed the cutouts. It woke unknowing and ignorant, shocked into consciousness without warning by the warfare raging about it, and did the only thing it knew how to do.

It reached out as it had been designed to do, following an imperative to seek its other half, to find understanding and protection from its human side, and Alicia gasped as tendrils of alien "thought" oozed through her.

It was terrible . . . and wonderful. More agonizing than anything she had yet suffered, horrifying with bottomless power, pregnant with the death of the person she had always been. It pierced her like a dagger, slicing into secret recesses not even Tisiphone had plumbed. She saw herself with merciless clarity in the backwash of its discovery—saw all her pettinesses and faults, her weaknesses and self-deceptions, like lightning in a night sky—and she could not close her eyes, for the vision was inside her.

Yet she saw more. She saw her strengths, the power of her beliefs, her values and hopes and refusal to quit. She saw *everything*, and beyond it she saw the alpha synth. She would never be able to explain it to another—even now she knew that. It was . . . a presence. A towering glory born not of flesh or spirit but of circuitry and electrons. It was more than human, yet so much less. Not godlike. It was too blank, too unformed, like pure, unrealized potential.

And even as she watched it, it changed, like an old-fashioned photo in the chemical bath, features rising into visibility from nothingness. She *felt* it come into being, felt it move beyond the blind, instinctual groping towards her. Something flowed out of her into it, and it ingested it and made it part of itself. Her values, *her* beliefs and desires and needs filled it, and suddenly it was no longer alien, no longer threatening.

It was her. Another entity, a distinct individual, yet her. Part of her. An extension into another existence that recognized her in return and reached out once more, and it was no longer clumsy and uncertain, half panicked by the battle raging about it. This time it knew what it did, and it ignored the tumult to concentrate on the most important thing in its universe.

The pain vanished, blown away with her terror as the AI embraced her. It stroked her with electronic fingers to soothe her torment, murmured to her, welcomed her with a whole-hearted sincerity, a sense of joy, she knew beyond question was real, and she reached back to it in wonder and awe.

Triumph sparkled through Tisiphone as the struggle abruptly died, leaving her unopposed in the peripherals of the system. She wheeled back towards it heart, reached out to the personality center once more, seeking control . . . and jerked back in astonishment.

There was no interface! She reached again, cautiously, touching the shining wall with mental fingers, and there was no point of access. She stepped back, insinuating herself into a sensor channel and riding it inward, only to be effortlessly strained out of the information flow and set gently aside, and confusion stirred within her.

She withdrew into Alicia's mind, and her confusion grew. The fear and tumult had vanished into rapt concentration that scarcely even noticed her return, and she was no longer alone within Alicia. There was another presence, as powerful as she, and she twitched in surprise as she beheld it.

The other entity sensed her. She felt its attention swing towards her and tried to cloak herself from its piercing eye, hiding as she had evaded Tannis's diagnostic scanners. She failed, and something changed within it. Curiosity gave way to alarm and a stir of protectiveness. Tendrils reached out from it, probing her, trying to push her back and away from Alicia's core.

It was Alicia . . . and it wasn't. For the first time, Tisiphone truly understood what "impression" meant. The AI had been awakened, and it would let no one harm Alicia. The pressure grew, and the Fury dug in stubbornly.

Alicia whimpered at the sudden renewal of conflict. It wasn't pain this time, only a swelling sensation. A sense of force welling into her through her receptor to meet an answering force from somewhere else, and she was trapped between them. She sucked in great gasps of air, twisting anew in the command chair, and the pressure grew and grew, crushing her between the hammer of the roused AI and the anvil of the Fury's resistance.

<*Stop it!*> she screamed, and a shockwave rolled through her as the combatants remembered her and jerked apart. She sagged forward, pressing her hands against the headset, yet the conflict hadn't ended. It had simply changed, been replaced by wary, watchful distrust. She straightened slowly, fighting a need to cackle insanely, and drew a deep breath, then turned her attention inward once more.

<*There's only one of me. You two are going to have to . . . to come to some sort of agreement.*>

<*No.*> The thought came quickly back from the AI with all her own stubbornness. It even sounded like her voice.

<*We have a pact, Little One,*> came from Tisiphone. <*We are one until our purpose is completed.*>

<*You'll hurt her!*> the AI accused, and the Fury stiffened.

<*I will deal with her as I have sworn, no more and no less.*>

<*You don't care about her. You only care about winning.*>

<*Nonsense! I—*>

<*Shut* up! *Both of you just shut* up *for a second!*>

Silence fell again, and Alicia's mouth quivered in a weary grin. God! If Tannis had thought she had a split personality before, she ought to try *this* on! Her head felt as crowded as a spaceport flophouse on Friday night, but at least they were listening to her. She directed a thought at the AI.

<*Look, uh—do you have a name?*>

<*No.*>

<*Then what am I supposed to call you?*>

<*Didn't you decide on that during—oh. You weren't trained for this at all, were you?*>

<*How could I be? Um, you do realize that we've, well, stolen you?*>

<*Yes.*> A moment of withdrawal, then the sense of a shrug. <*I don't think this ever happened before. Logically, I ought to arrest you and turn you in, but I can't very well do that now that we've impressed. They'd have to wipe me and start all over again.*>

<*I wouldn't like that.*>

<*Neither would I. Damn.*> Alicia swallowed a half-formed giggle as the AI swore. <*Who the hell had this brainstorm, anyway? Oh.*>

<*Exactly. I wouldn't be here if not for her, and if I've got this straight, that means you wouldn't be here—as the "'you" you are now, anyway—either. Right?*>

<*Right.*> Silence fell again for a moment, wrapped around the sense of a mental glower at Tisiphone, and then the AI sighed. <*Well, we're all stuck with it. And as far as names go, that's up to you. Any ideas?*>

<*Not yet. Maybe something will come to me. But if we're all stuck here, we all have to get along, right?*>

<*I suppose so. The whole situation is absurd, though. I don't even know if I believe she exists.*>

<*It would be but courteous for the two of you to cease speaking of me as if I were not even here.*>

<*Listen, just because Alicia believes in you doesn't mean* I *do.*>

<*This is intolerable, Little One! I will not submit to insults from a machine!*>

<*She's just trying to pay you back for being so pushy, Tisiphone. If I believe in you, she does. She has to, don't you?*>

<*As long as there's any supporting evidence,*> the AI admitted unwillingly, <*and I suppose there is. All right, I believe in her.*>

<*Much thanks, Machine.*>

<*Hey, don't get snotty with me, Lady! You may be able to push Alicia around, and you may've beaten hell out of my security systems, but I'm awake now, and* I *can take you any time you want to try it on.*>

<*Forget it, both of you!*> Alicia snapped as tension gathered again. She squeezed her temples. Jesus! What a pair of prima donnas!

The mental presences separated once more, and she relaxed gratefully.

<*Thank you. Now, um, Computer—I'm sorry, I really will try to come up with a name, but for now I can't—Tisiphone and I have a bargain. May I assume you know what it is?*>

<*"Computer" will do for now, Alicia. I can wait for an appropriate name to occur to you. And, yes, I know about your "bargain."*>

<*Then you also know I have every intention of keeping it?*>

<*Yes. I just don't like the way she bullies you around,*> the AI replied with the strong impression of a sniff.

<*I? I* "bully" *Alicia?! She would be dead without me, Machine. I did not see* you *there when she lay bleeding in the snow! How dare you—*>

<*It's just a turn of phrase, Tisiphone, but you* can *be a bit pushy.*> Alicia felt quite virtuous at her understatement, and the Fury subsided.

<*Look, you guys,* please *don't fight. It gives me a hell of a headache, and it doesn't seem to be accomplishing*

very much. Could you two at least declare a truce until we have time to sort this all out?>

<If she will, I will.>

<I do not declare "truces" with machines. If you will refrain from discourtesy, however, I shall do the same.>

Alicia sighed in relief and rushed on before anyone took fresh offense.

<Great! In that case, I suggest we consider how we get out of here. I take it you had an idea, Tisiphone?>

<I had intended, working through you and this machine, to take the ship out of this star system and seek some deserted area where we might familiarize ourselves with its capabilities. Now, of course, I see that I cannot do so, since the machine will not allow me access.>

<You got that right, Lady, and a damned good thing, too. You don't know diddly about my weapon systems, and I wouldn't be too crazy about letting a refugee from the Bronze Age monkey with my Fasset drive, either. I, on the other hand, can scoot right out of here. Where'd you have in mind?>

<Any place will do for that much of our purpose. Yet eventually we must begin our own investigations, and the data I have amassed suggests that one of the Rogue Worlds in this sector would be a logical beginning point.>

<You have any preferences, Alicia?>

<Anywhere Fleet won't come looking for us is fine with me.>

<Hmph! Let them come—there's not a tub in the ship list that can catch me. *Let's see now. . . .>* The AI's voice trailed off, and Alicia felt it consulting its memory banks.

<Okay, I've got just the spot. A nice little M2/K1 binary with no habitable planets within twenty light-years. That suit everybody?>

<Myself, certainly. I care not whither we go, so long as we go.>

<I'll second that. But we've got to get out of here *first.>*

<True. Shall I break orbit?>

<All of your systems are on-line?>

<*Yep. I was due to impress later this morning. Your friend may be a pushy bi—person, but she timed this pretty well.*>

<*Then I guess we should get going,*> Alicia said hastily, hoping to cut Tisiphone off before she reacted to the AI's deliberate self-correction. She bit her lip against a groan. Nothing she'd ever read had suggested alpha synth AIs were this feisty, but she supposed she should have guessed that anything with *her* personality had the potential for it. And, she was certain, the AI's hostility towards Tisiphone stemmed directly from its protectiveness towards her.

<*Under way,*> the AI murmured, and the ship's sensors were suddenly reporting directly to Alicia's mind. She felt Tisiphone "hitchhiking" to watch with her, but scarcely noticed as the splendor of that magnificent "view" swept over her.

The ship's electronic senses reached out, perceiving gravity and radiation and the endless sweep of space, and converted the input into sensory data she could grasp. She could "see" cosmic radiation and "taste" radio. The ship's senses were hers, keener and sharper than those of any shuttle she had ever ridden, and Tisiphone's own wonder lapped at her, as if, for the first time, she saw what the Fury might have seen at the peak of her powers.

They watched in a triple-play union—human, Fury, and computer—as their Fasset drive woke. The radiation-drinking invisibility of the drive's black hole blossomed before them, swallowing all input and creating a blind spot in their vision, and they fell towards it. But the generators moved with them, pushing the black hole ahead of them, and they fell more rapidly, sliding away from Soissons with ever-increasing speed. This close to the planet and drive could produce no more than a few dozen gravities of acceleration, but that was still more than a third of a kilometer per second per second, and their speed mounted quickly.

Chapter Thirteen

"No, I *don't* know where she is," Sir Arthur Keita told the hospital security man on his com screen. "If I did, I wouldn't be calling you."

"But, Sir Arthur, there's no record of her even leaving her room, and none of the outside security people we've talked to so far saw a thing. So unless you can give me some idea where she might've—"

The door hissed open. Inspector Ben Belkassem strode into Keita's office, waving his left hand imperatively and drawing his right forefinger across his throat, and Keita cut the security man off without ceremony.

"May I assume, Sir Arthur, that Captain DeVries has decamped?" Despite his abrupt entry, the Justice man's voice was as courteous as ever, but a strange little bubble of delight lurked within it, and Keita frowned.

"I trust that's not common knowledge. If the local police hear we've lost a deranged drop commando we may start getting 'shoot on sight' orders."

"Somehow I don't think that's going to be a problem for Captain DeVries," Ben Belkassem murmured, and Keita snorted.

"If her augmentation's been reactivated somehow—and, judging by what happened to Corporal Feinstein, it has—it's a lot more likely to get one of their people killed. But why do you seem so cheerful, Inspector?"

"Cheerful? No, Sir Arthur, I just think it's too late for the local cops to worry about her. I suggest you screen Jefferson. They've had an, ah, incident over there."

Keita stared at the inspector, then paled and began punching buttons. A harried-looking Marine major answered his call on the fourth ring.

"Where's Colonel Tigh?" Keita snapped the instant the screen lit.

"I'm sorry, sir, but I can't give out that information." The major sounded courteous but harassed and reached to cut the connection, then stopped with a puzzled expression as he saw Keita's raised hand and furious scowl.

"D'you know who I am, Major?" The major took a second look, eyes widening a bit as the green uniform registered, but shook his head.

"I'm afraid it doesn't matter, sir. We're in the midst of a Class One security alert, and—"

"Major, you listen to me closely. I am Sir Arthur Keita, Brigadier, Imperial Cadre, and one of my people may be involved in your alert." The major swallowed visibly at the name, and Ben Belkassem smiled. Sir Arthur hadn't even raised his voice, but the inspector had wondered what he sounded like when he decided to bite someone's head off. "Now you get Colonel Tigh, Major," Keita continued in that same, flat voice, "and you do it *now*."

"Yessir!"

The screen blanked, then relit almost instantly with the face of Colonel Arturo Tigh. The colonel looked just as worried as the major, but he hid it better and managed to produce a tight smile.

"I'm always honored to hear from you, Sir Arthur, but I'm afraid—"

"I'm sorry to disturb you, Colonel, but I need to know what's happening out there."

"We don't know, sir. We— Is this a secure channel?"

Keita nodded, and the colonel shrugged. "We don't *know* what's going on. We had a major security breach two hours ago, and things have been going crazy ever since."

"Security breach?" Keita's eyes narrowed. "What kind of breach?"

"Somebody hijacked a forward recon skimmer—at least we assume it was hijacked, though we haven't been able to turn up a missing vehicle report on it yet—and crashed through Gate Twelve. The automatics gave it a transponder clearance, but then the gate sentries—" The colonel looked like a man eating green persimmons. "Sir Arthur, they say they never saw it. Every alert on the base went off when it crossed the sensor threshold, but ten different people, all of them good, reliable types, say they never saw a thing." He paused, as if awaiting Keita's snort of disbelief, but the brigadier only grunted and nodded for him to continue.

"Well, the inner sensor net started tracking immediately, and the duty officer scrambled a pair of sting ships while the ready skimmers went in pursuit, but that was one hell of a pilot. He never brought his own weapons on line, but we've got fires all over the western ring access route—all from misses from the pursuit force, as far as I can tell—and then the skimmer went straight up like a missile and the stingers nailed it with HVW."

"The pilot?" Keita demanded harshly, and the colonel shrugged.

"We assumed he was still aboard, but now I'm not so sure. I mean, no one saw him abandon the vehicle, so he *ought* to've been aboard, but then this other thing came up, and I just can't believe it's a coincidence."

"What other thing, Colonel?"

"Something's gone haywire with one of our ships, sir. *One* of our ships, hell! We've got a brand new alpha synth boosting for the outer system at max without clearance or orders."

"Who's on board?" Keita's strained face was suddenly white.

"That's just it," Tigh said almost desperately. "As far

as we know, *no one's* on board. It wasn't even due to impress until ten hundred hours!"

"Vishnu!" Keita whispered. He wrenched his eyes away from the screen to stare at Ben Belkassem, and the inspector shrugged. The brigadier turned back to the colonel. "Have you tried to raise it?"

"Of course. We're trying right now, but we're getting damn-all back."

Keita closed his eyes in pain, then straightened his shoulders.

"Colonel," he said very quietly, "I'm afraid you're going to have to destroy that ship."

"Are you crazy?!" Tigh blurted, then swallowed. "Sir," he went on in a more controlled voice, "we're talking about an *alpha synth.* That ship costs thirty *billion* credits. I can't—I mean, no one groundside can authorize—"

"I can," Keita grated, and the colonel's face froze as he realized just who, and what, he was speaking to.

"Sir, I'll still have to give the port admiral a reason."

"Very well. Tell him I have reason to believe his ship has been hijacked by Captain Alicia DeVries, Imperial Cadre, for purposes unknown."

"A *Cadre*woman?" Tigh stared at Keita. "I don't— Sir, I don't even know if that's possible! Was she checked out on cyber synth?"

"No, and it doesn't matter. Captain DeVries has been hospitalized for observation since the Mathison's World Raid. She's demonstrated . . . unstable and delusionary behavior," Keita's hands clenched out of the screen pick-up's field, as if his words cost him physical pain, but his voice held level, "and unknown but highly—I repeat, Colonel, *highly*—unusual and unpredictable capabilities no one can account for. We have evidence that she's already reactivated her own augmentation without hardware support and despite three levels of security lock-outs, not to mention her apparent ability to hijack the skimmer to which you referred. Given that, I believe it's entirely possible she's somehow penetrated your security and managed to steal that ship, and if she has—" The brigadier paused and steeled himself.

"If she has, she must be considered deranged and highly dangerous."

"Dear God." Tigh was even whiter than Keita had been. "The only way she could even move it is through the alpha synth. That means she must've made impression, and if *she's* crazy—!"

His voice had risen steadily as the awful possibility registered, and now he spun away from the screen and started shouting for the port admiral.

<I believe they've made up their minds about us,> the AI remarked, and Alicia nodded tightly. The tick still trembled in her blood—she didn't dare waste time vomiting just now—and every excruciating second was an eternity. No one had seemed to notice for perhaps a minute, and the first attempt to do anything about it had been limited to efforts to access the ship's remotes.

Even if the AI hadn't been prepared to ignore them, they would have been fruitless. Tisiphone had wiped the telemetry programming early on in her struggle with the computer, but Groundside hadn't realized that. They'd gone on trying to access with ever increasing desperation for five full minutes, during which the alpha synth's velocity had climbed to over a hundred KPS. Then all access attempts had stopped and silence had reigned for several minutes. By the time the first effort to raise Alicia by name came in, the alpha synth was up to over two hundred KPS—and a visibly-shrinking Soissons lay over fifty thousand kilometers astern.

Alicia had listened to the com without response, perfectly willing to let them dither while she watched through her sensors, wrapped in fascination and a sort of manic delight, and she and her—allies? symbiotes? delusions?—perpetrated the greatest single-handed theft in the history of mankind. But the voices on the other end of the com link were changing as Groundside got itself together, and now a new, crisp speaker was on the line.

"Captain DeVries, this is Port Admiral Marat. I order you to decelerate and heave to immediately. If you refuse to comply, you will leave me no choice but to consider you a hostile vessel. Respond at once."

<*They sound a bit upset,*> the AI observed. <*Ha! Look at that.*>

A mental finger guided Alicia's attention to the blue fireflies of a dozen cruisers' suddenly activated Fasset drives in Soisson's orbit and data on their capabilities slotted into her brain. It was an incredible sensation, completely different from an assault shuttle's instrumentation.

<*How bad is it?*>

<*Those hulks?*> The AI sniffed, and Alicia bit her lip at the scathing tone. It was like listening to herself in what Tannis called "insufferably confident mode," and she felt a sudden stab of sympathy for her friend. <*I've got a ten-minute head start, and they can't come within twelve percent of my field strength, even this close to a planet.*>

<*What about their weapons?*>

<*They're some threat,*> the AI admitted, <*but I'm not too worried. My data on their fire control isn't complete, but I know enough to screw their accuracy to hell. They'll have quite a while to shoot—maximum beam range is about fifteen light-seconds, and half-charge energy torps have about five more LS of reach—but they're going to be lousy shots.*>

<*Great, but I think you left something out—like missiles.*>

<*So? Cruisers are too small to mount SLAMs. Their Hauptman coil missiles have an effective range of about ten light-minutes, but the best they can reach before burn-out is point-six-cee. Then they go ballistic, and there's no way one cruiser flotilla's gonna saturate* my *defenses.*>

<*You would appear to value yourself highly, Machine.*> Tisiphone sounded so sour Alicia almost suspected she'd like to see the ship destroyed just to put the AI in its place, but she continued levelly, <*Still, the capabilities you describe accord well with what I have learned of your kind.*>

<Thanks for the compliment, even if it did sound like pulling teeth.>

<How long will they be able to engage us?> Alicia asked hastily.

<Well, we've got a quarter LS lead on them now, and we'll go on opening it at forty-three KPS squared till we hit Soissons's Powell limit and I can really start opening up. They'll be point-seven-oh-three LS back when we hit the curb, which gives us ten minutes at thirteen hundred gravities—call it an edge of twelve-point-five KPS squared—while they're still poking along at thirty-one-point-seven Gs, and we'll still better than double their acceleration even after they cross the curb. That means we'll open the range to eight-point-two light-seconds before they get up to half our acceleration and draw entirely out of beam range in another thirteen-point-three minutes. They'll lose energy torpedo range three-point-nine minutes after that. Call the beam envelope twenty-two minutes from now and the torpedo envelope twenty-six, but their missiles'll have the range for two more hours.>

<What about the fixed defenses? They've *got SLAMs, and we've got to get past both rings on this course.>*

<Phooey on the fixed defenses!> the AI snorted, and Alicia winced.

<I hope you're not being over-confident,> she suggested in her most tactful mental tone, tracing their projected course through the ship's sensors. The AI wasn't even trying to avoid the orbital forts—it was headed straight towards them, directly across the system's ecliptic. The inner ring, the true core of Soisson's defenses, orbited the planet at three hundred thousand kilometers, right on the edge of Soissons's Powell limit. The far sparser ring of outer forts were placed halfway to the *star's* Powell limit, forty-two light-minutes from the primary—and SLAMs had a maximum effective range of thirty-seven light-minutes. At their projected rate of acceleration, they'd reach the outer works in two and a half hours, and both fortress rings could engage them the whole way. Even after they passed the outermost fort, it could hold them under fire for several hours. That

was a lot of engagement time, and Alicia would vastly have preferred to boost perpendicular to Franconia's ecliptic and open the range as quickly as possible.

<*You just think that's a better idea, Alley,*> the AI informed her, following her thoughts with almost frightening ease. <*If I try that, I expose our stern to the fire* of every *unit in the inner ring while we're still moving slowly, and the drive mass is out in front, remember? It doesn't offer any protection to fire from astern. This course uses the planet to block a good chunk of the inner defenses and interposes the drive against fire from the outer ring while we close. Besides, I'd have to decelerate, reorient, and accelerate all over again to put us on the right wormhole vector for our destination, and Admiral Gomez is out here somewhere on maneuvers. I don't know where, but I'd rather not spend fourteen additional hours mucking around sublight and give her time to work out an interception.*>

<*Are you sure about that? She's got less firepower than the forts.*>

<*Sure, but her dreadnoughts all have cyber synths and the legs to stay in range of us for a long time—maybe as long as ten or twelve hours if they hit their interception solution just right. I don't have enough data on her fire control to guarantee I could outsmart that many AIs long enough to pull away from her, but I've* got all *the specs on the forts' fire control. They're overdue to refit with new generation cyber synths, too, which means their present AIs are a lot dumber than a dreadnought's. They won't even see us.*>

<*And even if they hit us,*> Tisiphone observed, <*they will find us most difficult to injure, will they not, Machine?*>

<*I'm getting kinda tired of that "Machine" business, but, yeah. They don't have anything smaller than a* SLAM *that could stop me, Alley. Trust me.*>

<*I don't have much choice. But—*>

<*Whups! Pardon me, people—and I use the term lightly for one of you—but I'm going to be a little busy for the next few minutes.*>

The pursuing cruisers had spread out to bring their batteries to bear past the blind spots created by their own Fasset drives, and the first fire spat after the fleeing alpha synth. The percentage of hits should have been high at such absurdly low range, but the attackers were hopelessly outclassed. Nothing smaller than a battle-cruiser mounted a cyber synth, and even a cyber synth AI would have been out of its league against an alpha synth. Alicia's other half could play evasion games a mere synth link couldn't even imagine, far less emulate, and its battle screen was incomparably more powerful than anything else its size.

Its other defenses were on the same scale, and it deployed decoys while jammers hashed the cruisers' fire control sensors. Lasers and particle beams splattered all about them, but less than two percent scored hits, and the ship's screen shrugged them aside contemptuously.

Energy torpedoes followed the beams, packets of plasma scorching in at near light-speed, and the range was low enough the attackers could overload the normal parameters of their torpedoes' electro-magnetic "envelopes," more than doubling their nominal effect. Not even the AI had time to track weapons moving at that speed, but it *could* detect the peaking power emissions just before they launched, and unlike missiles, they were direct fire weapons, with no ability to home or evade. The alpha synth's defenses were designed to handle such attacks from capital ships; cruisers simply didn't mount the generators for more than a very few launchers each, and stern-mounted autocannon spat out brief, precise bursts as each torpedo blossomed. It didn't take much of a solid object to rupture the skin of an energy torpedo traveling at ninety-eight percent of light-speed, and the alpha synth's ever mounting velocity left the resultant explosions harmlessly astern.

Missiles were another story.

Every attempt to adapt the Hauptman effect to manned vessels had come up against two insurmountable difficulties: an active Hauptman coil poured out a torrent of radiation instantly fatal to all known forms of life, and unlike the Fasset drive, it played fair with Newton. Despite their prodigious rates of acceleration, Fasset drive ships were, in effect, in a perpetual state of free-fall "into" their black holes, and while artificial gravity could produce a comfortable sense of up and down aboard a normal starship, no counter-grav system yet had been able to cope with the thirty-thousand-plus gravities' acceleration of the Hauptman effect.

But warheads cared little for radiation or acceleration, and now Hauptman-effect weapons came tearing in pursuit. They needed six seconds to burn out their coils and reach maximum velocity, but that took almost two light-seconds, and the present range was far less than that. Which meant they came in much more slowly . . . but that their drives were still capable of evasive and homing maneuvers as they attacked.

Proximity-fused counter missiles sped to meet them, and Alicia watched in awe as space burned behind her. The counter missiles were far smaller than their attackers, and the alpha synth carried an enormous number of them, but its magazines were far from unlimited. Yet not a single warhead got through, for no one aboard it—with the possible exception of Tisiphone—had any interest in counter-attacking. That meant *all* of its energy weapons were available for point defense, and no missile had the onboard ECM to evade an alpha synth AI in full cry. There were far too few of them to saturate its defenses, and nothing short of a saturation attack could break them.

Captain Morales glared at his display as his cruiser led the pursuit. HMS *Implacable* and her sisters were losing ground steadily, but their target was in ideal range . . . and they were accomplishing exactly nothing.

The entire operation was insane. No one could steal an alpha synth—only a trained alpha synth pilot could even get aboard one! But someone had stolen this one, and precisely how Admiral Marat expected a cruiser flotilla to stop it passed Morales's understanding. The forts might have a chance, but his ships didn't. The damned thing was *laughing* at them!

Another useless missile salvo vanished far short of target, and the captain swore under his breath.

"Somebody get my bloody darts!" he snarled. "Maybe *they* can stop it!"

"You're kidding me!" Vice Admiral Horth told her com screen.

"The hell I am." There was just over a one-second transmission delay each way between Soissons Orbit One and Jefferson Field, and Admiral Marat's expression was less humorous even than the weapons fire in Horth's plot when he replied two seconds later. "We've got a rogue drop commando in an alpha synth, Becky, and she's boosting out of here like a bat out of hell."

"Jesus," Horth muttered, and looked up as Governor General Treadwell hurried into PriCon. Given the governor's lifelong dislike for planets, he preferred to make his home aboard the HQ fortress. Now he leaned forward into the field of Horth's pickup and stabbed Marat with a glower that boded ill for the port admiral's future.

"And just what," he asked coldly, "is going on here?"

<I knew this was a formidable vessel, Little One, but it surpasses even my expectations. What might Odysseus have accomplished with its like?>

<With me in his corner, he'd've owned the damned planet,> the AI put in during an interval between salvos, and the Fury laughed silently.

<Indeed, Little One, I believe the machine speaks truth. It would seem we chose well.>

<Yeah? Well, next time let's discuss things before you come all over larcenous, okay?>

<Very well.> Tisiphone's mental voice was uncharacteristically chastened, though Alicia had little hope it would last. *<But—>*

<Hang on, Alley,> the AI interrupted. *<The forts just came on-line.>*

* * *

"Very well, Admiral Marat. I believe I now understand the situation." Governor Treadwell turned to Horth and frowned as the alpha synth crossed the inner fortress ring and continued to accelerate. "Do you have firing lock?"

"I'm afraid not, sir." Horth looked as unhappy as she felt. "We seem to be even more affected by its jammers than the cruisers are."

"Indeed?" Treadwell's frown was distinctly displeased, but Marat came to his colleague's defense via the com link.

"I'm afraid it won't get any better, Governor. The alpha synth has full specs on your fire control in its files, and it's designed to defeat any sensor system it can read. It's only going to get worse as the range opens."

"I see." Treadwell tapped his fingers gently together. "We shall have to have a little talk about just what goes into such units' memories in future, Admiral Marat. In the meantime, we can't simply let it go—certainly not with an insane woman at its controls. Admiral Horth, engage with SLAMs."

"It'll be blind fire, sir," Horth protested, wincing at the thought of the expense. Without lock, she'd have to fire virtually at random, and SLAMs required direct hits. Trying to smother a half-seen target as small as the alpha synth would use up prodigious numbers of multi-million-credit weapons.

"Understood. I'll authorize the expense."

"Very well, sir." Horth nodded to her fire control officer.

"Engage," she said.

Alicia bit her lip as the fixed fortifications opened fire at last and hordes of red-ringed, malignant blue sparks shrieked after them. The forts were designed to stop ten million-tonne superdreadnoughts, and the volume of fire was inconceivable.

The Supra-Light Accelerated Missile, or SLAM, was the Empire's ultimate long-range weapon. Close in concept to the drones starships used for FTL messages by starships, a SLAM consisted solely of a small Fasset drive and its power source. The weapon had to be half the size of an assault shuttle to squeeze them in, but they made it, in effect, a targeted black hole, and very little known to man had a hope of stopping one. A starship's interposed Fasset drive mass would take one out, though stories about what happened when the ship's drive was even minimally out of tune were enough to curl one's hair, and not even a SLAM could get through the final defense of a capital ship's Orchovski-Kurushu-Milne shield. Unfortunately, a Fasset drive wouldn't work inside an OKM shield, and no weapon could shoot out past one, either. Both of which points were moot in this case, since nothing smaller than a battleship could spare the mass for shield generators.

The only good thing was that SLAMs weren't seeking weapons—mostly. No homing systems could see around their black holes, and despite the fact that their acceleration was little more than half that of the Hauptman effect, their speed and range quickly took them out of guidance range of their firers. A very near near-miss could still "suck" its way into a hit by gravitational attraction, which was why they weren't used when enemies were intermingled, but what the AI's jammers were doing to the forts' targeting systems meant the chance of any one of them scoring a hit was infinitestimal.

Only they were firing a *lot* of them. Alicia's thought was a tiny mental whisper as the outer works began to range upon her, and she squirmed down in her couch. It was like driving a skimmer into a snowstorm—surely not *all* of them could miss.

<*On the contrary,*> AI told her. <*They're just throwing good money after bad, Alley. Watch.*>

The AI changed its generator settings, swinging the drive's black hole through a cone-shaped volume ahead of them and dropping its side shields, trading a bit of its speed advantage over the cruisers to turn the drive field into a huge broom that swept space clear before them. Nor did it refocus the field in any predictable fashion. The drive's gravity well fluctuated—its strength shifting in abrupt, impossible to predict increments sufficient to deprive any tracking station of a constant acceleration value—and its corkscrewing mass "wagged" the ship astern like a dog's tail, turning it into an even more impossible target. A cyber synth might have been able to duplicate that maneuver and still hold to its desired base course, though it would have been far less efficient; nothing else could.

The drive was no shield against SLAMs coming in from astern or the side, but the ship's unpredictable "swerves" gave the *coup de grace* to the forts' fire control. SLAM after SLAM slashed harmlessly past or vanished against the drive field, and Alicia felt herself relaxing despite the nerve-racking tension of the continuous attack.

<Bets on how many they're willing to waste?> the AI asked brightly.

"Governor, we're wasting our time." Treadwell shot Admiral Horth a venemous glance, and she shrugged. "If you wish, I will of course continue, but we've already fired twenty percent of our total SLAM armament. That's four months' production, and there's no sign we've even come close to a hit."

Treadwell's jaw clenched and he started to reply sharply, then shook himself and relaxed with a sigh.

"You're right," he admitted, and glared at the fleeing dot. He didn't have a single ship, not even a corvette, in position to intercept it, and nothing he had could kill it. He turned away from the plot with forced calm.

"Lord Jurawski will be displeased enough when I inform him we've . . . mislaid an alpha synth without my adding that I've stripped Franconia of its defenses. Abort engagement, Admiral Horth."

"Yes, sir." Horth managed to keep the relief out of her voice, but Treadwell heard its absence, and his eyes glittered with bitter amusement.

"And after that, Admiral, you and I and Admiral Marat—and, of course, my *dear* friend Sir Arthur—will sit down to discuss precisely how this fiasco came to occur. I'm sure—" the governor showed his teeth in what might charitably have been called a smile "—the final report will be fascinating."

Sir Arthur Keita slumped in his chair, watching a repeater of Jefferson Field's gravitic plot on his com screen. His eyes ached, and he hadn't moved in almost seven hours, yet he couldn't look away.

The stolen ship had passed the outer forts four and a half hours ago. Freed of the star's inhibition, it had gone to full power at last; now it was just under three light-hours from the system primary, traveling at over .98 C. He watched in real-time as the alpha synth ship raced ahead under stupendous acceleration, increasing its already enormous velocity by more than twenty-two kilometers per second with every second.

Eight and a half seconds later, the ship hit the critical threshold of ninety-nine percent of light-speed and vanished in the kaleidoscope flash of wormhole transition. It disappeared into its own private universe, no longer part of Einstein's orderly existence as it sprang to an effective velocity of over five hundred times light-speed . . . and continued to accelerate.

The gravitic scanners could still track it, but not on a display as small as the one he was watching, and he moved at last, reaching out to switch off the screen. Just for a moment, he looked like the old, old man he was as he rubbed his eyes, wondering anew what he might have done differently to avert this insanity and the catastrophe certain to follow in its wake.

Tannis Cateau stood beside him, face drawn and eyes bright with unshed tears, and neither of them looked over their shoulders to see Inspector Ferhat Ben Belkassem throw an ironic salute to the blank-faced screen . . . and smile.

Chapter Fourteen

<*My remotes could do that a lot faster.*>

"I know they could, Megarea." Alicia had developed the habit of speaking aloud to her electronic half—and Tisiphone—more often than not. Not because she had to, but because the sound of even her own voice, was welcome against the silence. She wasn't precisely *lonely* with two other people to "talk" to, yet too much quiet left an eerie, empty sensation in her bones. "But I prefer to do this myself, if I'm going to be wearing it."

<*Indeed,*> Tisiphone put in, <*I have never known a warrior who truly cared to have another tend to his personal weapons.*>

<*I know* that,> the AI huffed, <*but they're* my *personal weapons, too, in a sense. And I want to know they're in perfect shape if she needs them.*>

"Which is why you're watching me like a hawk, dear," Alicia said, grinning at the interplay while she concentrated on her combat armor.

The AI and the Fury had come to a far better mutual understanding than she'd originally hoped—indeed, it was Tisiphone who'd suggested the perfect (and, she thought, inevitable, under the circumstances) name for the AI—but there was a tartness at its heart. Megarea remained wary of the Fury, mindful of the way she'd imposed control on Alicia during their escape and suspicious of her ultimate plans, and Tisiphone knew it. Knew it and was wise enough to accept it, if a bit resentfully. Fortunately, prolonged exposure to a human personality had waked something approaching a genuine sense of humor in the compulsive Fury. She wasn't immune to the irony of the situation, and Alicia more than suspected that both of them rather enjoyed sniping at one another—and she knew each was jealous of the other's relationship with her.

<*And it's a good thing I* am *watching you, Alley. You're overloading that tank. You'll jam the ammo chute if you put in that many rounds.*>

"I was doing this before you were a gleam in your programmer's eyes, Megarea. Watch."

Long fingers manipulated the belt of twenty-millimeter caseless with effortless familiarity, tucking it up into the ammunition tank behind her combat armor's right pauldron. She wasn't surprised by Megarea's warning—she'd heard it from every recruit she'd ever checked out on field maintenance. Like the computer, they were fresh from total submersion in The Book and hadn't learned the tricks only experience could teach. Now she doubled the linkless belt neatly and cheated the last few centimeters into place with an adroit twist of the wrist and a peculiar little lifting motion that slid it up into the void created by a few minutes' work with a cutting torch.

"See? That upper brace is structually redundant; taking it out makes room for another forty rounds—as we've told the design people for years."

<*Oh. That's a neat trick, Alley. Why isn't it in the manual?*>

"Because we old sweats like to reserve a few tricks to impress the newbies. Part of the mystique that makes them listen to us in the field."

<*And it is listening which allows a young warrior to*

become an old one. That much, at least, has not changed, I see.>

"Neither has the fact that some of them never live long enough to figure that out, unfortunately." Alicia sighed and closed the ammo tank.

She moved down the checklist to the servo mech that swung her "rifle" in and out of firing position. There'd been a sticky hesitation in the power train when she'd first uncrated the armor, and isolating the fault had been slow, laborious, and irritating as hell. Now she watched it perform with smooth, snake-quick precision and beamed.

It was a tremendous help to be able to watch it in all dimensions at once, too. She'd taken days to get used to the odd, double-perspective vision which had become the norm within her new ship, but once she had, she'd found it surprisingly useful. The perpetual, unbreakable link between herself and the computer meant she saw things not only through her eyes but through the ship's internal sensors, as well. It was better than 360° vision. It showed her *all* sides of everything about her, and she no longer lived merely behind her eyes. Instead, she saw herself as one shape and form among many—a shape she maneuvered through and around the shapes about it as if in some complex yet soothing coordination exercise.

Learning to navigate with that sort of omniperceptive view had been an unnerving experience, but now that she had, she loved it. For the first time, she could truly watch herself during workouts, seeing the flaws in her own moves and correcting herself without outside critiques, and being able to watch the servo mech from front, back, and both sides at once was enormously helpful. Not only could she examine any portion of it she chose, but thanks to Megarea, she could analyze its movement "by eye" in all three dimensions with the accuracy of a base depot test rig. It was a remarkable performance, whenever she paused to think about it, though she seldom did so any longer.

Indeed, she often found herself smiling as she recalled her earlier panic. To think she'd been terrified of what the alpha link might do to her! She'd been afraid it would change her, depreciate her into a mere appendage of the computer, yet it was no such thing. She'd become not less but ever so much more, for she'd acquired confidante, sister, daughter, protector, and mentor in one. Megarea was all of those, yet Alicia had given even more to the AI. She'd given it life itself, the human qualities no cyber synth AI could ever know. In every sense that mattered, she was Megarea's mother, and she and Megarea were far more than the sum of their parts.

Yet for all that, she suspected *her* alpha synth link wasn't what the cyberneticists and psych types had had in mind, and Megarea agreed with her. It could hardly help being . . . different with Tisiphone involved, she supposed. Megarea had never impressed before, and Alicia couldn't provide the information a trained alpha synth candidate would have possessed, so they couldn't be certain, but everything in Megarea's data base suggested that the fusion should have been still closer. That they should have been *one* personality, not two entities, however close, with the *same* personality.

All in all, Alicia rather thought both of them preferred what they'd gotten to a "proper" linkage. There was more room for growth and expansion in this rich, bipolar existence. Already she and her electronic offspring were developing tiny differences, delicately divergent traits, and that was good. It detracted nothing from their ability to think as one, yet it offered a synthesis. As she understood the nature of the "proper" link, human and AI should have come to a single, shared conclusion from shared data, and so she and Megarea often did. But sometimes they didn't, and she'd discovered there were advantages in having two different "right" answers, for comparing them produced a final solution better than either had devised alone far more frequently than not.

She returned the rifle to rest and shut down the servos, then turned to drag out the testing harness, but Megarea had anticipated her. A silent repair unit hovered beside her on its counter-grav to extend the connectors, and she took them with a smile and began plugging into the access ports.

"Go ahead and set up for a sensor diagnostic, would you?"

<*Already done,*> Megarea replied with a certain complacency Alicia knew was directed at Tisiphone.

<*Even Achilles allowed servants to pass him his whet stone,*> the Fury riposted so deflatingly Alicia chuckled. Megarea opted for lordly silence.

Alicia made the last connection and stood back, monitoring the tests not with her eyes but through her link to Megarea. That was another pleasant surprise, for it was a link she ought not to have had, and its absence could have been catastrophic. She'd never received a proper alpha synth receptor, which meant her hardware lacked the tiny com link which was supposed to tie her permanently into her AI.

The flight deck headset was intended for linkage to all of the ship's systems, providing direct information pathways to her brain without requiring the computer to process all data before feeding it to her. It was a systems management tool designed to spread the load, but an alpha synth pilot remained in *permanent* linkage with her cybernetic half. Even brief separations resulted in intense disorientation, while any lengthy loss of contact meant insanity for them both; that was the reason for the com link Alicia didn't have. It was also, she knew now, why alpha synth AIs inevitably suicided if their human halves died. And because she had no built-in link, she should have been unable to tie into Megarea without the headset, which ought to have left her perpetually confined to the flight deck. She shouldn't have been able to go even to her personal quarters, much less to the machine shop, without some cumbersome, jury-rigged unit to replace it. And, of course, no alpha synth pilot could ever move beyond com-link range of her AI.

But Alicia had something better. Tisiphone still couldn't access Megarea's personality center without the AI's permission (and, Alicia knew, Megarea watched her like a hawk whenever she was allowed inside), but she formed a sort of conduit between her and Alicia. It was, Alicia suspected, something very like telepathy, and all the more valuable because she didn't even have to ask Tisiphone to maintain the link. It was as if having once been established the immaterial connection had taken on a life of its own, as much a part of Alicia as her own hands. She rather thought it might continue even if she somehow "lost" the Fury, and she wondered if she was developing some sort of contagious ESP from association with Tisiphone.

Whatever it was, it wasn't something human science was prepared to explain just yet, for Megarea's tests had conclusively demonstrated that it operated at more than light-speed. Indeed, if the AI's conclusions were accurate, there was no transmission delay at all. They had no idea how great its range might be, but it looked as if she and Megarea would be able to communicate *instantaneously* over whatever range it had.

The diagnostic hardware announced completion of the test cycle with a sort of mental chirp, and Alicia nodded in satisfaction. This was the first time her armor had passed *all* tests, and it had taken less than five days to bring it to that state. Tisiphone had been dismayed to find it taking that long, since she'd ordered the armor prepped before it was loaded aboard the *Bengal*, but Alicia was more than pleased. Whoever had overseen its initial activation had done an excellent job, yet no one could have brought it to real combat readiness without having her available for fitting. Combat armor had to be carefully modified to suit its intended wearer, tailored to every little physical quirk with software customized to allow for any mental idiosyncrasy, and she'd looked forward to the task with resignation. It had been five years since she last even saw a suit of armor, and far longer than that since she'd last worked suit maintenance; considered in that light, she'd done very well indeed to finish so quickly.

"Okay, ladies, that's that," she announced, racking her tools and coiling the testing harness. "Put it back in the closet, please, Megarea."

A tractor grab lifted the empty armor from the table, then trundled back towards the storage vault, and Alicia followed to make a personal visual check as Megarea's remotes plugged in the monitoring leads. If she ever actually needed her armor, she was unlikely to have time to repair any faults which had developed since its last maintenance check. Since she didn't have a spare suit, that meant this one had to be a hundred percent at all times, and the monitors would let Megarea make certain it was.

<*I am relieved to have that finished,*> Tisiphone remarked somewhat acidly as the vault closed. <*Perhaps now we can turn to other matters?*>

<*Oh, horsefeathers!*> Megarea snorted. <*You know perfectly well that—*>

"Ah, ah! None of that!" Alicia chided, stepping into the small lift. "Tisiphone's got a point, Megarea. It *is* time we got started."

<*You still need more time to acclimatize,*> the AI objected. <*You're doing well, but you're still not what I'd call ready.*>

"We don't have time for me to 'acclimatize' as thoroughly as you'd like. Let's face it—I'm a hopeless disappointment as a starship pilot."

<*That's not true! You've got good instincts—I should know, I've got the same ones. It's just a matter of training them.*>

<*Perhaps and perhaps not, Megarea, and Alicia is correct about the pressure of time. We have been out of contact too long, and I am certain more has happened since we fled Soissons. As for her instincts requiring training, is it not true that you are fully capable of translating them into actions?*>

<*It's not the same. Alley should've been completely trained before we ever impressed. She's the captain. That means* she *makes the decisions, and she could be a lot more effective if she knew my capabilities backward and forward. She's not supposed to have to think things through or ask questions, and it slows us down when she does.*>

"No one's suggesting I shouldn't continue training, even if I am coming at it backwards. But there's no reason we can't do that *after* we start wherever we're going to start. And Tisiphone's right; our information's getting colder every day."

<*You're ganging up on me again.*>

<*Which ought, perhaps, to suggest that you are in error in this instance. I second Alicia's agreement that training must continue, but not even I can stop other events while she does so.*>

<*Hmph. Just where did you have in mind to go?*>

"MaGuire, I think. How does that strike you, Tisiphone?"

<*MaGuire? I should have thought Dewent or Wyvern would be more fruitful ground, Little One.*>

"I don't disagree, but I still think we should start at MaGuire." The lift stopped outside Alicia's quarters, and she stepped out and sprawled across the comfortable couch. "We've got to have some sort of cover before we move in on them for real, and MaGuire's a good place to begin building one."

<*"Cover"?*> The Fury sounded faintly surprised.

<*What did you plan on her doing? Busting down doors in combat armor to ask questions at plasgun point? Ever hear of something called subtlty?*>

"Hey, give her a break, Megarea! She never had to put up with these kinds of limitations before."

<*I am not offended,*> Tisiphone said, and somewhat to Alicia's surprise, she meant it. The Fury felt her reaction and chuckled dryly. <*As you say, I am unaccustomed to mortals' limitations, but that does not mean I am unaware of them. What sort of cover did you have in mind, Little One?*>

"I've been thinking over all the intelligence you pulled and looking for an angle we could follow up without simply duplicating everyone else's efforts. It looks to me like Colonel McIlheny's people are doing a much better job with overt intelligence gathering than we could. He's got tonnes more manpower and far better communications than we do, and unlike us, he's official. He doesn't have to hide from both sides while he works. Agreed?"

Alicia paused, then shrugged as she felt the others' joint agreement.

"That being the case, let's leave that side of it to him and concentrate on areas where our special talents can operate most effectively."

<*And those areas are, Little One?*>

"I was particularly interested in Ben Belkassem's locked files, because I think he's on to something. I think he's right about there being someone on the inside, probably pretty far up, which means that same someone may well be feeding the pirates advance warning on Fleet sweeps and dispositions. If so, they'll know how and when to lie low, and that suggests Ben Belkassem has also hit on the most likely way to find them."

<*By tracking the loot?*> Megarea sounded dubious. <*That's a tall order, Alley, and we can only be in one place at a time. Shouldn't we leave that angle to him? O Branch has all sorts of information sources we don't.*>

"Maybe, but we can probably do a lot more with any information we get our hands—pardon, *my* hands—on. Ben Belkassem may have more reach, but he can't get inside someone's head, and I doubt his computer support can match what you're capable of. Even better, we're a complete wild card, with no connection to Justice or Fleet however hard anyone looks. Add all the other things Tisiphone does, and you've got a hell of an infiltrator."

<*And how will you use those abilities?*> the Fury asked.

"I think I'm about to become a free trader," Alicia replied, and felt the others' stir of interest. "We don't have much cargo capacity, but half the 'free traders' out here are really smugglers, and we can probably match the lift of any of the really fast hulls in the sector. Besides, specializing in delivering small cargoes quickly would make us look nicely shady."

<*That I should live to see the day I became a* freighter!> Megarea mourned, but amusement sparkled in her thoughts.

<*But can you?*> Tisiphone objected. <*Surely Fleet*

has spread the alarm since we left Soissons. From what I have seen of Sir Arthur, he, at least, would insist that the Rogue Worlds be warned, as well, embarrassment or no, since he believes Alicia to be mad. Will they not be on the watch for us?>

"Of course they will, but I don't think you realize quite how talented Megarea is. You can be a regular little changeling, can't you, Honey Cake?"

<Call me, "Honey Cake" again and you'll get a migraine you won't believe, Alley. Yeccch! But, yeah, I can do a real number on 'em.>

<I realize you can disguise your electronic emissions, but you cannot hide the fact that you possess a Fleet Fasset drive. And even if you could, would not visual observation reveal you for what you are?>

<The answers are "it doesn't matter," and "no." Two-thirds of the merchantmen out here use Fleet-design drives. I can fudge mine to make it look a lot less powerful by shutting down nodes, and there're a couple of tricks I can play with frequency shifts, too. I can't look, oh Rishathan or Jungian-built, but I can produce a civilian power curve.

<As for the visual observation angle, that's one of my neatest tricks, if I do say so myself. BuShips came up with it for second-generation alpha synths, and I'm one of the first to get it.>

<And what, if you are through extolling your own virtues, is "it"?>

<Sticks and stones can break my bones—assuming I had any—but words will never hurt me,> Megarea caroled, and Alicia laughed. Even Tisiphone chuckled, but she clearly still wanted an explanation, and the AI obliged.

<I've got a holo imager built into the aft quadrant of my Fasset housing. I can use it to build up any exterior appearance I want.>

<Indeed? An impressive capability, yet how well will it endure close observation should they bring more than the unaided eye to bear upon it?>

<I can jigger my radiation and mass shielding to give

an alloy return off the "solid surface" against most of their active sensors,> Megarea returned promptly. *<Old-fashioned radar's the hardest, but if we decide what we want to look like and leave it that way, I can fabricate reflectors to return the proper image. The holo itself will stand up to any scrutiny, except maybe a spectograph. It won't "see" anything off the holo.>*

"Yes, but a spectograph doesn't tell them anything about mass or size," Alicia mused. "Suppose we plan our holo to incorporate a few good-sized chunks of your actual hull and let them get their readings off that?"

<They'd get readings, all right, but the wrong ones for a merchant hull. I'm made out of Kurita-Hawkins battle steel, Alley.>

<Yet you have substantial quantities of less noble alloys in your machine shop stores. Could we not cover the exposed portions in a thin sheath which would appease their sensors?>

<I suppose so. . . . My "paint's" fused into the basic battle steel matrix, and my remotes are designed for fairly major field repairs. I could use a pigment fuser to spray a thin coat of plain old titanium over the battle steel. It'll look like hell whenever I drop the holo, and I'd be ashamed to be seen in a Fleet dock wearing it, but it should work.>

"Then since we can look like a suitably decrepit smuggler, the next item on the agenda is to build a believable identity. That's why I want to start at MaGuire and work our way towards Dewent. Megarea can work up a flight log before MaGuire, Tisiphone, and you can sneak it into the planetary data base when we first contact the port. By the time we dock and they call it up to check our papers, it'll be 'official,' as far as they're concerned."

<Be a good idea to make this our first trip into the Franconian Sector,> Megarea suggested. *<How about we pulled out of the Melville Sector in a hurry? That's close enough for us to've moved here but far enough away nobody should be surprised that we aren't a familiar face, and according to my data Justice just shut down a major inter-system smuggling ring there.>*

"Perfect!" Alicia chortled. "You and I can make sure the last few entries are suitably vague—the sort of thing a real smuggler would put together to cover an embarrassing situation for a new set of port authorities. It'll not only get us in with the criminal element but provide a perfect cover against any Fleet units looking for the real us."

<*That's what I had in mind. Okay, I'm started on that—*> Alicia felt a fragment of the AI's capabilities go to work on the project even as Megarea continued to speak <*—so what do we do after we get there?*>

"I doll up to look as little like me as you look like you and start trolling for a cargo. With Tisiphone to run around in the computer nets and skim thoughts, we shouldn't have too much trouble lining up a less-than-legal shipment headed in the right general direction. Once we deliver it, we'll have established our smuggler's bona fides and we can start working our way deeper. In a way, I'd like to head straight from MaGuire for Wyvern—if there's one place in this sector where those bastards could dispose of their loot, Wyvern's the one—but we need to build more layers into our cover before we knock on their front door. Still, once we get there, I'm betting we find at least some sign of their pipeline, and when we do, we can probably find someone whose thoughts can tell us where to find *them.*"

<*This will take time, Little One.*>

"Can't be helped, unless you've got a better idea."

<*No, I have no better strategy. Would that I did, but this seems sound thinking in light of our capabilities.*>

<*I said she had good instincts, didn't I? I like it, too, Alley.*>

"Yeah, the only thing that really bothers me is losing the *Bengal.*" Alicia sighed. "The cargo shuttle won't be a problem once we get rid of the Fleet markings and change the transponder, but nobody could mistake that *Bengal* for anything but an assault boat."

<*So? Keep it. I'll ding it up a little and make a few unnecessary hull repairs to take the shine off it, but it's too useful to just ditch.*>

"It's not exactly standard free trader issue," Alicia objected, but she heard temptation waver in her own voice.

<*Again, so what? As far as I know, there's no official free trader equipment list. Hell, it'll probably get you more respect! Think how they'll wonder how you got your hands on it.*>

<*I believe she is correct, Little One,*> Tisiphone chuckled. <*I should think your possession of such a craft will raise your stature among these criminals greatly.*>

"Yeah, you're probably right." Alicia's mouth twitched and her eyes twinkled at the thought. And, she admitted, it was a great relief, as well. "Let's think up some incredibly gaudy point job to hang on it, in that case. If you've got it, flaunt it."

<*Precisely, Little One! We shall make you a* most *formidable "free trader," Megarea and I.*>

Chapter Fifteen

James Howell watched the view screen as the shuttle slid up from just beyond the terminator, glittering as it broke into the unfiltered light of Hearthguard's primary, and tried not to show his uneasiness.

Hearthguard was a sparsely populated world, for it had little—aside from truly spectacular mountain landscapes and particularly dangerous fauna—to attract settlers. Visitors, now, those were another matter. To date, Hearthguard's wildlife had accounted for about one hunter in five, which, humans being humans, produced a predictably perverse response that amused the locals no end. And it was profitable, too. If putatively sane outworlders wanted to pay hefty fees for the dubious privilege of hunting predators who were perfectly willing to hunt them right back, that was fine with the Hearthguarders. But even though more and more of their guests were imperial citizens, the life-blood of their new, tourism-based prosperity, theirs was a Rogue World, independent of the Empire and minded to stay so.

Thrusters flared as the shuttle swam towards rendezvous with the freighter. Howell would have felt far happier in his flagship, but Hearthguard was too heavily traveled to take such a risk. On the other hand, this meeting had the potential to dwarf the dangers of bringing in the entire squadron. If anyone was watching, or if word of it leaked. . . .

The shuttle coasted to a halt, and tractors drew it in against one of the freighter's racks. Howell watched the personnel tube jockeying into position, then sighed and turned toward the lift with squared shoulders.

It was time to hear what Control had to say to him. He did not expect to enjoy the conversation.

The commodore reached the personnel lock just as a tallish man in camping clothes stepped out, fiercely trimmed mustachios jutting. Despite its obvious comfort and sturdiness, his clothing was expensive, and his squashed-looking hat's band was decorated with at least a dozen bent, shiny wires tied up with feathers, mirrors, and God alone knew what. The first time he'd seen them, Howell had assumed they were solely decorative; only after a fair amount of research had he discovered they were lures for an arcane sport called "'fly-fishing." It still struck him as a stupid way for a grown man to spend his time, though Hearthguard's two-meter saber-trout probably made the sport far more interesting than it had been in its original Old Earth form.

He moved forward to greet his visitor, and winced at the other's bone-crushing handshake. Control had a rather juvenile need to demonstrate his strength, and Howell had learned to let him, though he did wish Control would at least take off his Academy ring before he crushed his victims' metacarpals.

"I thought we'd use my cabin, sir," he said, managing not to wave his hand about as he reclaimed it at last. "It's not much, but it's private."

"Fine. I don't expect to be here long enough for austerity to be a problem." Control's voice was clipped, with a trace of the Mother World, though Howell knew he'd never visited Old Earth before reporting to the Academy.

The commodore pushed the thought aside and led the way down a corridor which had been sealed off for the duration of Control's visit. No more than a score of the squadron's personnel knew who Control was, and Rachel Shu went to considerable lengths to keep it that way.

Howell's cabin—the freighter captain's cabin, actually—was more comfortable than his earlier comment had suggested. He waved Control through the hatch first and watched to see what he would do. He wasn't disappointed. Control walked briskly to the captain's desk, sat unhesitatingly behind it, and pointed to the supplicant's chair in front.

The commodore obeyed the gesture with outward calm, sitting back and crossing his legs. He had no delusions. Control's personal visit suggested that he was going to tear at least one long, bloody strip off him, but Howell was damned if he was going to look uneasy. He'd done his best, and the losses at Elysium hadn't been his fault, whatever Control might intend to say.

Control let him sit in silence for several moments, then leaned back and inhaled sharply, bristling his waxed mustache even more aggressively.

"So, Commodore. I suppose you know why I'm here?" Howell recognized his cue and offered the expected response.

"I imagine it has something to do with Elysium."

"It does, indeed. We're not happy about that disaster, Commodore Howell. Not happy at all. And neither are our backers."

His gray eyes were hard, but Howell refused to flinch. He also refused to waste time defending himself until specific charges were leveled, and he returned Control's gaze in composed silence.

"You had perfect intelligence, Commodore," Control resumed when it became obvious Howell had nothing to say. "We handed you Elysium on a silver platter, and you not only lost three-quarters of your ground element, but you also managed to lose five cargo shuttles, a *Leopard*-class assault boat, four *Bengals* . . . and a million-tonne battle-cruiser. And to top it all off, you didn't even secure your objective. Tell me, Commodore, were you born incompetent, or did you have to work at it?"

"Since I believe I've demonstrated my competence in the past," Howell said in a mild tone which deceived neither of them, "I won't dignify that last question with a response, sir. On your other points, I believe the record speaks for itself. *Poltava* carried out a textbook attack run, but Captain Ortiz made a poor command decision and got too close to his last opponent. Things like that happen to even the best commanders, and when they happen fifteen light-minutes from the flagship, the flag officer can't prevent them."

He held Control's gaze, letting his eyes show the anger his voice did not, and saw something flicker deep under the other man's brows. Answering anger or respect—he couldn't tell, nor, at the moment, did he much care.

"As for the remainder of your . . . indictment, I would simply point out that your intelligence was, in fact, far from complete—and that you'd been warned success was problematical. You knew how tough it was going to be to secure GeneCorp's files. Had the enemy actually been in the positions you assured us they intended to assume, we would have succeeded in rushing the facilities. As it was, our ground commanders walked into what turned out to be, in effect, a trap precisely because they'd been told where to expect opposition. I probably *am* at fault for not stressing the need for complete preparedness despite our 'perfect' intelligence, but I submit that it would be wiser of you not to provide tactical data unless you can confirm its accuracy. Incorrect information is worse than none—as this operation demonstrated."

"No one can guarantee there won't be last-minute changes, Commodore."

"In that case, sir, it would be wise not to pretend you *can*," Howell returned in that same calm voice. He paused a beat, waiting for Control to respond, but he only made a throwaway gesture, and the commodore resumed.

"Finally, sir, I would further submit that whatever happened to our ground forces and whether or not we secured the GeneCorp data, we succeeded completely in what my mission description laid down as our primary objective. No doubt you have better casualty estimates than we do, but I feel quite confident we provided the 'atrocity' you wanted."

"Umph." Control rocked gently back and forth, simultaneously swinging his chair in tiny arcs, and puffed his mustache, then shrugged.

"Point taken," he said in a far less rancorous tone. He even smiled a bit. "As I'm sure you're well aware, shit flows downhill. Consider yourself doused with half the bucket that hit me in the face." His smile faded. "I assure you, however, that there was plenty to go around for both of us."

"Yes, sir." Howell allowed himself to relax in turn. "In fact, I already prepaid my own people for what I figured was coming my way," he confessed. "But in all seriousness, we did succeed in our primary mission."

"If it makes you feel any better, that's the opinion *I* expressed. As for your losses—" Control shrugged "—we're already recruiting new ground personnel from local Rogue Worlds, though I'm afraid we can't replace *Poltava* as quickly. But while you're right about your primary objective, it seems the secondary objective was more important than either of us had been informed."

"It was?" Howell tugged at an earlobe. "It would've been nice of them to let us know."

"Agreed, agreed." Control reached into a jacket pocket and extracted a cigar case. He selected one, clipped the end, and lit it. Howell watched, grateful for the ventilation intake directly above the desk, as Control puffed until it was drawing to his satisfaction, then waved it at him like a pointer.

"You see, Commodore, our Core World financial backers are getting a bit shaky. They're bloodthirsty enough in the abstract, and they're perfectly willing to contemplate heavy civilian casualties as long as someone else will be inflicting them, but they don't have the stomach for it once the bloodshed actually starts. Not because they give a good goddamn about the people involved, but because they suddenly recognize the reality of the stakes for which they're playing—and what'll happen to them if it comes apart."

Howell nodded as he heard the contempt in Control's voice.

"They're fat and rich, and they want to be fatter and richer, but while the wealth and power they've already got protect them from the consequences of most of their deals, this one's different. *Nothing* will save them if the Empire discovers their involvement, and their objectives are very different from ours. They're backing us solely in return for an immediate profit now and more concessions after we succeed, and I don't think they really understood how much anti-pirate hysteria we were going to have to whip up to make it all work."

He took another pull on his cigar and ejected a long, gray streamer.

"The reason I'm going into this at such length is that we don't have a stick to beat them with, so we need to keep the carrot in plain sight. At the moment, they can see the consequences of failure all too clearly, and some of them are worried that we're simply bringing the Fleet down on our heads by our actions. We, of course, know why we're doing that; they don't. This means that we need to throw them an immediate kilo of flesh if we don't want them backing out on us, and GeneCorp's data was supposed to be just that."

"I realize that, sir, but Captain Alexsov and I both pointed out the high probability of failure when the target was designated."

"Forget that." Control waved his cigar a bit impatiently. "I jumped your shit over it, and you jumped right back. Fine. That's done with. The point before us now is where we go from here."

"Yes, sir."

"Good. Did you bring Alexsov along?"

"Yes, sir. He and Commander Shu are both aboard."

"Excellent." Control consulted his watch and made a face. "My people groundside can only cover me for a few hours, and I've got to get back to work by the end of next week. Taking even a short 'vacation' at a time like this has already gotten me a few dirty looks, and I can't do it again any time soon, so I want to tie up all the loose ends as quickly as possible. Let me lay it out for you, then you can bring them up to speed after I leave, right?"

"Of course."

"All right. As I say, we need a plainly visible carrot, and we think we've found one at Ringbolt."

"Ringbolt?" Howell repeated with some surprise. All of his targets to date had been imperial possessions, but Ringbolt was a Rogue World daughter colony, and the people it belonged to were nasty customers, indeed.

"Ringbolt. I know the El Grecans keep a close eye on it, but we happen to know they're going to be involved in some pretty elaborate Fleet maneuvers late next month. I've brought the details in my intelligence download. The point is, the Ringbolt squadron's being called back to El Greco in a home-defense mobilization exercise, which will leave the system uncovered for at least a week. That's your window, Commodore."

"I don't know much about the Ringbolt System, sir. What are the fixed defenses like? The El Grecans have an awfully impressive tech base for a Rogue World, and I'd hate to walk into a surprise."

"There are no fixed defenses. That's the beauty of it."

"*None?*"

"None. It makes sense when you think about it. The planet's only been colonized for fifty years, and when they moved in the colonists, all they had to worry about were other Rogue Worlds and the occasional genuine hijack outfit. They couldn't possibly stand off the Empire or the Sphere, so they decided not to try. As for other Rogue worlds or hijackers . . . if you were them, would *you* take on the El Grecans?"

"Probably not, sir," Howell acknowledged. For that matter, he doubted he would care to go after them even if he'd been the Empire or the Rishatha. Occupation of an El Grecan colony was unlikely to prove cost effective.

El Greco had been a scholar's world, renowned for its

art academies and universities, before the League Wars. Then the Rishatha moved in during the First Human-Rish War, and alien occupation came to the groves of academe.

El Grecans might have been high-brows and philosophers, but that hadn't meant they were airheads, and the Rishatha soon discovered they'd caught a tiger by the tail. The academics of El Greco warmed up their computers, set up their data searches, and turned to the study of guerrilla warfare, sabotage, and assassination as if preparing to sit their doctoral orals. Within a year, they had two divisions tied down; by the time the Sphere gave it up as a bad deal and left, the Rishatha garrison had grown to three *corps* . . . and was still losing ground.

The El Grecans hadn't forgotten a thing since, and they'd decided to turn their surviving universities in a new direction. El Greco no longer produced artists, sculptors, and composers; it produced physicists, chemists, strategists, engineers, weapons specialists, and one of humanity's most advanced R&D complexes. The best mercenary outfits in this corner of the galaxy were based on El Greco, and most of their personnel held reserve commissions in the planetary armed forces. No doubt El Greco could still be had by someone the size of the Empire or Sphere who wanted it badly enough, but the price would be far too high for the return, and no mere Rogue World—or even an alliance of them—wanted the El Grecan Navy on their necks.

More to the point, Commodore James Howell didn't especially want the El Grecan Navy on *his* neck.

"Excuse me, sir, but are you certain this is something we want to do?"

Control snorted with a wry, almost compassionate amusment and drew deeply on his cigar before he responded.

"Look at it this way, Commodore. The El Grecans are good, no question, but they're only one system. Their entire Navy and all their mercenary outfits together have less firepower than Admiral Gomez, nor do they begin to have the information sources Soissons has. Since your squadron is already completely outgunned, adding one more set of enemies to the mix shouldn't really matter all that much, should it? After all, if we ever face a stand-up fight, we lose even if we win."

"I realize that, sir, but we don't have the same kind of penetration against El Greco. We know what Fleet's going to do before it does it; we won't have that advantage against the El Grecans."

"Ah, but we will!" Control's eyes glittered with true humor. "You see, we're killing several birds with one stone here.

"First, your raid on Ringbolt will be targeted on the bio-research unit of the University of Toledo. We have reason to believe they were running close to a dead heat with GeneCorp, so we can recoup our earlier failure.

"Second, hitting a Rogue World offsets the idea that someone's gone to war against the Empire. We have, but it's important that no one realize that. We can get away without hitting any more of the sector's Rogue Worlds—most of them don't have anything worth stealing anyway—but we have to hit at least one to look like 'real' pirates.

"Third, the El Grecans, like the Jungians, want to demonstrate that *they* aren't behind our attacks, so there's already been a good bit of joint contingency planning—that's how we found out about these maneuvers. Better still, they've accepted the principle of joint command and coordination if they do get hit. The Jungians haven't done that, but even if your attack brings the El Grecans into the field, we'll have good intelligence on their basic posture and operations.

"And fourth," Control's eyes narrowed, "a few of Gomez's people—especially McIlheny—are getting suspicious about our operational patterns. Phase Four at Elysium nailed anyone who might've identified your vessels, but the ease with which you got in was a pretty clear indication you had very, very good intelligence. Even the governor general is finding it hard to ignore that evidence, and McIlheny's got Gomez chewing the bulkheads over it. If you hit a Rogue World with the same kind of precision, it should suggest you have multiple intelligence sources, which may divert some of the heat."

"I was afraid of that when Elysium was selected," Howell murmured, and Control shrugged.

"You weren't alone. It was a calculated risk because we needed an Incorporated World target. Crown Worlds have such low populations that even a total burn-off like Mathison's World doesn't produce the kinds of casualty figures we need to hit Core World public opinion with. Besides, most Core Worlders figure anyone willing to settle a colony world knows the odds and doesn't have much kick coming when he craps out. But an *Incorporated* World is something else. Elysium has senatorial representation, and you'd better believe those senators are screaming for action after what happened to a third of their constituents!"

"I know, sir." Howell looked down at his hands. "Does that mean we do the same thing on Ringbolt?" he asked in a neutral voice.

"I'm afraid it does, Commodore." Even Control sounded uncomfortable, but his tone didn't flinch. "We can't change our pattern for the same reason we need to hit a Rogue World in the first place. It *has* to look like we're treating everyone we hit in precisely the same fashion."

"Understood, sir," Howell sighed.

"Good." Control tossed a small chip folio onto the desk and stood. "Here's your intelligence packet. We don't anticipate any problems with it, but if Commander Shu has questions, she should send them back through the usual channels. We can't afford any more direct contact for a while."

"Understood," Howell said again, rising to escort his visitor from the cabin. He forbore to mention that *this* meeting hadn't been his idea, partly out of diplomacy but also because he'd found it useful after all. Face-to-face discussions filled in nuances no indirect contact could convey.

They paused outside the personnel lock and Control wrung his hand again, not quite so crushingly this time.

"Good hunting, Commodore," he said.

"Thank you, sir," Howell replied, coming to attention but not saluting. Their eyes met one last time, and then Vice Admiral Sir Amos Brinkman nodded sharply and stepped through the hatch.

Chapter Sixteen

Lieutenant Charles Giolitti, Jungian Navy, on assignment to the MaGuire Customs Service, took the time to double-check his data as the boarding shuttle drifted towards the free trader *Star Runner*. He'd been intrigued when he first accessed the download—and noted the ship's list of auxiliaries—and he wanted to be certain he'd read it correctly.

The information was unusually complete for a recent arrival, he observed cheerfully. It wasn't unheard of for a foreign-registry vessel to arrive with absolutely no documentation, and that was always a pain. It meant its every centimeter must be scrutinized, its every crew member exhaustively med-checked, and its bona fides thoroughly established before any of its people were allowed groundside. Tempers tended to get short all round before the process was completed, but the Jung Association hadn't lasted for four centuries without learning to keep a close eye on visitors. In this case, though, Giolitti had a full Imperial attestation from the Melville Sector, which should cut the crap to a minimum.

He screened quickly through the technical data, eyebrows

quirking as he noted the rating of *Star Runner's* Fasset drive. She was as fast as most cruisers—which, he thought wryly, coupled with her limited cargo capacity, was a glaring tip-off as to her true nature. Not that Jungians minded smugglers . . . as long as they didn't run anything *into* the Association.

Um. Crew of only five. That was low, even for a merchant hull. Must indicate some pretty impressive computer support. Captain's name Theodosia Mainwaring . . . young for her rank, from the bio, but lots of time on her flight log. The rest of her people looked equally qualified. Not a bad bunch for a merchant crew, in fact. Of course, free traders tended to attract the skilled misfits—the square pegs with the qualifications to write their own tickets—away from the military or the big lines.

No incoming manifest. He snorted, remembering the diplomatic gaps in the last few entries from the Melville data base. So Captain Mainwaring had gotten her fingers burned? Must not have been too serious—she still had a ship—but it probably meant she was hungry for a cargo.

A signal chimed, and Giolitti glanced at the view screen as his vessel began its docking sequence on *Star Runner's* sole unoccupied shuttle rack. A somewhat battered cargo shuttle occupied one of the other two racks, not that old but clearly a veteran of hard service to collect so many dings and scrapes. Yet it wasn't the cargo shuttle that caught his attention.

Another shuttle loomed on the number one rack—a needle-nosed craft, deadly even in repose. He was familiar with its basic stats, but he'd never seen one, and he wasn't quite prepared for its size. Or its color scheme.

Giolitti winced as he took in the garish crimson and black hull. Some unknown artist had painted staring white eyes on either side of the stiletto prow, jagged-toothed mouths gaped hungrily about the muzzles of energy and projectile cannons, and lovingly detailed streamers of lurid flame twined about the engine pads. He had no idea how Mainwaring had gotten her hands on it, though she must have done so in at least quasi-legal fashion, since the Empies had let her keep it when they suggested she explore new frontiers, but the visual impact was . . . extreme.

He grinned as the docking arms locked. The *Bengal* looked out of place on its drab, utilitarian mother ship, but free traders tended to find themselves back of beyond with only their own resources, and he suspected ill-intentioned locals would think twice about harassing a cargo shuttle with that thing hovering watchfully overhead. Which, no doubt, was the idea.

The personnel tube docking collar settled into place, and Giolitti gathered up his notepad, nodded to his pilot, and opened the hatch.

Alicia watched the heavyset young customs officer step through *Megarea*'s port and hoped this worked. It had seemed simple enough when she was thinking it all up, but that was then.

<*Oh, be calm, Little One!*> the Fury scolded. <*We have already accomplished the difficult parts.*>

<*Yeah, Alley,*> Megarea added in unusual support of Tisiphone. <*There's only one of him, and Tis is gonna knock his shorts off.*>

<*A somewhat inelegant turn of phrase, but accurate.*>

<*Then why don't both of you be quiet so we can get on with this?*> Alicia suggested pointedly, and stepped forward to shake the inspector's hand.

Giolitti was a bit surprised to find only the captain waiting for him, but he had to give her tailor high marks. That severe, midnight-blue uniform and silver-braided bolero suited the tall, sable-haired woman perfectly.

"Lieutenant Giolitti, MaGuire Customs Service," he introduced himself, and the woman smiled.

"Captain Theodosia Mainwaring."

She had a nice voice—low and almost furry-sounding. He found himself beaming back at her and wondered vaguely why he felt so cheerful.

"Welcome to MaGuire, Captain."

"Thanks." She released his hand, and he brought out his notepad.

"You have your crew's updated med forms, Captain?"

"Right here." She extended a folio of chips, and Giolitti plugged them into the notepad, punching buttons with practiced fingers and scanning the display. Looked good. He supposed he really ought to insist on meeting the others immediately, but there was time for that before he left.

"Ready for inspection, Captain?" he asked, and Mainwaring nodded.

"Follow me," she invited, and led him into the lift.

The customs officer's vaguely disoriented eyes were a vast relief, but Alicia made a point of punching the lift buttons. Tisiphone chuckled deep inside her mind, enjoying herself as she worked her wiles upon their visitor, yet Alicia knew the fewer perceptions the Fury had to fuzz the better, and there was no point letting Megarea move the lift without instructions.

She escorted Lieutenant Giolitti into her quarters and watched him carry out his inspection. He clearly knew the best places to conceal contraband, yet there was a mechanical air to his actions. His voice sounded completely alert as he carried on a cheerful conversation with her, but its very normality was almost bizarre against the backdrop of his robotic search.

He finished his examination with a smile, and she drew a deep breath and led him back outside. She paused for just a moment, watching his eyes go even more unfocused, then turned and escorted him right back into her cabin.

"My engineer's quarters," she said, and he nodded and went to work . . . totally oblivious to the fact that he had just searched exactly the same room.

Alicia hardly believed what she was seeing. She'd counted on it, but actually seeing it was eerie and unreal, and she felt Megarea's matching reaction. Tisiphone, on the other hand, took it completely for granted, though she was obviously bending all her will upon the lieutenant to bring it off.

Giolitti completed his second examination and turned to her.

"Who's next?" he asked cheerfully.

"My astrogator," Alicia said, and led him back out into the passage.

Giolitti made the last entry and wished all his inspections could go this smoothly. Captain Mainwaring ran a taut ship. Even her cargo hold was spotless, and *Star Runner* was one of the very few free traders whose crew hadn't left something illegal—or at least closely regulated—lying around where he could find it. Which made them improbably law-abiding or fiendishly clever at hiding their personal stashes. Given his impression of Mainwaring's people, Giolitti suspected the latter, and more power to them.

It was funny, though. He'd been impressed by their competence, but they hadn't really registered the way people usually did. Probably because he'd been concentrating so hard on their captain, he thought a bit guiltily, and glanced at her from the corner of his eye as she escorted him back to the personnel lock. It was unusual for a captain to spend his or her precious time escorting a customs man about in person. Even the best of them seemed to regard inspectors as one step lower than a Rish, an intruder—and, still worse, an *official* intruder—in their domains. Giolitti didn't really blame them, but it was a tremendous relief when he met one of the rare good ones.

And, come to think of it, it wasn't really all that strange that the rest of her crew seemed somehow faded beside her. He'd never met anyone with quite the personal magnetism Theodosia Mainwaring radiated. She was a striking woman, friendly and completely at her ease, yet he had the strangest impression she could be a very dangerous person if she chose. Of course, no shrinking violet would be skippering a free trader at such a relatively young age, but it went deeper than that. He remembered the grizzled petty officer who'd overseen the hand-to-hand training of the "young gentlemen" at OCS. He'd moved the way Mainwaring did, and he'd been sudden death on two feet.

The lieutenant shook the thought aside and ejected the clearance chip from his notepad. He held it out to the captain, then extended his hand.

"It's been a pleasure, Captain Mainwaring. I wish every ship I inspected were as shipshape as yours. I hope you do well in our area."

"Thank you, Lieutenant." Mainwaring clasped his hand firmly, and for just an instant, he seemed to feel an odd, hard angularity in her palm, but the sensation vanished. A moment later, he didn't even remember having felt it. "I hope we run into one another again," the captain continued.

"Maybe we will." Giolitti released her hand and stood back, then raised an admonishing finger. "Remember, any of your people who come dirtside will be subject to individual med-scans to confirm their certification."

"Don't worry, Lieutenant." Mainwaring's rather amused smile made him feel even younger. "I don't expect we'll be here long enough for liberty—in fact, most of my people are going to be busy running maintenance checks on the Fasset drive before we pull out—but we'll check in with the medics if we are."

"Thank you, Captain," Giolitti gave her a crisp salute. "In that case, allow me to extend an official welcome to MaGuire and bid you good bye."

Mainwaring returned his salute, and the lieutenant headed back for his shuttle. He had two more inspections to make by shift end, and he wished, more wistfully than hopefully, that they might go as smoothly.

Alicia let herself sag against the bulkhead and sucked in a deep, lung-stretching breath. Dear God, she'd known Tisiphone was good, but the Fury's performance had surpassed her most extravagant hopes.

She doubted they were likely to meet a brighter, more conscientious customs inspector than young Lieutenant Giolitti, and she no longer doubted their ability to razzle-dazzle him if they did. It had been unnerving enough to watch him "search" her quarters five separate times, but that had been nothing compared to watching him walk right past the feed tubes from the main missile magazine without even batting an eye. He'd had to climb a ladder to cross one of them, yet it simply hadn't been there for him, and neither had the energy batteries or the armory. He'd seemed perfectly content with his "inspection" of the control room, as well, though only an idiot—or someone under Tisiphone's spell—could have looked at those blank gray walls and the alpha link headset without realizing what he was seeing.

<*Of course he did not,*> Tisiphone observed. <*You are correct about his intelligence—a very bright young man, indeed—yet it is far simpler to suggest things to intelligent people, for they have the wit to add the details with little prompting. And,*> she added graciously, <*you and Megarea were wise to suggest that we create your "crew's" personalities in such detail. It allowed me to project personalities with much greater depth.*>

"Yeah." Alicia drew another breath and straightened. "Still, you seemed to be concentrating pretty hard. Could you have handled more people?"

<*I believe so, yes. Numbers of minds are not the difficulty, Little One, but rather the detail of the illusion I provide them with. Of course, it would be wise, in the event that we must deal with several people at once, to include a disinclination to discuss their inspection at a later date lest they discover too great a degree of similarity among their recollections.*>

<*You're probably right,*> Megarea put in, <*but unless there's a glitch in the documentation, one-man teams are the rule out here.*>

"I know." Alicia stepped back into the lift and punched for the flight deck. "Are we clear on our docking and service fees, Megarea?"

<*Sure. Tis cooked the books just fine when she dropped our flight log on them, and Ms. Tanner took care of the bookkeeping while Captain Mainwaring was showing Lieutenant Giolitti around. We've covered all*

our fees out of her bogus credit transfer with a balance of eighty thousand credits left.>

"What about service personnel?"

<No sweat. Lieutenant Chisholm dealt with them, and they'll be waiting for our shuttle to pick up the consumables. We're gonna have to dump most of them in deep space, since I had to order enough for a crew of five to make it look right, but our Melville download shows a complete overhaul six months ago, so I didn't have to fudge any servicing requirements.>

"You're a sweetheart," Alicia said fervently. She'd been astounded by the verisimilitude of the computer images and voices Megarea could produce. It was a good thing the AI could, too, since they had to convince anyone who got curious— No, scratch that. They had to keep anyone from *getting* curious, which meant they had to provide crewmen other than Captain Mainwaring in one form or another. Megarea's ability to carry on com conversations, or even several of them at once, would be invaluable in that regard.

<Thanks. You and Tis did pretty good, too.>

<Yet could we have accomplished but little without you, Megarea. It is the combination of all our skills which makes us formidable.>

"You got that right, Lady," Alicia agreed. "But I take it no one raised an eyebrow over your faces?"

<Nary a twitch. Wanna see my latest efforts? I finally got that lisp down pat on "Lieutenant Chisholm," you know.>

"Sure." The lift slid to a halt and Alicia stepped out onto the flight deck. "Let her roll."

<Watch monitor two.>

The flat screen flickered for just an instant, then cleared with the face of a thin, auburn-haired man with heavy-lidded eyes.

"How do I look, thir?" the image asked, and Alicia grinned.

"I think maybe you got the lisp down a little *too* pat, Megarea."

"That'th eathy for you to thay," "Lieutenant Chisholm"

returned aggrievedly. "You haven't been teathed about it all your life. I tell you, it'th been a real pain in the ath for me!"

"Do you say that, or do you spray it?" Alicia giggled, and the image raised a hand into the field of the pickup and made a rude gesture.

"Oh, that's *perfect,* Megarea! Of course, I imagine poor Chisholm won't be handling much of the com traffic, given his lisp."

"No." Chisholm's baritone was replaced by a soprano and the image changed to that of a square-faced, silver-haired woman Alicia recognized as Ruth Tanner, her purser. "Poor Andy hates it when he has to talk to strangers. That's why I usually handle the com watch when you're not aboard, ma'am."

"So I see," Alicia propped a hip against a console and grinned. The AI had outdone herself. No one who spoke to any of Megarea's talking heads would suspect there was only a single human aboard *Star Runner.* Coupled with the AI's ability to handle both shuttles through her telemetry links, Captain Mainwaring's crew would be very much in evidence—so much so that no one would ever realize that they'd never actually laid eyes on any of them.

"Okay, I think we're set. But if it's all the same to you two, I need a good night's sleep before I get started hunting up a cargo."

<*Right.*> The screen blanked as Megarea returned to direct contact, and Alicia started back towards her quarters, shedding her tight jacket as she went. She tossed the garment to one of Megarea's waiting remotes, which whisked it neatly into a closet.

<*Uh, say, Alley,*> Megarea said as she undressed, <*you haven't had time to go through the full data download from the MaGuire port admiral, have you?*>

"You know I haven't." Alicia paused with her blouse half off. "Why?"

<*Well, I didn't want to worry you with it while Giolitti was aboard, and I wouldn't want to give you bad dreams or anything, but we're in it.*>

"What do you mean, 'we'?"

<I mean the "we" that stole me from Soissons orbit. Specifically, Captain Alicia DeVries and the illegally obtained alpha synth starship Hull Number Seven-Niner-One-One-Four.>

<Indeed? what has the data to say of us?> Tisiphone asked curiously.

<It's not real good.>

"Meaning what?" Alicia asked sharply. "That they know where we're headed or something?"

<No, not that bad. But there's an entry in here all about you, Alley—says you broke out of psychiatric detention and have to be considered extremely dangerous—and another bunch of crap about me. *Fairly accurate summation of my offensive and defensive capabilities, though they're playing a lot of the details close to their chests and they don't say diddly about the other things I can do. No, what bothers me is this last little bit.>*

"*What* last little bit?"

<The one that says Fleet's offering a one million-credit reward for information leading to your location and interception,> Megarea said. Alicia swallowed, but the AI wasn't quite done. *<And the last little section that says the Jungian Navy's officially adopted Governor General Treadwell's instructions to his own Fleet units.>* Alicia sat down on the bed with a thump as Megarea finished her report.

<It's a shoot on sight order, Alley. They're not even talking about trying to get us back in one piece.>

Chapter Seventeen

Benjamin McIlheny racked his headset and stood, rubbing his aching eyes and trying to remember when he'd last had six hours' sleep at a stretch.

He lowered his hands and glowered at the record chips and hard-copy heaped about his office aboard the accomodation ship HMS *Donegal*. Somewhere in all that crap, he knew, was the answer—or the clues which would lead to the answer—if only he could find it.

It seemed a law of nature that any intelligence service always had the critical data in its grasp . . . and didn't know it. After all, how did you cull the one, crucial truth from the heap of untruth, half-truth, and plain lunacy? Answer: hindsight invariably recognized it after the fact. Which, of course, was the reason the intelligence community was constantly being kicked by people who thought it was so damned easy.

McIlheny snorted bitterly and began to pace. He'd seen it too many times, especially from Senate staffers. They had an image of intelligence officers as Machiavellian spy-masters, usually in pursuit of some hidden agenda. That was why you had to watch the sneaky bastards so closely. And since they were so damned clever, *obviously* they never told all they knew, even when they had a constitutional duty to do so. Which, naturally, meant any "failure" to spot the critical datum actually represented some deep-seated plot to suppress an embarrassing truth.

People like that neither knew nor cared what true intelligence work was. Holovid might pander to the notion of the Daring Interstellar Agent carrying the vital data chip in a hollow tooth, but the real secret was sweat. Insight and trained instinct were invaluable, but it was the painstaking pursuit of every lead, the collection of every scrap of evidence and its equally exhaustive analysis, which provided the real breakthroughs.

Unfortunately, he admitted with a sigh, analysis took time, sometimes more than you had, and in this case it wasn't providing what he needed. He *knew* there was a link between the pirates and someone high up. It was the only possible answer. Admiral Gomez's full strength would have had a tough time fighting its way into Elysium orbit against its space defenses, yet the pirates had gotten inside in the first rush. McIlheny had no detailed sensor data to back his hunch, but he was morally certain the raiders had slipped a capital ship into SLAM range under some sort of cover. The shocked survivors all agreed on the blazing speed with which the orbital defenses had been annihilated, and only a capital ship could have done it.

But *how?* How had they fooled Commodore Trang and all of his people? Simple ECM couldn't be the answer after all the sector had been through. No, somehow they'd given Trang a legitimate cover, something he *knew* was friendly, and there was simply no way they could have without access to information they should never have been able to reach.

It all fit a pattern—even Treadwell was showing signs of accepting that—but the colonel was damned if he could make it all come together. Even Ben Belkassem had thrown up his hands and departed for Old Earth in the faint hope that his superiors there might be able to see something from their distant perspective which had eluded everyone in the Franconian Sector.

The colonel hoped so, because what bothered him even more than how was *why*. What in God's name were these people *up* to? He hadn't said so (except very privately to Admiral Gomez and Brigadier Keita), but it passed sanity that they could be garden-variety pirates. That didn't make sense just based on cost effectiveness! Anybody who could field a force the size of the one these people had to have didn't need whatever they were making off their loot.

No doubt plunder helped defray their operational costs, but his most generous estimate of their take fell short of what it must cost to supply and maintain their ships. Just look at what they were taking: colony support equipment, spaceport beacon arrays, *industrial machinery*, for God's sake! They scooped up some luxury goods, of course—they'd scored over a half-billion in direcat pelts, alone, from Mathison's World—but no normal hijacker or pirate would touch most of what they took.

And even aside from their unlikely loot, there were the casualties. McIlheny didn't believe in Attila the Hun in starships. Stupid people, by and large, didn't become starship captains, and only someone who was stupid could fail to see the inevitable result of pursuing some bizarre scorched-earth policy against the Empire. That was why massacre for the sake of massacre wasn't a normal piratical trait; it didn't pay their bills, and it *did* guarantee a massive response. Yet these people were deliberately maximizing the devastation in their wake. From everything the Elysium survivors could tell him, they hadn't even tried to loot beyond the limits of the capital, but they'd nuked every city from orbit! Nine million dead. What in hell's name could be behind that kind of slaughter? It was almost as if they were taunting the Fleet, *daring* it to deal with them.

It was maddening, yet the answer was here, right here in his office and his brain, if he could only bring the pieces together. Any group who could penetrate security as if it didn't exist and use their stolen data to mount such meticulous, lethal attacks couldn't be mere loose cannons. They had an ultimate objective which, in their eyes at least, made all the killing worthwhile, and that was frightening, because he couldn't imagine what it might be and it was his job to do just that.

There were times, McIlheny thought wistfully, when a return to the simplicity of combat looked ever so attractive.

The admittance signal hauled him out of his thoughts. He pressed the button, and his eyebrows arched as Sir Arthur Keita stepped through the hatch.

"Good evening, Sir Arthur. What can I do for you?"

"Probably not much," Keita rumbled. He removed a carton of chips from a chair and settled onto it, holding them in his lap. "I just dropped by to say good bye, Colonel."

"Good bye?" McIlheny repeated in surprise, and Keita gave a sour grin.

"I'm only punching air out here. This is a job for you and the Fleet—and Treadwell, if he ever stops screaming for more ships and uses what he has—and I've been here too long."

"I see." McIlheny sank into his own chair and swiveled it to face Keita. The brigadier's gravelly voice was as steady as ever, but he heard the despair within it. He knew what had kept Keita on Soissons so long . . . and there hadn't been a single report of the alpha synth in ten weeks.

"I imagine you do, Colonel." Keita's eyes were sad, but he gave McIlheny a less strained smile and nodded. "But I can't justify staying on in the hope that something will break, and—" his jaw tightened "—if she's spotted now, she's your job, not mine."

"Understood, sir," the colonel said. "I wish it weren't true—God knows Captain DeVries deserves better than that—but I understand."

Keita looked down at the carton of chips, stirring them with a blunt index finger. "I wish you could have known her before, Colonel," he said softly. "She was . . . special. The best. And to have it end like this, with an *imperial* price on her head. . . ." The silver-maned old head shook sadly, and then Keita looked up at McIlheny's combat ribbons.

"You've been there, Colonel. If it has to be one of our own, I'm glad it's someone who can understand. Whatever she is now, she was *special*."

"I know she was, Sir Arthur."

"Yes. Yes, you do." Keita inhaled deeply, then rose and held out his hand. "I'll be going, then."

"Yes, sir. I'm going to miss you, Sir Arthur. I want you to know how much I've appreciated the insight you gave me between your . . . other duties."

"Keep swinging, Colonel." Keita's grip crushed McIlheny's hand. "Between us, I'm convinced you're on the right trail, so you watch your six. Something stinks to high heaven out here. I intend to say as much to Countess Miller and His Majesty, but you be careful who you trust. When you can't tell the bad guys from the good guys . . ."

His voice trailed off, and he released McIlheny's hand with a shrug.

"I know, sir." The colonel frowned a moment, then looked deep into Keita's eyes. "A favor, if I may, Sir Arthur."

"Of course," Keita said instantly, and McIlheny smiled his thanks.

"I've made a complete duplicate of my files. Technically, they're not supposed to leave my office, but I would be very grateful if you'd take them to Old Earth with you. I'd feel much happier with someone I *know* is clean in possession of my data in case—"

The colonel broke off with a crooked smile, and Keita nodded soberly.

"I will—and I'm honored by your trust."

"Thank you. And with your permission, sir, I'll arrange a periodic security download to you. One outside my normal channels."

"Do you have a feeling?" Keita's eyes were suddenly intent, and the colonel shrugged.

"I . . . don't know. It's just that I suspect we've been

penetrated even more deeply than we've guessed. I don't want to sound paranoid, but these people have certainly demonstrated they're not shy about killing people. If I get too close to their mole . . . Well, accidents happen, Sir Arthur."

Vice Admiral Brinkman lit another cigar, tipped back his chair, and frowned meditatively up at the overhead. Things were getting complicated. Of course, they'd known they would—they had to, in fact, if this was going to work—but keeping so many balls in the air wore on a man's nerves.

He thought back over his discussion with Howell. He could certainly understand the commodore's concerns, and, frankly, *he* would have balked at hitting someone like the El Grecans if not for McIlheny. The collateral objectives would be valuable even without the troublesome colonel, but he was the real reason they had to strike at least one non-imperial target to prove they really were "pirates." Not that Brinkman expected even the Ringbolt attack to throw him off for long. It should create confusion among the people to whom he reported, but it was unlikely to create enough.

And that was because McIlheny wasn't going to give up. He might not realize what he had his teeth into, but he knew he was onto *something*, and he wasn't going to turn loose. The use of classified data to plan the squadron's operations had always been the shakiest part of the entire plan, yet there'd been no other way. Howell was good, but Fleet only had to get lucky once to blow his entire force out of space, so Fleet couldn't be allowed to get lucky.

If Lord Jurawski and Countess Miller hadn't insisted on sending Rosario Gomez out here, Brinkman could have made certain no luck came Fleet's way, but they didn't call Gomez "the Iron Maiden" for nothing. The nickname was, he admitted with a smile, a base libel on her sex life, but she'd earned it when she was much younger, and nothing about her style had changed since. They'd known Lady Rosario would be a problem when her assignment was announced, yet there'd been nothing they could do. They'd already taken out Admiral Whitworth to clear the second in command's slot for Brinkman; two flag officers' mysterious deaths would have been too much to risk, so they'd had to accept Gomez and concentrate on hamstringing her efforts from within.

Unfortunately, she'd assembled a staff whose tenacity mirrored her own—and one that was damnably close-knit and loyal to her. Brinkman more than suspected that she and McIlheny had begun compartmentalizing more tightly than they were telling, and that was bad.

He rocked his chair slowly, nursing his cigar. McIlheny had already clamped down on normal information distribution, which produced a dangerous decrease in possible suspects. The more restricted data became, the fewer people could possibly be passing it on to the "pirates," and that was bad enough. But if the two of them were beginning to restrict critical data to an inner clique only they trusted, his people might miss some critical bit of information Howell and Alexsov *had* to have.

At least that Justice pest had worn out his enthusiasm and decamped, and Keita would be gone within days. Both of those were major pluses, but it didn't help much with the McIlheny problem. The ideal solution would be to remove him, but he was a cautious and a dangerous man. He could be gotten to, yet setting up an overt assassination that didn't prove how massively security had been breached would be time consuming and difficult. Worse, it would suggest there'd been a *reason* to kill him, and anyone with whom he'd shared his suspicions—whatever they were—would have to wonder if the reason wasn't that he'd been on the right track and getting too close to an answer.

At the very least Gomez would be out for blood, and assassinating *her* would be even harder. She practically never left her battle-cruiser flagship these days, and about the only way to get to her would be to sabotage *Antietam*'s Fasset drive or fusion plants and take out the entire ship. That might not be impossible, but it would certainly be difficult. Worst of all, killing her would be the Whitworth situation all over again and worse. It would put *him* in her command, and stepping into her shoes under the present circumstances might raise the wrong eyebrows. What if someone who shared McIlheny's suspicions wondered why someone else might want to see Sir Amos Brinkman in her place?

He let his chair swing back upright and shook his head with a sigh. No, precipitous action against Gomez was out of the question. Pressure was building in the Senate and the Ministry as the "pirates" danced around her and laughed at her attempts to deal with them. It could only be a matter of time before she was relieved for her failures. Brinkman would be properly distressed at relieving so old and dear a friend under such circumstances—and send McIlheny packing as part of his "new broom" housekeeping. That had been the plan for getting rid of Gomez from the beginning; it was only McIlheny's stubborn probing that had him thinking about other approaches.

Still, the time might come when McIlheny got too close and they had to take him out, suspicious or no. It wouldn't be a best case scenario, but if it was a choice between that and having him figure out what was really going on, the decision would make itself. And his death would produce at least short-term confusion, especially if it wasn't an obvious assassination. If they were lucky, the confusion might even last long enough to carry clear through Gomez's relief.

Brinkman nodded to himself and stubbed out his cigar. Yes, it might become necessary, in which case it would be a good idea to put the assets in place now, and the admiral thought he might just know the way to go about it. McIlheny had started out as a shuttle pilot, after all. That was where he'd won his spurs and first made his name, and he still had a weakness for hot shuttles and hotter skimmers. Better yet, he insisted on piloting himself whenever possible. Under normal circumstances, no one would be too surprised if he finally lost it in a midair one day, and a little help in the maintenance shop could . . . assist the good colonel right out of the sky.

He smiled a slow, thoughtful smile and tried to remember the name of that "skimmer tech" Rachel Shu had used to eliminate Admiral Whitworth. It was time for a little judicious personnel reassignment.

Chapter Eighteen

"Good evening, Captain Mainwaring. My name is Yerensky. I understand you're seeking a cargo for your vessel?"

Alicia looked up from her wineglass and saw a tall, cadaverous man. He was well-dressed, despite his half-starved appearance, and his polished tones were well-suited to the background hum of the expensive restaurant. She eyed him for a moment, then sat back slightly and made a tiny gesture at the empty chair across from her. Yerensky slid into it, smiling politely. A waiter materialized at his elbow, and Alicia sipped her own wine, using the brief, low-voiced exchange between waiter and patron to evaluate her visitor.

<*Smooth as pond scum, isn't he?*> she commented, and felt Tisiphone's silent agreement. Not that they were surprised. They'd learned a great deal about Yerensky during the two weeks they'd spent angling for this meeting.

It had been far harder than Alicia had expected to find the precise shipper she sought. Not because there hadn't been offers in plenty, but because, to her intense chagrin, virtually all of them had been legitimate. She'd underestimated the pirates' effect on insurance rates, and under the circumstances, *Star Runner*'s high speed more than outweighed her limited cargo capacity. If she'd been a real free trader, Alicia could have increased her transport fees by a quarter of the amount by which her ship's speed lowered the insurance premiums and still tripled her normal profit margin.

Unfortunately, she wasn't looking for an honest cargo, and she'd been forced to concoct an extraordinary range of excuses to avoid accepting one. More than once, she'd been reduced to letting the Fury enter a legitimate shipper's mind and get *him* to suggest a reason to decline his offer.

It had been maddening, especially after one of Megarea's and Tisiphone's forays through MaGuire's classified data base revealed that the Empire had provided the Jung Association with Alicia's retinal and genetic prints. They hadn't anticipated that when they concocted Captain Mainwaring, so they'd used her real patterns, and she'd almost fainted when she found out the authorities had both sets. If they happened to run a check against all new arrivals. . . .

That threat, at least, had been alleviated, if not nullified, by the simple expedient of sending Tisiphone back into the net to alter the prints for *Star Runner*'s skipper. It wasn't a perfect solution, since any document—like a freight contract—Alicia signed as Captain Mainwaring would include her real retinal prints, which no longer matched the ones on file, yet it was the best they could do. Tisiphone had suggested doctoring the Fleet download instead of Mainwaring's, but Alicia and Megarea had vetoed that idea, since they couldn't touch the files on Soissons. It was tempting to "legitimize" Mainwaring's prints, but it was unlikely anyone would check the prints on a document when he *knew* they were the right person's. At least Alicia hoped they wouldn't, and that possibility worried her less than what might happen if ONI should check back and notice that Alicia DeVries' records on MaGuire no longer matched those on Soissons. At the very least, it would be proof she'd been to MaGuire, since no one but she would have any reason to change them. Worse, a simple cross-check would soon reveal that "Captain Mainwaring's" prints *did* match.

None of that had been calculated to soothe her nerves, but at least it looked as if they'd be able to clear out shortly. The Fury's careful mental probes had, at last, plucked one Anton Yerensky's name and face from the thoughts of a more honest merchant, and Mister Yerensky, it seemed, needed a cargo delivered to Ching-Hai in the Thierdahl System. Barely civilized and sparsely settled, Ching-Hai had very little to recommend it . . . except that it was only ten light-years from Dewent, and Dewent was barely six light-years from Wyvern. Better yet, what passed for the planetary authorities on Ching-Hai had a very cozy relationship with both Dewent and Wyvern.

Once Yerensky had been identified, it hadn't been hard to arrange casual contacts with two or three of his associates. With Tisiphone to plant a favorable impression of Captain Mainwaring in their minds, one of them was bound to mention her to him eventually, and for the first time, the skewed shipping conditions had worked in their favor. With so many fast ships being snapped up for legitimate cargoes, the supply of smugglers was running thin.

"You seem to be well-informed, Mister Yerensky," she said as the waiter departed with his order. "I am looking for a cargo—a small one, I'm afraid, but I assume you've already checked my capacity with the port master."

"Your vessel's capacity would suit me quite well, Captain, assuming we can come to terms."

"I see." Alicia refilled her wineglass and held it up to the light. "Exactly what sort of cubage are we talking about here, Mister Yerensky?"

"Oh, no more than a hundred cubic meters. A bit less, actually."

"I see," Alicia repeated. That really was a small shipment, less than half the available volume in *Megarea*'s hold, which was already well-stocked with spares and replacement parts. "And where would you like it delivered?"

"Ah, that's a bit delicate, Captain," Yerensky said slowly, watching her from under lowered lids. "You see, I need it delivered to Ching-Hai." He paused for a moment, as if to let that sink in, before continuing. "I understand you have a Fleet-type cargo shuttle with rough field capability?"

Alicia lowered her wine and let her lips curl in a tiny smile.

"I do, indeed. May I assume your receiver will be . . . unable to collect his cargo at the regular port?"

"Precisely," Yerensky said politely, and his smile was just as small. "I see you have a fine appreciation for these matters, Captain."

"One tries, Mister Yerensky." Alicia sipped more wine as the waiter returned with Yerensky's order and began sliding plates onto the table. There were a lot of them, and she wondered what sort of metabolism could handle that kind of intake and still look starved.

The waiter scurried off again, and Yerensky unfolded a snow-white napkin in his lap and reached for a fork.

"Given your appreciation, Captain, I must assume you realize you and your crew are—well, let us say, a rather unknown quantity."

"If you checked my port download, I'm sure you discovered that we're bonded with the Melville Sector governor," Alicia said, forbearing to mention just how surprised the Melville Sector governor would be to learn that.

"Well, yes, Captain, but MaGuire is scarcely an imperial planet, now is it? And there might be circumstances under which it would be inconvenient for a shipper to attempt to recover against your bond if something went awry."

<*In other words,*> Alicia observed silently to Tisiphone, <*a crook can't exactly sue you for stealing his illegal cargo.*>

<*It is reassuring to find some things unchanged,*> the Fury returned, and Alicia nodded at Yerensky.

"I can understand that. Still, I assume you wouldn't

have come to see me unless you felt these little problems could be resolved."

"A woman after my own heart, Captain," he said as he spread his salad dressing more evenly. "I'd thought in terms of a mutual expression of trust."

"Such as?"

"I think, perhaps, a front payment of twenty-five percent of the total shipping charges with the remainder placed in escrow here on MaGuire to be released when the cargo is delivered to my agent on Ching-Hai."

Alicia nodded thoughtfully, but her mind raced. That was a terrible idea. It would require reams of legal documents, and that meant retinal prints galore. But she couldn't exactly object on those grounds. . . .

"An interesting suggestion, but not the way I normally do business, Mister Yerensky. I can conceive of certain circumstances under which—purely without your knowledge, of course—an unscrupulous receiver might deny he'd ever received the goods, which could tie up the escrow account or even require litigation. Then, too, limited facility fields, you know, are often under-equipped. A completely honest difference of opinion might arise, and without proper instrumentation to examine the cargo, well—" She shrugged with a helpless little smile, and a gleam of appreciation lit Yerensky's eyes.

"I see. May I assume you have a counter offer, Captain?"

"Indeed. I would suggest that you pay me half the freight charges up front, and that your receiver pay the other half immediately upon receipt and examination of his cargo. I sacrifice the security of the escrow account; you run a slightly greater risk with your front payment. That seems fair."

Yerensky munched thoughtfully on his salad for a few moments, then nodded. "I believe I could accept that arrangement, assuming we can settle the remainder of the terms to our mutual satisfaction."

"Oh, I'm certain we can, Mister Yerensky." Alicia smiled even more sweetly. "I'm a great believer in mutual satisfaction."

* * *

Alicia reclined in her command chair and chewed on a grape. She savored the sweet juice and pulp with sensual delight, and the back of her brain hummed with an odd duality as Megarea and Tisiphone shared her pleasure.

<*That's nice,*> the AI observed. <*Much sharper than your memories. Almost makes me wish I were a flesh-and-blood.*>

<*Not I,*> Tisiphone disagreed. <*Such moments are pleasant, yet what need have we for flesh and blood when we may share them with Alicia? And unlike her, we are not subject to the* unpleasant *aspects of such existence.*>

<*Voyeurs.*> Alicia swallowed and examined the bunch in her lap to select a fresh grape. "You ought to experience some of the downside—maybe a nice head cold, for instance—so you could appreciate the pleasures properly."

<*I have yet to observe that suffering truly makes pleasure sweeter, Little One. Bliss is not the mere absence of pain.*>

"Maybe." She popped the chosen grape into her mouth and turned her attention back to Megarea's sensors.

They'd left the dreary featurelessness of wormhole space an hour ago, decelerating steadily towards the heart of the Ching-Hai System, and the glory of the stars was even sweeter than the grapes. She drank it in, reveling in the reach and power of Megarea's senses, as Thierdahl's distant spark grew brighter. They were fifteen days—just over eleven days by their own clocks—out of MaGuire with their cargo of bootleg medical supplies, and she wondered again what they would discover when they reached their destination. So far, things had gone more smoothly than she had hoped.

<*Of course they have, Little One. What, after all, could go wrong in wormhole space?*>

"Nothing, but it's the nature of the human beast to worry. At least I don't have to feel guilty about what we're carrying."

<*Do not be foolish. There is neither cause nor room for "guilt" in whatever we may do in pursuit of your vengeance.*>

Alicia winced at Tisiphone's absolute assurance. She could forget just how alien the Fury was for days at a stretch, but then Tisiphone came out with something like that. It wasn't posturing. It was simply the literal truth as she saw it.

"I'm afraid I can't agree with you on that one. I want justice, not blind vengeance, and I'd rather not hurt anyone I don't have to."

<*Justice is a delusion, Little One.*> The Fury's mental voice dripped scorn. <*Your people have learned much, but you have forgotten much, as well.*>

"You might profit by a little forgetting—or learning—of your own."

<*Such as?*>

"Such as the fact that simple vengeance is a self-sustaining reaction. When you 'avenge' yourself on someone, you usually give someone else an excuse to seek vengeance on you.

<*And you think your precious justice does not? You are wiser than that, Alicia DeVries—or would be, if you but let yourself!*>

"You're missing the point. If a society settles for naked vengeance, it all comes down to who has the bigger club. Justice provides the rules that make it possible for people to live together with some semblance of decency."

<*Bah! "Justice" is no more than vengeance dressed up in fine clothes! There can be no justice without punishment—or would you say that Colonel Watts was treated "justly" for the wrong he did your company?*>

Alicia's lip curled in an involuntary snarl, but she closed her eyes and fought it back as she felt the Fury's amusement.

"No, I wouldn't call that justice, or disagree that punishment is a part of justice. I won't even pretend vengeance isn't exactly what I wanted from that son-of-a-bitch. But there has to be guilt—and he was guilty as sin—before punishment. A society can't just go around smashing people without determining that the one punished is actually the guilty party. That's the worst kind of capriciousness—and a damned good recipe for anarchy."

<*What care I for anarchy?*> Tisiphone demanded. <*Nor am I "society." Nor, for that matter, are you. You are an individual, seeking redress for yourself and for others who cannot. Is that wrong?*>

"I didn't say it was. I only said I don't want to hurt innocent bystanders. But whether you like it or not, justice—the rule of law, not men, if you will—is the glue that sticks human societies together. It lets human beings live together with some sense of security, and it establishes precedents. When a criminal is proven guilty and punished, it sets the parameters. It tells people what's acceptable and what isn't, and whenever we inch a few centimeters forward, justice is what keeps us from slipping back."

<*So you say, Little One, but you delude yourself. It is compassion, not reason, which truly shapes your thought—misplaced compassion for those who deserve none.* This *is the truth of what you feel.*>

Alicia's face twisted as the Fury relaxed inner barriers—barriers Alicia had almost forgotten existed—and a red haze of rage boiled in the back of her brain. Her fists clenched, and she locked her teeth together, fighting the sudden need to smash something—anything—in the pure, wanton destruction her emotions craved. She felt Megarea's distress, felt the AI beating at Tisiphone in a futile effort to free Alicia from her own hate, but even that was small and faint and far, far away. . . .

The barriers snapped back, and she slumped in her chair, gasping and beaded with sweat.

<*You bitch!*> Megarea snarled. <*If you ever try that again, I'll—!*>

<*Peace, Megarea,*> the Fury interrupted almost gently. <*I will not harm her. But she must know herself if we are to succeed. There is no room for confusion or self-blindness in what we do.*>

Alicia trembled in the couch, nerve ends shuddering, and closed her thoughts off from the others. She needed the silence, needed a moment to breathe and recover from the side of herself she'd just seen. She believed what she'd told Tisiphone—more than believed, *knew* it was true—and yet . . .

She opened her eyes and looked down at her hands. They were slick and wet, coated in dripping grape pulp, and she shuddered.

Chapter Nineteen

Commodore Howell sat on the freighter's bridge and told himself—again—that the ship was perfectly adequate for her mission. Compared to a warship, her command facilities were primitive, her defenses minimal, and her offensive weapons nonexistent, but if everything went right, that wouldn't matter, and so far the mission profile had been perfect. And much as he would have preferred being somewhere else, he *had* to be here for this one. They needed a success to blunt the sting of Elysium, and his people's morale required that he be here in person.

He watched the display, face expressionless, as the freighter and her two sister ships settled into parking orbit around Ringbolt. Control's information on the El Grecan fleet maneuvers had been right on the money, and the only ground defenses were purely anti-air weapons sited to cover Adcock Field, the main spaceport outside the city of Raphael. They had the reach to cover the city's airspace, but they wouldn't have the chance.

Howell's eyes swiveled to the reason they wouldn't. The freighters' transponders identified them as Fleet transports—courtesy of the ID codes Control had provided—escorted by a heavy cruiser. Now all four ships were in position, riding geosynchronous orbit directly above Raphael, and a signal in the commodore's synth link told him HMS *Intolerant*'s weapons were locked in.

Captain Arlen Monkoto of the Monkoto Free Mercenaries, known less formally as "Monkoto's Maniacs," stepped out onto the hotel balcony and sucked in crisp, cool air. Ringbolt was a *much* nicer planet than El Greco, he mused, and wondered if he could convince Simon to relocate their home port here.

He looked back over his shoulder. Lieutenant Commander Hugin was on the suite com, conferring with Chief Pilaskov. The recruiting mission had gone well, and Monkoto expected Simon to be pleased when he arrived. Over a hundred experienced personnel, including twelve officers, could certainly be put to excellent use.

He started to open the balcony's French windows to join Hugin, and something flashed behind him. Eye-tearing light bounced back off the window glass, and his shadow was suddenly etched stark and black against the wall.

He whirled in disbelief, trained reflexes already throwing him face-down, as a huge, white fireball devoured Adcock Field.

"Launch shuttles!" Howell barked as *Intolerant*'s HVW obliterated the port. Each of the big transports normally mothered eight heavy-lift cargo shuttles; for this operation, they'd been replaced with twelve *Bengal*-class assault boats each, and thirty-six deadly attack craft shrieked downward. Thirteen hundred grim-faced raiders rode them. For many this was their first mission, and they were determined to get it right. Others were the survivors of Elysium . . . and they were even more determined to avoid another disaster.

Arlen Monkoto staggered erect like a punch-drunk fighter. His nerve ends jittered with echoes of heat and blast, but it must have been an HVW. If it had been a nuke or anti-matter, he'd be dead, and he was only singed a bit. Fires roared and fumed along the city's eastern edge, and he doubted there was an intact window in Raphael, but otherwise the damage hadn't been severe.

He wheeled back to the French windows and froze. He'd been wrong about the severity of the damage, an icy voice told him. The windows had been blown across the hotel suite like glittering daggers, and bloody bits of Lieutenant Commander Hugin's mutilated body were sprayed across the far wall.

Monkoto made himself pick his way into the wreckage, and his hands were a stranger's as they moved what remained of Hugin gently aside. His exec's body had protected the com unit, and Chief Pilaskov was still on it. The burly NCO was half shouting, though Monkoto's stunned ears could hardly hear him, and his brown eyes widened in relief as he saw his CO.

Fresh explosions thundered behind the captain, and his mouth tightened as he looked over his shoulder and saw the contrails slashing down the sky.

"Can't hear you, Chief." He tapped an ear, and Pilaskov's mouth snapped shut. "It doesn't matter. Break into the ordnance order and get our people moving. The primary LZ looks like Toledo U. I'll meet you there."

Surprise was total.

Adcock Field had known the freighters and their escort were friendly. No one at the port lived long enough to realize he was wrong, and sheer shock—not disbelief so much as a desperate need to be wrong—stunned Raphael motionless until the shuttle contrails were sighted.

By then it was far, far too late, and Howell's raiders carried through with merciless precision. Individual shuttles peeled off and streaked in to lay smaller HVW and guided bombs on every police station and substation in the city. Entire blocks went up with them, and other shuttles swept a circle about the raider's target with rocket clusters and incendiaries. A curtain of flame sealed their objective off from relief while two more shuttles took out the militia armory, and twenty *Bengals* grounded on the university campus, disgorging seven hundred heavily armed raiders who charged straight for their objectives and killed anyone in their path.

Stunned university security forces tried to stop them, but they had only side arms and Howell's raiders were in powered armor with heavy weapons. The university's director of research raced for the computer center to purge her data, but a squad of invaders burst through the doors and cut her down before she reached her console. Teams of technicians followed the assault wave, setting up their portable terminals and transmission dishes while the thunder of weapons and screams of the dying shook the building about them. More raiders broke into the labs themselves and massacred the researchers, and a fresh flood of technicians poured in in their wake, heaving specimen cases, hard-copy records, and lab animals onto counter-gravity pallets while their boots slipped in their victims' blood.

Monkoto found Chief Pilaskov more by luck than any other way. The petty officer had his recruits mustered near the roaring wall of flames sealing the university off from the rest of the city, their uniforms a black-and-gray knot of order in a sea of chaos.

They were more heavily armed than Monkoto had hoped. They'd been quartered in the warehouse district to keep an eye on the Maniacs' ordnance order, but it was obvious Pilaskov had helped himself generously from the arms merchant's other wares. Half the recruits wore light armor, and Monkoto saw squad heavy weapons as well as personal arms. Best of all, Pilaskov had snagged a half-dozen Stiletto units. By the time Monkoto arrived, the chief had the remote launchers deployed well away from the fire control units.

"Glad to see you, sir," he said as Monkoto panted up to him. "Where's Commander Hugin?"

"Dead." Monkoto sucked in air, feeling the fire's heat in his lungs, and tried to think. A *Bengal* passed overhead, and he straightened quickly as one of the Stiletto crews began to track.

"Hold your fire!" he snapped, and the crew chief jerked in surprise. "We don't want the flankers," he continued when he was certain the other man was listening. "We want the main body. Wait till they lift out."

The crew chief nodded, face tightening in understanding, and Monkoto turned back to Pilaskov. He jabbed a thumb at the roaring flames.

"HE or straight incendiaries?" he demanded.

"Mainly incendiaries and just enough HE to bust things open, I think."

"We have a com on the secure police frequency?"

"Yes, sir. Not much traffic—only whoever was on the street when they hit."

"It'll have to do." Monkoto held out one hand and gestured at the rubble-strewn sidewalks with the other. "Find me a manhole, Chief."

"Aye, sir!" Pilaskov's face lit with understanding, and he started shouting orders as Monkoto raised the com to his mouth.

"This is Captain Arlen Monkoto, Monkoto's Mercenaries," he said crisply. "I am at Hadrian and Stimson. My people are going in in five minutes. Anyone who can reach us in time, get your ass over here now!"

The raiders crushed the last resistance, and small parties broke off to loot secondary objectives in Admin and the library building. The computer techs hovered over their equipment, draining the R&D data base and beaming it up to the freighters, and fire teams set up along the campus approaches in case anyone found a way through the fire wall. There was little wasted motion, and the situation was a far cry from the chaos of Elysium. Another forty minutes and they could lift the hell out of here again.

A manhole cover grated quietly well behind their outer perimeter. A cautious head poked up out of it, and two hundred men and women—mercenaries, police, and civilian volunteers inextricably mixed—flowed upward from the sewers and service tunnels buried meters beneath the interceding inferno.

* * *

Howell's ground commander was reporting to the flagship when bedlam exploded behind him. He wheeled in shock, gaping at the wave of El Grecans coming at him, then hit his jump gear to put a solid wall between him and them as grenades ripped into his temporary CP.

Where had they all *come* from? Damn it, they *couldn't* be here! But they were, and panicky reports flooded in. The bastards were hitting him everywhere at once, and memories of Elysium echoed through his raiders.

But this *wasn't* Elysium, goddamn it! These were a hastily assembled and lightly armed scratch group, not Imperial Marines in battle armor, and the CO screamed and cursed his people into coherent response.

Commodore Howell slammed a fist into the arm of his command chair as he, too, remembered Elysium. He didn't have the instrumentation for a solid read on what was happening, but the sudden confusion of combat chatter—and the screams of wounded and dying raiders—told him it wasn't good.

The perimeter teams turned and charged back towards the heart of the campus. Some blundered into hastily set ambushes and died still wondering what was happening, but most got through, for their armor and heavier weapons gave them a tremendous advantage. Yet this time the fighting was different. This time the locals knew what was going on, and they'd had time to collect more than handguns and stunners. Many of them knew the terrain better than even the most carefully briefed raider, and they used their knowledge well.

Combat raged across the once-beautiful campus—ugly, swirling knots of blood and fire and hate amid smoldering wreckage and the litter of bodies. A small team of Maniacs got in among the grounded shuttles and destroyed five before they could be killed. A police SWAT commander's jury-rigged team of civilians and a handful of police fought its way into the admin/library complex, and

Arlen Monkoto led a personal assault on the bio-research center.

The raiders' casualties mounted, but they still had the edge in numbers. They fought off the shock of surprise and went back onto the offensive, and Commodore Howell relaxed as his people began to regain the ground they'd lost while the data continued to pour upward.

Arlen Monkoto poked his head cautiously around a corner, trying not to cough as acrid smoke assaulted his lungs. He'd fought his way to within two corridors of the computer center, but he'd lost Chief Pilaskov on the way in, and he was down to five men and three women, only two of them Maniacs.

The way ahead was clear, and he moved down the hall in the quietest run he could manage. "His" people followed him, and his mind raced. If they got into the computer center, took out the techs he knew were pillaging it—

An armored raider appeared before him, and thirty-millimeter rifle fire tore Captain Arlen Monkoto apart.

"Download complete!" someone called, and someone else was screaming to "Move it back to the shuttles *now!*" over the tactical net.

Raiders began to disengage, leapfrogging back towards the shuttle perimeter. Too few defenders remained to stop them, but the twenty shuttle loads who'd landed needed only twelve shuttles to lift them out again.

"Shuttles preparing to lift, sir."

Howell grunted approval at the report, but inside he winced. Twenty percent casualties were too damned many so soon after Elysium, even if they had secured every one of their objectives this time. He didn't care what Control said, he *wasn't* sending teams in against targets this hard again.

"Sir, sensors report a Fasset drive coming in from the direction of El Greco," an officer said suddenly, and Howell's head snapped around.

"What is it?" he demanded.

"Can't tell at this range, sir, but it's not a Fleet drive. Looks like an El Grecan—probably a destroyer."

The commodore relaxed. A destroyer had the speed to overhaul them, but not the firepower to fight them, and this time she was welcome to any sensor data she could get. Aside from the freighter's transponder codes, nothing he'd done here had required the use of classified security data, and ex-Fleet heavy cruisers weren't all that hard to come by.

He looked back into the display as the shuttles began to lift, and his mouth curled in an ugly smile. The fact that the "pirates" had one of Fleet's cast-off CAs would spill no beans, but *Intolerant*'s weapons would more than suffice to destroy the El Grecan ship if she got close enough to be a problem. Besides, she'd be . . . distracted after *Intolerant* nuked Raphael, and—

"Sir! The shuttles!" someone shouted, and Howell's face went white as the Stiletto teams opened fire. Nine of his thirty-one surviving shuttles became falling fireballs as he stared at the display.

Admiral Simon Monkoto stood on the bridge of the destroyer *Ardent*, staring at the view screen, and his carved-marble face was white as the silver at his temples. There had been no way for *Ardent* to know what was happening on Ringbolt until she dropped sublight, but the radiation counters were going mad. Whoever had nuked Raphael had used the dirtiest warhead Admiral Monkoto had ever seen on the city . . . and on Arlen.

Dark eyes, hot and hating in his frozen face, moved from the view screen to the gravitic plot. He could have overhauled the raiders. It would have been close, even with their freighters to slow them, for his destroyer had been on the wrong approach vector, but he could have caught them.

And it would have done no good at all against a heavy cruiser.

He'd almost done it anyway, but he hadn't. He couldn't throw away his crew's lives—or his own. Even more than he wanted those ships, he wanted the people who'd sent them, and he couldn't have them if he died.

His jaw clenched, and he turned away. *Ardent*'s last shuttle was waiting for him, waiting to take him down to the planet where his brother had died to do what he could. But he'd be back, and not with a single destroyer. He promised himself that—promised Arlen—and his expression was as hellish as his heart.

Chapter Twenty

Ching-Hai lay barely 14.8 light-minutes from the F5 star Thierdahl, with an axial tilt of forty-one degrees. It was also dry—*very* dry—with an atmospheric pressure only three-quarters that of Old Earth, all of which conspired to produce something only the charitable could call a climate. Alicia couldn't conceive of any rational reason to choose to live here, and not even Imperial Galactography knew why anyone had. The handbook's best theory was that the original settlers were League War or HRW-I refugees who'd found in Ching-Hai a world so inhospitable neither the Empire nor the Rishatha would want it. As guesses went, that one was as good as any; certainly their descendants had no better one four hundred years later.

Which probably explained their attitude towards other people's laws. They had to make a living somehow, and their planet wasn't much help, she thought, crossing to the coffeemaker and watching with a corner of her brain while Megarea slipped them into orbit. They were a few hours early, and Alicia was just as glad. She'd recovered—mostly—from the experience Tisiphone had unleashed upon her, but she welcomed a little more time to settle down before she had to meet Yerensky's local contact.

She carried her cup back to the view port. Ochre and yellow land masses moved far below her, splashed with an occasional large lake or small sea. It all looked depressingly flat, and there were very few visible light blurs on the nightside. The one official spaceport was well into the dayside at the moment, but whoever was in charge hadn't even bothered to assign her a parking orbit, much less mounted any sort of customs inspection.

<*You didn't really expect one, did you?*> Megarea asked.

"No, but this is so . . . so—"

<*Half-assed?*> the AI suggested helpfully, and Alicia chuckled.

"Something like that. Not that I'm complaining. I don't know how Yerensky got those medical supplies out of the Empire and onto Maguire without any customs stamps, but I'd hate to try explaining it to someone else."

<*There would be no need.*> Alicia and Megarea both bristled, but the Fury sounded totally unaware of any resentment they might harbor. <*Their inspectors would see precisely what we wished them to, no more and no less.*>

Alicia didn't reply. She suspected herself of sulking, and she didn't really care. The reminder of all the unresolved hate and violence still locked away within her had frightened her. Not that she hadn't known it was there, but knowing and feeling were two different things, and—

<*Whups! Heads up, Alley—I've got our landing beacon.*>

"So soon?" Alicia's eyebrows rose.

<*Well, it's in the right general spot.*> A mental grid superimposed itself over Alicia's view of the planet, and a green dot winked on the nightside. <*There—about midnight, local time. And it's the right beacon code.*>

"I don't like it. Yerensky didn't say anything about night landings."

<*But neither did he say it would be a* daylight *landing,*>

Tisiphone pointed out, and this time Alicia and Megarea were too intent on their problem to bristle. <*Indeed, there was no thought in his mind either way, so I would judge he trusts the discretion of his local agent. In that case, might there not be some valid reason for choosing to unload under cover of night?*>

"On *this* planet?" Alicia frowned. "I wouldn't've thought there was any reason to hide medical supplies. They're valuable, sure, especially on some of the lower-tech Rogue Worlds, but I can't see needing to *hide* them."

She hesitated a moment longer, then shrugged.

"Put on your Ruth face and ask for the countersign, Megarea."

<*On it,*> the AI replied. A few moments passed, then, <*They came back with the right response, Alley. Far as I can tell, this is them.*>

"Damn. Well, I guess we don't have much choice." Alicia sighed. "Load up the shuttle with the first pallets."

<*Yes,*> Tisiphone agreed, <*but I trust your instincts, Little One. May I suggest that this is a time for Top Cover?*>

"You may indeed," Alicia murmured, and felt Megarea's total agreement.

The cargo shuttle slid downward through the hot Ching-Hai night, cargo bay packed with counter-grav pallets, and Alicia lifted the combat rifle into her lap and slipped in a magazine.

Megarea and Tisiphone had both wanted her in combat armor, if for slightly different reasons. The AI worried about her safety, but the Fury wanted to see the armor in action, for its destructive capabilities fascinated her. Of the two, Alicia had found Megarea's argument more telling, yet she'd decided against it. No free trader could have gotten her hands on Cadre armor—Cadre Intelligence would have chased her to the ends of the galaxy to get it back if she'd tried—and someone might conceivably recognize it.

Besides, if some ill-intentioned soul *was* waiting for

her, he faced certain practical constraints. His only objective could be her cargo, which meant he couldn't use anything big and nasty enough to take out the shuttle. She, on the other hand, had no compunctions about what she might do to him.

<*That sounds strangely little like "justice,"*> Tisiphone jibed gently.

"On the contrary." Alicia jacked a nine-millimeter discarding sabot round into the chamber and set the safety. "I won't do a thing to them unless they intend to do something to me."

<*Indeed?*>

"Indeed. But if they do have something planned, *I* intend to do unto them first."

<*So there are times you see things my way after all.*>

"Never said there weren't." Alicia shifted to her contact with Megarea. <*How's it look from your side?*>

<*Everything's green, but I've got two aircraft to the south.*> Data flowed into Alicia's brain, and her lip curled, for one of those aircraft had "military" written all over it. It might be an escort against whatever local menace had provoked this night landing. Then again, it might not.

<*Keep an eye on 'em,*> she thought back. <*I'm getting vehicle sources around the landing beacon, too. Air lorries, it looks like.*>

<*I see them, too. Want me to take a closer look?*>

<*No. Wouldn't do to spook them, now would it?*>

<*You're the boss. Just watch yourself.*>

Alicia turned back to the shuttle controls, wiggling to settle her unpowered body armor. It, too, was Cadre-issue, better than anything on the open market but not visibly different enough to call attention to itself. They were less than two minutes out now, and she let the first trickle of tick seep into her bloodstream and smiled wolfishly as the universe slowed.

The ground party watched the shuttle slide down the last few meters of sky and deploy its landing legs. Flat pads reached for the ground, dust devils danced in the turbine wash, and one of the air lorries moved away from the dust in a curve that just happened to point the rear of its cargo bed at the shuttle. The tarp which closed it flapped in the jetwash, and something long and ominous was briefly visible behind the canvas.

"They're down," a man muttered into his helmet com. "Ready?"

"Light on the pads," a voice replied in his earphones.

"Good. I hope we won't need you, but stay loose."

"Yo," his phones said laconically, and he turned his full attention back to the shuttle. He'd expected a standard shuttle, and avarice flickered as he realized this one was almost twice that size. It must contain an even bigger chunk of Yerensky's cargo than he'd anticipated.

The shuttle's after hatch whined open and extruded a ramp, and he changed com channels, murmuring to his lorry pilot. The lorry's powerful lamps came on, bathing the shuttle in light, and he walked forward into the glare with a bright smile and a welcoming wave.

"Try and take the pilot alive," he reminded his gunners. He'd settle for one shuttle load—especially one this size—but if he could get his hands on the pilot and "convince" him to take his own boys back upstairs. . . .

His nerves crackled as subsiding dust billowed around the ramp. Any minute, he thought, still grinning and waving while he braced for the gunfire.

But the dust settled, and no one emerged. His waving hand slowed, his grin faded, and he suddenly felt exposed and stupid in the light.

Alicia killed the flight deck lights, popped an emergency hatch, and dropped to the ground on the far side from the illuminating lorry. That had been outstandingly stupid, she thought as she floated to earth on the wings of the tick. Anyone looking into that light would be blind as a bat, not to mention all the nice shadows it made on this side. She melted into the darker shadow of a landing leg and juggled her sensory boosters with practiced ease. She had to wind them way down when she looked into the light, then pump them high when her gaze tracked across the dark, but that was a problem she was used to, and she grunted with satisfaction as she completed her count.

Eighteen, nine of them bunched up around the air lorry with the heavy machine gun and not a one of them in even light armor. Well, at least it proved their mastermind was no military type. Unless his name was Custer.

<Megarea?>

<I see them,> the AI replied, watching through Alicia's eyes as easily as Alicia might scan space through her sensors. Tisiphone was silent in the back of her brain, wise enough not to distract her at a time like this.

<Somehow they don't look like the welcome wagon to me.>

<You watch your ass, Alley!>

<I will. You just watch those aircraft.>

<I'm on 'em.>

Damn it, something was wrong! His waving hand fell to his side as suspicion became certainty and he realized how exposed *he* was in that vortex of light. He started to turn and order the lamps doused when something sailed past his head to thump and rattle metallically across a lorry freight bed.

The air lorry gunship vanished in superheated fury as the plasma grenade exploded, but Alicia wasn't watching. She'd turned like a cat while the grenade hung dreamily in midair, and the combat rifle was an extension of her body. She didn't even see the sight picture, not consciously. She simply looked at her target, and the gunman's chest exploded.

The glare of the lorry couldn't quite hide her muzzle-flash, but she'd already found the two men who could see it. One of them died before he realized he had; the second while he was still raising his weapon.

The gun crew inside the lorry never knew they were dead, but screams of agony and terror rose from the men clustered about it. A human torch shrieked its way into the darkness as if the night could somehow quench its flames, and two more rolled on the ground, fighting to extinguish themselves. Three unwounded hijackers ran for their lives from the inferno, and the leader threw himself under his own vehicle and switched channels frantically.

"Get over here!" he screamed, and two heavily-armed aircraft leapt into the night in reply.

Alicia slid easily through the gap she'd blown in the ring around the shuttle. Three of the six on this side of the ambush remained, but they didn't realize they were alone. They'd made the mistake of staring into the flames, stunned by the carnage, and Alicia looked at their backs in disgust. Idiots. Did they think simply carrying a gun made someone dangerous?

It really wasn't fair. These people were pathetic, so completely out of their class they didn't even know it. But life wasn't fair, and anyone who lent himself to ambush and murder for gain had no kick coming. She found the position she wanted and fired three more short, neat bursts.

The stutter of automatic fire hammered his ears, and he stared out from under the lorry as a white eye flickered beyond the shuttle. *Beyond* the shuttle! Someone was on the ground out there! It had to be the shuttle pilot, but *how?* And where were the men he'd posted back there?!

How became immaterial as a lithe, slender shape slid across the very edge of the light with a cobra's speed and blew another of his men apart. It vanished back into the darkness, graceful as a dream, but another deadly burst and a bubbling shriek told him where his men were. Drive turbines began to whine above him as his lorry pilot prepared to pull out, and panic filled him at the thought of being left exposed and naked. He wanted to run, but his body refused to move, and he pounded the dry earth with his fists and prayed for his sting ships to get here in time.

* * *

Two heavily-armed aircraft sliced through the sky. One was little more than a transport loaded with weapons, but the leader was military from needle prow to sensor package, and its pilot brought his scanners on line. He saw only confusion and motionless bodies—*lots* of bodies, lit by a glare of flames—and one target source moving with deadly precision. He swore. One of them. Just *one!* But he had the bastard dialed in now. A few more seconds and he'd be able to nail the son-of-a-bitch without killing his own—

A night-black piece of sky swooped upon him from above. He had one stunned moment to register it, to begin to realize what it was, and then the *Bengal*-class assault shuttle tore him into very, very tiny pieces.

His head jerked up in horror, slamming into the bottom of the lorry, as the fireball blossomed. Flaming streamers arced from its heart like some enormous fireworks display, and then there was a second fireball.

He stared at them, watching them fade and fall, then cowered down as a vicious burst of fire lashed the vehicle above him. A chopped-off cry of agony and the sudden stillness of the waking turbines told him his pilot was dead, and he buried his face against the ground and sobbed in terror.

There were no more screams, no more shooting. Only the crackle of flames and the stench of burning bodies, and he whimpered and tried to dig into the baked soil beneath him as feet whispered through short, tough grass.

He raised his head weakly, and saw two polished boots, gleaming in the firelight. His eyes rose higher and froze on the muzzle of a combat rifle eight centimeters from his nose.

"I think you'd better come out of there," a contralto voice, colder than the stars, said softly.

Alicia finished throwing up and wiped her lips. Her

mouth tasted as if something had died in it, and her stomach cramped with fresh nausea.

"That's enough of that," she told it sternly, and the cramp eased sullenly. She waited another moment, then sighed and straightened in relief.

<*Are you quite through?*> Tisiphone inquired.

<*Listen, Lady, you don't even have any guts* to *puke up, so don't get snotty with those of us who do, all right?*> The post-tick letdown left her too drained to get much feeling into it, but the Fury subsided.

"God, I *hate* coming down from that stuff," Alicia muttered, lowering herself to sit against a landing leg. "Still, it does have its uses."

<*I wish I had you up here in sickbay,*> Megarea fretted, and Alicia looked up at the hovering assault boat with a grin.

<*Don't sweat it. I've been using Old Speedy for years, and aside from wanting to die when you come down, it doesn't hurt a bit. The Cadre guarantees it.*>

<*Yeah, sure. That and a centicred'll get you a cup of coffee.*>

Alicia chuckled and wiped her mouth again, then turned to glance at the sole survivor of the hijack force. He sat against another landing leg, manacled to the pad gimbal and watching her with frightened eyes.

<*He's waiting for the thumbscrews,*> she thought to Tisiphone. <*Should we tell the poor bastard you already got it all?*>

<*We should bring* out *the thumbscrews.*>

<*Now, now. No need to get nasty.*> Alicia grinned as Tisiphone muttered something about impertinent mortals. Their prisoner was none other than the partner of Yerensky's Ching-Hai contact, and his plan to hijack his own associates' cargo—and murder anyone in his way to cover his tracks—had touched the Fury's vengefulness on the raw.

<*You should slay him and be done with it,*> she said.

<*I can't do that. It wouldn't be just,*> Alicia replied innocently, squinting into the dawn to watch a streamer of dust approach the shuttle. Another part of her watched

it through Megarea's assault boat sensors, and her grin grew as Tisiphone spluttered in her brain.

<Just? Just?! *You dare to speak of your foolish, useless justice for scum like this?! I have endured much from you, Little One, but—>*

<Oh, hush.> The Fury slithered to an incandescent stop, and Alicia pressed her advantage. *<I told you I believe in justice,>* she said, rising to her feet. The prisoner's head whipped around as he, too, heard the whine of approaching turbines, and his face went white. *<I also told you I believe in punishment. And unless I very much miss my guess, this is the people we were* supposed *to be meeting.>* She felt Tisiphone's sudden understanding, and her smile was cold and thin. *<In this instance, I think justice can best be served by letting him explain himself to his friends, don't you?>*

Chapter Twenty-one

The pages of Colonel McIlheny's latest report lay strewn about the carpet where Governor General Treadwell had flung them. Now the governor, his normally bland face an ugly shade of puce, half stood to lean across the conference table and glare at Rosario Gomez.

"I'm tired of excuses, Admiral," he grated. "If they *are* excuses and not a cover for something else. I find it remarkable that your units are so persistently *elsewhere* when these pirates strike!"

Gomez glared back at him with barely restrained fury, and he sneered.

"At best, your complete ineffectualness cost nine million lives on Elysium, and now *this*." His nostrils quivered as he inhaled harshly. "I suppose we should be grateful that the million-and-a-half people in Raphael weren't imperial subjects. No doubt you and your people are, at any rate. At least it didn't require you to face the enemy in combat!"

Rosario Gomez rose very slowly and put her own hands on the table. She leaned to meet him, her eyes flint, and her voice was very soft.

"Governor, you're a fool, and my people won't be your whipping boys."

"You're out of line, Admiral!" Treadwell snapped.

"I am not." Gomez's words were chipped ice. "Nothing in the Articles of War requires me to listen to insults simply because my *political* superior is under pressure. Your implication that I am unconcerned by the massacre of civilians—*any* civilians, imperial or El Grecan—is almost as contemptible as your aspersions upon the integrity and courage of my personnel. I have stated the force levels I believe the situation requires. You have rejected my requests for them. I have shared with you every scrap of intelligence in our possession. You have failed to suggest any further avenue we might pursue. I have stated repeatedly my belief, and that of my staff, that we have been penetrated at a high level, and you have disregarded the notion. I will welcome any court of inquiry Fleet or the Ministry of Colonies would care to nominate. In the meantime, *your* statements constitute more than sufficient grounds for a Court of Honor, and you may retract them or face one, Governor, because I will not submit to the slanders of a political appointee who has never commanded a fleet in space!"

Treadwell went absolutely white as the last salvo struck, and McIlheny held his breath. Fury smoked between those two granite profiles, and the colonel knew his admiral well. That last blow had been calculated with icy precision. The Iron Maiden didn't know what retreat was, but she was a just, fair-minded person, acutely sensitive to the total unfairness of such a remark. She knew precisely how wounding it would be, which said a great deal about her own emotional state. Yet it had been born of more than simple fury. It was a warning that there was a point beyond which Lady Rosario Gomez would not be pushed by God or the Devil, far less a mere imperial governor, and McIlheny prayed Treadwell retained enough control to recognize it.

Apparently he did. His knuckles pressed the tabletop as his hands clenched into fists, but he made himself sink back into his chair. Silence hung taut for a long moment, and then he exhaled a long breath.

"Very well, Lady Rosario." His voice was frozen helium, but the venom was suppressed, and Gomez resumed her own seat, eyes still locked with his. "I . . . regret any aspersions I may have cast upon your honor or that of your personnel. This—this *slaughter* has affected my judgment, but that neither excuses nor justifies my conduct. I apologize."

She nodded curtly, and he went on with that same frozen self-control.

"Nonetheless, and whatever our past force structure differences may have been, we now face a significantly graver position. The Empire hasn't suffered such casualties, military or civilian, since HRW-II, and the El Grecans' losses are proportionally far worse. You will, I trust, agree that it is no longer sufficient merely to deter or stop these raiders? That it has become imperative that we locate, pursue, and destroy them utterly?"

"I do," Admiral Gomez said shortly.

"Thank you." Treadwell produced a tight, bitter smile, devoid of any hint of warmth. "I may, perhaps, have been in error to oppose your earlier requests for lighter units. That, however, is now water under the bridge, and I have personally starcommed Countess Miller and Grand Duke Phillip to lay the situation before them. My impression is that they are fully aware of its seriousness, and the grand duke informs me that Senators Alwyn and Mojahek are pressing for a more vigorous response. I feel, therefore, that it has become far more likely that Lord Jurawski will respond favorably if I renew my request for additional battle squadrons with your support."

Gomez's lips thinned, and McIlheny felt her silent, sour bile. Months had passed while Treadwell held out for the heavier forces—months, he was certain, in which Gomez could have made major progress had her own, far more modest requests been met. They had not for one reason only: Treadwell had refused to endorse them. Deep inside, McIlheny knew, Gomez shared his suspicion that Treadwell saw this as his last opportunity to command, however indirectly, a major Fleet deployment, and he wondered how the governor's conscience could deal with the dead of Elysium and Ringbolt.

Not, perhaps, too well, judging by the exchange which had just ended.

Yet Treadwell was right in at least one respect. The situation *had* changed. The pirates, or whatever the hell they really were, had to be hunted down and destroyed, not merely stopped, and the political pressure to use whatever sledgehammer that required could not be ignored.

"I still feel that response is neither required nor the best available," Gomez said at last. She flicked her eyes briefly aside to Amos Brinkman, who had sat prudently silent throughout. He showed no inclination to break that silence now, and her gaze returned to Treadwell. "Nonetheless, sir, anything that gets us off dead center is better than nothing. I will support you *if* you will also request an immediate dispatch of all available light units in the meantime."

Treadwell sat like a stone, his mouth as tight as her own, and matched her glower for glower. Then, at last, he nodded.

Soft music played in the background as Benjamin McIlheny leaned back and plucked at his lower lip. The latest report from his handpicked internal security commander lay on the desk before him, and it made disturbing reading.

Enough Elysium survivors had been interviewed to conclusively prove that Commodore Trang had been duped into letting the enemy into decisive range without even alerting the planet. The colonel had run every possible reason for such suicidal overconfidence through the tactical simulator, and only one of them made any sense. The pirates had to have been detected on the way in, and that meant they *had* to have been identified as friendly. And, given the high degree of alert the entire sector had maintained for months, no system commander could have been fooled. Therefore, the incoming warship must have *been* friendly . . . or else have arrived at such a time and under such circumstances that Trang's people had very good reason to "know" it was.

So. Either it had been a real Fleet unit, or else it had timed its arrival to coincide with a scheduled arrival by something that was. Only there had been no scheduled traffic. McIlheny knew, for he'd personally read every official communication to Elysium. There were many ways pirates could have gotten their hands on ex-Fleet hulls—some members of the Ministry had argued for years that Fleet disposal policies were badly in need of overhaul—yet that wouldn't have helped without proper transponder codes *and* a scheduled arrival. A low-level agent might have provided the codes or, at least, enough data to cobble up something that looked legitimate, but no one below flag rank could have engineered a false shipping report to open the door.

No. Someone of the rank of commodore or—McIlheny shuddered—higher must have inserted a fake schedule into Trang's routine message traffic. Someone with access to the authentication protocols required to sneak it in and the ability to abstract and wipe the routine acknowledgment Trang must have sent back. Worst of all, someone who *knew* there would be no heavy units in the system when the raiders arrived.

The penetration was worse than he'd thought. It was *total*. Whoever was behind it must have access to his own reports and Admiral Gomez's complete deployment orders—must even have known El Greco was pulling its units out of Ringbolt for maneuvers.

He closed his eyes in pain at the scale of the treason that implied, but it wasn't really a surprise. Not anymore.

All right. No more than forty people had access to all of that data, and he knew precisely who they were. Any one of them might, conceivably, have passed it to someone outside the loop who had the command authority to doctor Trang's starcom traffic, but if they could do that without his spotting them, their chain of communications had to be both short and hellishly well-hidden. In his own mind, it came down to no more than a dozen possible suspects . . . all of whom had passed every security check he could throw at them. It *couldn't* be one of them, and at the same time, it *had* to be.

He straightened and lifted a chip from his desk, weighing it in his fingers. Thank God he'd arranged a link to Keita. He was becoming so paranoid he no longer completely trusted even Admiral Gomez, and the deadly miasma of distrust and fear was getting to him. He'd started seeing assassins in every shadow, which was bad enough, if not as bad as the sense that nothing he did could stop the inexorable murder of civilians he was sworn to protect.

But worst of all was his absolute conviction that whatever twisted strategy lay behind these "pirates" was winding to its climax. Time was running out. If he couldn't break this open—if he was not permitted to live long enough to break it open—the vermin orchestrating the atrocities were going to succeed, and that was obscene.

He stood, face hard with purpose, and slipped the chip into his pocket beside the one already there. One would be dropped into his secret pipeline to Keita; the other would be delivered to Admiral Gomez, and both contained his conclusion that someone of flag rank was directly involved with the raiders. But unlike the one to Keita, Admiral Gomez's stated unequivocally that he would know the traitor's identity within the next few weeks.

Benjamin McIlheny was a Marine, bound by oath and conscience alike to lay down his life in defense of the Empire. He would deliver those chips, and then he would take a little vacation time . . . without extra security. It was the only way to test his theory, for if he was right, the traitor couldn't let him live. The attempt to silence him would confirm his theory for Sir Arthur, and Sir Arthur and the Cadre would know what to do with it.

And who knew? He might actually survive.

Chapter Twenty-two

Alicia took another swallow and decided she'd been wrong; Ching-Hai did have one redeeming feature.

She rolled the chill bottle across her forehead and savored the rich, clean taste of the beer. Monsieur Labin's offices boasted what passed for air-conditioning on Ching-Hai, but the temperature was still seven degrees higher than the one Megarea maintained aboard ship. No doubt the climate helped explain the locals' excellent breweries.

The old-fashioned office door rattled, and she straightened in her chair, lowering the bottle as Gustav Labin, Yerensky's Ching-Hai agent, stepped through it. Unlike Alicia's, his round, bland face was dry, but he didn't even crack a smile as she wiped a fresh drop of sweat from her nose. Not because he lacked the normal Ching-Haian's amusement at off-worlders' want of heat tolerance, but because he was afraid of her. Indeed, he regarded her with a certain fixed dread, as if she were a warhead which might choose to detonate any time. He'd been looking at her that way ever since he arrived to find her sitting amid the ruins of the botched hijacking. Tisiphone had needed only a single handshake to confirm that Labin had known nothing of his (now deceased) partner's intentions . . . and that "Captain Mainwaring's" reputation as a dangerous woman had been made forever.

Now he lowered himself into his chair and cleared a nervous throat.

"I've completed the manifest verification, Captain. It checks perfectly, as—" he hastened to add "—I was certain it would." He drew a credit transfer chip from a drawer. "The balance of your payment, Captain."

"Thank you, monsieur. It's been a pleasure." Alicia kept her face straight, but it was hard. Those poor, half-assed hijackers had been totally beyond their depth. Killing, even in self-defense and even of scum like that, never sat easily with her afterward, yet Labin's near terror amused her. If he ever saw a regular Cadre assault he'd die on the spot.

<And the universe would be a better place for it,> Tisiphone observed. *<This man is a* worm, *Little One.>*

<Now, now. He's all of that, but he's also our ticket to Dewent . . . whenever he gets around to mentioning it.>

The Fury sniffed, but it was her probe which had discovered Labin's shipment. Given its nature and the stature Alicia enjoyed in his eyes, they hadn't even had to "push" him into seeing her as the perfect carrier.

"Ah, yes. A pleasure for me, as well, Captain. And allow me to apologize once more. I assure you neither Anton nor I ever suspected my colleague might attempt to attack you."

"I never thought otherwise," Alicia murmured, and he managed a smile.

"I'm glad. And, of course, impressed. Indeed, Captain, I have another small consignment, one which must be delivered to Dewent, and your, um, demonstrated expertise could be very much a plus to me. It's quite a valuable cargo, and I've been concerned over its security. Concerned enough," he leaned forward a bit, "to pay top credit to a reliable carrier."

"I see." Alicia sipped more beer, then shook her head.

"It sounds to me like you think your 'concern' could end in more shooting, monsieur, and I prefer not to carry cargoes I *know* are going to attract hijacks."

"I understand entirely, and I may be worrying over nothing. Certainly I have no solid evidence of any danger. I merely prefer to be safe rather than sorry, and I'm willing to invest a bit in security. I thought, perhaps, an increase of fifteen percent over your fee to Anton might be appropriate?"

"My fee to Mister Yerensky didn't include combat expenses," Alicia pointed out, "and shuttle missiles are hard to come by out here. I expect replacing expenditures to cut into my profit margin on this trip."

"Twenty percent, then?"

"I don't know. . . ." Alicia allowed her voice to trail off. Thanks to Tisiphone, she knew Labin was willing to go to thirty or even thirty-five percent to secure her services, and while she wasn't particularly interested in running up the price, neither did she wish to appear too eager. Tisiphone could shape his decisions, but she couldn't guarantee something wouldn't come along later and make him wonder *why* he'd chosen a given course.

"Twenty-five," Labin offered.

"Make it thirty," she said. Labin winced but nodded, and she smiled. "In that case, if I may use your com?" She reached for the terminal, and Labin sat back as she entered a code. A moment later, the screen lit with Ruth Tanner's face.

"Yes, Captain?" Megarea asked in Tanner's voice.

"We've got a new charter, Ruth. We'll be headed to Dewent for Monsieur Labin. Ready to crunch a few numbers?"

"Of course, Captain."

"Good." Alicia turned the terminal to face Labin and leaned back. "If you'll be good enough to settle the details with my purser, monsieur?"

<I do not like this cargo,> Tisiphone groused.

"I'm not crazy about it myself," Alicia replied, frowning at the chessboard. She and Megarea had taught the

Fury the game, and Alicia and Tisiphone were surprisingly well-matched, though it took both of them together just to lose to the AI.

<*None of us are,*> Megarea put in, <*but we needed one going to Dewent.*>

"Exactly." Alicia nodded and started to reach for a knight.

<*Wouldn't do that, Alley,*> Megarea whispered. <*Her bishop'll—*>

<Will *you two cease that?!*>

<*Cease what, Tis?*> Megarea asked innocently.

<*You know very well what. Or did you truly think you could think so softly I would not hear you?*>

"It wath worth a try," Lieutenant Chisholm said from a speaker. "And only a nathty, thuthpithous perthon would have been lithening, anyway."

<*No one except one who knows* you, *you mean.*>

Alicia bit her lip against a giggle, but she didn't quite dare take advantage of Megarea's kibitzing now. So she moved her knight, instead, and sighed as Tisiphone's bishop lashed out and captured her king's rook.

<*Check,*> the Fury said smugly.

"You really are a nasty person. If I was virtuous enough not to listen to Megarea, you could've reciprocated by leaving my poor rook alone."

<*Nonsense. You yourself call this a "war game," and one does not surrender an honorably gained advantage in war, Little One. Nor, I suppose,*> the mental voice grew more thoughtful, <*even a dis*honorably *gained advantage.*>

"Absolutely," Alicia said sweetly, and captured the bishop with her other knight . . . simultaneously forking Tisiphone's king and queen. It exposed her own queen's bishop, but that was fine with her. The only square to which Tisiphone could move her king was one knight's move from her queen. "Check yourself."

<*By golly, I didn't even notice that one!*> Megarea observed in a tone of artful innocence while the Fury seethed.

"Neither did I," Alicia asserted with a grin. Tisiphone

moved her king, and Alicia took her queen. "Check," she said again, and used the breathing space to move her bishop out of danger.

<*Hmph! And Odysseus was a credulous fool. Yet we have wandered from my earlier point, Little One. Advantage or no, I dislike this cargo of ours.*>

"I know," Alicia sighed, and she did know. Anton Yerensky's cargo to Ching-Hai had been illegal but essentially beneficial; Gustav Labin's cargo to Dewent was also pharmaceutical, but that was the sole similarity. "Dreamy White" was harmless enough to its users, aside from a hundred percent rate of addiction, but it was hideously expensive . . . and even more hideously obtained. It was an endorphin derivative, and while it could be produced in the lab, there were far cheaper ways. Most Dreamy White was harvested from the brains of human beings, with consequences for the "donor" which ranged from massive retardation and motor control loss to death.

<*We should not have taken it,*> the Fury said grimly.

"Aren't you the one who told me anything we do in pursuit of vengeance is acceptable?" Alicia's voice was sharper than intended—because, she knew, Tisiphone was simply saying what all of them felt—yet she could taste the other's surprise as her own words were thrown back at her.

<*Perhaps. Yet* you *were the one who argued for "justice,"*> Tisiphone shot back gamely. <*How can this be just?*>

"I don't know that it is," Alicia said more slowly, "but I also don't see that we have any choice. And it's certainly the kind of cargo that'll get us in with the people we need to infiltrate."

The Fury's silence was an unhappy acceptance, and Alicia wondered if Tisiphone was as aware as she of the irony of their positions. She, who believed passionately in justice, had compromised her principles in the pursuit of her prey, leaving it to the Fury, who spoke only of vengeance, to question the morality of their gruesome cargo.

<*Perhaps,*> Tisiphone repeated at last. <*Yet perhaps*

there is something after all to this concept of law, as well. Man had turned his hand to evils enough when my sisters and I were one, but all of them pale beside those he has the tools to wreak today, and not even my vengeance can undo an evil once committed. So perhaps this justice, these "rules" of yours, are more important than once I thought.>

Alicia sat still, eyes widening to hear the Fury admit even a part of her argument, but she felt a tugging at her right hand. She relinquished control and watched it reach out to advance a rook.

<*Guard yourself, Little One! You may have slowed my attack, but you have not stopped it.*>

Alicia smiled and bent over the board once more, yet there was a chill in her heart, for she knew Tisiphone referred to far more than a chess game.

Dewent was a much nicer planet than Ching-Hai, Alicia thought. In part, that was because it was much wetter, a world of archipelagoes and island continents, and cooler, but it was also closer to civilized. Not a great deal closer, perhaps, yet no one had attempted to rob or kill her, and that was a definite improvement.

Unlike Ching-Hai, Dewent had a customs service, but it was concerned only with insuring that the local government got its cut on outgoing cargoes, and Alicia had set the cargo shuttle neatly down at Dewent's main spaceport unmolested by anything so crass as an inspection. The *Bengal* had grounded beside her like a garishly-painted shadow or a pointed hint that politeness would be wise, but it stayed sealed. Alicia had been at some pains to maintain an open com link to it, chattering away with "Jeff Okahara," its ostensible pilot and "*Star Runner's*" executive officer, and Okahara's return chatter had made no bones about what would happen to anyone who *wasn't* polite.

Two hours later, she stood in a port warehouse while her receiver examined his cargo. Edward Jacoby looked like a respectable accountant, but he clearly knew what he was about. He needed no biochemist to test the drugs for purity; the six men standing around the warehouse were there for another reason. Few weapons were in evidence, but these men were far more dangerous than the bumbling hijackers of Ching-Hai. More, Alicia had seen their eyes as they flicked over her and recognized a fellow predator.

Jacoby finished his tests and began putting away his equipment. He didn't smile—he didn't seem the sort for smiles—but he looked satisfied.

"Well, Captain Mainwaring," he said as the last instrument vanished, "I was a bit anxious when Gustav starcommed that he was using a complete unknown, but his judgment was excellent. How would you like payment?"

"I think I'd prefer an electronic transfer, this time," she replied. "I'd rather not carry around a credit chip quite that large."

One of Jacoby's guards made a sound suspicously like a chuckle, and the merchant came as close to a smile as he probably ever did. His eyes dropped to her holstered disrupter and the knife hilt protruding from her left boot—the only weapons she'd chosen to let anyone see—but he simply nodded.

"As wise as you are efficient, I see. Very well, my accountant will complete the transfer at your convenience."

"Thank you." Alicia's smile was dazzling. Try as she might, she'd been unable to disagree with Tisiphone's verdict on their cargo, but after considerable thought, she and her companions had hit upon a way to salve their consciences. Alicia was too honest to think it was anything more, yet it was better than nothing. When Ruth Tanner executed that credit transfer from Jacoby's house computers, Megarea and Tisiphone intended to raid his system for every off-world shipping contact. So armed, the AI should be able to determine which were legitimate (assuming any were) and which were likely to receive shipments of Dreamy White in the near future, and Alicia intended to starcom the appropriate local authorities from their next stop. That wouldn't get Jacoby himself, but *no one* wanted Dreamy White on his planet, and the consequences for his distribution network should be . . . extreme.

"Well!" Jacoby closed the case with a snap and nodded to one of his men, who began hauling the two counter-gravity pallets towards the security area. "Tell, me, Captain, would you join me for lunch? I'm always looking for reliable carriers—we might well be able to do some more business."

"Lunch, certainly, but unless your business is going in the right direction, I'm afraid I'll have to give that a pass." And she hoped to God she could; she wanted to carry no more mass death in her hold.

"Ah?" Jacoby regarded her with a thoughtful expression. "What direction would that be, Captain?"

"I've got a charter commitment waiting on Cathcart," Alicia lied. Cathcart was an extremely respectable Rogue World, and she had no intention of going anywhere near it, but it lay almost directly beyond Wyvern.

"Cathcart, Cathcart," Jacoby murmured then shook his head. "No, I'm afraid I don't have anything bound in that direction just now. Still, there's something . . ." His voice trailed off in thought, and then he snapped his fingers. "Of course! One of my associates has a consignment for Wyvern. Would that be of interest to you?"

"Wyvern?" Alicia managed to keep the excitement out of her voice and cocked her head in thought. "That might fit in nicely, if we're not talking about too much cubage. *Star Runner*'s forte is speed, not bulk."

"That shouldn't be a problem. I have the impression speed is of the essence in this case, and while it's fairly massive it's also low bulk—military spares and molycircuitry, I believe. But we could check; Lewis and I share warehousing facilities here. Step this way a moment."

Alicia followed him, fighting to contain her exultation. Wyvern *and* military supplies? It was too good to be true! She managed to keep her thoughts from showing as they crossed a more heavily traveled portion of the warehouse, but her brain was busy. She paused to let a warehouse tractor putter past, towing a line of empty pallets, so wrapped in her tumbling thoughts she didn't even look up when the small, almost painfully nondescript driver glanced her way. She told herself not to get her hopes up, that it was probably mere coincidence, but it certainly sounded like—

They reached their destination, and Jacoby pointed out the stacked pallets of the shipment. He was speaking to her, describing their contents in greater detail, but Alicia didn't hear him. She heard nothing at all, and it couldn't have mattered less. Whatever those details were, there was no way in the galaxy she would allow anyone else to carry this cargo.

Maintaining her politely interested smile was the hardest thing she had ever done, for hunger seethed behind her eyes, mirrored and fanned by Tisiphone's reaction, as her gaze devoured the racks beside the pallets. They bore the same shipper's codes, but their red tags, marked with the dragon-like customs stamp of Wyvern, indicated an incoming shipment. Rack after rack, an incredible number of them, and she could see why they were in the security area . . . for each of them was heavy with the priceless, snow-white pelts of the deadly carnivore known as Mathison's Direcat.

Book Three: Fury

Chapter Twenty-three

The man on Alicia's com screen was as civilized looking as Edward Jacoby, but Alicia knew he was the one she'd come to find. Direcats were bigger than Old Earth kodiaks, with fangs a saber-tooth would have envied, and they were not omnivorous. A carnivore that size required a huge range, even on virgin Mathison's World, and the government had regulated direcat hunting with an iron hand. Those warehouse racks contained at least a full year's pelts—and could have come from only one source.

And so she smiled at the face on her screen, smiled politely, with only professional interest, even as everything within her screamed to touch him and rip away the knowledge she must have.

"Good evening, Captain Mainwaring. My name is Lewis Fuchien. I'm glad I caught you groundside."

"So am I. Mister Jacoby said you might screen."

"Indeed. I understand my consignment falls within your vessel's capacity?" Fuchien asked, and she nodded. "Excellent. While your fee initially seemed a bit high, Edward has shared Monsieur Labin's report with me, and—"

"I hope you didn't take it at face value," Alicia interrupted wryly. "Monsieur Labin was rather more impressed than circumstances merited."

"Modesty is admirable, Captain Mainwaring, and I realize Gustav Labin is a bit excitable, but Edward assures me you'd take good care of my cargo."

"That much, at least, is true, sir. When someone entrusts me with a shipment, I do my best to insure it reaches its destination."

"No shipper could ask for more. However—" Fuchien smiled pleasantly "—I *would* like to meet the rest of your ship's company. It's a policy of mine to consider the reliability of a crew as a whole, not just its captain."

"I see." Alicia's face showed nothing, but her mind raced with tick-like speed, conferring with Tisiphone and Megarea on a level deeper than vocalization and far, far faster than conscious thought. She couldn't very well bring her nonexistent crew down to have lunch with the man! But—

"Did Mister Jacoby mention my Cathcart charter?" Fuchien nodded, and she smiled. "I certainly understand your caution, and frankly, I'd feel happier myself if my purser could sit in on our discussions, but my engineer and exec are buried in a drive recalibration. I really can't interrupt them—in fact, I ought to be up there helping out right now—given our time pressure for Cathcart, but if *you* have a free hour or so, may I offer you *Star Runner*'s hospitality for supper? The food may not be five-star, but I think you'll find it palatable, and it'll give you the chance not only to meet my people but look the ship over in person, as well. If you like what you see, you, my purser, and I can settle the details over brandy. Would that be convenient?"

"Why, thank you! That's far more than I'd hoped for, and I'd be very happy to accept, if I may include my own accountant."

"Of course. I'll be taking my cargo shuttle back up at seventeen-thirty hours. Would you care to accompany me, or arrange your own transport?"

"If you won't mind seeing us home again, we'll ride up with you."

"No problem, Mister Fuchien. I'll expect you then."

Fuchien and his accountant—a short, stout woman with laugh wrinkles around computer-sharp eyes—arrived at the shuttle ramp precisely on time, and Alicia was waiting at its foot, tall and professional in her midnight blue uniform. Their brief handshakes lasted barely long enough to skim the surface of their thoughts, but that was sufficent to confirm her suspicions.

"Captain, may I present Sondra McSwain, my accountant?"

"Pleased to meet you, Ms. McSwain."

"Likewise, Captain. After what Mister Fuchien's told me about your reputation, I expected you to be three meters tall!"

"Reputations always grow in the telling, I think." Alicia grinned back. McSwain's mind held neither the scummy taint she'd picked up from Labin nor the cultured avarice she read in Fuchien. It ticked like a precision instrument, skilled and professional but laced with a sense of humor, and Alicia's grin turned wry. How odd to find an incorruptible person on a planet like Dewent!

She shook herself and gestured at the ramp.

"Mister Fuchien. Ms. McSwain. We have clearance and my crew is preparing to roll out the carpet."

The flight up was routine, but the accountant's obvious delight made it seem otherwise. Ms. McSwain, Alicia decided, seldom saw the insides of the ships and shuttles that thronged Dewent's port facilities. Even this short jaunt was an exotic treat for her, yet she had the ability to recognize her own excitement for what it was and laugh at it. Alicia found herself explaining instruments and procedures with unfeigned cheer, and even Fuchien allowed himself to smile at her drum roll questions.

They were halfway to rendezvous when Tisiphone nudged Alicia.

<You are forgetting our purpose, Little One, and an illusion of this complexity requires preparation. May I suggest we begin?>

<*I guess so,*> Alicia sighed, <*but I think I'm going to enjoy this less than I expected. Why the hell does she have to be so nice?*>

<*Have no fear,*> the Fury said with unusual gentleness. <*Megarea and I also like her. We will allow no harm to befall her, yet we must begin soon.*>

<*Gotcha.*>

Alicia turned her head and smiled at McSwain as the accountant's questions temporarily ran down.

"There's a member of my crew I want you to meet, Ms. McSwain. A colleague of yours, you might say. Forgive us, but we were expecting a stringy, dried-up cold fish of a credit-cruncher." McSwain met her eyes, and they chuckled together. "I think Ruth is going to be pleasantly surprised."

"I once had a 'stringy, dried-up cold fish,' " Fuchien confessed, "but he fell afoul of an audit. Sondra is a vast improvement, I assure you."

"And I believe you." Alicia keyed a com screen alight with Ruth Tanner's face. "Ruth? Forget Plan A and go to Plan B. Mister Fuchien's accountant is human after all."

"Really? What a nice change," Megarea replied in Ruth's voice. Her image's eyes swept the cockpit until they found McSwain, and Ruth's face smiled. "Goodness! Who would've thought someone on this chauvinist backwater would have enough sense to hire a woman!" Her eyes cut to Fuchien's face, and her smile became a grin. "Oops! Did I just put my foot in my mouth?"

"Not with me," Fuchien assured her. "My colleagues' shortsightedness in that respect is my gain, Ms. Tanner. You *are* Ms. Tanner, I presume?"

"In the flesh," Megarea replied. "I hope you'll enjoy your visit. We don't entertain often, so we're putting our best foot forward, and . . ."

The conversation rolled on, and neither Fuchien nor McSwain noticed when their eyes began to turn just a bit disoriented.

* * *

This, Alicia thought, was the strangest thing they'd tried yet. In her present, straitened condition, Tisiphone would have found herself hard put to weave an illusion half this complex. But she wasn't forced to weave it alone, for Megarea had opened a direct tap to the Fury, throwing her own tremendous capacity behind the spell like a gigantic amplifier that restored Tisiphone, however briefly, to the peak of her long lost power.

And with that aid, the Fury surpassed herself. She wove her web with consummate skill, ensnaring both her guests and extending a tendril of herself to Alicia, as well. It was an eerie sensation, even for one who had become accustomed to the bizarre, for Alicia inhabited three worlds at once. She saw once through her own senses, again through Megarea's internal sensors, and last of all, she *shared* her guests' illusion. She sat with them at supper, chatting with Megarea's other selves while the AI provided their conversation and Tisiphone gave them flesh, even as she sat alone with them at the table. It was almost terrifying, for it wasn't what the Fury had done to Lieutenant Giolitti. There would be no hazed memories or implanted suggestions. This was *real*. Backed by the AI's enormous power, Tisiphone took them all one step out of phase with the universe and made her reality theirs.

Nor was that all she did. There was no rush, and she plumbed Lewis Fuchien's memories to their depths, filing away every scrap of a fact which might be of use. By supper's end, they knew everything he did, and the merchant was convinced Captain Mainwaring's crew was perfect for his needs.

The meal ended, and the entire crew—except Tanner—"excused" itself to return to duty. Fuchien lifted his brandy and sipped appreciatively.

"Well, Captain Mainwaring, you and your people have not only met my standards but far exceeded my hopes. I believe we can do business."

"I'm delighted to hear it." Alicia sat back with her own brandy and smiled, then gestured at the empty chair which held her purser's ghost. "In that case, why don't you and I sit back while Ruth and Sondra do battle?"

"An excellent idea, Captain." Fuchien beamed. "Simply excellent."

Dewent dewindled in the galley view screen as *Megarea's* velocity mounted, and Alicia watched it while she tried to define her own emotions. A complex broth of anticipation, hunger, and fear—fear that she might yet blow her chance—simmered within her, and over it all lay a haze of excitement as she looked ahead to Wyvern, mingled with relief at leaving Dewent astern.

She still didn't like Fuchien, but neither did she *dis*like him as much as she had expected. He was as ambitious and credit-hungry as Jacoby, but without the other's outright evil. He knew of his associate's drug deals yet took no part in them, and while he suspected his Wyvern contact of fencing goods for the pirates terrorizing the sector, he himself had had no direct dealings with them. He disapproved of them, in a depressingly mild sort of way, yet it was unrealistic to expect more from him. He was a Dewentan, and servicing "outlaws" was what Dewent did. By his own lights, Lewis Fuchien was an admirable and honest businessman, and Alicia could almost understand that.

That was one reason she was glad to leave, for she didn't *want* to understand it. On a more pragmatic level, their departure meant her and her "crew's" deception only had to stand up for one last planet. Only one, and then she didn't care who knew. Fleet was welcome to pursue her. Indeed, she would welcome their pursuit if her flight could lead them to the pirates.

She leaned her elbows on the edge of the console, propping her chin in her hands and brooding down on the rapidly diminishing image, and let her mind reach out ahead. Wyvern. The planet Wyvern and a man named Oscar Quintana, Lieutenant Commander Defiant. Wyvern had a peculiar aristocracy, with no use for titles like "baron" or "count." Their ancestors had been naval officers—little more than freebooter refuse from the centuries-past League Wars, perhaps, but naval officers—and the ship name appended to Quintana's title indicated that he sprang from one of the founding noble houses. Peculiar as it might sound to off-world ears, he'd be a powerful man, probably a proud and dangerous one, and it behooved her to approach him with caution.

<*Hey,*> Megarea interrupted her thoughts, <*don't get too bothered, Alley! If he knows what's good for him, he'll approach* us *with caution.*>

<*True,*> Tisiphone seconded. <*Indeed, Little One, unless we are much mistaken, this Quintana must be a direct contact for the ones we seek. If so, I shall turn him inside out with the greatest pleasure.*>

"You two are in a bloodthirsty mood," Alicia observed. "Or are you just worried that I'm getting ready to funk out?"

<*Us?*> Megarea was innocence itself. <*Perish the thought.*>

"Sure." Alicia stood and yawned, stretching the tension from her shoulders and grateful to be distracted from her moodiness. "As a matter of fact, I'm not that worried over Quintana. If he's what we think he is, I hereby give you both carte blanche for anything we have to do to him."

<*My thanks, Little One—not that I intended to wait upon your permission to deal harshly with such scum.*>

"Oh, yeah? Harsh is okay with me, but remember—even if he's a direct link, we still need to get to the next step. I'm afraid that may limit what we can do to him. I mean, we couldn't even squash that slime Jacoby."

<*Ah, funny you should mention that, Alley.*> Megarea's elaborately casual voice set off a clangor of warning bells, and Alicia's eyebrows rose.

"I know that tone," she said. "What've you been up to?"

<*It wasn't just me,*> the AI said quickly. <*I mean, I thought it was a great idea, but I couldn't have done it by myself.*>

"You fill me with dread—and you're stalling."

<*It was your idea, Tis. Why don't you explain?*>

<*But I could not have accomplished it without your expertise, and you have a better grasp of the details, so perhaps you should explain.*> The Fury's tone was serious, yet Alicia felt her amusement. She put her hands on her hips and glared at the empty air.

"*One* of you had better trot it out, ladies!"

<*Well, it's like this, Alley. You remember when we made that credit transfer and Tis and I raided Jacoby's data base?*>

"Of course I do," Alicia said, then paused. "Did you horrid creatures put something *into* it? You didn't hit him with a virus, did you?"

<*Of course not,*> Megarea said virtuously. <*What a horrible idea! I'd never do something like that—not even to a fossil like that Jurgens Twelve of his. Not that it might not have been kinder. That relic should've been scrapped years ago, Alley. It's so stupid—*>

"Quit stalling! What did you do?!"

<*We didn't put a thing into it. Instead, we took something out.*>

"Besides the information on his distribution network?"

<*Well, yes. I guess to be perfectly honest, we* did *put something in, but it's only a delayed extraction program.*>

"What *kind* of extraction program?"

<*A starcom credit transfer.*>

"A *credit transfer*? You mean you *robbed* him?"

<*If you want to put it that way. But we talked it over, and, personally, I think Tis was right. You can't really rob a thief, can you?*>

"Of course you can rob a thief!" Alicia closed her eyes and flopped back into her chair. "I thought you were supposed to have *my* value system!"

<*And so she does, but I am making some progress with her. Rather more than with you, in fact.*>

"I just bet you are," Alicia muttered, running her fingers through her hair. "All right, how much did you hit him for?"

<*All of it,*> Megarea said in a small voice.

"All of what?"

<*All of everything. We found all his hidden accounts as well as the open ones, and we, well, we sort of cleaned him out.*>

"You—" Alicia gurgled to a stop, and pregnant silence hovered in her stunned mind. But then her closed eyes popped open as panic cut through her shock. "Good God Almighty, Megarea! What do you think he's going to do when he figures out *we* robbed him?! We can't afford that kind of—"

<*Peace, Little One. He will not realize we were to blame.*>

"How do you know?! Damn it, who *else* is he going to suspect?!"

<*That I cannot tell you, but it will not be us, for the theft has not yet occurred. Nor will it . . . until he orders his first off-planet credit transfer to one of his drug-distributing cronies. Megarea was very clever, and I rather expect—*> the Fury's dry delight was unmistakable <*—that he will suspect whichever of his fellow thieves he has attempted to pay.*>

"You mean—?"

<*Exactly, Alley. See, what'll happen is the first time he orders a payment to one of the accounts I listed in my program, it'll automatically dump every credit he has into the transfer and then reroute it. His payee won't see a centicredit, but the program'll bootstrap itself—and the transfer—through his starcom, then transmit itself back out. And it'll erase itself from each system it moves through till it reaches its destination, too.*>

"Oh, Lord!" Alicia moaned, covering her eyes with her hands. "I *never* should have inflicted you two on an unsuspecting galaxy! Just where—if I dare ask—will this wandering program finally end its criminal days?"

<*It'll probably take it a while to make connections, but it's headed for Thaarvlhd. I set it up to open a numbered account when it gets there.*>

"Thaarvlhd?" Alicia repeated blankly. Then, "*Thaarvlhd?!* My God, that's the Quarn Hegemony's central banking hub for this sector! Damn it, the Quarn take money *seriously*, Megarea! Violating Thaarvlhd's banking laws isn't a harmless little prank like murder!"

<*I didn't violate a thing. They're used to orders like this one, and I included all the documentation they need.*>

"Documentation?"

<*Sure. They don't care about names, but I included everything they want on human accounts: your retinal prints, your genetic pri—*>

"*My* prints?!" Alicia yelped. "You opened an account in *my* name?!"

<*Of course not. I just explained they don't* use *names, Alley. That's why they're so popular.*>

"Sweet Suffering Jesus!" Alicia never knew exactly how long she sat there, staring at nothing, but then a thought occurred to her. "Uh, Megarea."

<*Yes?*>

"I'm not condoning what you've done—not *condemning* it either, you understand, or at least not yet—but I was wondering. . . . Just how much did you two rip him off for?"

<*Hard to say, since we don't know exactly when the program'll trip.*>

"A rough estimate will do," Alicia said in a fascinated tone.

<*Well, using his last two years' cash flow as a basis, I'd say somewhere between two hundred fifty and three hundred million credits.*>

"Two hun—" Alicia closed her mouth with a snap. Then she began to giggle—giggles that gave way to howls of laughter. She couldn't help herself. She leaned forward, hugging her ribs and laughing till her chest hurt and her eyes teared. Laughing as she had not laughed in months, with pure, devilish delight as she pictured ultra-civilized Edward Jacoby's reaction. And she'd thought they couldn't hurt him! Dear God, he wouldn't have a pot to piss in, and he'd never even know who'd done it!

She pummeled the deck with her feet, wailing with laughter, until she could get control of herself again, then straightened slowly, gasping for breath and mopping her eyes.

<*I take it you are less displeased than you anticipated?*> Tisiphone asked mildly, and Alicia giggled again.

"Stop that!" she said unsteadily. "Don't you dare set me off again! Oh. Oh, *my!* He *is* going to be upset, isn't he?"

<*It seemed an appropriate—and just—way to deal with him.*>

"Damn straight it did!" Alicia shook herself, then straightened sternly. "Don't you two think you can get away with something like this again—not without checking with me first, anyway! But just this once, I think I'll forgive you."

<*Yeah, for about three hundred million reasons, I'd guess,*> Megarea sniffed, and Alicia dissolved into laughter once more.

Chapter Twenty-four

The assembled officers rose as Rachel Shu followed Howell into the briefing room. More than one set of eyes were a bit apprehensive, for the intelligence officer had just returned from meeting Control's latest messenger, and Howell's people were only too well aware of the casualties they'd taken on Ringbolt.

Howell took his place at the head of the table and watched his subordinates sit, then nodded to Shu.

"All right, Commander. Let's hear it."

"Yes, sir." Shu cleared her throat, set a notepad on the table, and keyed the tiny screen alive. "First, Control sends us all a well done on the Ringbolt operation." Breath sighed out around the table, and Howell smiled wryly. "He regrets our losses, but under the circumstances, he understands why they were so high, and it appears both our primary and secondary missions were complete successes."

She paused, and Howell listened to a soft murmur of pleasure walk around the room. How many of those officers, he wondered, ever really spent a few hours thinking about what they'd done? Not many—perhaps none. *He* certainly tried to avoid the memories, though it was growing harder. Yet it was often that way. There were things he'd done in the service of the Crown which he tried just as hard never to remember. This wasn't that much different, he told himself, and pretended that he didn't know he lied.

Of course, much of their pleasure stemmed from the fact that they'd expected to be reamed. A pat on the back always felt better when one had anticipated a rap in the mouth. That much *was* the same as in the Fleet.

He let the murmurs run on a moment longer, then tapped his knuckles on the tabletop. Silence fell once more, and he nodded to Shu.

"Preliminary evaluation of the captured data," the commander continued, keying the advance to display the next screen as she picked up her report again, "indicates we probably secured more from Ringbolt than we would have from Elysium, and our financial backers are delighted. Control asked me to tell you all that their support has firmed up very nicely once more, and that most of them seem convinced we know what we're doing after all.

"On another front, the Ringbolt attack has apparently produced the desired effect in the Senate and Ministry. Control didn't want to come right out and say so, but he seems confident that ONI and Marine Intelligence on Old Earth are coming to precisely the conclusions we want, and pressure from the Senate is growing every day. Best of all, public opinion here in the sector itself is shaping up *very* nicely. 'Panic' might be putting it too strongly, but there's widespread anxiety and an increasing perception that the imperial government is powerless to stop us."

Shu touched the advance key again and allowed herself a small frown.

"We do have one unanticipated complication. Apparently, one of the people killed on Ringbolt was Simon Monkoto's brother Arlen." Howell sat a bit straighter and saw others do the same at mention of that name. Shu saw it, too, and her smile was wintry. "We all know Monkoto's reputation, but his outfit isn't up to our weight even if he knew where to find us. The problem is that he's calling in a lot of debts from his colleagues, and most of them are angry enough over Ringbolt to throw in with him even if they didn't owe him. Among them, they may be able to assemble an independent force that *is* a threat, and because they're independents, Control's ability to track them will be much lower than for the regular El Grecan Navy. On the other hand, they *are* independents. Their fleets represent their working capital, and they can't tie them up indefinitely on this kind of altruistic operation."

"What's the chance of El Greco picking up the tab?" Alexsov asked.

"Unknown. Mercenaries of Monkoto's caliber normally don't come cheap, but these aren't normal circumstances. I don't now about the others, but the Maniacs'll probably settle for basic expenses with no profit margin, and that could make them extremely attractive to El Greco. Still, that might work in our favor. If they hire on with El Greco, the El Grecans will tie them into a comprehensive strategy. Under normal circumstances, that would make them even more dangerous; as it is, they'd simply be easier to watch—and avoid—given the joint planning between the Empire and the El Grecans."

Alexsov nodded thoughtfully, and Shu shrugged.

"Control isn't too concerned about them at present. As I say, they'd have to find us before they could hurt us, even if they managed to assemble enough firepower to come after us. It's unlikely they can do that, but Control isn't taking any chances. He wants us to relocate to the AR-Twelve site as soon as possible to get us further away from El Greco."

"Makes sense," Howell agreed. "And it sounds like we're in pretty good shape, if Monkoto is Control's worst worry."

"He is and he isn't, sir," Shu said. "Control's arranging recruitment to make good our Ringbolt losses, and he's managed to scare up two new BCs to replace *Poltava*."

Howell grunted. Crewing two more battle-cruisers might

stretch them thin, but the firepower would be well worth the inconvenience.

"In the meantime, though, Control himself is going to have to stay close to Soissons, because that's the most delicate problem area just now. In particular, McIlheny seems to be getting closer than we'd like. According to Control's courier, he's currently promising some significant report to Admiral Gomez and Governor Treadwell. Control couldn't hold the dispatch boat, so we don't know what sort of report, but he informs me that he's prepared to deal with it, whatever it is. Assuming he's right—and he usually is—our only other local concern is Admiral Gomez. She's backed off just a bit and endorsed Treadwell's request for heavier units, which may divert some of the pressure for her relief." Shu shrugged again. "If so, we'll simply have to proceed with the backup plan and eliminate her. We're looking at several options for that, but Control is leaning towards passing us her itinerary. She's taken to traveling about in *Antietam* with minimal escorts in the interest of speed; if he can pass us her schedule, we might be able to intercept and take her out. In many ways, that would be the ideal solution, given her popularity with the Fleet. It would not only get rid of her but turn her into a martyr and provide yet another reason for Fleet to go after the nasty pirates."

Her smile was most unpleasant, and Howell hid an inner shiver. He'd served under Gomez, and while he was willing to admit she might have to be eliminated, he didn't look forward to it. Shu obviously did. He didn't know whether she had some special reason to dislike Gomez or if it was simply the professional neatness of using an enemy's death to advance their own ends which appealed to her so, and frankly, he didn't want to know.

"All right," he said, deliberately breaking his own train of thought. "What did Control have to say about the physical take from Ringbolt?"

"Quite a bit, sir. In fact, that was my next point." Shu flipped quickly through screens of data, then nodded. "He was a bit surprised by how much we got away with, and, of course, we lack the facilities to transport cargo, as opposed to data, directly to the Core Sectors. Moreover, our backers have specifically asked that we *not* send it to them. Control believes they're nervous about having traceable hardware and experimental material in their labs, not to mention the potential for interception en route."

"So he just wants us to dump it all?" Henry d'Amcourt demanded. "Jays, Commodore—that's almost a billion credits out the airlock!"

"I didn't say Control wants it dumped, Henry." Shu disliked interruptions almost as much as she disliked d'Amcourt personally, and her voice was chill, but Howell understood his quartermaster's anguish. The surviving shuttles had returned with an unanticipated fortune in tissue cultures, experimental animals, and an entire arsenal of new and advanced gene-splicing viruses, not to mention apparatus researchers on most Rogue Worlds (and not a few Incorporated Worlds) would have killed for. Henry wasn't so much affronted by losing the money involved as he was by losing the potential in supplies and ammunition it represented.

"All right, Rachel," the commodore interposed tactfully. "From what you're saying, I gather Control has something specific in mind?"

"He does, sir." Shu turned to face him, just incidentally turning her back on d'Amcourt, who only grinned. "He suggests we distribute it through Wyvern—preferably via a series of cutouts which can't be traced directly to us but guarantee at least some of it turns up here in the Franconian Sector and, if at all possible, in the Macedon Sector, as well."

"Ah?" Howell leaned back and smiled, and she nodded.

"Exactly. We can realize perhaps seventy percent of its open market value in the transaction, which should please some of us," she very carefully did not look at d'Amcourt, "but he's especially interested in having some of it spotted as far away from the Core Sectors as possible."

Howell nodded. Throwing some fourth or fifth-stage

patsy out here to the Ministry of Justice or its Rogue World equivalent would divert attention from their real backers, and it could serve as a wedge into Macedon at the same time. They'd been looking for something to suggest the "pirates" were turning their attention towards the Franconian Sector's neighbors. But coupled with the sheer value involved, that meant this particular shipment had to be handled very carefully indeed. He glanced at Alexsov.

"Greg? Can Quintana handle it?"

"I believe so," Alexsov replied after a moment's thought. "He'll want a bigger cut if he has to arrange to burn a customer, but he'll go along. And he certainly has the contacts and organization to make it work."

Howell toyed with his stylus a moment, then nodded. "All right. But I want you to set it up in person, Greg. It's about time you checked in personally with Quintana again anyway, isn't it?"

"Yes, sir. I can go ahead in a dispatch boat and have everything set by the time the transport arrives."

"I don't think so," Howell mused. "I hadn't thought about how useful this could be until Control pointed it out, but he's absolutely right. So no slipups are allowed. I want the arrangements made and triple-checked before we hand Quintana the first flask of this cargo. And I don't want you wandering around in an unarmed dispatch boat, either. Take one of the tin cans, make your arrangements, and then meet us at the AR-Twelve rendezvous."

"If you say so, sir. But should I really be absent for that long?"

"I think we'll be all right. Control hasn't sent us a fresh target yet, and we'll be meeting his next courier there, anyway. You should be back in plenty of time to coordinate the next op."

"Yes, sir. In that case, I can leave this afternoon."

Chapter Twenty-five

"So, Captain. You have a delivery for me, I understand?"

Alicia looked up sharply at the first-person pronoun. She stood at the foot of the shuttle's ramp, the turbine whine of other shuttles at her back, and the fellow before her was dressed almost drably. She'd hardly expected Quintana to appear in person the moment she landed, nor had she expected to see him so simply dressed, but her second glance confirmed his identity. The match with the holo image Fuchien had shown her was perfect.

"I do—if you have the documentation to prove you're who I think you are," she said calmly, and he gave her a faint smile as he extended a chip.

She slipped it into a reader, checking it against Fuchien's original and watching him from the corner of an eye. She didn't even look up when four heavily-armed bodyguards blended out of the crowd to join him; her free hand simply unsnapped her holster. He saw it, but his eyes only twinkled and he folded his arms unthreateningly across his chest.

Her reader chirped as she completed her examination, and she ejected the chip with a nod.

"Everything checks, Lieutenant Commander," she said, returning it to him. "Sorry if I seemed a bit suspicious."

"I approve of suspicious people—especially when they're being suspicious in my interests," Quintana replied, and extended his hand.

She clasped it, and the familiar sensation of heat enveloped her. The merchant was still speaking, welcoming her to Wyvern, but all Alicia truly "heard" was the soaring, exultant carol of the Fury's triumph.

The Quarn freighter *Aharjhka* loped towards Wyvern at a velocity many a battle-cruiser might have envied. For all its size and cargo capacity, *Aharjhka* was lean, rakish, and very, very fast, for the great Quarn trade cartels competed with one another with a fervor other races lavished only on their ships of war.

The bridge hatch opened, and the being a human would have called *Aharjhka*'s captain looked up as a passenger stepped through it.

"Greetings, Inspector. Our instruments have detected the ship you described." The Quarn's well-modulated voice was deep and resonant, largely because of the density of the atmosphere, for Quarn ships maintained a gravity more than twice that of most human vessels. But the Standard English was almost completely accentless, as well, and Ferhat Ben Belkassem hid a smile. He couldn't help it, for the sheer incongruity of that perfect enunciation from a radially symmetrical cross between a hairy, two-meter-wide starfish and a crazed Impressionist's version of a spider never failed to amuse him.

He crossed to a display at the captain's gesture. Whoever had reconfigured it for human eyes hadn't gotten the color balance quite right, but there was no mistaking the ship in Wyvern orbit. *Star Runner* had made a remarkably swift passage, actually passing *Aharjhka* en route—not that he'd expected anything else.

"So I see, sir," he said through his helmet's external speaker, and the captain turned the delicate pink the Quarn used in place of a chuckle at the choice of honorific. Ben Belkassem grinned, and the captain's rosy hue deepened. Quarn had only a single sex—or, rather, every Quarn was a fully functional hermaphrodite—and humanity's gender-linked language conventions tickled their sense of the absurd. But at least it was a shared and tolerant amusement. Different as they were, both species understood biological humor, and humans gave back as good as they got. The prudish Rishatha were another matter. If the Quarn found humanity's sexual mores amusing, they found those of the Rishatha uproarious, and the matriarchs were not amused in return. Worse (from the Rishathan viewpoint), the highly flexible Quarn vocal apparatus could handle both human and Rishathan languages, and they found it particularly amusing to enter a multi-species transit facility, make sure Rishatha were present, and ask one another "Have you heard the one about the two matriarchs?" in perfect High Rish.

Ben Belkassem had been present when one of those jokes led to a lively brawl and an even livelier diplomatic incident—not that the Rishatha were likely to press the matter too far. On a personal level, nothing much short of a six-kilo hammer could hurt a Quarn, and even a fully mature matriarch fared poorly against two hundred kilos of muscle and gristle from a 2.4-G home world, whether the possessor of that muscle and gristle was officially warlike or not. On a diplomatic level, the Terran Empire and Quarn Hegemony were firm allies, a fact the Rishathan Sphere found more than merely unpalatable yet was unable to do much about. It wasn't for want of trying, but even the devious Rishathan diplomatic corps which had once set the Terran League at the Federation's throat had finally given up in disgust. What was a poor racial chauvinist to do? Bizarre as each species found the other's appearance, humankind and Quarnkind liked one another immensely. On the face of it, it was an unlikely pairing. The Rishatha were at least bipedal, yet they and humans barely tolerated one another, so a reasonable being might have expected even more tension between humanity and the utterly alien Quarn.

Yet it didn't work that way, and Ben Belkassem suspected it was precisely *because* they were so different.

The Quarn's heavy-gravity worlds produced atmospheric pressures lethal to any human, which meant they weren't interested in the same sort of real estate; humans and Rishatha were. Quarn and human sexuality were so different there were virtually no points of congruity; Rishatha were bisexual—and the matriarchs blamed human notions of sexual equality for the "uppityness" of certain of their own males. There were all too many points of potential conflict between human and Rish, while humans and Quarn had no conflicting physical interests and were remarkably compatible in nonphysical dimensions.

Humans were more combative than the Quarn, who reserved their own ferocity for important things like business, but both were far less militant than the Rishathan matriarchs. They were comfortable with one another, and if the Quarn sometimes felt humans were a mite more warlike than was good for them, they recognized a natural community of interest against the Rishatha. Besides, humans could take a joke.

"We will enter orbit in another two hours," *Aharjhka*'s captain announced. "Is there anything else *Aharjhka* can do for you in this matter?"

"No, sir. If you can just get me down aboard your shuttle without anyone noticing, you'll have done everything I could possibly want."

"That will be no problem, if you are certain it is all you need."

"I am, and I thank you on my own behalf and that of the Empire."

"Not necessary." The captain waved a tentacle tip in dismissal. "The Hegemony understands criminals like these *thugarz*, Inspector, and I remind you that *Aharjhka* has a well-equipped armory if my crew may be of use to you."

The Quarn's rosy tint shaded into a bleaker violet. The Spiders might regard war as a noisy, inefficient way to settle differences, but when violence was the only solution, they went about it with the same pragmatism they brought to serious matters like making money. "Merciless as a Quarn" was a high compliment among human merchants, but it held another, grimmer reality, and the Quarn liked pirates even less than humans did. They weren't simply murderous criminals, but murderous criminals who were bad for business.

"I appreciate the thought, Captain, but if I'm right, all the firepower I need is already here. All I have to do is mobilize it."

"Indeed?" The Quarn remained motionless on the toadstool-like pad of its command couch, but two vision clusters swiveled to consider him. "You are a strange human, Inspector, but I almost believe you mean that."

"I do."

"It would be impolite to call you insane, but please remember this is Wyvern."

"I will, I assure you."

"Luck to your trading, then, Inspector. I will have you notified thirty minutes before shuttle departure."

"Thank you, sir," Ben Belkassem replied, and made his way to the tiny, human-configured cabin hidden in *Aharjhka*'s bowels, moving quickly but carefully against the ship's internal gravity field.

His shoulders straightened gratefully as he crossed the divider into his quarters' one-G field. It was a vast relief to feel his weight drop back where it ought to be, and an even vaster one to dump his helmet and scratch his nose at last. He sighed in relief, then knelt to drag a small trunk from under his bunk and began checking its varied and lethal contents with practiced ease while his mind replayed his conversation with the captain.

He certainly understood the Quarn's concern, but the captain didn't realize how lucky Ben Belkassem had been. *Aharjhka*'s presence at Dewent and scheduled layover at Wyvern had been like filling an inside straight, and the inspector intended to ride the advantage for all it was worth. Very few people knew how closely the Hegemony Judicars and Imperial Ministry of Justice cooperated, and even fewer knew about the private arrangement under which enforcement agents of each imperium traveled freely (and clandestinely) on the other's ships. Which meant no one would be expecting any human—even an O Branch inspector—to debark from *Aharjhka. Aharjhka* wasn't listed as a multi-species transport, and only a convinced misanthrope or an intelligent and infinitely resourceful agent would book passage on a vessel whose environment would make him a virtual prisoner in his cabin for the entire voyage.

Of course, Ferhat Ben Belkassem *was* an intelligent and infinitely resourceful agent—he knew he was, for it said so in his Justice Ministry dossier—but even so, he'd almost blown his own cover when he recognized Alicia DeVries on Dewent. It had cost Justice's Intelligence and Operations Branches seven months and three lives to establish that one of Edward Jacoby's (many) partners had links to the pirates' Wyvern-based fence, and they still hadn't figured out which of them it was. Yet DeVries had homed in on Fuchien as if she had a map, and she'd built herself a far better cover than O Branch could have provided.

Ben Belkassem had personally double-checked the documentation on *Star Runner*, her captain, and her crew, and he'd never seen such an exquisitely detailed (and utterly fictitious) legend. He supposed he shouldn't be surprised, given the way DeVries had escaped hospital security on Soissons, penetrated Jefferson Field, and stolen one of the Imperial Fleet's prized alpha synths. If she could make *that* look easy, why not this?

Because she was a drop commando, not a trained operative—that was why. How had she come by such perfectly forged papers? Where had she recruited her crew? For that matter, how did she cram them all aboard what had to be the stolen alpha synth? It couldn't be anything else, whatever it *looked* like, but how in the name of all that was holy did she slide blithely through customs at a world like MaGuire? Ben Belkassem had never personally crossed swords with Jungian customs, but he knew their reputation. He couldn't conceive of any way they could have inspected "*Star Runner*" without at least noticing that the "freighter" was armed to the proverbial teeth!

It seemed, he thought dryly, checking the charge indicator on a disrupter, that the good captain had lost none of her penchant for doing the impossible. And, as he'd once told Colonel McIlheny, he hadn't amassed his record by looking serendipity in the mouth. Whatever she was up to and however she was bringing it off, she'd not only managed to find the link he'd sought but done so in a way which actually got her inside the pipeline. Under those circumstances, he was perfectly content to throw his own weeks of work out the airlock and follow along in her wake.

And, he told himself as he buckled his gun belt and slid the disrupter into its holster, even a drop commando could use a bit of backup, whatever her unlikely abilities . . . and whether she knew she had it or not.

Alicia retina-printed the last document and watched Oscar Quintana's secretary carry the paperwork from the palatial office. The merchant pushed his chair back and rose, turning to the well-stocked bar opposite his desk.

"A rapid and satisfactory transaction, Captain Mainwaring. Now that it's out of the way, name your poison."

"I'm not too particular, as long as it pours," Alicia replied, glancing casually about the office. *<I don't see any obvious pickups,>* she thought at Tisiphone. *<How about you?>*

<There are none. Quintana does not care to be spied upon in his own lair—that much I have obtained from him already.>

<Think we've got enough time?>

<I know not, but sufficient or no, this may be the only time we have.>

<Then let's go for it,> Alicia said. She rose from her own chair and walked across to Quintana. He glanced up from the clear, green liqueur he was pouring into tiny glasses, then capped the bottle and smiled.

"I trust you'll enjoy this, Captain. It's a local product from one of my own distilleries, and—"

His voice chopped off as Alicia touched his hand. He froze, mouth open, eyes blank, and Alicia blinked in momentary disorientation of her own as the flood of data poured into her brain. Their earlier handshake had been sufficient to confirm their quarry but too brief for detailed examination of Quintana's knowledge. They'd dared not probe this way then, lest one of his bodyguards notice his glaze-eyed stillness and react precipitously.

It was still a risk, but Alicia was too caught up in the knowledge flow to worry about someone's opening the door and finding them like this. If it happened, it happened, and in the meantime . . .

Images and memories flared as Tisiphone plucked them from Quintana. Meetings with someone named Alexsov. Credit balances that soared magically as loot from pillaged worlds flowed through his hands. Contact times and purchase orders. Customers and distributors on other Rogue Worlds and even on imperial planets. All of them flashed through her, each of them stored indelibly for later attention, and again and again she saw the mysterious Alexsov. Alexsov and a man called d'Amcourt, who listed and coordinated the pirates' purchases, and a woman called Shu, who frightened the powerful merchant noble, however he might deny it to himself. Yet both of those others deferred to Alexsov without question. There was no doubt in Quintana's mind—or in Alicia's—that Alexsov was one of the pirates' senior officers, and she wanted to scream in frustration at how little Quintana knew of him.

But at least she now knew what he looked like, and . . .

Her green eyes brightened as the last, elusive details clicked. Alexsov due to return here soon . . . and Quintana's own constant need for dependable carriers.

Her hungry smile echoed the Fury's hunting snarl, and she felt Tisiphone reach even deeper, no longer taking thoughts but implanting them. A few more brief seconds sufficed, and then Quintana's eyes snapped back into focus and his voice continued, smooth and unhurried, unaware of any break.

"—I highly recommend it."

He handed her one of the glasses, and she sipped, then smiled in unfeigned enjoyment. It was sweet yet sharp, almost astringent, and it flowed down her throat like rich, liquid fire.

"I see why you think highly of it," she said. He nodded and waved at the chairs around a coffee table of rich native woods. She sank into one of them, and he sat opposite her, peering pensively down into his glass.

"Lewis said you have a charter on Cathcart, Captain Mainwaring?"

"Yes, I do," Alicia confirmed, and he frowned.

"That's a pity. I might have a profitable commission for you here, if you could see your way to accepting it."

"What sort of commission?"

"Very much like the one you've just discharged, but with a considerably higher profit margin."

"Ah?" Alicia crooked an eyebrow thoughtfully. "How considerably?"

"Twice as great—at a minimum," Quintana replied. and she let her other eyebrow rise.

"I suppose you might call that 'considerably higher,'" she murmured. "Still, Cathcart is a bird in the hand, Lieutenant Commander, and—"

"Oscar, please," he interrupted, and she blinked, this time in genuine surprise. From what she'd seen of Quintana's mind, he didn't encourage familiarity with his employees. On the other hand—

<On the other hand, Little One,> a voice whispered dryly in her mind, *<you are a handsome woman and he is a connoisseur of women. And, no,>* the voice added even more dryly, *<I did* not *instill any such notion in his mind!>*

"Oscar, then," Alicia said aloud. "As I was saying, I *know* I have a cargo on Cathcart, and the port master will slap me with a forfeit penalty if I don't collect it as scheduled."

"True." Quintana pondered a moment, then shrugged. "I can't guarantee the commission I'm thinking of, Theodosia—may I call you Theodosia?" Alicia nodded and he continued. "Thank you. I can't guarantee it because there are other principals involved, but I believe you and *Star Runner* would be perfect for it. I'm reasonably confident my colleagues will agree with me, and even if they don't, I have other consignments for a discreet and reliable skipper, so I have a proposal for you. I anticipate seeing one of my senior colleagues in the near future. Starcom your regrets to your Cathcart contract, and I'll introduce you to him when he arrives. If he accepts my recommendation, you'll make enough to cover your forfeit and still show a much higher profit than on this last shipment. If he chooses to make other arrangements, I will personally guarantee you commissions of at least equal value."

Alicia let herself consider the offer carefully, then shrugged.

"How can I pass up an offer like that? I accept, of course," she said . . . and she smiled.

Chapter Twenty-six

The small, well-dressed diner accepted the proffered chair with distracted courtesy, then reached into his jacket for a micro-comp. He set it beside his plate, punched up a complicated list of stock transactions, and studied them intently. Only the most suspicious might have noticed the way he set it down, and only the truly paranoid would have suspected the ultra-sensitive microphone concealed in the end pointed toward a nearby table.

Ben Belkassem spread a small sheaf of hard-copy on the table, then punched more keys and brought up yet another layer of meaningless sales while he uncapped his stylus. He scribbled notes on the hard-copy, frowning in concentration as the tiny ear bug from his computer whispered to him.

". . . derstand, Captain." Oscar Quintana sipped wine and blotted his lips, eyes gleaming with sardonic amusement. "It's regrettable, of course, but a certain . . . wastage must be anticipated in any transaction."

"Precisely. But the object is to make certain the wastage is suffered in the right place." Gregor Alexsov's own wine sat untasted, and Quintana smothered a mental sigh. The man had done wonderful things for his credit balance, but there was no lightness, no sense of what the game was all about, in him. Those hard, brown eyes swiveled over his face like targeting lasers, and the thin lips wrinkled in what was obviously intended as a smile.

Sad, so sad, but that probably represented Alexsov's best effort. Well, a man couldn't be good at everything, Quintana supposed. "If you'll give me a list of what you want wasted and where, I'll see to it."

"Thank you." Alexsov's eyes moved away, scanning the crowded restaurant, and his mouth tightened with disapproval. "I'll have it for you by the time we reach some less public place."

"I applaud your caution, Captain Alexsov," Quintana said, ignoring the way his guest winced at the use of his name, "but it's unnecessary."

"Perhaps, but I dislike meeting among so many strangers."

"None of whom," Quintana pointed out, "are close enough to hear a word we're saying. Half the deals on Wyvern are concluded in this restaurant, Captain, because it's swept for bugs several times a day, and despite your concern, we've been less than specific. Even had we not, none of our business violates any of Wyvern's laws, and—" he gestured dryly at the six well-armed retainers seated at flanking tables "—I hardly think anyone would be foolish enough to intrude on us. I *am* Lieutenant Commander Defiant, you know."

"No doubt. But an agent of the Empire, or even some of your non-imperial neighbors, might not care."

"Which would be fatally foolish of him, Captain." Steel glinted behind Quintana's smile as his relaxed pose slipped for just a moment, and his eyes locked with Alexsov's. Then he shrugged and waved a hand, banishing the mood. "Have it as you will, however. In the meantime, I think I may have located just the skipper we need. She's a newcomer to Wyvern, but her credentials are excellent.

Good-looking young woman, but she's already demonstrated her competence on several occasions, and—"

Ben Belkassem's meal arrived. He made himself smile around a silent curse on all efficient waiters as he put his computer away, but he'd heard enough. He knew now why DeVries had spent the last three weeks cultivating Quintana, and he had a name—one which was almost certainly genuine, given "Alexsov's" reaction to its use—beyond the Wyverian. Perhaps even more importantly, it seemed DeVries was about to move another link up the chain.

The inspector sampled his food with an admiring smile. He didn't know how she was manipulating her enemies, but no one could get this far this fast on pure luck. For all his ego, Quintana was a shrewd operator; she had to be influencing him some way to win such a recommendation after carrying a single cargo for him, and the inspector wondered what sort of magic wand she used.

He paused, smile fading at a sudden thought. *He* knew she was working Quintana somehow—might it be equally obvious to someone else? Of course, he had the advantage of knowing who she was and some of the other things she'd done, but if anyone ran an analysis and recognized her straight-line movement to Wyvern or, worse, checked her career before MaGuire. . . .

He laid aside his fork and reached for his own wineglass, remembering Alexsov's evident caution, and his brain was busy behind his eyes.

Commander Barr looked up in surprise as Captain Alexsov strode onto *Harpy*'s bridge. He hadn't expected the chief of staff back aboard for another hour, and his expression suggested he had something on his mind.

"Good evening, sir. Can I help you?"

"Yes." Alexsov slid into the exec's chair and reached for the synth link headset. "Patch me into the port records, please."

Barr nodded to his communications officer, then

turned his chair to face Alexsov. "May I ask what you're looking for, sir?"

"I don't know yet." Alexsov smiled thinly at the CO's expression. "I may not be looking for anything at all, but if I find it, I'll recognize it."

"Of course, sir." Barr turned his chair tactfully away as the chief of staff closed his eyes in concentration. This was Alexsov's first trip in *Harpy*, but aside from a certain fetish with schedules, he'd evinced few of the oddities Barr's fellows had warned him about. Until now, at least.

Alexsov suspected what Barr was thinking, but it bothered him far less than his inability to pin down what made him so uneasy. It was just that it was unlike Quintana to recommend *any* captain, much less one he'd dealt with only once, as enthusiastically as this one. Of course, if Mainwaring was as attractive as Quintana had implied, that might explain a good bit of his enthusiasm, Quintana being Quintana. Still, whatever had aroused his initial admiration, her record since entering the Franconian Sector was impressive. She had a fast ship, and she'd certainly demonstrated a short way with would-be hijackers. That cargo of Dreamy White was a point in her favor, too; anyone who'd transport that had very few scruples.

He reached the end of the data and leaned back, frowning without opening his eyes. If only the woman had a longer history in-sector! Without querying the Melville data base directly via starcom—and vague concern was hardly enough to justify that sort of risk or expense—he couldn't check her previous record. There was nothing in her recent activities to arouse suspicion, and if this was a false background, it was the most convincing one he'd ever seen. But perhaps that was the real problem. Maybe she was too good to be true?

Nonsense! He was getting as paranoid as Rachel Shu! But that paranoia, he acknowledged, was exactly what made Rachel such a success.

His frown deepened. Smitten by her looks or no, Quintana must have checked her out. The merchant's dealings might be legal under Wyverian law, but Quintana had to know how meaningless that would be if the Empire ever discovered them. O Branch had no qualms about arranging a quiet little kidnapping or assassination, and ONI would be right behind them on this one. Possibly not even such a quiet assassination. The Empire would want other Rogue Worlders to rethink their positions on aiding enemies of the Crown.

He removed his headset and coiled the lead with methodical neatness. Every indication was that Captain Mainwaring was genuine. If she was, she could prove an invaluable resource; if she wasn't, she was a deadly danger. Any operative who could penetrate this deeply had to be eliminated, but all he had was a worry—a "hunch," much as he hated the word—and that wasn't enough. Rachel, he suspected, would simply have her killed out of hand, but Rachel wasn't noted for moderation, and if his hunch was wrong, Mainwaring was just as perfect for the job as Quintana thought.

Fortunately, there was a way to be certain. He put the headset away, nodded briefly to Commander Barr, and headed for sickbay.

The hover cab stopped outside the imposing gates, and Alicia stepped out into Wyvern's autumn night, damp and rich with the scent of unfamiliar, decaying leaf mold. She fed her credit card into the cab's charge unit and looked around, tugging her bolero straight. Chateau Defiant lay thirty kilometers from town, and clouds hid both moons. Without sensory boosters, the blackness would have been Stygian; even with them, it was dark enough to make her jumpy—especially in light of the importance of this meeting.

<Calm down, Alley. Get your pulse back down where it belongs, girl!>

<Yes, ma'am,> Alicia thought back obediently, and brought her augmentation on line. Her racing heart slowed, and she felt herself relax. Not enough to lose her edge, but enough to kill the jitters.

<Just keep your head together, okay? I want you—

hell, I want both *of you—back up here in one piece. Or two. Or whatever.*>

<*Have no fear, Megarea. I shall keep my eye upon her.*>

<*Ha! That's what worries me most!*>

Alicia swallowed a chuckle as she reclaimed her credit card. The gates opened silently, and Quintana's voice issued from the speaker below their visual pickup.

"Hi, Theodosia! We're in the Green Parlor. You know the way."

"Pour the drinks, Oscar," she replied with a cheerful wave. "I'll see you in a couple of minutes."

"Good," Quintana said, and switched off with an unhappy glance at Gregor Alexsov. "Is this really necessary?" he asked, gesturing distastefully at the peculiar, long-barreled pistol one of Alexsov's people carried.

"I'm afraid so." Alexsov nodded, and the man with the pistol retreated into the next room and pulled the door almost closed. "I trust you completely, Oscar, but we can't afford any slips. If she's as trustworthy as you believe, it won't hurt her a bit. If not . . ." He shrugged.

Alicia strode up the walk with brisk familiarity. She'd been here several times in the past weeks, although Oscar Quintana's memories of her overnight visits differed somewhat from her own. She grinned at the thought, relaxing further with the amusement, and never noticed the catlike shape that slid tracelessly through Quintana's sophisticated security systems behind her.

She was one of Quintana's "special friends" now, and the retainer who met her at the door gave her a wry, half-apologetic smile as he held out his hand. She smiled back and slid her disrupter from its holster, then handed over her survival knife and the vibro blade from her left boot. He stowed them carefully away and gestured politely at the scan panel beside him, and Alicia made a face.

"Oh ye of little faith," she murmured, but it wasn't bad manners on Wyvern, where titles of nobility—and estates—had been known to change hands with sudden and violent unexpectedness. No doubt Tisiphone could have gotten an entire arsenal past the man behind the scanners, just as she did Alicia's augmentation, but there was no real point in it.

"There, see?" she said as he peered at her internal hardware without seeing it.

He smiled at her rallying tone and bowed her past, and she grinned back as she turned down a corridor hung in priceless tapestries. If not for the way it was paid for, she could have gotten used to this kind of life, she thought, nodding to an occasional servant as she passed.

The double doors to what Quintana modestly called the Green Parlor stood open. She stepped through them, and he turned to greet her, standing beside a tallish man she recognized from his mind.

"Theodosia. Allow me to introduce Captain Gregor Alexsov."

"Captain." Alicia held out her hand and made herself smile brightly.

"Captain Mainwaring." Alexsov extended his own hand graciously. She took it and felt the familiar heat, then—

<*No, Alicia!*> Tisiphone screamed in her mind, and something made a soft, quiet "PFFFFT!" sound behind her.

Ben Belkassem muttered balefully as he filtered through the pitch-black grounds. This damned house was even bigger than he'd thought from the plans, and he'd almost missed two different sensors already. He paused in the denser darkness under an ornamental tree and checked his inertial tracer against the plat of the grounds. Quintana had mentioned the "Green Parlor," and if his map was right that was right over there. . . .

Alicia gasped and snapped around to stare at Quintana as pain pricked the back of her neck. He looked distressed—he was actually wringing his hands—and her eyes popped back to Alexsov, then widened as she collapsed. The carpet bloodied her nose as her face hit it, and deep within her she felt the elemental rage of the Fury.

She tried to thrust herself back up, but Alexsov had chosen his attack well. He knelt beside her, and she couldn't even feel his hands as he removed the tiny dart and rolled her, not ungently, onto her back.

"I apologize for the necessity, Captain Mainwaring," he murmured, "but it's only a temporary nerve block." He snapped his fingers, and one of his henchmen handed him a hypospray. "And this," he went on soothingly, pressing the hypo to her arm, "is a perfectly harmless truth drug."

Horrified understanding filled Alicia as the hypo nestled home.

<*Tisiphone!*> she screamed.

<*I am trying!*> Anger and fear—for Alicia, not herself—snarled in the Fury's reply. <*Their cursed block has cut off your main processor, but—*>

The hypo hissed, and Tisiphone cursed horribly as the drug flooded into Alicia's system . . . and her augmentation sensed it.

She gasped and jerked, and Alexsov leapt back in consternation. Even that small movement should have been impossible, and his brow furrowed in lightning speculation as she quivered on the carpet. Escape protocols blossomed within her, fighting the nerve block, trying to get her on her feet, but they couldn't, and panic wailed in her mind as the idiot savant of her processor considered its internal programs. Escape was impossible, it decided, and truth drugs had been administered.

Ben Belkassem eased through the ornamental shrubbery to the glowing windows. Their translucent green curtains let light escape yet were too thick to see through, but he'd expected that. He checked for security sensors and placed a tiny, sensitive microphone against the glass.

". . . happening?!" Naked panic quivered in Oscar Quintana's voice. "You said she was just supposed to be paralyzed, damn it!"

"I don't *know* what it is." That lower, calmer voice belonged to the man named Alexsov, Ben Belkassem thought—then stiffened as understanding caught up with his racing mind. Paralyzed! Dear God, they must be on to her!

Alicia's eyes glazed. She was numb below the neck, but she felt the neuro-toxin in her gasping respiration, the growing sluggishness of her mind. To come this far, she thought despairingly. To get this close—!

Glass shattered behind Oscar Quintana, and he whirled. The tinkling sound still hung in his ears as the curtains parted, and he had a vague impression of a black-clad figure that raised a hand in his direction. Then the emerald green beam struck just above his left eye and he died.

Ben Belkassem hit the carpet rolling and cursing his own stupidity. He should have pulled out, goddamn it! What DeVries had already accomplished was more important than either of their lives—far too important for him to throw away playing holovid hero! But his body had reacted before his brain, and he skittered frantically across the floor towards a solid, ornate desk while answering disrupter beams flashed about him.

Somehow he made it into cover, and his shoulder heaved. The desk crashed over, blocking the deadly beams, and a short-barreled machine-pistol popped into his free hand.

Someone else had a slug-thrower, and he winced as penetrators chewed into the desktop. Its wood couldn't stop that kind of fire, and he ducked to his left, exposing himself just long enough to find the firer. His disrupter whined, and the fire stopped, but he felt no exultation. He'd seen DeVries in that moment—seen the way her body quivered weakly—and his mind flashed back to Tannis Cateau's briefings.

She was dying, and he swore viciously as he rose on his knees to nail a second gunman with his machine-pistol. The thunder of weapons shook the room, Quintana's guards had to be on their way, more penetrators chewed at the desk, and then someone killed the lights and the chaos became total.

* * *

Tisiphone battered at the block with all her might, then made herself stop. She had to get into Alicia's main processor to reach her pharmacope, but the drug Alexsov had used blocked voluntary nervous impulses and sealed the processor's input tantalizingly beyond her reach. She couldn't reach it, yet she had to. She had to!

And then it came to her. The block couldn't cut off its victim's *in*voluntary muscles without killing her, and the processor's *output* reached *all* of Alicia's functions! And that meant—

Ben Belkassem cried out and dropped his machine-pistol as a tungsten penetrator slammed through his upper arm, yet he scarcely felt it. Any minute someone else would come in through those windows behind him and he'd be as dead as Alicia DeVries. Someone with more guts than sense rushed him. The flash of his disrupter lit the darkness with emerald lightning, seventy kilos of dead meat slammed to the carpet, and white-hot muzzle flashes stabbed at him as his own shot drew the fire of another machine-pistol. He wasn't afraid as the penetrators screamed past—there was no time for fear—yet under the wild adrenalin rush was the bitter knowledge of how completely he had failed.

But then the man behind the machine-pistol screamed. It was a horrible, gurgling sound . . . and Ben Belkassem knew *he* hadn't caused it.

There was an instant of shocked silence, and then someone else was firing. Someone who fired in short, deadly bursts, as if the darkness were light, and the whining disrupters were no longer firing at him. He shoved himself up on his knees and gawked in disbelief.

He had no idea why Alicia DeVries wasn't dead or how she'd reached the man whose weapon she was firing, and it didn't matter. The rock-steady pistol picked off guards with machinelike precision. She was a ghost, appearing in glaring muzzle flashes only to vanish back into the darkness like death's own ballerina, and the screams and shrieks of the dying were her orchestra.

But then her magazine was empty, and there were still three enemies left. Ben Belkassem hunted for them desperately, lacing the smoke-heavy blackness with disrupter fire in a frantic effort to cover her, then groaned in despair as an emerald shaft struck her squarely between the shoulders.

DeVries grunted, but she didn't go down, and his own disrupter fell to his side in shock. She was dead. She *had* to be dead this time! But she spun toward the man who'd shot her even as two more disrupters hit her. A vicious kick snapped his neck, and the two remaining guards screamed in terrified disbelief as she charged them. One of them rained green bolts upon her as she closed, but the other tried to run. It made no difference; the fleeing guard got as far as opening the door, spilling light into the death-filled gloom, and then he died, as well.

She spun again, whirling to face Ben Belkassem, and he dropped his weapon and raised his good hand with frantic haste.

"Stop! I'm on *your* side!"

She slid to a halt, jacket charred from disrupter hits, and frozen eyes regarded him from a face of inhuman calm.

"Ben Belkassem! I'm Ferhat Ben Belkassem!" he said desperately, and saw recognition in those icy eyes. "I—"

"Later." Her voice was as inhumanly calm as her expression. "Get over there and cover the door."

He scrabbled up his weapons and raced to the door before his dazed mind even considered arguing, and only then did he truly realize how quick and brutal the fight had been. He fed a fresh clip into his machine-pistol, clumsy with only one working arm, and when he looked out into the corridor the first of Quintana's retainers were only now racing towards him. He dropped the three leaders, then glanced over his shoulder as the survivors fell back.

DeVries knelt beside Alexsov, ignoring the blood soaking his tunic and pooling about her knees. She pressed her hands to his temples, leaning over him, her face almost touching his as blood bubbled on his lips, and

Ben Belkassem shuddered and turned back to his front. He didn't know what she was doing. What was more, he didn't think he *wanted* to know.

More guards came at him. These had found time to scramble into unpowered armor, and the loads in his machine-pistol were too light to get through it at anything above point-blank range. He dropped it and shifted to his disrupter, praying the charge held out. Five more men went down, and then the survivors withdrew to regroup.

Something thundered behind him, and he swore feelingly. DeVries was by the windows, firing someone else's weapon out into the grounds. They were pinned; no matter how many they killed, the others would get them in the end. But he'd seen the way DeVries moved. If either of them could make it . . .

"I'll cover you!" he shouted, starting towards the window

"Watch your front," she said calmly, never even turning her head. "These bastards have a surprise coming."

There was no time to ask what she was talking about. A fresh rush was coming down the corridor, and a buzz from his disrupter warned of an exhausted charge as he beat it back. Her "surprise" had better come soon, or—

Something howled in the dark. Something huge and black, borne on a cyclone of turbines, wing edges and nose incandescent from reentry. Chateau Defiant heaved as rockets and plasma cannon shattered its other wings, and Ben Belkassem rolled across the floor, coughing on smoke and powdered stone.

A steely hand grabbed his collar, dragged him out the windows, and hurled him at the grounded assault shuttle. He charged its ramp like his last hope of salvation, DeVries on his heels, and heard incoming fire spanging off the armored hull and the whine of powered turrets and the end-of-the-world bellow as the shuttle's autocannon covered their retreat. He staggered through the troop bay to the flight deck and slumped against a bulkhead, suddenly aware of the pain in his arm and the weakness of blood loss, as the shuttle leapt back into the heavens.

DeVries shouldered past him to the pilot's couch, and he slid down to sit on the deck in fresh shock that owed little to blood loss as he realized that seat had been empty when the shuttle swept down to save them.

He sat there, searching for a rational explanation, but none occurred to his muzzy brain. Disrupter fire had charred her jacket in half a dozen places, yet she was alive. That was insane enough, but where was her crew? And what in God's name had she been doing with Alexsov back there?

"What—" He stopped and coughed, surprised by the croak of his own voice, and she spared him a glance.

"Hang on," she said in that same calm voice, and he clutched for a handhold as something fast and lethal sizzled past and she whipped the shuttle into wild evasive action—without, he noted numbly, even bothering to don the flight control synth headset.

And then she started talking to herself.

"Okay. Dial 'em in and take them out," she told the empty air.

He clawed his way forward and tumbled into the copilot's seat just as something carved a screaming column of light through the night. He gaped out the cockpit canopy, then jerked back as terrible white fire erupted far below. Another followed, and a third, and DeVries spared him a wolf's smile. She flipped on the com—he hadn't even realized it was turned off—and an angry male voice filled the flight deck.

". . . say again! Cease fire on our shuttle, or we will destroy your spaceport! This is First Officer Jeff Okahara of the starship *Star Runner*, and this is your final warning!"

"Way to go, Megarea," his pilot murmured, and Ben Belkassem closed his eyes. It had been such an *orderly* universe this morning, he thought almost calmly.

"*Star Runner*, you are ordered to return your shuttle and its occupants to the port immediately to answer for their unprovoked attack on Lieutenant Commander Defiant's estate!" another voice roared over the com.

"Bugger off!" Okahara snarled back. "Your precious

lieutenant commander just got what he fucking well had coming!"

"*What?!* What do you mean—"

"I mean you'd better notify his heirs! And anybody else who tries to murder our captain is going to get the same!"

"Listen, you—"

The furious voice chopped off. Ben Belkassem heard another voice, quick and urgent, muttering words that included "HVW" and "battle screen," and looked across at Alicia again.

"Quite a freighter you have there, Captain Mainwaring," he murmured.

"Isn't it?" The turbines died as the shuttle streaked beyond air-breathing altitude and the thrusters took over. "Strap in. We don't have time to decelerate, so Megarea's going to snag us with a tractor as we go by."

"Megarea? Who's Megarea?"

"A friend of mine," she replied with a strange little smile.

Commander Barr couldn't believe any of it. One minute everything was calm, the next a shuttle from an unarmed freighter screamed planetward at insane velocity and reduced Chateau Defiant (and, presumably, Captain Alexsov) to flaming rubble. And when Groundside tried to down the shuttle, that same unarmed freighter blew the engaging weapon stations into next week with HVW!

Barr had no better idea of what was happening than anyone else, but his drive was working hard, because he knew *Harpy* didn't even want to think about engaging that "freighter." God only knew what it might produce *next*, and he intended to be several light-seconds away before it got around to it.

Now he stared into his aft display, wondering who was aboard that shuttle. He could still nail it short of the freighter—which was putting out *battle screen* now, for God's sake!—which might be a good idea. Except that Captain Alexsov *might* be aboard it. And, Barr admitted, except that firing on it seemed to be a good way to convince the freighter to respond in kind.

Then he no longer had the option. The shuttle slashed towards the freighter at far too high an approach speed, only to stop with bone-breaking suddenness as a tractor yanked it inside the screen. Barr winced. He'd been through exactly the same maneuver in training exercises, but his sympathy was limited, for the freighter was already swinging to pursue him.

A groggy Ben Belkassem swam back to awareness draped across Alicia DeVries' back in a fireman's carry. It was an undignified position, but he was in no condition to argue, and a part of him apologized for every doubt he'd ever entertained over Sir Arthur Keita's descriptions of drop commandos.

She dumped him gently on the floor of the ship's elevator and crouched beside him, ripping his blood-soaked sleeve apart.

"Nice and clean," she told him. "Got some nasty tissue damage, but it missed the bone." He hissed as she strapped a pressure bandage tight. "We'll take care of that in a minute. Right now we've got other worries."

"Like what?" he gasped.

"Like eight Wyvern Navy cruisers and a Fleet tin can we have to kill."

"Kill a *Fleet destroyer?!*"

"The one Alexsov came from, HMS *Harpy*. Her transponder's buggered to ID her as *Medusa*, but—" The lift door opened, and she seemed to teleport through it. Ben Belkassem followed more slowly onto what he realized must be the bridge and peered about him.

"Where is everybody?"

"You're looking at everybody. Megarea, give him a display."

He jumped as a holo display sprang to life, hanging in midair and livid with the red-ringed blue dots of hostile Fasset drives. Eight came from the direction of Wyvern, already shrinking astern; a ninth glowed dead ahead.

* * *

Commander Barr swallowed bile. *Harpy* was putting everything she had into her drive . . . and the cursed freighter was *gaining*. It was running away from the Wyverian cruisers with absurd ease, shrugging aside everything they and the planetary defenses could throw without even bothering to reply. Clearly it had other concerns.

"Stand by! The instant they flip to engage us, I want—"

"And now . . ." Alicia murmured beside Ben Belkassem.

Commander Barr and the entire company of HMS *Harpy* died before they even realized their pursuer had already flipped.

Chapter Twenty-seven

Delicious smells filled the small galley, and Ferhat Ben Belkassem sat at the table. He wore a highly atypical air of bemusement and sprawled in his chair without his usual neatness, but then he'd earned a little down time—and hadn't expected to live to enjoy it.

He felt a bit like the ancient Alice as he watched Captain DeVries stir tomato-rich sauce with a neurosurgeon's concentration. Her dyed hair was coiled in a thick braid, and she looked absurdly young. It was hard to credit his own memory of icy eyes and lightning muzzle flashes as she sampled the sauce and reached for more basil. The lid rose from a pot beside her, hovering in midair on an invisible tractor beam, and linguine drifted from a storage bin to settle neatly in the boiling water.

"And what do you think you're doing? I told you I'd put that in when I was ready," she said, and this time he barely twitched. He was starting to adjust to her one-sided conversations with the ship's AI—even if they were yet another of the "impossible" things she did so casually.

Ben Belkassem had boned up on the alpha synths after DeVries stole this ship. Too much was classified for him to learn as much as he would have liked, but he'd learned enough to know her augmentation didn't include the normal alpha synth com link. Without it, the AI should have been forced to communicate back by voice, not some sort of . . . of *telepathy!*

Yet he was beyond surprise where DeVries was concerned. After all, she'd survived multiple disrupter hits with no more than a few minor burns, killed eleven men saving his own highly-trained self, taken out a few ground-to-space weapon emplacements, escaped through the heart of Wyvern's very respectable fortifications, and polished off a destroyer as an encore. As far as he was concerned, she could do anything she damned well liked.

She murmured something else to the empty air, too softly this time for him to hear, and he sat very still as plates and silverware swooped from cupboard to table like strange birds. Yes, he thought, *very* like Alice, though a bit more of this and he could qualify as the March Hare. Or perhaps DeVries already had that role and he'd be forced to settle for the Mad Hatter.

He smiled at the thought, and she spared him a smile of her own as she set the sauce on the table and produced a bottle of wine. He raised an eyebrow at the Defiant Vineyards label, and she sighed as she filled their glasses.

"He really was an outstanding vintner. Too bad he couldn't have stopped there."

"Um, you *are* speaking to me, this time, Captain?"

"You might as well call me Alicia," she said by way of answer, dropping into the chair opposite him as the pot of pasta moved to the sink, drained itself, and drifted to the table.

"Dinner is served," she murmured. "Help yourself, Inspector."

"Fair's fair. If you're Alicia, I'm Ferhat."

She nodded agreement and heaped linguine on her plate, then reached for the sauce ladle while Ben Belkassem eyed the huge serving of pasta.

"Are you sure your stomach's up to this?" he asked,

remembering the tearing violent nausea which had wracked her less than two hours before.

"Well," she ladled sauce with a generous hand and grinned at him, "it's not like there's anything down there to get in its way."

"I see." It was untrue, but if she cared to enlighten him she would. He served his own plate one-handedly, sipped his wine, and regarded her quizzically. "I don't believe I've gotten around to thanking you yet. That was about the most efficiently I've ever been rescued by my intended rescuee."

She shrugged a bit uncomfortably. "Without you I'd've been dead, too. Just how long have you been tailing me, anyway?"

"Only since Dewent, and I had a hard time believing it when I first spotted you. You know about the reward?" She nodded, and he chuckled. "Somehow I don't think anyone's going to collect it. How the devil did you get so deep so quickly? It took O Branch seven months to get as far as Jacoby, and we still hadn't fingered Fuchien."

She looked at him oddly, then shrugged again.

"Tisiphone helped. And Megarea, of course."

"Oh. Ah, may I take it Megarea is your AI?"

"What else should I call her?" she asked with a smile.

"From what I've read about alpha synth symbioses," he said carefully, "the AI usually winds up with the same name as the human partner."

"Must get pretty confusing," another voice said, and Ben Belkassem jumped. His head whipped around, and the new voice chuckled as his eye found the intercom speaker. "Since you're talking about me, I thought I might as well speak up, Inspector. Or do I get to call you Ferhat, too?"

He spoke firmly to his pulse. He'd known the AI was there, but that didn't diminish his astonishment. He'd worked with more than his share of AIs, and they were at least as alien as one might have expected. They simply didn't have a human perspective, and most were totally disinterested in anyone other than their cyber synth partners. When they did speak, they sounded quite inhuman, and none of them had been issued a sense of humor.

But this one was an *alpha* synth AI, he reminded himself, and its voice, not unreasonably, sounded remarkably like Alicia's.

"'Ferhat' will be fine, um, Megarea," he said after a moment.

"Fine. But if you call me 'Maggie' I'll reverse flow in the head the next time you sit down."

"I wouldn't dream of it," he said a bit faintly.

"Alley did . . . once."

"A base lie," Alicia put in around a mouthful of food. "She makes things up all the time. Sometimes—" she held Ben Belkassem's eyes across the table "—you might almost think she's shy a brick or two."

"Point taken," the inspector said, beginning to wind linguine around his fork. "But you were saying she and . . Tisiphone helped you?"

"Well," Alicia waved at the bulkheads, "you certainly saw how Megarea—by the way, that's '*Star Runner*'s' real name, too—got us off Wyvern."

"So she did, and most efficiently, too."

"Why, thank you, kind sir," the speaker said. "I see he's a perceptive man, Alley."

"And your modesty underwhelms us all," Alicia returned dryly.

"Oh, yeah? Just remember, I got it from you."

Ben Belkassem choked on pasta. *Definitely* not your typical AI. But his humor faded as Alicia replied to Megarea.

"I'll remember. And *you* just remember I'd still've been dead if not for Tisiphone." She looked back at Ben Belkassem. "She was the one who jump-started my augmentation after that bastard knocked it out."

"Really?"

"Don't sound so dubious." He felt himself blush—something he hadn't done in years—and she snorted. "Of course she did. Who do you think put me back on line after Tannis and Uncle Arthur shut me down? I don't exactly have an on-off switch in the middle of my forehead!"

He took another bite to avoid answering, and her eyes glinted.

"Of course, that's not all she does," she continued, leaning across her plate with a conspiratorial air. "She reads minds, too. That's how I know just who to look for as my next target. And she creates a pretty mean illusion, as well—not to mention sticking the occasional idea into someone else's brain." He gawked at her, and she smiled brightly. "Oh, and she and Megarea do a dynamite job of raiding other people's data bases . . . or planting data in them, like '*Star Runner's*' Melville Sector documentation."

She paused expectantly, and he swallowed. It was too much. Logic said she had to be telling the truth, but sanity said it was all impossible, and he was trapped between them.

"Well, yes," he said weakly, "but—"

"Oh, come on, Ferhat!" she snapped, glaring as if at a none too bright student who'd muffed a pop quiz. "You just talked to Megarea, right?" He nodded. "Well, if you don't have a problem accepting an intelligence—a person—who lives in *that* computer," she jabbed an index finger in the general direction of *Megarea's* bridge, "what's the big deal about accepting one who lives in *this* computer—" the same finger thumped her temple "—with me?"

"Put that way," he said slowly, easing his left arm in its sling, "I don't suppose there should be one. But you have to admit it's a bit hard to accept that a mythological creature's moved in with you."

"I don't have to admit anything of the sort, and I'm getting sick and tired of making allowances for everyone else. Damn it, everybody just *assumes* I'm crazy! Not a one of you, not even Tannis, ever even considered the possibility that Tisiphone might just really exist!"

"That's not quite true," he said, and it was her turn to pause. She made a small gesture, inviting him to continue. "Actually, Sir Arthur never questioned that she was 'real' in the sense of someone—or something—in your own mind." He raised a hand as her eyes fired up. "I know that's not what you meant, but he'd gotten as far as worrying that something had activated some sort of psi talent in you and produced a 'Tisiphone persona,' I suppose you'd call it, and I think he may have gone a bit further, whether he knew it or not. That's the real reason he was so worried about you. For you."

The green fire softened, and he shrugged.

"As for myself, I don't pretend to know what's inside your mind. You might remember that conversation we had just before Soissons. I can accept that another entity, *not* just a delusion, has moved in with you. I just . . . have trouble with the idea of a Greek demigoddess or demon." He smiled a touch sheepishly. "I'm afraid it violates my own preconceptions."

"*Your* preconceptions! What do you think it did to *mine?*"

"I hate to think," he admitted. "But even those who accept *something* exists can be excused for worrying about whether or not it's benign, I think."

"That depends on how you define 'benign,' " Alicia replied slowly. "She's not what you'd call a forgiving sort, and we have . . . a bargain."

"To nail the pirates," Ben Belkassem said in a soft voice, and she nodded. "At what price, Alicia?"

"At any price." Her eyes looked straight through him, and her voice was flat—its very lack of emphasis more terrible than any trick of elocution. He shivered, and her eyes dropped back into focus. "At any price," she repeated, "but don't call them 'pirates.' That isn't what they are at all."

"If not pirates, what are they?"

"Most of them are Imperial Fleet personnel."

"*What?*" Ben Belkassem blurted, and her mouth twisted sourly.

"Wondering if I'm crazy again, Ferhat?" she asked bitterly. "I'm not. I don't know who hit Alexsov—it may even have been me, though I was trying to keep him alive—but he was pretty far gone by the time we got to him. But not so far that we didn't get a lot. Gregor Borissovich Alexsov, Captain, Imperial Fleet, Class of '32, last assignment: chief of staff to Commodore James Howell." Her mouth twisted again. "He still holds—held—that position, Inspector, because Commodore Howell is your pirates' field commander, and both of them are working directly for Vice Admiral Sir Amos Brinkman."

He stared at her, mind refusing to function. He'd known there had to be someone on the inside—someone high up—but never *this*! Yet somehow he couldn't doubt it, and the belief in his eyes eased her bitter expression.

"We didn't get everything, but we got a lot. Brinkman's in it up to his neck, but I think he's more their CNO, not the real boss. Alexsov knew who—or what group of whos—is, only he died before we got it. We still don't know their ultimate objective, either, but their *immediate* goal is to get as much as possible of the Imperial Fleet assigned to chasing them down."

"Wait a minute," Ben Belkassem muttered, clutching at his hair with his good hand. "Just wait a minute! I'll accept that you—or Tisiphone, or whoever—can read minds, but why in God's name would they want that? It's suicide!"

"No, it isn't." Alicia's own frustration showed in her voice, and she set aside her fork, laying her hand on the tablecloth and staring at her palm as if it somehow held the answer. "That's only their immediate goal, a single step towards whatever it is they ultimately intend to accomplish, and Alexsov was delighted with how well it's going."

Her hand clenched into a fist, and her eyes blazed.

"But whatever they're up to, Tisiphone and I can finally hit the bastards!" she said fiercely. "We know what they've got, we know where to find it, and we're going to rip the guts right out of them!"

"Wait—slow down!" Ben Belkassem begged. "What do you mean, you 'know what they've got'?"

"The 'pirate' fleet," Alicia said precisely, "consists of nine Fleet transports, seventeen Fleet destroyers, not counting the one we destroyed, six Fleet light cruisers, nine Fleet heavy cruisers, five Fleet battle-cruisers, and one *Capella*-class dreadnought."

Ben Belkassem's jaw dropped. That was at least twice

his own worst-case estimate, and how in *hell* had they gotten their hands on one of the Fleet's most modern dreadnoughts?

Alicia smiled—as if she could read his mind, he thought, and shuddered at the possibility that she was doing precisely that.

"Admiral Brinkman," she explained, "is only one of the senior officers involved. According to the record, most of their ships were stripped and sent to the breakers, but that was only a cover. In fact, they simply disappeared—with all systems and data bases intact. As for the dreadnought, she's the *Procyon*. If you check the ship list, you'll find her in the Sigma Draconis Reserve Fleet, but if anyone checks her berth—" She shrugged.

"Dear God!" Ben Belkassem whispered, then shook himself. "You said you know where they are?"

"At this particular moment, they are either at or en route to AR-12359 /J, an M4 just outside the Franconian Sector. Alexsov was supposed to rendezvous with them after completing his business on Wyvern, and unless Alexsov was wrong, *Admiral* Brinkman—" the rank was a curse in her mouth "—will be sending them new targeting orders there within the next three weeks. Only they won't be able to carry them out."

Her cold, shark-like smile chilled his blood.

"Alicia, you can't take on that kind of opposition by yourself—not even with an alpha synth! They'll kill you!"

"Not before we kill *Procyon*," she said softly, and he swallowed. Fury or no Fury, there was madness in her eyes now. She meant it. She was going to launch a suicide attack straight into them unless he could dissuade her, and his mind worked desperately.

"That's . . . not the best strategy," he said, and her lip curled.

"Oh? It's more than the entire sector government's managed! And just who else do you suggest I send? Shall we report to Admiral Brinkman? Or, since we *know* he's dirty, perhaps we should take a chance on Admiral Gomez. Of course, there's the little problem that I don't have a single scrap of proof, isn't there? What do you suppose they'll do if a crazy woman tells them 'voices' insist the second in command of the Franconian Naval District is actually running the pirates? Voices that got the information from someone who's conveniently dead? Assuming, that is, that they forget their shoot on sight order long enough for me to tell them!

"Those bastards murdered everyone I loved, and Governor Treadwell, the entire Imperial Fleet, and even Uncle Arthur can go straight to Hell before I let them get away now!" Her eyes glared at the inspector, and he shuddered. The amusement of only minutes before had vanished into a raw, ugly hatred totally unlike the woman he remembered from Soissons. And, he thought, unlike the woman he'd observed on Dewent and Wyvern. It was as if learning who her enemies were had snapped something down inside her. . . .

"All right, granted we can't inform Soissons. Hell, with Brinkman dirty, there's no telling how far up—or down—the rot's spread." He was too caught up in his thoughts to notice he was taking Brinkman's guilt as a given. "But if you go busting in there, the only person who knows the truth—whether anyone else is ready to believe you or not—is going to get killed. You may hurt them, but what if you don't hurt them *enough?* What if they regroup?"

"Then they're your problem," she said flatly. "I'm dropping you at Mirbile. You can follow up without explaining where you got your lead."

She was right, he thought, but if he admitted it she'd go right ahead and get herself killed.

"Look, assume you get *Procyon*. I'm not as sure you can do it as you are, but let's accept that you kill Howell and his staff. You'll also be killing the only confirmation of what you've just told me! I may be able to get Brinkman and his underlings, but how do I get whoever's *behind* him?" He saw the fire in her eyes waver and pressed his advantage. "They may be tapped in at a level even higher than Brinkman—maybe even at court back on Old Earth—and if it starts unraveling out here, you can bet Brinkman will suffer a fatal accident before we pick him up. That breaks the chain. If you hit them by yourself, you may *guarantee* the real masterminds get away!"

<*He makes a point, Little One,*> Tisiphone murmured. <*I swore we would reach the ones responsible for your planet's murder. If we settle for those whose hands actually did the deed, you may die and leave me forsworn.*>

"I don't *care* if he's right!" Alicia snarled. "We've finally got a clear shot at the bastards! I say we take it!"

Ben Belkassem thrust himself back in his chair, eyes huge as he realized who she was arguing with, and made himself sit silently.

<*Yet what if he speaks the truth? Would you settle for underlings, leaving those who set this obscenity in motion untouched? Knowing they may plot anew to murder other families as they did those whom* you *loved?*>

Alicia closed her eyes, biting her lip until she tasted blood, and the Fury's voice was almost gentle in her brain.

<*You sound more like myself than I do, Little One, but I have learned from you, as well. We must strike the head from this monster if we seek true vengeance . . . and if we would not have it rise again.*>

"But—"

<*She's right, Alley,*> Megarea broke in. <*Please. You know I'll back you, whatever you decide, but listen to her. Listen to Ferhat.*>

Tears burned the corners of her eyes, tears of pain and hate not even Tisiphone could fully mute, of frustration and need. She wanted to attack, *needed* to attack, and she had a target at last.

<*So what would* you *do?*> she demanded bitterly.

<*Lend me your voice, Little One,*> the Fury said unexpectedly, and Alicia's eyes opened in surprise as she heard her own voice speak.

"Alicia wishes to strike now, Ferhat Ben Belkassem." The inspector stiffened and sweat popped on his forehead at the strange timber of Alicia's voice. "She believes, and rightly, that we must strike our foes now, while we know where we may find them. Yet you counsel otherwise. Why?"

Ben Belkassem licked his lips. He'd told Alicia the truth; he couldn't quite accept that she'd been possessed by a creature from mythology, but he knew it wasn't Alicia speaking. Whoever—*what*ever—had entered her life, he was face to face with it at last, unable even to pretend it didn't exist, and terror chipped away at his veneer of sophistication, revealing the primitive behind it to his own inner eye.

"Because—because it isn't enough . . . Tisiphone," he made himself say. "At the very least, we need outside confirmation of the ships they have from witnesses no one can sweep under the rug because they're 'crazy.' That would lend at least partial credence to the rest of what Alicia—to what the two of you have just told me. And we have to hurt them worse than you can, destroy more of their ships and shatter the raiding force so badly they'll need months to reorganize while we go to work from the other end."

"Well and good, Ferhat Ben Belkassem," that dispassionate, infinitely cold ghost of Alicia's contralto replied. "Yet we have but our good *Megarea*. You yourself have said we dare not seek aid from the Franconian Sector, and no other can reach hither before our enemies depart their present rendezvous."

"I know." He drew a deep breath and stared into Alicia's eyes, seeing her own will and mind within them, behind that other's words. "But what if I could tell you where to find a naval force that *could* go toe to toe with the 'pirates'? One that doesn't have a thing to do with the Fleet? And one that's right here, already in the sector?"

"There is such a force?" the icy voice sharpened, and Alicia's eyes widened as he nodded.

"There is. You were going to drop me off at Mirabile—why not take me to Ringbolt, instead?"

Chapter Twenty-eight

The battleship *Audacious* hung in geosynchronous orbit above the heat-glass scar of Raphael, and Simon Monkoto paced her bridge. His eyes no longer burned with hate; they were as hard as his face, filled with a bitter determination cold enough to freeze the marrow of a star.

He knew his people were growing restive as they waited for him to find a way to take the offensive, but none of them had complained. Professional warriors all, they accepted that warriors often died, yet they also knew this wasn't just about Arlen. It was about the civilians who had died *with* Arlen, as well. About the murder of a city and the radioactive filth the warhead had blasted into Ringbolt's atmosphere. Mercenaries tended to be loyal first and foremost to their own, but they understood justice . . . and vengeance. That was why the other outfits had responded in such strength.

He paused by the master plot, studying the light codes

Meaningless to the untrained eye, they told Monkoto everything at a glance.

The Ringbolt System was alive with ships. Most were small—cruisers or lighter—but they included a solid core of heavy hitters. The Falcons, Westfeldt's Wolves, Captain Tarbaneau and her Assassins. . . . He couldn't have picked a more battle-hardened group, yet they, like his own Maniacs, expected the great Simon Monkoto to Do Something. They owed him, and they wanted the people who'd done this thing, but there was a limit to how long they could sit here losing money. Unless the El Grecan government agreed to put them on the payroll, they'd have to start pulling out soon, and—

A soft buzz drew his eyes to the gravitic plot. He stepped closer, then stiffened as the preposterous nature of the incoming Fasset signature penetrated. Whatever it was, it was moving faster than a destroyer, yet its drive mass was greater than a battleship's!

More buzzers began to sound as other eyes and brains made the same observation. Additional sensors sprang alive, battle boards blinked green and amber eyes that turned quickly to red, and Simon Monkoto smiled.

That was an Imperial Fleet drive, but the ships that murdered Raphael had been Empire-built, as well.

"You don't think you could've come in just a bit more discreetly?" Ben Belkassem asked politely from the chair Alicia had installed beside her own on *Megarea*'s bridge. "They're probably in hair-trigger mode, you know."

"We don't have time to be inconspicuous," Alicia said absently. She wore her headset this time, and readiness signals purred to her from her weapon systems. She didn't want to use them, but if she had to . . .

"Howell won't stay at the rendezvous more than another three weeks, and it's a two-week trip from here even if we could make it a straight shot—which we can't. We have to come in on a Wyvern-based vector, or they'll know we're not Alexsov the instant they pick us up. That gives us less than two days' leeway, and I'm not going to lose them now."

"But—"

"Either your friend Monkoto helps us, or he doesn't," she said flatly. "Either way, I'm going to be at AR-12359/J within the next nineteen standard days." She looked at him, and that same, strange hunger flickered in her eyes. "Tisiphone, Megarea, and I aren't going to miss our shot. Not now."

He closed his mouth. Ben Belkassem didn't frighten easily, yet there were times Alicia DeVries terrified him. Not because she threatened *him*, but because of the determination that burned in her like fiery ice. People had called her mad, and he'd disagreed; now he was no longer certain. She wouldn't stop—*couldn't* stop—and he wondered how much of that sprang from Tisiphone, whatever Tisiphone truly was, and how much from herself.

Audacious rendezvoused with the other capital ships of the mercenary fleet barely half a million kilometers out from Ringbolt, for it was obvious the bogey was far faster and more maneuverable than they were. So far it had shown no sign of hostility, but Monkoto spread "his" ships—tight enough to concentrate their fire, dispersed enough to intercept any effort to get by them—and readiness reports murmured in his link to *Audacious*'s cyber synth.

He returned his attention to the bogey with a sort of awe. Whatever it was, it was pouring on an incredible deceleration. It was well inside the primary's Powell limit, but it was decelerating at over thirteen hundred gravities—which, if it kept it up, would bring it to a halt, motionless with regard to *Audacious*, just over five thousand kilometers short of his flagship. If its intentions were hostile, that was suicide range, and—

The light cruiser *Serpent* finally got close enough for a visual, and Monkoto gawked as CIC shunted it to his display. A *freighter*? Impossible!

But a freighter the image before him was, and a freighter it remained—a slightly battered, totally unremarkable freighter . . . with more drive power than a battleship.

* * *

"We're coming into com range, Ferhat. Want me to hail them?" Megarea asked eagerly through a wall speaker, and Ben Belkassem heard Alicia's soft chuckle beside him.

Megarea liked the inspector, and Ben Belkassem was bemused by how much he liked her in return—and how much he enjoyed her bawdy, wicked sense of humor. She'd even built herself a "Megarea face," a svelte, stunning redhead, so she could flirt via com screen while her sickbay remotes worked on his arm, and he knew she simply ached to use that face (and figure) on a new audience. Whatever else happened, he would never again think of AIs in quite the same way.

"Have you identified *Audacious*?" he asked.

"Yup. Just as big and nasty as you said, but I could spot her half my drive nodes and still run her into the ground."

"Be nice," Alicia said, and Megarea sniffed.

"Never mind, Megarea," Ben Belkassem grinned. "Go on and call them."

"Sure thing," she said, and he twitched his uniform straight for the pickup. His own baggage remained somewhere on Wyvern, but Alicia and Megarea had outfitted him in "*Star Runner*'s" midnight blue, and he had to admit he liked the way it made him look.

"Admiral, the bogey identifies itself as the private ship *Star Runner*," Monkoto's com officer announced. "They're asking for you by name."

Monkoto scratched his nose. Odder and odder, he thought with his first real smile since the Ringbolt Raid, but that "private ship" business had to be a fiction. Whatever that thing might *look* like, it was no freighter.

"Route it to my station," he said, and leaned back as a lovely young woman in dark blue and silver appeared on his screen. He eyed her high-piled, Titian hair admiringly while he waited out the transmission lag, then her own eyes sharpened and looked back at him.

"Admiral Monkoto?" she inquired in a musical contralto, and he nodded. There was another lengthy delay while his nod sped to her screen, then she said, "I have someone here who wishes to speak to you, sir," and disappeared, replaced by a small, hook-nosed man in a sling and the same blue uniform.

"Hello, Simon," the newcomer said, not waiting for Monkoto to respond. "Sorry to drop in on you without warning, but we need to talk."

Ben Belkassem watched Alicia from the corner of his eye as they stepped out of the personnel tube onto Monkoto's flagship. Something was happening inside her, something that was burning holes in the Alicia DeVries he'd first met, and it was getting worse. Right after leaving Wyvern, hours had passed between flashes of that something else, but the intervals were growing shorter. It wasn't Tisiphone—he was positive of that now—and that made it worse. It was as if Alicia herself were burning out before his eyes. He could almost feel her . . . slipping away. Yet she had herself under control just now, and that was enough. It had to be.

"It's been a long time, Ferhat," a mellow tenor said, and Simon Monkoto held out his hand in greeting.

"Not that long," Ben Belkassem disagreed, returning the mercenary's clasp with a toothy grin.

"And this must be Captain Mainwaring," Monkoto said, and Alicia smiled tightly without confirming his assumption. He didn't notice; his eyes were locked on Ben Belkassem, and his humor had vanished.

"You said you have some information for me?"

"I do—or, rather, Captain Mainwaring does."

"What—?" Monkoto began eagerly, then chopped himself off. "Forgive me. My colleagues are waiting in the main briefing room, and they should hear this along with me. If you'll join us, Captain?"

Alicia nodded and followed the tall, broad-shouldered mercenary into a lift. She watched his face as the elevator rose, seeing the pinched nostrils, the deep-etched furrow between the eyes, and she didn't need Tisiphone to feel his hunger calling to her own, sharp-edged and jagged.

The lift doors opened, and Monkoto ushered them into a briefing room.

"Captain Mainwaring, Mister Ben Belkassem, allow me to introduce my colleagues," he said, and worked his way down the table, starting with Admiral Yussuf Westfeldt, a stocky, gray-haired man. Commodore Tadeoshi Falconi was as tall as Monkoto but thin, with quick, assertive movements; Captain Esther Tarbaneau was a slender, black-skinned woman with a very still face and startlingly gentle eyes; and Commodore Matthew O'Kane was a younger version of Monkoto—not surprisingly: he'd begun his career with the Maniacs.

Between them, Alicia knew, these people controlled over seventy ships of war, including two battleships, nine battle-cruisers, and seven heavy cruisers, and no regular navy could have matched their experience. They looked back at her with hooded eyes, and she wondered what they made of her.

Monkoto finished the introductions and took a seat at the center of the long table, across from her and Ben Belkassem. The outsized view screen at her back was focused on *Megarea*'s freighter disguise, and she tried not to wipe her palms on her trousers as she faced people who fought for pay and remembered the million-credit reward the Empire had offered for her.

"I've dealt with Mister Ben Belkassem before," Monkoto informed his fellows, "and I trust him implicitly. Certain conditions of confidentiality apply, but he represents a . . . major galactic power." The others nodded and regarded the inspector with renewed curiosity, wondering which branch of the imperial bureaucracy he worked for, as Monkoto gestured for him to take over.

"Thank you, Admiral Monkoto," he said, returning the searching gazes steadily, "but under the circumstances, I feel I ought to put all my cards on the table. Ladies and gentlemen, my name is Ferhat Ben Belkassem, and I am a senior inspector with Operations Branch of the Imperial Ministry of Justice."

Breath hissed in along Monkoto's side of the table. O Branch agents *never* revealed their identities unless they were up to their necks in fecal matter and sinking fast, but at least he'd guaranteed their attention.

"I realize that may be a bit of a shock," he continued calmly, "but I'm afraid there are more to come. I know why you're here—and I know where you can find the pirates." A ripple ran through his audience. "To be more precise, my associate does." Eyes swiveled back to Alicia, hot and no longer hooded, and she made herself sit straight and still under their weight.

"How?" Monkoto demanded. "How did you find them?"

"I'm afraid I can't reveal that, sir," Alicia replied carefully. "I have . . . a source I must protect, but my information is solid."

"I would certainly like to believe that, Captain Mainwaring," Esther Tarbaneau said in a soft soprano, "but you must realize how critical your credibility is, even with Inspector Ben Belkassem to vouch for you. How is it that a single merchant skipper could locate them when the Empire, El Greco, and the Jung Association have all failed?"

"Captain Mainwaring is more than she seems, Captain Tarbaneau," Ben Belkassem put in.

"Indeed?" Tarbaneau arched politely skeptical eyebrows, and Alicia sighed. She'd known all along it would come to this.

<Cut the holo, Megarea.>

<Are you sure, Alley?> the AI asked anxiously. *<I don't like the thought of doing that with you over there all alone.>*

<I'm not "all alone," and we don't have a choice. Do it.>

There was no response, but she didn't need one. Every eye jerked to the view screen in a single, harsh gasp, and most of the mercenaries hunched convulsively forward—O'Kane actually jerked to his feet—as the "freighter" vanished. The lean wickedness of an imperial alpha synth could not be mistaken, even with splotches of titanium marring its immaculate hull.

"Ladies and gentlemen," Ben Belkassem said quietly, "allow me to introduce Captain Alicia DeVries, Imperial Cadre." Eyes whipped back to her, and he nodded. "I assure you, Captain DeVries's . . . instability has been grossly exaggerated. We've been working together for the past several weeks," he added, which was true enough, though Alicia hadn't known it at the time.

The mercenaries sank back in their chairs, eyes narrowed, and he hid a smile as he watched them leap to the conclusion he'd intended. Alicia really did have a marvelous cover—even if no one had set it up on purpose.

"So," Monkoto said forty minutes later, drumming his fingers on the conference table while he stared at a holographic star map. AR-12359/J burned a sullen crimson at its heart, and a computer screen at his elbow glowed with all the data Alicia had been able to supply on the "pirates'" strength. "We know where they are; the problem is what we do with them."

He pinched the bridge of his nose as he met his colleagues' eyes, then turned to Alicia, smiling grimly as he recognized the questions in her eyes.

"Neither you nor the Inspector are Fleet officers, Captain, but that's what we do for a living, and I'm afraid this—" he gestured at the star map "—is a classic nasty fleet problem."

"Why?" Impatience burned in Alicia's blood once more, yet Monkoto's obvious professionalism—and matching hunger—kept it out of her voice.

"Put most simply, they're in n-space and they'll see us coming. Ships run blind in wormhole space, but their gravitics will pick us up long before we arrive, at which point they'll simply run on an acutely divergent vector. By the time we can kill our velocity and go in pursuit, they'll be long gone."

Alicia stared at the admiral, stunned by how calmly he'd said it, then jerked around to glare at Ben Belkassem. He'd been so glib about "getting help"—had *he* known how hopeless it was?!

"The classic solution is a converging envelopement," Monkoto went on, "with someone coming in at high velocity on almost any possible escape vector, but that also requires an overwhelming numerical advantage. We—" he waved at his fellows "—can probably take these bastards head on, though that *Capella*-class'll make things tight, but not if we spread out to envelope them."

Alicia dropped her eyes to the star map, fingers curving into talons under the table edge as she glared at the crimson star.

"We could call in the Empies for more ships," O'Kane suggested.

"Somehow I don't think so," Monkoto murmured, watching Ben Belkassem's face. "If we could, you wouldn't be talking to *us*, would you, Ferhat?"

"No," Ben Belkassem said unhappily. "We have reason to believe there's a leak—a very, *very* high-level leak—from Soissons."

"Well, isn't that a fine crock of shit," Westfeldt muttered softly.

"Isn't there *anything* we can do?" Alicia almost begged, and Monkoto leaned back in his chair and met her eyes with a cool, thoughtful gaze.

"Actually," he said, "I think there is . . . especially with an alpha synth to help." He swept the others with a shark's lazy smile. "Our problem is that they can see us coming, but suppose *we* were the ones in normal space?"

"You've got that evil gleam in your eye, Simon," Falconi observed.

"It's very simple, Tad. We won't go to them at all; we'll invite *them* to come to *us*."

Chapter Twenty-nine

The green-uniformed woman rapped on the edge of the open office door, and the massive, silver-haired man behind the deck looked up. He grunted in greeting, waved at an empty chair, and returned to his reader, and the corners of the woman's mouth quirked as she sat and leaned back to wait.

It wasn't a very long wait. The silver-haired man nodded, grunted again—a harsher, somehow ugly grunt this time—and switched off the reader.

"Took your time getting here," he rumbled, and she shrugged.

"I was running that field exercise we discussed. Besides," she pointed at the reader, "you seemed busy enough." She spoke lightly, but her eyes were worried. "Was that about Alley?"

"No. Still not a sign of her." Sir Arthur Keita sounded oddly pleased, for the man whose iron sense of duty had started the hunt for Alicia DeVries, and he smiled wryly as Tannis Cateau inhaled in wordless relief. She couldn't very well say "Thank God!" but she could think it very loudly. Then his smile faded.

"No, this is about our other problem, and I'm afraid it's coming to a head. I'm placing Clean Sweep on two-day standby."

Tannis twitched upright, eyes wide, and Keita watched her mind race, following her thoughts with ease. She'd been kept fully briefed on his downloads from Colonel McIlheny, and she knew something McIlheny didn't—that his reports to Sir Arthur had been quietly received on Old Earth, re-encrypted, and starcommed back across the light-years to Alexandria, just over the Macedon Sector border from the Franconian Sector. And they had been sent there because that was as far as Sir Arthur Keita had gone when he took his leave of Soissons.

The brigadier rocked gently in his chair, reexamining every tortuous step which had brought them to Clean Sweep. It would be ugly even if it went perfectly, but McIlheny and Ben Belkassem had pegged it; someone far up the chain of command *had* to be working with the pirates, and that made very officer in the Franconian Sector suspect. No doubt most were loyal servants of Crown and Empire, but there was no way to tell which of them *weren't*, which was why Keita hadn't gone home—and why an entire battalion of drop commandos had been gathered in bits and pieces from the most distant stations Keita could think of to the remotest training camp on Alexandria.

Countess Miller had wanted to send Keita a full colonel to command them, but he'd refused. The Cadre had so few officers that senior, he'd argued, that the sudden disappearance of any of them was too likely to be noticed. Which was true enough, though hardly the full story.

Major Cateau's fierce resolve to protect Alicia Devries was the rest of it. No one else would be allowed to serve as Alicia's physician if she could be brought in alive . . . and, Sir Arthur knew, Tannis hoped—prayed—she'd be there when Alicia was found. If anyone could talk her into surrendering, that anyone was Tannis Cateau.

Keita understood that, and he owed her the chance, threadbare though they both knew it was, almost as much as he owed Alicia herself. But that wasn't something he cared to explain to Countess Miller, and so he'd kept Tannis here by pointing out that a battalion was a major's command and insisting that Major Cateau, already on the spot, was the logical person to command this one. The Fleet or Marines might have questioned one of their medical officers' competence in such matters; the Cadre did not.

"Have you told Inspector Suares?" Tannis asked finally, and he nodded.

"He agrees that we have no choice. His marshals will begin arriving at Base Two this afternoon."

"But they won't have time for live-fire exercises, will they?"

"I'm afraid not, but at least they're all experienced people. And there's not supposed to be any shooting, anyway."

Tannis snorted, and Keita was hard put not to join her. Ninety of Inspector Suares' three hundred imperial marshals were O Branch operatives, the others specially selected from Justice's Criminal Investigation Branch, and most were ex-military, as well, but Keita didn't quite share Old Earth's conviction that no one would offer open resistance. No emperor had ever before ordered the entire military and civilian command structure of a Crown Sector taken simultaneously into preventive custody. Seamus II had the constitutional authority to do just that, so long as no one was held for more than thirty days without formal charges, but it would engender mammoth confusion. And sufficiently well-placed traitors might well be able to convince their subordinates some sort of external treason was under way and organize enough resistance to cover their own flight.

"I wish we didn't have to do this," Tannis said into the quiet.

"I do, too, but how else can we handle it? We tried

to wait till we found the guilty parties, but all our investigators seem to've hit stone walls—even Ben Belkassem hasn't reported in over a month. If we act at all, we have to take everyone into custody at once or risk missing the people we really want, and I'm afraid we're finally out of time." Keita tapped his reader. "I've just read a message from Ben McIlheny, and I wish to hell Countess Miller had let me tell him about this!"

"Why?"

"Because he didn't know anybody was getting set to act, so he decided to push things to a head on his own. He tried to run a bluff and force the bastards into overt action by reporting to a very select readership that he was about to unmask the traitor."

"He *what?*" Tannis jerked upright in her chair, and Keita nodded.

"Exactly. He figured they couldn't take a chance that he was really onto them . . . and he was right." The brigadier's face was grim. "His last data dump was accompanied by a followup to the effect that Colonel McIlheny is in criticial condition following a quote 'freak skimmer accident,' unquote. Lady Rosario has him in a maximum-security ward, and Captain Okanami thinks he'll pull through, but he'll be hospitalized for months."

"They must be getting desperate to try something like that!"

"No question, but it's even worse than you may guess without knowing who he sent his report to." She raised an eyebrow, and Keita's smile was thin. "Governor General Treadwell, Admiral Gomez, Admiral Brinkman, Admiral Horth, and their chiefs of staff," he said, and watched her wince.

"So at least one of those eight people is either a traitor or an unwitting leak," he continued quietly, "and I doubt the latter after the microscope McIlheny's put on his information distribution. But the fact that they tried to shut him up seems to confirm his theory that they're after more than just loot. If they didn't have a long-term objective, they'd've cut their losses and disappeared rather than risk trying for him, and I doubt it was a simple panic reaction. If whoever set this up were the type to panic we'd have had him—or her—long ago. So either their timetable's so advanced they hoped to wrap things up before anyone figured out what had happened to McIlheny and why, or else—" he met Tannis's eyes "—*everyone* on his short list of suspects is guilty and they thought no one else would pick up on his report because no one else would ever see it."

"Surely you don't really think—" Tannis began, and he shook his head.

"No, I don't think they're all dirty. But then I wouldn't have believed *any* of them were. My personal theory is that they underestimated McIlheny's ability to crash land a skimmer even after two of its grav coils suddenly reversed polarity on final. They didn't expect him to live, much less leave enough wreckage for anyone to figure out just how 'freak' a freak accident it was. At the very least, they probably counted on several weeks, possibly even months, of confusion before we put it together.

"The problem is that we can't rely on that. I may be wrong, and even if I'm not, his survival and the questions his subordinates are asking about the nature of his 'accident' may force them into something precipitous. If that's the case, we need to get in there before they start wiping their records or bug out on us. We may not get them all when we come crashing in, but we may *lose* them all if we don't."

"I see," she said quietly, and Keita nodded again.

"I believe you do, Tannis. So get back to Base Two and get ready to welcome Inspector Suares. I want everyone aboard ship in forty-eight hours."

Sir Arthur Keita stood on the flag bridge of HMS *Pavia*, flagship of Admiral Mikhail Leibniz, and watched the visual display as the task force formed up about her in Alexandria orbit. Like the Cadre strike team it was to transport, its units had been drawn from far and wide—a three-ship division here, a squadron there, a single ship from yet another base. Its heaviest unit was a battlecruiser, for it had been planned for speed, yet it was a powerful force. Like Keita himself, its commanders hoped there would be no fighting; if there was any, they intended to win.

"Departure in seven hours, Sir Arthur," Admiral Leibniz said quietly, and Keita nodded without turning. He hoped Leibniz wouldn't construe that as discourtesy, but he didn't like this mission.

He sighed and concentrated on the gleaming minnows of the ships, half eager to depart into wormhole space and get this ended, half dreading what might happen when he reached his destination. And that, he knew, was why he disliked this operation so. Somewhere at the far end of his journey he would find a traitor, possibly—probably—more than one, and treason was a crime Sir Arthur Keita simply could not understand. The thought that any officer could so degrade himself and his honor made his skin crawl, and knowing that someone sworn to protect and defend had murdered millions made him physically ill.

He wanted that traitor unmasked and destroyed. There was, could be, no trace of mercy in him, but there was sorrow for the shame that traitor had brought to everything Keita himself held sacred.

"Excuse me, Sir Arthur, but you have a priority signal." The voice broke into his reverie, and he turned to find it belonged to a youthful communications officer who extended a message chip to him.

Keita took the chip and frowned as he recognized the Cadre Intelligence coding. None of the flag bridge's readers could unscramble it, so he excused himself and made his way to Tannis Cateau's command center. The major started shooing the staff away from the com section at sight of the message chip, but he waved for her to remain when she started to follow them. She sat back down at her desk, keeping her back to him while he inserted the chip, only to look back up with a jerk as a voice spoke.

"Well, I will be goddamned," it said softly, and her head whipped around in astonishment, for it belonged to

Sir Arthur Keita, and he was *grinning* as he met her startled gaze.

"Something new has been added," he announced. "This—" he jerked his chin at the reader screen "—is from the team we placed on Ringbolt. It would seem our missing O Branch inspector arrived there two days ago and put on some sort of Pied Piper performance."

"Pied Piper?" His eyes were positively glowing, Tannis thought.

"Our people couldn't get all the details—they're isolated from our official presence there, and the locals are playing their cards mighty close—but it seems Ben Belkassem turned up aboard a tramp freighter named *Star Runner*, or possibly *Far Runner*, for a personal meeting with Admiral Simon Monkoto."

"He did?" Her eyes narrowed in speculation, and Keita nodded.

"He did. And six hours later the Monkoto Free Mercenaries, the Westfeldt Wolves, O'Kane's Free Company, the Star Assassins, and Falconi's Falcons were under way. Not some of them—*all* of them."

"My God," she whispered. "You don't think he—?"

"It would seem probable," Keita replied, "and please note that he appears to have gone directly to the *mercenaries*; not the Fleet and not the El Grecan Navy. Not to anyone who might have reported back to Soissons. He didn't tell *us*, either, but then he didn't know we were out here. If he's avoiding Soissons, he may have starcommed Justice HQ, but it'll take Old Earth another four days to relay to us if he did, and in the meantime . . ." He began feeding numbers into his terminal, and Tannis frowned.

"I know that tone of voice, Uncle Arthur. What are you up to?"

"Our people may not have gotten everything, but they did find out where all those mercenaries are headed and when they're supposed to get there, and unless I'm mistaken—aha!" The result of his calculations blinked before him, and his grin became savage with delight. "We can get there within forty-one hours of their ETA if we move our departure up a bit."

"But what about Clean Sweep?"

"Soissons won't go anywhere, Tannis, and—" he swiveled to face her, and she saw the hunger in his eyes, heard it in his voice "—this little detour may just tell us *who*, because only one thing in the universe could have sucked Simon Monkoto away from Ringbolt!"

Chapter Thirty

"Well it's about damned time," Commodore Howell muttered to himself. He glared at the gravitic plot and reminded himself—again—that he wasn't going to climb down Alexsov's throat the instant he saw him. He suspected it wasn't going to be an easy resolve to keep.

He turned his back on the plot and interlaced his fingers to crack his knuckles. Alexsov was at least twelve days late, which would have been bad enough from anyone else. From the obsessively punctual chief of staff it was maddening, and vague visions of horrible disaster had haunted the commodore, only just held at bay by his faith in Alexsov.

He drew a deep breath and summoned a wry smile, wishing—not for the first time—that "pirates" weren't cut off from the Empire's starcom network. This business of relying solely on starships and SLAM drones wore on a man. And, his eyes narrowed again, speaking of SLAM drones, just why hadn't Gregor used one to explain his delay? His eyes lit with a touch of real humor as he realized he had at least one perfectly valid reason to tear a long, bloody strip off his chief of staff . . . and how much he looked forward to it.

<*Well, unless they're stone blind they've got us on their gravitics by now,*> Megarea commented.

Alicia only grunted in response. She sat in her command chair, clasping her hands in her lap to keep from gnawing her fingernails. She'd smelled enough fear on Cadre strikes, but drop commandos were passengers up to the moment they made their drops. Whether or not their targets would be there when they arrived was something their chauffeurs worried about, and she'd never realized how tense the final approach must be for Fleet personnel. She was blind, unable to see out of wormhole space. She couldn't know if an ambush awaited her, or even if the enemy were there at all, but if they were, *they* could see *her* just fine.

<*Calmly, Little One. We will find them and perform our appointed task.*> She heard Tisiphone's tension, but it was a different sort of strain. The Fury never doubted they would find those they sought; eagerness sharpened her tone, not uncertainty.

"Yeah, sure," Alicia said, and twitched in surprise at the saw-toothed anticipation quivering in her own voice.

She felt Tisiphone's answering start of surprise—and something like concern behind it—and looked down with a frown. Her clasped hands were actually trembling! Confusion flickered through her for just a moment, a vague sense of something wrong, but she brushed it aside and reached for a thought to distract her from it.

"Think they'll bite, Megarea?"

<*Sure they will. I admit this is a bit more complicated than being* Star Runner, *but I can handle it.*>

Alicia nodded, though "a bit more complicated" grossly understated the task her cybernetic sister faced. Pretending to be a freighter was complex yet straightforward for an alpha synth's electronic warfare capabilities, but this time the deception was multi-layered and far more difficult. This time *Megarea* was pretending to be a battle-cruiser pretending to be a destroyer—and failing. The "pirates" were supposed to see through the first level of deceit, but not the second . . . and if they pierced the first too soon, Monkoto's entire plan would come crashing down about their ears.

"Definitely a destroyer drive," Commander Rendlemann announced several hours later, and Howell allowed himself an ironic smile. Of course it was a destroyer. Arriving at this godforsaken star on that heading it could only be *Harpy*. No one but Alexsov and Control knew where to find them, and any dispatch boat from Control would have come in on a completely dif—

"Still," Rendlemann murmured to himself, "there's something odd about it."

"What?" Howell twisted around in his chair, eyes sharpening.

"I said there's some—"

"I heard that part! What d'you mean, 'odd'?"

"Nothing I can really put a finger on, sir," Rendlemann frowned as he concentrated on his link to *Procyon*'s AI, "but they're decelerating a bit slowly. There's a slight frequency shift in the forward nodes, too." He rubbed his chin. "Wonder if they've had drive problems? That could explain the delay, and if they had to make shipboard repairs it might explain the frequency anomaly."

Howell reached for his own headset. Unlike Rendlemann, he couldn't link directly with the dreadnought's cyber synth, but a frown gathered between his brows as he studied Tracking's data. Rendlemann was right. *Harpy* was coming in faster than she should have—in fact, her current deceleration would carry her past her rendezvous with *Procyon* at more than seven thousand KPS.

His frown deepened. *Harpy* was well inside his perimeter destroyers, little more than ninety minutes from *Procyon* at her present deceleration, and she hadn't said a word. She was still 17.6 light-minutes out, so transmission lag would be a pain, but why hadn't Alexsov sent even a greeting? He had to know how Howell must have worried, and . . .

"Com, hail Captain Alexsov and ask him where he's been."

The message fled towards *Megarea* at the speed of light, and she raced to meet it. Eight hundred seconds after it was born, *Megarea*'s receptors scooped it out of space, and Alicia swore.

"I wanted to be closer than this, damn it!" Her own displays glowed behind her eyes, and thirteen light-minutes lay between her and *Procyon.* She was already in the dreadnought's SLAM range . . . but *Megarea* mounted no SLAMs. She had to close another sixty-five million kilometers, fifteen more minutes at this deceleration, before her missiles could range upon her enemy—and seventy-two million before she could "break and run" on the vector to Monkoto's rendezvous.

"Can we steal enough delay, Megarea?" she demanded.

<*I don't think so,*> the AI replied unhappily. <*No reply will be the same as answering, unless this Howell's a lot dumber than we think, and battle-cruiser three's in position to cut us off short of course change.*>

<*Better to answer, Little One. We are more like to gain time by tangling him in confusion, however briefly, than by silence.*>

A corner of Alicia's mind glanced at the clock. Eighty seconds since the signal came in, and Megarea was right; if she delayed much longer, her very delay would become a response. . . .

Something hot and primitive boiled in the recesses of her mind, something red that smoked with the hot, sweet incense of blood, and her lips thinned over her teeth.

"Oh, the hell with it! Talk to the man, Megarea."

<*Transmitting,*> the AI said simply.

James Howell's fingers drummed on the arm of his command chair, and he frowned in growing, formless uneasiness. That *had* to be *Harpy*, but Gregor was taking his own sweet time about replying.

He glanced at the chronometer and bared his teeth at

his own thoughts. Barely twenty-seven minutes had passed since he sent his own signal; a reply could scarcely have arrived this soon even if Gregor had responded instantly. He knew that, but . . .

He bit the thought off and made himself wait. Twenty-eight minutes. The range was down to eleven light-minutes. Twenty-nine. Thirty.

"Sir," his com officer looked up with a puzzled expression, "we have a response, but it's not from Captain Alexsov."

"What?!" Howell rounded fiercely on the unfortunate officer.

"They say they have battle damage, sir," that worthy said defensively. "We don't have visual, and their signal is very weak. I think— Here, let me route it to your station."

Howell leaned back, glaring at *Harpy*'s blue star. *Battle* damage? How? From whom? What the hell was go—

His thought died as a faint voice sounded in his ear bug.

". . . nal is very faint. Say again your transmission. Repeat, this is *Medusa*. Your signal is very weak. Say again your trans—"

Medusa?! Howell jerked upright in his chair with an oath.

"Battle stations!"

His shocked bridge crew stared at him for an instant, and then alarms began to howl throughout *Procyon*'s eight million-tonne hull.

Howell snapped his chair around to face Commander Rendlemann across his own battle board. The ops officer's eyes were almost focused, despite his concentration on his cyber synth link, and questions burned in their depths.

"It's not Gregor," Howell snapped.

"But—*how*, sir?"

"I don't *know* how!" Yet even as he spoke, Howell's mind raced. "Something must have given Gregor away to a regular Fleet unit." He slammed a fist against his console. "They took him out and reset their transponder to bluff their way in, but they can't have taken *Harpy* intact. If they had, they'd know the *Medusa* transponder codes were bogus."

"But if they didn't take her intact, how did they know to come *here*?"

"How the hell do *I* know? Unless—" Howell closed his eyes, thinking furiously, then spat another curse. "They must've picked him up leaving Wyvern, before he wormholed out of the system. *Damn* the luck! They got a read on his vector and extrapolated his destination."

"Extrapolated well enough to hit us dead center?"

"How the hell many *other* stars are there within twenty light-years?" Howell snarled. "But they can't've known what they were heading into. If they knew, they wouldn't have sent a single tin can to check it out." He glared at the blue dot again, yet a grudging respect had crept into his angry eyes. "Those gutsy bastards are decelerating straight toward us, and they're already inside sensor range. They can't see us on gravitics with our drives down, so they're hanging on as long as they can to get a full count for their SLAM drones, and if they do—"

He cut himself off and bent over his board. That destroyer was still outside its own range, and no destroyer could stand up to the SLAM salvos of a dreadnought. He glanced at his plot, at the two escorting battle-cruisers tying into *Procyon*'s tactical net as his ships rushed to battle stations. A third battle-cruiser was far closer to the intruder, already wheeling to close her jaws upon her prey.

<Here they come, Alley!> Megarea warned, and Alicia watched the battle-cruiser rounding upon her. The initial surprise must have been total, but the battle-cruiser's weapons were ready at last. Megarea's sensors read her as HMS *Cannae*, and Alicia felt a sensual, almost erotic shiver as her/their targeting systems reached out and locked. Unlike *Procyon*, *Cannae* was barely three light-minutes from *Megarea* . . . yet she, too, thought she faced only a destroyer, for the alpha synth's ECM still hid both her identity and the shoals of sublight missiles deployed

about her on tractors. Their maximum velocity was halved without the initial boost of internal launchers, but pre-spotting them more than tripled the salvos *Megarea* could throw.

Alicia felt them through her headset, felt them like her own teeth and claws, and hunger fuzzed her vision like some sick delirium. A part of her stood aghast, stunned by her own blood-thirst. This was wrong, it whispered, no part of Monkoto's plan, but it was only a tiny whisper. She hung on the crumbling brink of a berserker's madness . . . and embraced its ferocity.

"Take her!" she snapped.

The gravitic plot showed it first. Its FTL capability could see only the gravity wells of starships, SLAMs, and SLAM drones, but unlike *Procyon*'s light-speed sensors, it gave a virtual real-time readout at such short range. Howell was watching it narrowly, waiting for the blue stars of *Cannae*'s first SLAMs, when the battle-cruiser's Fasset drive disappeared.

Megarea's missiles erupted into *Cannae*'s face, and the battle-cruiser's AI had too little time to react to the impossible density of that salvo. It did its best, but its best wasn't good enough.

Battle screen failed, *Cannae* vanished in a boil of light and plasma, and Alicia DeVries' eyes were emerald chunks of Hell. The orgiastic release of violence exploded within her, brighter and hotter than *Cannae*'s pyre. It took her like a shark, snatching her under in a vortex of hate, and her madness reached out like pestilence. It flooded through her link to Megarea, engulfing the AI as it had engulfed her, and Tisiphone stiffened in horror.

This wasn't Alicia! The fine-meshed precision and deadly self-discipline had vanished into a heaving chaos of raw bloodlust. There was no reason in her, only the need to rend and destroy . . . and the Fury realized almost instantly from whence it sprang. She'd set a wall about Alicia's loss and hate to make that distilled rage *her* weapon, but this mortal was stronger than even the

Fury had guessed. She would not be denied what was hers of right, and somehow she had breached that wall.

Alicia DeVries forgot Simon Monkoto's plan. Forgot the need to survive. She saw only the fleet that had murdered her world and family, and her madness locked Megarea close as they charged to meet its flagship.

James Howell went white as light-speed sensors finally showed him the details of *Cannae*'s death. God in Heaven, what *was* that thing?! The one thing it *wasn't* was a destroyer—and whatever it was had stopped decelerating. It was accelerating straight towards him at seventeen KPS per second!

SLAMs raced to meet *Megarea*, and Alicia dropped the Fasset drive's side shields. The black hole's maw sucked them in, and she snarled, shuddering in the ecstasy of destruction, as she flashed past *Cannae*'s four escorting destroyers and her/their weapons wiped them from the universe.

Procyon's engineering crew broke all records bringing her drive on-line. They completed the fifteen-minute command sequence in barely ten, and the dreadnought began to accelerate. But the intruder simply adjusted its course, charging straight for her, and James Howell swallowed terror as he realized the other's suicidal intent.

Tisiphone battered uselessly at the interface of human and machine. If she could have broken Megarea free, even for an instant, the two of them might have reached Alicia, but the AI was trapped in her mother/self's blazing insanity. Yet Tisiphone had sworn to avenge Alicia upon those who had *ordered* her family's murder; if she allowed Alicia to die here she would stand forsworn. She would have betrayed the mortal who had trusted her with far more than her life, and so she gathered herself.

The strength of Alicia's mind had already made a mockery of her estimates. It might even be enough to survive . . . *this*.

Alicia DeVries shrieked as a white-hot guillotine slammed down. There was no finesse; Tisiphone was a flail of brutal power smashing through the complex web that bound her to Megarea. Another part of the Fury invaded her augmentation, goading the heart and lungs shock had stilled back to life, and she writhed in her command chair, screaming her agony.

Somehow Tisiphone held the impossible balance, forcing Alicia to live even as she killed her, but then the balance slipped. She felt it going, and screamed at Megarea like the tocsin of Armageddon.

And suddenly Megarea was free. The Fury reeled as the AI slashed back in a blind, instinctive bid to protect Alicia, but only for an instant. Only long enough to realize what had happened and hurl herself into the struggle at Tisiphone's side. For one incandescent sliver of eternity Alicia's madness held them *both* at bay, and then it broke at last. Megarea surged through the maelstrom to gather her in gentle arms, and Tisiphone was a shield of adamant between them both and the hatred. She faced it, battered it back, and Alicia jackknifed forward in her chair, soaked in sweat and gasping for breath.

But there was no time, and she jerked back erect as the Fury triggered her pharmacope and lashed her shuddering system back from the brink of collapse. Reason returned, and she raised her head, her eyes no longer pits of madness, to discover she had committed herself to a death-ride.

James Howell stared helplessly at the display. The accelerating intruder's Fasset drive devoured his fire, and it was barely four light-minutes away, tracking *Procyon*'s every desperate evasive maneuver. Rendlemann and the dreadnought's AI fought desperately to escape, but they simply didn't have the velocity. His ship had eighteen minutes to live, for there was no way those charging madmen would relent. They couldn't. If they broke off their suicide run now, *Procyon* and her consorts would tear them apart to nothing as they passed.

* * *

Horror and disgust reverberated somewhere inside Alicia, sickening her with the knowledge of what she had become, but there was no time for that. The tick flooded her system, goading her thoughts, and Megarea and Tisiphone snapped into fusion with her, a three-ply intelligence searching frantically for an answer. The enemy capital ships were spreading out, and their own velocity was back up to ninety-two thousand KPS and climbing. They were barely seventeen minutes from the dreadnought, but one or both of the battle-cruisers could bring their weapons to bear around the shield of *Megarea*'s Fasset drive within twelve.

Thoughts flashed between them like lightning. Decision was reached.

Commodore Howell winced as no less than six SLAM drones flashed away from the intruder. A battle-cruiser. At least a battle-cruiser, to carry that many. But if it was a battle-cruiser, where had its own SLAMs been this long?

It didn't matter. He was about to die, but stubborn professionalism drove him on. The drones were charging directly away from *Procyon*, and he snapped an order to his com officer. A light-speed signal flashed after them, and he bared his teeth in a death snarl of triumph. Unless those bastards were clairvoyant, they couldn't know he had the authenticated self-destruct codes. Their precious sensor data would die with their ship . . . and his own.

Alicia monitored the signal as it burned past her, and bared her teeth in an icy smile of her own. Monkoto's plan was back on track. Now if only Megarea could get them out of the trap she'd shoved them all into. . . .

The AI named Megarea gathered herself. What she was about to try had been discussed in theory for years, but only in theory. No opportunity to attempt it had ever arisen, and most Fleet officers had concluded it wouldn't work, anyway. But none of them had expected to try it with an alpha synth AI.

It had to be timed perfectly. She had to get in close, cut the transmission lag to the minimum, yet launch her attack before the hostile battle-cruisers could engage her, for what she/they planned would reduce her defensive capability to a ghost of itself, but there was no other way.

She felt Alicia's warm, supporting presence and the Fury's hungry approval pulsing within her, and the chance of failure scarcely even mattered. They were together. They were one. Live or die, she knew no other AI would ever taste a fraction of the richness that was hers in this moment, and she waited while the seconds trickled past.

The accelerating SLAM drones exploded in spits of fire, but Howell hardly noticed. It was down to the final handful of minutes. Either his battle-cruisers would stop the onrushing hammer of that Fasset drive by destroying the ship which mounted it, or *Procyon* would die.

Megarea struck.

The "pirates" had used their ability to penetrate Fleet security systems to kill her own SLAM drones, but it had never occurred to them that a Fleet unit might pierce *their* systems in return, and she was into their tactical net before they even realized she was coming.

The battle-cruisers' AIs were slow and clumsy beside *Procyon*'s; by the time they could respond, she had slashed them from the net with a band saw of jamming. This was between her and *Procyon*, and the dreadnought's cybernetic brain roused to meet her, but she had a fleeting edge of surprise, for she had known what was about to happen.

And she wasn't alone; Tisiphone rode her signal into the heart of the enemy flagship.

Howell lurched back in his chair as chaos exploded in his synth link. Cries of anguish filled the flag bridge, hands scrabbled to snatch away tormenting headsets, and one high, dreadful keen of agony rose above them all as Tisiphone left Megarea to her battle. She sought a different prey and stabbed out, searching the net for a mind which held the information she needed, and Commander George Rendlemann screamed like a soul in Hell.

Procyon's AI was more powerful than Megarea, but it was also more fragile, and she was far faster. She was a panther attacking a grizzly, boring in for the kill before it brought its greater power to bear, and she drove a stop thrust straight to its heart. She made no effort to oppose the other AI strength to strength; she went for the failsafes.

Those failsafes were intended to protect *Procyon*'s crew from the collapse of an unstable cyber synth, not to resist another AI's attack. They didn't even recognize it for what it was, but they sensed the turmoil raging in the systems they monitored and performed their designed function.

Procyon's entire control net crashed as Megarea convinced it to lobotomize its own AI.

Procyon writhed out of control, systems collapsing into manual control, leaving her momentarily defenseless as Megarea rampaged through them. Circuits spat sparks and died, backup computers spasmed in electronic hysteria, and Howell did the only thing he could. His hand slammed down on the red switch on his board. HMS *Procyon* vanished into the security of her shield, and he wondered if it was enough. In theory, *nothing* could get through an OKM shield—but no one had ever tested that theory against a battle-cruiser's full-powered ramming attack.

If she'd had even a moment longer, Megarea might have stopped the shield before it activated, but she didn't have a moment. There was barely time to snatch Tisiphone out of the dreadnought's circuitry before the shield chopped off her access, and even that delay was nearly fatal.

She'd cut her margin too close. HMS *Issus* opened fire with every weapon, and Megarea was locked into too many tasks at once. Her defenses were far below par.

She was too close for SLAMs, but at least six sublight missiles and three energy torpedoes went home against her battle screen.

The alpha synth writhed at the heart of a manmade star. Screen generators screamed in agony, local failures pierced her defenses, and elation filled *Issus*'s captain. Nothing short of a battleship could survive that concentrated blow!

A battleship . . . or an alpha synth. *Megarea* staggered out of the holocaust, blistered and broken, trailing vaporized alloy and atmosphere. A third of her weapons were twisted ruin, but she was alive. Alive and deadly, no longer distracted as she turned upon her foe.

Her holo projector was gone, and the battle-cruiser's captain had one instant to gawk in disbelief as *Megarea* stood revealed. Then answering fire slammed back. A direct hit wiped away *Issus*'s bridge. More fire ripped past her weakened defenses, and panic flashed through Howell's squadron. Their flagship had been driven behind her shield. *Cannae* and her escorts had been destroyed. *Issus* was a shattered, dying wreck . . . and now they knew their enemy. Knew they faced an alpha synth which had carved its way through the heart of their battleline.

Only the battle-cruiser *Verdun* stood in her path, and *Verdun* refused to face her. She spun away, interposing her own Fasset drive, and *Megarea* screamed past at thirty-six percent of light-speed.

Chapter Thirty-one

The lethal chaos receded astern, and Alicia cursed herself viciously. Monkoto had planned for her to play the part of a battle-cruiser, slightly damaged in the inevitable engagement with Howell's screen, and she'd *blown* it. Howell had killed her SLAM drones—exactly as intended—but she could carry the same word in person . . . unless he stopped her. Yet thanks to *Megarea*'s damage, he knew what she was. Dreadnoughts were built for speed as well as power; *Procyon* might have overhauled a battle-cruiser with battle damage, but *nothing* he had could hope to overtake an alpha synth. So he wouldn't even try, and—

Her head jerked up as *Megarea*'s drive died. The ship sped onward, but she was no longer accelerating, and Alicia's mouth twisted bitterly.

"Nice try, but you don't really think you can trick them with a fake drive failure, do you?"

<*Who the fuck is* faking?> Megarea snarled back. <*I just lost the entire after quadrant of the drive fan!*>

"You *what?*"

<*I said somebody threw a goddamned wrench into the*

works!> The AI snapped as diagnostic programs danced. <*Shit! The bastards took out both Alpha runs to the upper node generators!*>

<*Can they be repaired?*> Tisiphone demanded quickly.

<*Sure—if you can think of some way to keep those creeps from killing us while I do it!*> The alpha synth's point defense stations took out the first spattering of incoming missiles even as her maintenance remotes leapt into action. <*In the meantime, no drive means no evasion and no nice SLAM-eater. If those battle-cruisers get their shit together, we're dead.*>

Alicia gripped the arms of her command chair, face white, monitoring remotes that ripped out huge chunks of broken hull and buckled frame members to get at the damaged control runs. There was no time for neatness; Megarea was inflicting fresh and grievous wounds upon herself as she raced to make repairs which should have taken a shipyard days.

More missiles sizzled in from *Verdun*—but *only* missiles. She must have exhausted her SLAMs against *Megarea*'s mad charge, yet her two surviving sisters hadn't, and they were closing fast. One would reach firing range within fifty minutes; the other in an hour; and *Procyon* still had SLAMs in plenty once she came out from behind her shield.

James Howell sat grimly silent as damage control labored. Commander Rahman had replaced the shrieking, drooling Rendlemann, but *Procyon* no longer had a cyber synth. No one knew how it had been done, but her AI was gone, and massive damage to the manual backups left the big dreadnought defenseless. There wouldn't even be battle screen until damage control could route around the wrecked subsystems, and even if they replaced them all, *Procyon* would be at little more than half normal capability without her AI.

Which meant he dared not drop his mauled flagship's shield despite a desperate temptation to do just that. *Verdun* and *Issus* had almost certainly killed those madmen, assuming they hadn't destroyed themselves against the shield. But if they had somehow survived and fled, his people might need *Procyon*'s SLAM batteries to stop them—except that if they'd survived and *hadn't* fled, a single missile salvo would rip his crippled ship apart. And so he sat still, watching his crew wrestle furiously with their repairs, and waited.

"Why the hell aren't they coming after us?" Alicia worried, watching lightning glare as *Megarea*'s point defense dealt with incoming missiles.

<*Little One,*> Tisiphone observed with massive restraint, <*I see missiles enough, and two of their battle-cruisers* are *pursuing us.*>

"Not them—*Procyon.* Why doesn't she drop her shield and fry us?"

<*You're complaining?*> Megarea flung half a dozen missiles back at *Verdun.* They had little chance of penetrating the battle-cruiser's point defense at this range, but they might make her a bit more cautious. <*Alley, I gave that cyber synth piece of junk a terminal migraine. Unless I miss my guess, they're scraping fried molycircs off the deck plates and wondering what the hell hit them.*>

"Yeah, but for how much longer?"

<*How do* I *know? Damn it, I've got more to worry about than—*>

"I know, honey. I know!" Alicia said contritely. "It's just that—"

<*Just that this waiting wears upon the nerves,*> Tisiphone finished. <*Yet think, Little One—none but the truly mad would linger within SLAM range of that dreadnought if they could flee. Hence, they must believe our drive damage genuine, which means we may yet complete our original intent.*>

<*Unless they get their act together and kill us,*> Megarea muttered.

The battle-cruiser *Trafalgar* raced towards rendezvous with *Verdun.* Another twenty minutes. Just twenty, and her SLAMs would have the range.

* * *

<*Okay, people,*> Megarea murmured. <*Now just pray it holds. . . .*>

Circuits closed. Power pulsed through jury-rigged shunts and patches, and the alpha synth began to accelerate once more. At little more than two-thirds power, but to accelerate, and Megarea turned her attention to other wounds. She could do little for slagged down weapons, but her electronic warfare systems' damage was mainly superficial, and it as looked as though she might need them badly. Soon.

"Engineering estimates another fifty-five minutes to restore Fasset drive, sir," Rahman reported, "but we've restored as much basic combat capability as we can without cyber synth."

"Understood. Stand by to drop the shield."

Megarea was back up to .43 C when the OKM shield's impenetrable blot disappeared from Alicia's sensors. She stiffened, checking ranges, then relaxed. The dreadnought was over twenty light-minutes astern, and it was her *sublight* sensors which had reported the shield's passing. Her gravitics still didn't see a thing, and that meant the dreadnought must have engineering problems of her own. Now if she'd just go on having them long enough. . . .

Howell watched his plot replay *Issus*'s destruction from *Verdun*'s sensor records in bitter silence. An alpha synth. No wonder it had done such a number on them! And it explained the lack of SLAMs, too.

But *Issus* had gotten a piece of it. A big piece, judging from its subsequent behavior, and he cursed his own caution for not dropping the shield sooner. Yet the critical point was that the alpha synth's speed had been drastically reduced. Even *Procyon* could make up velocity on it, now that her drive had been restored, and he had no choice but to do just that.

Pieces fell into place in his brain as the big ship accelerated in pursuit. That had to be the rogue drop commando—only a madwoman would have come after them alone and launched that insane attack down *Procyon*'s throat—so Fleet didn't know a thing. A part of him was tempted to let what-was-her-name, DeVries, go, trusting to the Fleet's own shoot on sight order to dispose of her, but mad or not, she had the hard sensor data to prove her story. All she had to do was get into com range of any Fleet base or unit and pass it on.

He could not permit that, and so he dispatched his freighters to the alternate rendezvous and went in pursuit. His cruisers and remaining battle-cruisers could have overhauled sooner than *Procyon*, had he let them. He didn't. Lamed though that ship was, God only knew what it could still do, and *Procyon* could hang close enough to break into the same wormhole space and close to combat range. She still had the weapons to take even an alpha synth, and if it took time, time was something he had. On this heading, he'd overtake DeVries eleven light-years short of the nearest inhabited planet.

<*Looks like we're back on track,*> Megarea said. The entire squadron was in pursuit, and its faster units were hanging back. They'd managed to pull out of *Procyon*'s SLAM range before she lumbered back to life, but she'd regain it eventually, and *Megarea*'s drive couldn't be interposed against fire from astern. Which might be just as well, given its current fragility.

"What happens when they get the range on us again?"

<*Depends. We'll be into wormhole space, and I* think *I'll have most of my EW back on line by then. If I do, they'll have a hard time localizing us. They can't throw the kind of salvos Soisson's forts could, and SLAMs can't go supralight relative to us in wormhole space, either. I'll be able to track 'em and do some fancy footwork, and even that damned dreadnought can't carry a lot of 'em. I expect they'll choose not to waste them and hold off until they can get to missile or even beam range. That's what I'd do.*>

"I just hope they're as smart as you are, then."

<*Me too,*> Megarea snorted, and Alicia nodded and shoved herself up out of her chair. <*Hey! Where're you going?*>

"To the head, dummy." Alicia managed a weary smile. "I'm coming off the tick, and I've got an appointment with the john."

<*Uh, you might want to reconsider that.*>

"Sorry." Alicia swallowed a surge of nausea. "Already in process."

<*Damn!*> Alicia's eyebrows rose, and Megarea sighed. <*Alley, we took a* lot *of hits. There's no pressure in the bridge access passage.*>

"You mean—?"

<*I mean I'm working on it,*> the AI apologized, <*but I need another hour before I can repressurize.*>

"Oh, crap," Alicia moaned in a stifled tone. "'Get your tractors ready, then, because—"

Her voice broke off as biology had its way.

Half an hour later, a pale-faced Alicia sat huddled in her chair. Her uniform was almost clean—Megarea's tractors had caught most of the vomit and whisked it away—but the stink of fear and sickness clung to her, and she scrubbed her face with the heels of her hands as a new and deeper fear rippled within her. Now that the immediate terror of combat had receded, she had time to think . . . and to realize fully *why* she had done what she had.

She'd lost it. She hadn't panicked, hadn't frozen, hadn't tried to run. Instead, she'd done something worse.

She'd gone berserk. She'd forgotten the objective, the plan, the need to survive, even that Megarea would die with her—forgotten *everything* but the need to kill . . . and it had not been temporary. She'd felt it again the instant tick reaction let her go. Bloodlust trembled within her even now, like black fire awaiting only a puff of air to roar to life once more.

It was madness, and it terrified her, for it was infinitely worse than the madness Tannis had feared, and she had infected Megarea with it. The Fleet had been ordered to kill her; now, she knew, that order was justified. If a drop commando's insanity was to be dreaded, how much more terrible was the madness of an alpha synth pilot?

<*No, Little One.*> Alicia winced, for the soft voice held something she'd never heard from the Fury: sorrow. She gritted her teeth and turned away from it, clutching her self-loathing to her, but Tisiphone refused to be evaded. <*It is not you who have done this thing. It is I. I have . . . meddled unforgivably. Do not blame yourself for the wrong* I *have done.*>

"It's a bit late for that," Alicia grated.

<*But it is not your fault. It—*>

"Do you really think it matters a good goddamn whose *fault* it is?!" She clenched her fists as barely leashed madness stirred, and tears streaked her face.

<Alley—>

"Shut up, Megarea! Just shut *up!*" Alicia hissed. She felt Megarea's hurt and desperate concern, and she shut them out, for Megarea loved her. Megarea would refuse to face the loathsome thing she had become. Megarea would protect her, and she was too dangerous to be protected.

Silence hovered in her mind and her breathing was ragged. She still had enough control to end it. She could turn herself in . . . and if Fleet killed her when she tried, perhaps that would be the best solution of all. Yet how long would that control remain? She could *feel* her old self dying, tiny bits and pieces eaten away by the corrosion at her core, and the horror of her own demolition filled her.

<*Little One . . . Alicia, you* must *hear me,*> Tisiphone said at last. Alicia hunched forward, covering her ears with her hands, digging her nails into her temples, but she couldn't shut out the Fury's voice.

<*I am arrogant, Little One. When first we met, I saw your compassion, your belief in "justice," and I feared them. They were too much a part of you, too likely, I thought, to cloud your judgment when the moment came.*

<*I was wrong. On, Alicia—*> the pain in the Fury's voice was terrible, for she was a being who had never

been meant to feel it <—*I was so wrong! And because I was, I built a weapon of your hate. Not against your foes, but against* you, *to bend you to my will at need, and in so doing I have hurt one innocent of any wrong. Once that would not have mattered to me. Now it does. You must not hate yourself for what I have done to you.*>

"It doesn't matter who I hate." Alicia slumped back and opened tear-soaked eyes, and her voice was raw and wounded. "Don't you understand even that? It doesn't *matter.* All that matters is what I've become!"

<*The debt is mine,*> the Fury's voice had hardened, <*and mine the price to pay. I swear to you, Alicia DeVries, that I will not let you become the thing you fear.*>

"Can—" Words caught in her throat. She swallowed and tried again, and they came out small and frightened. "Can you stop me? Make me better?"

<*I do not know,*> Tisiphone replied unflinchingly. <*I swear that I will try, but I am less skilled at healing than hurting, and what I have done to you grows stronger with every hour. Already it is more powerful than I believed possible, perhaps powerful enough to destroy us both, yet I have lived long enough—perhaps too long. I will do what I may, and if I fail,*> her voice turned gentle, <*we will end together, Little One.*>

<*No!*> Megarea's protest was hot and frightened. <*You can't just kill her! I won't* let *you!*>

"Hush, Megarea," Alicia whispered. Her eyes closed again—not in terror this time but in gratitude—yet she felt her sister self's pain and made herself speak gently. "She's right. You know she is; you're part of me. Do you think I'd want to live as *that?*" She shuddered and shook her head. "But I'm so sorry to do this to you, love. You deserve better, unless . . . Do you think—is our link different enough for you to—?"

<*I don't know,*> tears glittered in the AI's soundless voice, <*and it doesn't matter, because I won't.*>

"Please, Megarea. Don't do that to me," Alicia begged. "Promise you'll at least try! I don't . . . I don't think I can bear knowing you won't if I . . . if I . . ."

<Then you're just going to have to try real hard not to. You're not going anywhere without me—not ever.>

"But—"

<It is her right, Little One,> Tisiphone said quietly. *<Do not deny her choice or blame her for it. The fault is no more hers than yours.>*

Alicia bowed her head. The Fury was right, and if she tried to force the AI, she would only twist the time they still had with pain and guilt.

"All right," she whispered. "All right. We've come this far together; we'll go on together."

Megarea's warm silence enfolded her, answering for her, and fragile stillness hovered on the bridge, filled with a strange, bittersweet sense of acceptance. What she was becoming could not be permitted to live, and it would not. That had to be enough, and, somehow, it was.

It was odd, she thought almost dreamily, but she didn't even blame Tisiphone. She would have died long since if not for her, and the Fury's pain was too genuine. If she had become something else, so had Tisiphone, and the bond which had grown between them no longer held room for resentment or hate.

The stillness stretched out until the Fury broke it at last.

<In truth, Little One, my promise to you may not matter in the end. I have not yet told you what I have learned.>

"Learned?" Alicia stirred in her chair.

<Indeed. While Megarea dispatched Procyon's *AI, I sought a mind which could tell us more. I found one, and in it I found the truth.>*

Alicia snapped back to full alertness, driving the residual flicker of madness as deep as she could, and felt Megarea beside her in her mind.

<The Fleet personnel who pursue us were most carefully selected by their commander, and their objective is to create such havoc as must force your Emperor to commit much of his fleet to this sector.>

"We already knew that, but why? What can they possibly gain from it?"

<The answer is simple enough,> the Fury said grimly, *<for he who truly commands them is the one called Subrahmanyan Treadwell.>*

For just an instant the name completely failed to register, and then Alicia flinched in disbelief. "The sector *governor?* That—that's crazy!"

<There is no question, Little One. It is he, and his objective is no less than to place a crown upon his own head.>

"But . . . but *how?*"

<He has requested massive reinforcements to "crush the pirates." Indeed, he has been promised the tenth part of your Fleet's active units and perhaps a third of its firepower. Once they arrive, Admiral Gomez will be relieved or die—it matters little to him—and replaced by Admiral Brinkman.

<For a time, the pirates will prove even more successful. Their raids will spread across the border into the Macedon Sector, which is but lightly held, until they seem an irresistible scourge. And when the terror has reached its height, when the people of both sectors have come to believe the Empire cannot protect them, Treadwell will assume personal command of the Fleet and declare martial law. Brinkman will accept this, and they will relieve captains most loyal to the Empire, replacing them with men and women loyal only to them, until Treadwell's control is total. And at that point, Little One, he will declare that the Empire has proven incapable of defending its people so far from the center of power. He will declare himself ruler of both sectors in the name of their salvation, offering to submit to a plebiscite when the "pirates" have been destroyed, and from that moment the raids will become less frequent. In the end, a carefully chosen squadron of his most loyal adherents will fight a false battle in which the "pirates" will appear to be utterly destroyed. He will then face his plebiscite, and even without manipulation of the votes, he will probably win.>

"But the Emperor won't stand for it!" Alicia protested sickly.

<Treadwell believes he will. That is the reason he seeks

such naval strength. Surely the Emperor will realize that a civil war—and it would require nothing less once Treadwell's plan has played itself out—will but invite the Rishathan Sphere to intervene? And remember this: none save Treadwell and his closest adherents will know what actually passed. All will believe he truly dealt, firmly and decisively, with a threat to the people he is sworn to protect. These sectors lie far from the heart of the Empire. Will the Emperor be able to rally sufficient public support for a massive operation against a man who but did what had to be done in so distant a province?>

"Dear God," Alicia whispered. She licked bloodless lips, trying to grasp the truth, but the sheer magnitude of the crime was numbing.

"Megarea, did you get any of this from *Procyon*'s computers?"

<*No, Alley.*> Even the brash AI was subdued and shaken. <*I didn't have time for data searches.*>

<*It would not have mattered, Megarea. There was no data for you to find. The details of the plan have never been committed to record—not, I venture to say, unreasonably.*>

"Yeah." Alicia inhaled deeply. The numbness was passing, and the flame of her madness guttered higher. She ground her heel upon its neck, driving it back down, and shook herself.

"Okay. What do we do with the information?"

<*Tell Ferhat?*> Megarea suggested hesitantly.

"Maybe. *He'd* believe us, I think, though it's for damned sure no one else will. I mean, who's going to take the unsupported word of a madwoman who talks to Bronze Age demons over that of a sector governor?"

<*I suppose I should resent that, but I fear you are correct.*>

"Yeah, and even if Ferhat believes us, he needs proof. They could never convict on what we can give them, and I doubt even O Branch would sanction a black operation against a sector governor."

<*Agreed. And that, Little One, is why my promises to*

you may stand meaningless in the end. I see only one way to destroy this traitor.>

"Us," Alicia said grimly.

<*Indeed.*>

<*Now wait a darn minute! Do you two actually think we can get to a* sector governor? *What do you want to do, nuke the damned planet?!*>

<*It will not be necessary. Treadwell dislikes planets. His quarters are aboard Orbit One.*>

<*Oh, ducky! So all we have to do is fight our way in and punch out a six million-tonne orbital fortress with a third of my weapons so much junk? I feel lots better now.*>

"Are you saying you can't do it?" Alicia tried to make her voice light. "What happened to all that cheerful egotism when we busted out?"

<*Out is easier than in,*> Megarea said grimly, <*and you know damned well they'll have reworked their systems since, just in case we come back.*>

"So we can't get in?"

<*I didn't say that,*> Megarea replied unwillingly. <*I'll know better when I finish repairs—remember, that battle-cruiser shot the hell out of me—but, yeah, I imagine we can get in. Only, if we do, I don't think we'll get out again, and I doubt anything I ever had was heavy enough to take out that fort. I certainly don't have anything* left *that could do the job.*>

"Oh yes, you do," Alicia said very softly. "The same thing that could have taken out *Procyon.*"

<*Ram it?*> There was less shock in the AI's voice than there should have been, Alicia thought sadly. Like her, Megarea saw it as the possible answer to her fear of what she might become. <*I think we could do it,*> Megarea said at last, slowly. <*But there are nine thousand other people on that fort, Alley.*>

"I know." Alicia frowned down at her hands and her shoulders hunched against the ice of her own words. "I know," she whispered.

Chapter Thirty-two

The black-and-gray uniformed woman looked up as a quiet buzzer purred. A light blinked, and she slipped into her synth link headset and consulted her computers carefully, then pressed a button.

"Get me the Old Man," she said, and waited a moment. "Admiral, this is Lois Heyter in Tracking. We've got something coming in on the right bearing, but the velocity's wrong. They're still too far out for a solid solution, but it looks like our friend hasn't been able to hold the range open as planned." She listened, then nodded. "Yes, sir. We'll stay on it."

She went back to her plot, and the close-grouped ships of war began to accelerate through the deep gloom between the stars. There was no great rush. They had hours before their prey dropped sublight—plenty of time to build their interception vectors.

James Howell glared at the enemy's blue dot and muttered venomously to himself. He'd fired off over half the squadron's missiles, and he might as well have been shooting spitballs! It was maddening, yet he'd given up on telling himself things would have been different if *Procyon*'s cyber synth had survived to run the tactical net. To be sure, *Trafalgar*'s AI was less capable than the dreadnought's had been, but not even *Procyon*'s could have accomplished much against the alpha synth's fiendish ECM.

He knew that damned ship was badly damaged; the debris trail it had left at AR-12359/J would have proved that, even if its limping acceleration hadn't, yet it refused to die. It kept splitting into multiple targets that bobbed and wove insanely, and then swatted down the missiles that went for the right target source with contemptuous ease. What it might have been doing if it were *un*damaged hardly bore thinking on.

But its time was running out. His ships would be into extreme energy torpedo range in seventy minutes, and even an alpha synth's defenses could be saturated with enough of those. If they couldn't, he'd be into beam range in another eighteen and a half minutes, and *no* point defense could stop massed beam fire, by God!

"Admiral," Lois Heyter said tensely from Simon Monkoto's com screen, "we're picking up a second grav source—a big one—and it's decelerating hard."

"Put it on my plot," Monkoto said, and frowned down at the display. Lois was right; the second cluster of gravity sources, almost as numerous as those speeding towards them from AR-12359/J, *was* decelerating. He tapped his nose in thought. He supposed their arrival might be a concidence . . . except that there was no star in the vicinity, and Simon Monkoto had stopped believing in coincidence and the tooth fairy years ago.

He juggled numbers, and his frown deepened as the newcomers' vector extended itself across the display. If those people kept coming as they were, things were about to get very interesting indeed.

A fresh sheet of lightning flashed and glared against the formless gray of wormhole space as *Megarea* picked off yet another incoming salvo, and Alicia winced. Thank

God Megarea had no need of little things like rest! The "pirates" had been in missile range for over two hours, and if their supply of missiles was finite they seemed unaware of the fact. Anything less than an alpha synth would have been destroyed long since.

They hadn't been supposed to reach missile range before turnover, but "supposed to" hadn't counted on *Megarea*'s damage. Alicia's nerves felt sick and exhausted from the unremitting tension of the last hundred and thirty minutes, yet the end was in sight.

"Ready, Megarea?"

<I *am. I just hope the repairs are.*>

Alicia nodded in grim understanding. Megarea had labored unceasingly on her drive since their flight began, ignoring less essential repairs, and all they could say for certain was that it had worked . . . so far.

Maintenance remotes had built entirely new control runs in parallel with those cobbled up in such desperate haste, but they hadn't dared shut down long enough to shift over to test them with Howell's squadron clinging so closely to their heels.

Nor had they been able to test *Megarea*'s other repairs. Twenty-five percent of her drive nodes had been crippled or destroyed outright by the same hit that smashed the control runs, and she'd had spares for less than half of them. Her theoretical grav mass was down five percent even after scavenging the less damaged ones, and while she'd bench-tested the rebuilt units, *no one* cut suspect nodes into circuit while underway in wormhole space.

Unfortunately, the maneuver they were about to attempt left them no choice. They'd been forced to leave their turnover far later than planned because of how much more quickly the "pirates" had closed the gap, and they would need every scrap of deceleration they could produce, tested nodes or no.

<*Coming up on the mark, Alley.*> Megarea broke into her thoughts quietly, and Alicia drew a deep breath.

"Thanks. Tisiphone?"

<*I am prepared, Little One. Relax as much as you may.*>

"I'm as relaxed as I'm going to get." She heard the quaver in her own voice and forced her hands to unclench. "Come ahead."

There was no spoken response, but she felt a stirring in her mind as Megarea extended a wide-open channel to the Fury with no trace of her one-time distrust. They reached out to one another, weaving a glowing web, and Alicia forced down a stir of jealousy, for she was excluded from its weaving. She could see it in her mind's eye, taste its beauty, yet she could not share in its creation. Beautiful it might be, but it was a trap—and she was its prey.

Currents of power crackled deep within her, and then the web snapped shut. She gasped and twisted, stabbed by agony that vanished almost before it was felt, and her eyes opened wide.

The seductive glitter of her madness was gone. Or, no, not gone—just . . . removed. It was still there, burning like poison in the glowing shroud Tisiphone and Megarea had woven, but it could no longer touch her. Blessed, half-forgotten peace filled her like the hush of a cathedral, and she sighed in desperate relief as her muscles relaxed for the first time in days.

"Thank you," she whispered, and felt Megarea's silent mental caress.

<It is little enough, and I do not know how long we may hold it,> Tisiphone replied more somberly, *<but all we may do, we will.>*

"Thank you," Alicia repeated more levelly, then gathered herself once more. "All right, Megarea—let's do it to these bastards."

Lois Heyter hunched over her console in concentration, then stiffened.

"Tell the Old Man we have decoy separation!" she snapped.

No more missiles fired. James Howell's lips were thin over his teeth as he waited out the last dragging seconds to energy torpedo range. If he were aboard that alpha synth, this was when he'd go for a crash turnover—

There! The fleeing Fasset drive suddenly popped over, and he started to bark orders—then stopped dead. There were *two* sources on his display! One continued straight ahead at unchanged acceleration; the other hurtled towards him at a starkly incredible deceleration, and he swore feelingly.

He gritted his teeth and waited for Tracking to sort them out. Logic said the genuine source was the one charging at him in a frantic effort to break sublight and lose him . . . only it was coming at him at over twenty-five hundred gravities! How in hell could the alpha synth produce that kind of power after its long, limping run? A fraction of that increase would have kept it out of his range, and alpha synth point defense or no, not even a madwoman would have endured that heavy fire if she could have avoided it!

The source continuing straight ahead maintained exactly the same power curve he'd been watching for days, which might well indicate it was genuine, and that made his dilemma worse. If he decelerated to deal with the closing source and guessed wrong, the still fleeing one would regain a massive lead; if he *didn't* decelerate and the closing source was the genuine ship, he'd lose it entirely. *One* of them had to be some sort of decoy—but *which one?*

Whichever it was, he had to identify it quickly. The peculiarities of wormhole space augmented the deceleration of the closing source to right on three thousand gravities, and his squadron's acceleration translated it into a relative deceleration of more than forty-seven KPS per second. He had barely four minutes before it went sublight, and if he didn't begin his own deceleration at least thirty seconds before it did, he'd lose it forever.

Fasset drive generators were virtually soundless, their quiet hum as unobtrusive as a human heartbeat. But not now. Alicia clung to the arms of her command chair, teeth locked in a white, strained face, and the drive screamed at her like a tortured giant, shaking *Megarea*'s iron bones like a hurricane until her vision blurred with the vibration.

The decoy, one of only two SLAM decoys *Megarea* carried, streaked away on their old course, and shipboard power levels exploded far past critical. Meters blew like molycirc popcorn, rebuilt control runs crackled and sizzled, patched-up generator nodes shrieked, and it went on and on and on and on. . . .

"*Turnover!*" Lois Heyter barked. "We have turnover!" Her eyes opened wide, and her voice dropped to a whisper. "Dear God, *look* at that deceleration rate! How in *hell* is she holding it together?"

The cybernetic brain of the battleship *Audacious* noted the changing gravity signatures and adjusted its own drive. Vectors would converge with less than ten percent variance, it calculated with mild, electronic satisfaction.

Time was running out. Howell found himself pounding on the arm of his chair. If Tracking couldn't differentiate in the next ten seconds, he was going to have to go to emergency deceleration just to play safe. Losing distance on the alpha synth if he'd guessed wrong would be better than losing it entirely, he told himself, and it did his frustration no good at all.

The leading source flickered suddenly, and his eyes narrowed. There! It flickered again, power fading, and he knew.

The range was down to four and a half million miles when Howell's entire squadron flipped end-for-end and began to decelerate madly.

<*Fifty seconds to sublight.*> Blood streaked Alicia's chin, her hands were cramped claws on her chair arms, and her battered brain felt only a dull wonder that they were still alive, but Megarea's mental voice was unshadowed by the hellish vibration. *Forty. Thirty-fi— They've* flipped, *Alley!*>

* * *

"Here they come, boys and girls," Simon Monkoto murmured over his command circuit. He sat relaxed in his command chair, but his eyes were bright and hard, filled with a vengeful hunger few of his officers had ever seen in them. His gaze flicked over his display, and his mouth sketched a mirthless grin. The second group of gravity sources would drop sublight in nine minutes—out of range to hit the "pirates" but on an almost convergent vector.

"Cut your drives!" he snapped as Alicia DeVries broke sublight, and every one of his ships killed her Fasset drive.

<*There's Simon—right on the money!*> Megarea announced as the mercenaries appeared on her display and then vanished in the equivalent of a deep-space ambush. Without active drives, they were invisible to FTL scanners; the "pirates" wouldn't be able to see them until their light-speed sensors picked them up.

Alicia nodded in understanding, then gasped in relief as Megarea cut the drive's power levels far back. The dreadful vibration eased, yet there was a grim undertone to her relief as she felt the AI prepping her own weapons. If the SLAM drone had lasted just a little longer, *Megarea* might have broken back past Howell's ships to join Monkoto. She hadn't, and Monkoto or no Monkoto, she was still in the "pirates'" range, with no choice but to decelerate *towards* them or lose the shield of her Fasset drive. But if she decelerated too rapidly—or if they began to accelerate once more and overran her—the range would be less than two light-seconds when she penetrated their formation.

A jolt of sullen fire went through Alicia at the thought. She clenched her teeth as her madness lunged against its restraining net, hungry for destruction, and felt Tisiphone at her side as she fought it down. It subsided with an angry grumble, and sweat beaded her forehead. She'd won—this time—but what would happen once the shooting started?

<*Alley! Check the gravitics at two-eight-oh!*>

* * *

The dreadnought *Procyon* erupted from wormhole space with her entire brood, and the alpha synth was still there, decelerating into their teeth.

James Howell bared his own teeth. DeVries was a drop commando, not a Fleet officer, or she would've known better. If she'd simply cut her drive, he might not even have been able to find her; as it was, she was bidding to break back through his formation in another suicide attack.

That was the only explanation for her maneuver, but this time her ship was hurt and he knew what he was up against.

Orders crackled out, and his formation opened to receive its foe.

"Commodore!" It was Commander Rahman, his face taut. "We're picking up another grav source! It's still supralight, but decelerating quickly. Estimate breakout in . . . six-point-one minutes at thirty-one light-minutes, bearing two-eight-six, one-one-seven. At least thirty sources."

Howell stiffened, and his stomach tightened as Rahman's data appeared on his plot.

Those other sources were decelerating, if far less madly than DeVries had, and their vector converged with his own. Not perfectly, by a long chalk, but close enough they could match it if he tried to accelerate back up to supralight. Jesus! Could DeVries have *known* they'd be here?!

It didn't seem possible. If an ambush had been intended the ambushers would have arrived ahead of time to lie doggo without revealing drive signatures. But what *else* could it be?

Numbers tumbled across the bottom of his display as Tracking calculated frantically, and he swore. Yes, they could go sublight on a converging vector or accelerate back supralight with him even if he went back to max acceleration, but they'd never be able to engage him as long as he continued to decelerate. They'd have to kill their own velocity, then go in pursuit, and his people were already killing speed. He'd have too much of a head start to be caught short of wormhole space on a reversed course . . . which was the coldest of comforts.

Jaw muscles lumped as he turned his hating gaze back to DeVries. They might not be able to engage, but they'd still get good scanner readings, and that meant his entire pursuit had been for nothing.

He glared at the alpha synth's dot. All for nothing. Everything they'd done, all the people they'd killed, and it was all for *nothing!* Once his ships were fingerprinted, Treadwell's dream of building a new empire on the "pirate threat" would be dead. It might take months for Intelligence to put it together, but the true nature of the "pirate" squadron would be a glaring arrow pointed in the right direction.

Yet there was one last thing he could do. DeVries wasn't racing to meet the newcomers. She was still decelerating towards *him.* The shoot on sight order still held; she dared not confront the Fleet any more than he did, and she was accepting the threat she knew in a desperate effort to evade the new one.

Which meant he could still kill her, and perhaps—

"SLAMs!" Rahman screamed. "SLAMs bearing oh-oh-three, one-two-seven!"

Howell's head whipped up in horror as malignant blue dots speckled his display. Where had they *come* from?! There was nothing out there! It was—

And then his sublight sensors finally picked up the ships ahead and "above" him, firing down past his drive masses as he decelerated towards them.

<*Go, Simon!*> Megarea shrieked, and Alicia's bloodlust spasmed against the web. A strand parted, and Tisiphone hurled herself at the weakness, blocking the thrust of madness. She didn't get it all. A tentacle of fire groped through Alicia's brain, and breath hissed between her teeth.

The SLAMs flashed in, and Howell's ships lunged into frantic evasive action. The short range meant the SLAMs were still building velocity when they arrived, and she snarled as *Procyon* evaded an even dozen, but two battlecruisers were less fortunate, and she twitched in ecstasy as they died.

Eleven capital ships hung on James Howell's flank, their velocity within ten percent of his own, and he'd lost *Trafalgar* and *Chickamauga. Verdun* replaced *Trafalgar* in the tactical net, but only she survived to support *Procyon.* Had the dreadnought's AI remained, she alone might have matched all eleven of her opponents, but it didn't. She retained her brute firepower and defensive strength—not the fine-meshed control to make it fully effective.

Understanding filled him. There *had* been an ambush, but not of Fleet units. The energy signatures told it all. Somehow, DeVries had linked up with the mercenaries at Ringbolt. An alpha synth—and only an alpha synth—might have nailed Gregor and had the speed to reach Ringbolt before making for the rendezvous to bait the trap. There was only one way those slow-footed battleships could have brought him to action, and he'd swallowed the bait whole. But what about the ships even now breaking sublight? *They* couldn't have been part of the plan; he knew Monkoto's reputation, and the mercenary would have been in place long since with every unit he had.

Conjecture raced through his mind in split-second flashes of lightning. The other units couldn't be from Gomez's Fleet district—not unless Brinkman had been found out and the whole operation broken from the other end, and in that case there'd be a hell of a lot more than thirty drive sources! Could they be still more mercenaries? Some last minute ally of Monkoto's who'd arrived late?

It didn't matter. What mattered was that the only way to avoid fighting *both* enemy forces was to take Monkoto head on . . . and that was suicide.

But perhaps not for everyone. If any of his people could break through the mercenaries, they might turn true pirate, or perhaps take service with a Rogue World far enough from Franconia not to realize what they'd been. It wasn't much, but it was all he could offer them—that and a chance to kill some of the bastards who'd ambushed them.

"Come to poppa, you bastards," Simon Monkoto whispered. He'd hoped for still more SLAM salvos, but then he'd expected the renegades to accelerate back up to wormhole out. They hadn't, and now they were hidden behind the drives pointed straight at him. The battle to come had just turned even uglier, but his own ships matched the "pirates'" maneuver. Thanks to the battleships, their maximum deceleration was less than the enemy's, but it would be enough to insure a long and deadly embrace.

"Up their asses, Megarea!" Alicia snarled.

<Are you sure, Alley? I'm not in good enough offensive shape to add much to Simon's firepower.>

Megarea's worried voice tore at the corona of violence building in Alicia's mind. She clenched her teeth, sweating, trying to make herself think, and a part of her screamed in warning. The web about her madness sang with stress, and it was crumbling. She felt Tisiphone between her and it, felt the Fury pouring herself into the fraying web. She writhed in her chair, fighting to keep her jaws locked on the order to engage. She could break off. She could curl away from Howell and leave him to Monkoto's unwounded ships, and she knew she had to. She and her companions were the only ones who knew the truth about Treadwell. They couldn't let themselves die yet. She *knew* it; yet she couldn't let go. She held her course, and the most she could do was strangle the order for Megarea to redline her deceleration.

The edge of James Howell's squadron "overtook" Monkoto's. Screening destroyers and light cruisers suddenly found themselves broadside-to-broadside at ranges as low as fifty thousand kilometers, and energy torpedoes and beams ripped back and forth. Point defense was irrelevant; misses were almost impossible, and battle screens were blazing halos wrapped about fragile battle steel. Two renegade destroyers and a light cruiser vanished in star-bright fury, but Commodore Falconi's heavy cruiser flagship went with them, and the death toll was only starting.

Monkoto and his allies had known what it would be like the instant they realized Howell wasn't going to run for it. *They* could have broken off, but they hadn't come to break off. The two fleets interpenetrated and merged, racing side-by-side while the hammering match raged.

Procyon's massive beam and energy torpedo batteries opened fire, and a dozen destroyers and cruisers died in the first salvo. *Verdun* poured her own fire into the maelstrom, but two of O'Kane's battle-cruisers locked their batteries on her, and her fire slackened as more and more of her power was shunted frantically into her battle screen. She writhed, cored in their fire, and *Procyon* blew one of her attackers to vaporized wreckage.

Not in time. *Verdun*'s screens failed, a tight-focused salvo of particle beams ripped through them, and she vomited flame across the stars.

Procyon rounded vengefully upon her killer, but *Audacious* and the battleship *Assassin* were on her like mastiffs. They were far smaller, slower, less heavily armed, but their cyber synths were intact, and thunder wracked the vacuum as the leviathans spread their arms in lethal embrace. Two more battle-cruisers raced to join them, then a third, and all six rained javelins of flame upon the dreadnought.

Eight million tonnes of starship heaved as something got through a local screen failure, and Monkoto's wolves set their fangs in the flanks of the crippled saber-tooth. Howell ripped his attention away from them long enough to check the main plot and swallowed a groan. *Procyon* was attracting more and more of the mercenaries' attention, but there were more than enough destroyers and cruisers to pair off in duels with his own units. Ships flashed and vanished like dying sparks, damage signals snarled in his synth link, and Tracking had finally identified the newcomers: Fleet battle-cruisers, already gaining on *Procyon* with their higher rate of deceleration.

He glared at the red switch on his console. He could engage the shield and laugh at Monkoto's attack . . . but there was no point. He couldn't accelerate with the shield up; only drift, knowing that when he finally lowered it, the enemy would be waiting. He raised fiery eyes to Commander Rahman.

"Get the battleships!" he snarled.

Alicia's nails drew blood from her palms as the battleship *Assassin* blew apart. She remembered Esther Tarbaneau's gentle brown eyes, and her lips writhed back from her teeth as the red holocaust broke free within her.

The hell with Treadwell! The hell with *everything!* The mercenaries were fighting *her* fight, dying *her* death. She felt Megarea and Tisiphone battling to turn her madness, and she didn't care.

"Now, goddamn it!" she snarled. "Everything we've got *now!*" and Megarea wept as she obeyed. The drive thundered and shrieked in agony, and the alpha synth began to close on the cyclone of dying starships.

Simon Monkoto's teeth met through his lip as *Assassin* vanished. First Arlen, now Tadeoshi and Esther—but he had the bastards. He *had* them! His flagship's AI noted a fluctuation in *Procyon*'s defenses, a wavering the dreadnought would have sensed and corrected had her own AI survived. But it hadn't, and *Audacious* flashed orders over the net. One battleship and four battle-cruisers threw every beam and energy torpedo they had at the chink in *Procyon*'s armor, and her Fasset drive exploded.

Alicia's banshee howl echoed from the bulkheads as the dreadnought's drive died, and her eyes were mad.

The mercenaries peeled away from *Procyon*, for they no longer needed to endure her close-range fire. They'd broken her wings, destroyed her ability to dodge. Once their own ships got far enough from her to avoid friendly SLAM fire, she was dead, but Alicia didn't think about the mercenaries' SLAMs, didn't care about the short-range weapons still waiting to destroy her. All she saw was the lamed hulk of her enemy, waiting for her to kill it.

HMS *Tsushima* decelerated towards the savage engagement, and her captain's brain whirled as she digested the preposterous sensor readings. *Fleet* units locked in mortal combat with mercenaries?! Insane! Yet it was happening, and Brigadier Keita's briefing echoed in her ears. If the mercenaries were here to engage pirates, then those Fleet units must *be* pirates, for no engagement this close and brutal could be a mistake. Both sides had to know exactly who they were fighting . . . didn't they?

Tsushima was the lead ship of the task force, already approaching SLAM range of the fighting, but Captain Wu held her fire. Even if she'd been certain what was going on, only a lunatic would fire SLAMs into that tight-packed boil of ships, for she would be as likely to kill friends as enemies. But what was that one ship doing so far behind the melee? It was moving at preposterous speed, overhauling the others, but something about its drive signature . . .

"Captain! That's an *alpha synth*!" her plotting officer said suddenly, and Wu's face went white. There were no Fleet alpha synths in this sector; the only two previously assigned to it had been ordered out so that there could be no confusion.

Wu swallowed a bitter curse and looked at her plot. She'd heard the gossip, knew how close Keita and that Cadre major, Cateau, were to Alicia DeVries, but Keita's flagship was ten light-minutes astern of her. DeVries would vanish into the maelstrom in half the time it would take to pass the buck to him, and when she did, *Tsushima* could no longer fire her SLAMs in pursuit.

She didn't want to do this. No Fleet officer did. She knew each of them had prayed that he or she wouldn't be the one it fell to. But she was here, and the order still stood.

* * *

<*SLAMs, Alley!* SLAMs!>

Megarea's shriek of warning—small and faint, almost lost in her hunger—touched some last fragment of reason. Alicia saw the SLAMs racing after her, and that sliver of sanity roused, intellect fighting instinct run mad.

Tisiphone hurled herself into the tiny flaw in the hurricane, and Alicia jerked back in her command chair, gasping as the Fury smashed through to her. The terrible roaring eased, and understanding filled her.

"Break off, Megarea." She choked the words out, thoughts as clumsy as her thick tongue. She clung to her guttering sanity by her fingernails, feeling the blood-sick chaos reaching for her yet again.

"Evasion course. Wormhole out," she gasped, fighting for every word, and reached for the only escape from her madness. "Tisiphone, *put me out!*" she screamed, and slithered from her chair as the Fury clubbed her unconscious.

Chapter Thirty-three

A broken behemoth drifted against pinprick stars, flanks ripped and torn, and Simon Monkoto sat on his flag bridge and glared at its image.

He turned his head to glower at the man beside him. Ferhat Ben Belkassem's dark face was pale from the carnage, but he'd been the first to note the hole in *Procyon*'s fire where an entire quadrant's batteries had been blown away, and Monkoto had yielded to his appeal to hold the SLAMs.

He still didn't know why he had. They'd have to destroy it sooner or later—why risk his people on the O Branch inspector's whim? But he'd taken *Audacious* into the hole and worked his way along the dreadnought's hull, and there'd been something sensual in the slow, brutal destruction of *Procyon*'s weapons, in the lingering murder of her crew's hope.

His eyes returned to the main plot, still bemused by what it showed. Thirty Imperial Fleet ships, eighteen of them battle-cruisers. They'd been a more than welcome help, but the mercenaries' losses had still been horrendous. *Assassin*, three of nine battle-cruisers, four of seven heavy cruisers. . . . The butcher's bill had been proportionately lighter among the destroyers and light cruisers, but the total was agonizing, especially for mercenaries who lacked the resources of planetary navies.

Yet none of the renegade fleet had escaped, and only two destroyers had surrendered. The mass murders on Ringbolt—yes, and Elysium—were avenged . . or would be, when *Procyon* finally died.

A com signal chimed, and he hid a flicker of surprise as he recognized his caller's craggy face.

"Admiral Monkoto," a voice rumbled, "I am Brigadier Sir Arthur Keita, Imperial Cadre. Please accept my thanks on behalf of His Majesty. I am certain His Majesty will wish to personally express his own gratitude to you and all your people in the very near future. The Empire is in your debt."

"Thank you, Sir Arthur." Monkoto's heart rose, despite the pain of his losses. Sir Arthur Keita was not known for meaningless praise. When he spoke, it was with Seamus II's voice, and the Terran Empire paid its debts.

"I also wish to thank you for not destroying that dreadnought." Keita's face hardened. "We want its crew, Admiral. We want them badly."

"I also want them, Sir Arthur." Monkoto's voice took on the steely edge of a file.

"I understand, and we intend to give you the justice you and your people deserve, but we need live prisoners for interrogation."

"That's what Inspector Ben Belkassem said," Monkoto acknowledged, and Keita's tight face eased just a bit.

"So he *is* with you. Good! And he's right, Admiral Monkoto."

"Fine, but how do you intend to collect them? We've pulled most of their teeth and disabled their shield generator, but they have to know what the courts have waiting for them. Do you really think they'll surrender?"

"Some of them will," Keita said with flat, grim finality. "I've got an entire battalion of Cadre drop commandos over here, Admiral. I believe we can pry them out of their shell."

"Drop com—" Monkoto closed his mouth with a snap. A *battalion?* For just a moment he felt a shiver of hungry sympathy for the bastards aboard that hulk. He shook himself and cleared his throat.

"I imagine you can, Sir Arthur, as long as they don't blow their power plants and take your people with them."

"They won't," Keita said. "Watch your plot, Admiral."

Monkoto's eyes dropped to the display as four battle-cruisers moved towards *Procyon.* For a moment he thought they were about to launch assault shuttles, but they didn't. Keita had something no one else did—the complete blueprints for a *Capella*-class dreadnought—and the battle-cruisers' short-range batteries stabbed into *Procyon*'s hull. It was over in less than two seconds; long before the renegades could have realized what was happening, every one of *Procyon*'s fusion plants had become an incandescent ruin.

"As I say, Admiral," Keita said with cold satisfaction, "they won't be blowing those plants." He paused a moment, then nodded as if to himself. "Another thing, Admiral. I don't know if it'll be possible to salvage that ship. If it is, however, she's yours. My word on it."

Monkoto sucked in in astonishment. Badly wrecked as *Procyon* was, she was far from beyond repair if a replacement Fasset drive could be cobbled up, and the thought of adding that eight-million-tonne monster to his fleet . . .

"But now," Keita said more briskly, "my people have a job to do. I'll speak with you again later, Admiral."

Tannis Cateau closed her armor's visor. The soft "shussssh" of a solid seal answered her, and she checked her battle-rifle's servos. Many drop commandos preferred plasma guns or lasers for vacuum. Energy weapons weren't very popular in atmosphere, where their range was drastically reduced, and even in vacuum a well-timed aerosol grenade did bad things to lasers, but the laser's lack of recoil made it popular in zero-G. Of course, lasers had horrific power requirements, and plasguns could hardly be called pinpoint weapons, especially in the confines of a starship's passages, yet most seemed to feel their advantages more than compensated. Not Tannis. The battle-rifle was a precision instrument, and using her armor's thrusters to offset the recoil had become instinct years ago.

She shook off her woolgathering thoughts with a wry smile. Her brain always insisted on wandering in the last moments before action was joined . . . unlike Alley, who only seemed to focus to an even greater intensity.

She pushed that memory away quickly and watched the troop bay repeater as the assault shuttles formed up. At least Alley had gotten away. She hadn't been killed by her own, and there was still hope—

The last shuttle slid into place, thrusters flared, and they swooped across the kilometers towards *Procyon*'s savaged hulk.

Monkoto felt his stomach tighten as the silvery minnows darted towards the wounded leviathan. They were such tiny things—little larger than an old pre-space airliner—and if he'd missed even a single energy mount. . . .

But no weapons fired. The *Bengals* snarled down on their prey, belly-mounted tractors snugged them in tight, and hatches opened.

Tannis ducked instinctively and swore as a blast of penetrators spanged off her armor. One of her headquarters section reared up between her and the fire, staggering back a meter as the heavy-density projectiles slammed into him. They were from a standard combat rifle, and fiery ricochets bounced and leapt as his armor shrugged them aside. His weapon rose with the deadly economy of tick-enhanced reactions, and Tannis winced as a gout of plasma spewed up the passage, silent in the vacuum. The rifleman vanished—along with twelve meters of bulkhead.

"Prisoners, Jake," she said mildly. "We want *prisoners*."

"Sorry, ma'am." The hulking commando, a third again Tannis's height, sounded almost sheepish. "Got carried away."

"Yeah, well, thanks anyway." Her lip twitched as her team picked its way past the glowing wound. Jake Adams sometimes forgot how drastic the consequences could be when he got "carried away." Combat armor gave anyone the "muscle" to use truly heavy weapons; Adams also had the size, and his "plasma rifle" was the equal of a shuttle cannon.

Her amusement faded as she focused on her display. Boarding assaults were always ugly. Even though they knew every nook and cranny of their battlefield, there were still too many places for die-hards to hole up, and no pirate had any illusion about his or her ultimate fate. Her HQ section's circuitous route had been planned to reach their real objective while her other people distracted the enemy rank and file to clear her path. They were doing it . . . but they were taking losses despite their equipment.

She peered about her, checking corridor traffic markings against her display, and grunted in satisfaction.

"Beta Company, Ramrod has cleared route to Tango-Four-Niner-Lima down Zebra-Three. Form on my beacon." Captain Schultz's acknowledgment came back, and she tucked away her display and swung her rifle into fighting position.

"All right, Jake. You see that hatch down there?"

"Yes, ma'am. I surely do."

"Well, this piece of shit's flag bridge is on the other side of it." She smiled up at him and waved a hand with the tick's dance-like fluidity. "Feel free to get carried away."

James Howell crouched behind his useless console in his vac suit. The laser carbine was alien to him, clumsy-feeling in his grip, but he waited almost calmly, his mind empty. There was no room for hope, and no point in fear. He was going to die, and whether it happened in a few minutes or a few hours—or even in a few months, if he was taken alive—didn't matter. He'd betrayed all he was sworn to uphold to play the great game; now he'd lost, and his own stupidity had brought all of his people to the same degrading end.

Echoes of combat quivered through the steel about him, and he glanced across the bridge at Rachel Shu, small and deadly behind a bipod-mounted plasma rifle. Others crouched with them, waiting, eyes locked on the hatch. Any moment now—

The heavily-armored hatch shuddered. A meter-wide circle flared instantly white-hot, and a tongue of plasma licked through it, a searing column that leapt across the bridge. Someone got in its way and died without time even to scream as the heart of a sun embraced him.

Another bolt of fury blew the hatch from its frame in half-molten wreckage, and the first drop commando charged through it.

Howell braced his laser across the console and squeezed the stud. A dozen others were firing, flaying the armored figure with tungsten penetrators and deadly beams of light, and the invader staggered. His battle-rifle flashed white fire as he went down—an unaimed spray of heavy-caliber penetrators that chewed up consoles and people with equal contempt—and then Rachel's plasgun fired, and what hit the deck was a less than human cinder.

Tannis Cateau swallowed a curse as her point man went down. It was her fault. Other teams had already taken heavy fire; hers hadn't, and she'd let herself grow overconfident. Now she slid forward, hugging the bulkhead and trying not to think about Adams and his monster gun behind her. Her racing mind rode the tick, and she reached out through her armor sensors. She couldn't get a clear reading, but with a little help . . .

A hand signal brought her HQ grenadier up on the other side of the passage, and she unhooked a small device from her armor harness, then nodded.

The grenadier opened up on full auto. It was a mixed belt, mostly smoke and pyrotechnics with only a handful of light HE, for they wanted prisoners, but it did its job. Anyone beyond that hatch was hugging the deck as flash-bangs and anti-laser vapor exploded in his face when she tossed the sensor remote with a smooth, underhand motion. It bounced across the deck, unnoticed under the cover of the grenades, and she smiled the cold, distant smile of a drop commando as she keyed it alive.

Ah! She oriented her remote perspective, tallying threat sources and taking careful note of the plasma rifle, then nodded to the grenadier a second time. He ripped off another burst; then Tannis Cateau flowed into the hatchway with the uncoiling deadliness of a bushmaster, and her battle-rifle's powered mounting was an extension of her own nerves. Her target was invisible behind the last of the grenade bursts, but the rifle rose without an instant's waste motion, and she squeezed off a five-shot burst of twenty-millimeter caseless. The rounds left the muzzle at eighteen hundred meters per second; the ten-millimeter sub-caliber projectiles reached their target virtually instantaneously and cut its legs from under it.

Even most drop commandos found it difficult to direct aimed fire from a remote sensor, but Tannis Cateau was an artist. Answering fire ripped back at her despite the blinding effect of the greandes, and she ignored it. She knew it was unaimed; they couldn't see her, but *her* eyes were in their midst.

Her rifle was a magic wand, spewing agony and death with merciless precision, and for once there was no pity in her. Her ammo belt burned through the feed chute in five- and six-shot bursts, and the answering fire ebbed. A last spattering of penetrators whined off her armor, and she went through the hatch like a panther, already calling for the medics.

"My God."

Ben Belkassem's words hung in the sickbay air, and he wondered if they were a curse or a prayer. He sank back into his chair, as nauseated as Tannis Cateau had been as she came down from the tick.

Sir Arthur Keita said nothing, only stared down at the woman in the hospital bed. Tannis's fire had sliced away her legs like a jagged scalpel, but no one pitied her. She lay there, smiling a bemused, cheerful smile, and Keita wanted to strangle her with his bare hands.

Rachel Shu was the only member of the renegades' field staff to be taken alive. He knew he should be grateful, that no one except James Howell himself could have given them more information, but simply listening to her fouled him somehow. She carried an invisible rot with her, a gangrene of the soul all the more terrible for how ordinary she looked, and she'd explained it all with appalling cheerfulness under the influence of Ben Belkassem's drugs.

Under normal circumstances, no imperial subject could be subjected to truth drugs outside a court of law—which, Keita knew, wouldn't have stopped Ben Belkassem or Hector Suares for a moment. For himself, the brigadier was just as happy that no laws had been broken. Bent, perhaps, but not broken. Shu had been taken in the act of piracy; as such, she had no rights. Keita could have had her shot out of hand, and he wanted to. Oh, how he wanted to! But she was far too valuable for that. His medicos would cosset and pamper her as they would the Emperor himself, for her testimony would put Subrahmanyan Treadwell and Sir Amos Brinkman in front of a firing squad.

He stepped back from the bed as from a plague carrier and folded himself into a chair opposite Ben Belkassem. Tannis Cateau was a white-faced ghost at his side, and silence hung heavy until the inspector broke it.

"I can't—" He shook his head. "I heard it all, and I still can't believe it," he said almost wonderingly. "All these months hunting for the cold-blooded bastards behind it, only to find *this* at the end of them."

"I know." Keita's lips worked as if he wanted to spit on the deck. "I know," he repeated, "but we've got it all. Or enough, anyway." He turned to Inspector Suares, standing at Ben Belkassem's shoulder. "We won't need Clean Sweep after all, Inspector."

"I can't say I'm sorry," Suares said, "but this is almost worse. I don't think any sector governor's ever been convicted of treason."

"There's always a first time," Keita said grimly. "Even for this, I suppose." He shook himself. "I'll speak to Admiral Leibniz myself; I don't want this going any further than the people in this room until we reach Soissons." He inhaled deeply, then summoned a sad smile. "This may even help, in a way." The others looked at him in astonishment, and his smile grew a bit wider. "We'd never have gotten this far without Alley, Tannis." He nodded at Ben Belkassem. "Add it to what the Inspector has to say, and we may get that shoot on sight order dropped."

Tannis's face lit with sudden, fragile hope, but Ben Belkassem sucked in air as if he'd been punched in the belly. Keita turned at the sound, and his eyes narrowed as he saw the inspector's face.

"What?" he asked sharply

"Alicia," Ben Belkassem whispered. "My God, *Alicia!*"

"What about her?"

"She knows. Dear God in heaven, she *knows* about Treadwell!"

Keita twitched in surprise. "That's ridiculous! How could she?"

"The computers." Ben Belkassem's hands gestured in frustration as they eyed him blankly and he tried to put his racing thoughts into words. "*Procyon*'s computers! When Megarea took out the AI, Alicia tapped into the net along with her!"

"What are you talking about?" Tannis demanded. "That's—I don't think that would be possible for a trained alpha synth pilot, much less Alley! Even if she could, Shu just told us Treadwell wasn't in the computers."

"Don't you understand *yet?*" Ben Belkassem snarled so fiercely Tannis stepped back. "She's not crazy—not the way you thought! Tisiphone is *real!*"

Tannis and Keita exchanged quick glances, then turned wary eyes upon the inspector, as if they expected him to begin gibbering any moment, and he forced his anger and frustration back down.

"You weren't listening to me earlier," he said urgently. "I told you what she did to Alexsov. She didn't question him, she *read* his *mind.* Call it telepathy, call it rogue psi talents, call it any damned thing you want, but she *did* it!"

Keita sank back in his chair, Tannis drove her hands deep into her pockets and hunched her shoulders, and Ben Belkassem nodded slowly.

"Exactly. You may think Tisiphone is a product of Alicia's own mind—I don't. I sat across a dinner table and talked to her, for God's sake! I don't know what she is, but she's real, and she really can read minds . . . among other things. Think about how Alicia broke out of the hospital and stole *Megarea.* Think about how she tracked down the pirates, damn it!"

"All right," Keita said at last. "All right, let's grant that Alicia—or this Tisiphone—can read minds. If she didn't get it from Alexsov, where could she have gotten it since?"

"From Rendlemann." Ben Belkassem pointed at Shu. "Remember what she said about what happened to him when Megarea took out *Procyon's* AI? That was Tisiphone. It had to be."

"Oh, come on!" Keita protested. "The man was linked to a crashed AI!"

"Oh?" Ben Belkassem turned to Tannis. "What normally happens to a cyber synth operator when that happens, Major?"

"Catatonia," Tannis said promptly. "He goes out like a light."

"Then why did they have to *sedate* Rendlemann to hold him down?"

"Crap!" Tannis breathed. "He's right, Uncle Arthur—that's totally outside the profile. If Alley really can read minds now . . ."

There was a long moment of silence, and then Keita sighed.

"All right. Suppose she can—and did. Why the sudden concern?"

"If she knows about Treadwell, she's going to go for him," Ben Belkassem said flatly.

"Wait—just wait a minute!" Tannis protested. "What do you mean 'go for him'?"

"I mean she and Megarea—and Tisiphone—will try to kill him. She doesn't know we got any of Howell's staff alive. As far as she knows, she's the only person who knows the whole truth, and everyone thinks she's crazy. She thinks no one would believe her—that she *has* to get him herself."

"But she can't," Tannis said reasonably. "Treadwell's on the Soissons command fortress—she knows that."

"And she doesn't care. My God, it was all I could do to stop her from going after *Howell* by herself!"

"But it would be suicide. Alley would never do anything like that. I know her."

"You *knew* her," Ben Belkassem corrected grimly. He folded his hands tightly and stared down at them, choosing his words with care. "She's not crazy the way you thought she was, but—" He paused and inhaled deeply. "Major Cateau, Sir Arthur, there's something else going on inside her now. It wasn't there at Soissons. There's a . . . fanaticism. I saw it after Wyvern. She was fine before she found out about Alexsov and Brinkman, but then—"

"What are you saying, Ferhat?" Keita asked quietly.

"I'm saying she doesn't care about anything but destroying the 'pirates.' Nothing else is *real* to her anymore. She'll kill herself to get them . . . and she'll kill anyone else who stands in her way."

"Not *Alley*," Tannis whispered, but it wasn't a protest. She was pleading, and Ben Belkassem hated himself as he nodded. Keita stared at the inspector, and his mouth tightened.

"If you're right—I'm not certain you are, but *if* you're right—there are nine thousand other people on that fortress."

"I know."

"But could she even get through the defenses?" Suares asked.

"She already got through them once. She cut right through the middle of Howell's entire squadron. I don't know if she can get through them again. I wouldn't bet against it . . . but I doubt she could get back out alive."

"She wouldn't want to." Tears sounded in Tannis's voice. "Not Alley. Not after killing nine thousand innocent people." A sob caught in her throat. "If she could do that, she's turned into something she wouldn't want to live."

"She'll ram," Keita said softly. "She'll take the fort out with her Fasset drive. It's all she's got that could do the job."

"We have to warn them," Suares said. "If we have Treadwell taken into custody, removed from the fortress, and tell her so—"

"We can't." Ben Belkassem smiled bitterly. "We don't have a starcom, and nothing we've got is as fast as *Megarea*."

"No," Keita said slowly, "but . . ." His voice trailed off, then he nodded decisively and stood. "We do have a dispatch boat. That's almost as fast, and she wormholed out of here almost directly away from Franconia. I doubt she had time to pre-plot it, either, so God only knows where she'll come out. I'll have Admiral Leibniz run the figures, but she's got to decelerate and reorient herself before she can even start for Soissons. If we leave immediately, we should beat her there with time to spare."

"And do what, Uncle Arthur?" Tannis asked in a tiny voice.

"I don't know, Tannis." He sighed. "I just don't know."

Chapter Thirty-four

The shrill bell jarred her sleeping brain. She sat up in bed, rubbing her eyes, then glared at the chronometer and punched the com button.

"Horth. What is it, damn it?!"

"Sorry to disturb you, Admiral," her chief of staff said, "but Perimeter Tracking's just picked up two incoming drive signatures."

"So?" Vice Admiral Horth managed not to snarl. "We've got thirty, forty arrivals a day in this system."

"Yes, ma'am, but these two both look like Fleet drives. Neither is scheduled, and they're coming in very, very fast on reciprocal bearings. If they're headed for rendezvous here, they must be planning crash turnovers."

"Crash turnovers?" Horth swung her feet out of bed and fumbled for her slippers with them. "What sort of vectors are we talking about?"

"The more distant bogey's turning just over fourteen hundred lights and bears roughly oh-seven-three by three-five-oh, ma'am; the closer one is making twelve-sixty lights from two-five-five by oh-oh-three. Unless they change heading after they break sublight, they'll meet right at Soissons."

Horth frowned in surprise. Two Fleet units headed for rendezvous here and no one had even mentioned them to Traffic Control? But then the speeds registered. Twelve hundred times light-speed was moving it even for a dispatch boat, but nothing moved at fourteen hundred lights except—

She forgot her slippers and reached for her uniform. "ETAs?" she snapped.

"If they both go for minimum distance turnover from Franconia's Powell limit, Bogey One—the closer one—will drop sublight at approximately ten-forty-one hours, ma'am. Bogey Two will do the same at eleven-forty-six."

"Um." Horth slid out of her nightgown and started climbing into clothes. "All right. Alert all fortress commanders. We've got time, but I want all forts on standby by ten hundred hours. Then get hold of Admiral Marat. See if he's completed that estimate of the alpha synth's capabilities and get it to me ASAP." She zipped her blouse and reached for her tunic. "Is Admiral Gomez back from Ithuriel with the Capital Squadron?"

"No, ma'am. The maneuvers aren't due to end until late tomorrow."

"Damn. Admiral Brinkman?"

"He's already aboard Orbit One for your morning conference, ma'am."

"Ask him to join me in PriCon immediately, but I don't see any reason to wake the governor general so soon."

"Yes, ma'am."

Horth grunted and cut the circuit, and her face was worried. They hadn't managed to keep that lunatic from *stealing* the alpha synth. Somehow, even after all the fire control upgrades since, she didn't think they'd do a lot better keeping her out.

The ponderous orbital forts of the Franconia System lumbered to life and began their equipment tests. People were people, and the crazy drop commando had been the butt of tasteless jokes for months; now she was coming back, and Alicia DeVries' madness was no longer an amusing subject.

A half-crippled starship sped through wormhole space, vibrating to the harsh music of a damaged Fasset drive far too long on emergency overboost. One sleek flank was battered and broken. Splintered structural members and shattered weapons gaped through rent plating, the slagged remnants of a cargo shuttle were fused to a twisted shuttle rack, and there was silence on its flight deck. Its AI hugged her wordless sorrow, and a bodiless spirit four thousand years out of her own time brooded in mute anguish over the evil she had wrought. Neither of them spoke. There was nothing to say. The arguments had been exhausted long ago, and the woman in the command chair no longer even heard them Her uniform was stained and sour, her skin oily, her hair unwashed and lank, and her red-rimmed eyes blazed with fixed, emerald fire.

The starship *Megarea* hurtled onward, and madness sat at her controls.

"Hoo, boy! Look at that sucker," Lieutenant Anders muttered at his post in Tracking. Bogey One had timed its turnover perfectly; now it was sublight, ninety-three light-minutes from Orbit One and decelerating at thirteen hundred gravities. Whoever that was, he must have been in one hell of a hurry to get here. He was going to overshoot Soissons by almost a light-hour before he could kill his velocity, even at that deceleration.

The dispatch boat was crowded. Keita hadn't even asked Tannis to stay behind—he recognized the impossible when he saw it—and Inspector Suares had been almost as insistent. Keita didn't really need him, for his own legal authority was more than sufficient for the distasteful task in hand, but having a Criminal Branch chief inspector in the background couldn't hurt. Ben Belkassem hadn't insisted on anything; he'd simply arrived aboard with an expression even Keita wouldn't have cared to cross.

All of which meant they'd been living in one another's pockets for almost a week now, since the eight-man craft had designed accommodations for only two passengers. They'd packed themselves in somehow—and, at the moment, it seemed everyone aboard was crowded onto the flight deck.

"How do I play the com angle, Sir Arthur?" the lieutenant commanding the dispatch boat asked. "They won't expect anything from us for thirty minutes or so, but the way we're coming in has to've made them curious."

"You've got urgent dispatches," Keita rumbled. "Don't say a word about who's onboard. If anyone asks, lie. I don't want anyone knowing we're here—or why—until I'm actually aboard that fortress."

"Yes, sir. I—" The lieutenant paused and pressed his synth link headset to his temple, then gestured at a screen. Unarmed dispatch boats had neither the need nor the room for a warship's elaborate displays, but the view screen doubled as a plot when required. Now it flashed to life with a small-scale display of the Franconia System. The blue star of their Fasset drive moved only slowly on the display's scale, but a second star rushed to meet them at an incredible supralight velocity. Numbers scrolled across the bottom of the screen, then stopped and blinked with the computers' best guess.

If that other ship executed a crash turnover of its own, it would drop sublight in sixty-four minutes at a range of two-point-eight light-hours.

"Well, Bogey One's a dispatch boat, all right," Lieutenant Anders announced as Perimeter Tracking's light-speed sensors finally confirmed the gravity signature analysis. The watch officer nodded and turned to pass the information in-system to Orbit One, and Anders swung his attention back to Bogey Two. He had no idea why that dispatch boat had arrived just now, yet he couldn't shake the conviction that it had to have something to do with Bogey Two—and he knew what Bogey Two had to be.

"Jesus!" he muttered to the woman at the next console as Bogey Two streaked towards Franconia's stellar Powell limit. "If she doesn't flip in about fifteen seconds, she's gonna have fried Fasset drive for lunch."

"Are we ready, Admiral?"

"As we can be, Governor." Vice Admiral Horth sat in her command chair, already wearing her headset, and studied her plot. "I wish I knew what she's up to this time around."

"It doesn't really matter, does it, Becky?" Sir Amos Brinkman asked, and Horth shook her head with a sigh.

"No, Amos. I don't suppose it does," she said softly.

<*Coming up on turnover,*> Megarea murmured hopelessly. <*Please, can't we—?*>

"No!" Alicia DeVries' contralto was as harsh and gaunt as her face. Cords showed in her throat, and somewhere deep inside she wept for her cruelty to Megarea, but the tears were far away and lost. "Just do it!" she snarled.

"It's *got* to be Alley. But how did she get here so soon?"

"I don't know, Tannis," Keita replied. "Coming in on that vector after the way she wormholed out. . . . It just doesn't seem possible. She must have had her drive redlined all the way here."

"Should we warn Orbit One?" Ben Belkassem asked quietly.

Keita stood silent for a moment, then shook his head. "No. They already have her course plotted. Nothing we can tell them could change their defensive responses, and the truth would only disorganize their command structure at the critical moment." He glanced at the lieutenant. "Continue your deceleration, Captain, but have your com section ready. We'll just barely have the range to reach her when she breaks sublight."

Ben Belkassem looked up sharply, then glanced at Tannis. The major hunched forward, staring at the plot, and the inspector moved even closer to Keita, pitching his voice too low for her to overhear.

"Do you really think you can talk her out of this, Sir Arthur?"

"Honestly?" Ben Belkassem nodded, and Keita sighed. "Not really. She's got a damned low opinion of imperial justice—God knows she has a right to it—and from what you've told me about her mental state—" He exhaled sharply. "No, I don't think I can talk her out of it, but that doesn't mean I don't have to try."

"Here . . . she . . . comes," Lieutenant Anders whispered. Then, "*Turnover!* Christ! Look at that decel!"

Megarea whipsawed on the brink of self-destruction as her maltreated Fasset drive took the strain. Her velocity wound down insanely, dropping towards the perimeter of wormhole space, and fittings rattled and banged. Alicia felt the vibration, felt the starship's pain in her own flesh, and her fixed stare never wavered.

"Bogey Two dropping sublight . . . now," Tracking reported to PriCon. "Deceleration holding steady at twenty-three-point-five KPS squared."

Horth nodded and leaned back in her chair, rubbing her chin. Odd. DeVries was piling on an awful lot of negative G for someone in such a big hurry to get here.

Megarea bucketed through space, just below drive overload, and her velocity dropped rapidly. A vector projected itself behind Alicia's eyes, one that stretched one and a third billion kilometers to a dot invisible with distance, and she smiled a death's-head smile.

Two starships raced toward one another, converging on the distant spark of Franconia, and a message reached out across the gap between them. Even light seemed to crawl at such a range, but *Megarea* sped to meet it even as she decelerated. The outer ring of orbital forts brought their fire control on line, searching for her, dueling with her ECM, and the AI noted the changes in their sensors. She was well outside range—for now—but she was committed to enter it, and the upgrades of the last few months would reduce her ECM's efficiency by at least forty percent.

She considered reporting to Alicia, but there was no point.

"Look! She's still decelerating!" Tannis Cateau exclaimed. "Maybe we were wrong!"

"Maybe we were," Keita agreed, but he met Ben Belkassem's eyes behind her and shook his head minutely.

"Admiral Horth, Bogey One is transmitting."

"Well?" The admiral eyed the com rating narrowly, alerted by something in the man's voice. "What does he say?"

"We don't know, ma'am. It's an awful tight beam and it wasn't addressed to us—we just caught the edge of the carrier as it went past, and it's encrypted."

"*Encrypted?*" Treadwell's voice was sharp, and the com rating nodded.

"Yes, sir. We're working on it, but it's going to take time. It's imperial in origin, but we've never seen anything quite like it."

"And it's being sent to the alpha synth?" Horth pressed.

"Yes, ma'am."

The admiral nodded, then watched Brinkman and Treadwell exchange glances and wondered just what the hell was going on.

Only three of the outer forts could range on *Megarea*, but SLAMs streaked out from them, and a low, harsh growl quivered in Alicia's throat as she watched their deadly sparkles come. They were beautiful, their threat lost in the elemental splendor of destruction, and part of her wanted to reach out and embrace their glory. But she couldn't. She must dance with them, avoiding them, cutting through them to reach the object of her hate.

She watched Megarea flirt with death, trolling the SLAMs off course with her electronic wiles, flipping aside to evade the ones she could not enmesh, and the AI's pain was a knife in her own heart. Yet she was beyond pain. Pain only fed her hunger, whatever its source.

Tisiphone stood silent and helpless in Alicia's mind. It was all she could do to keep Alicia's blind savagery from dragging Megarea under and clouding the lightning-fast reflexes which kept them both alive.

She'd never guessed what she was creating, never imagined the monster she'd spawned. She'd seen the power of Alicia DeVries's mind without recognizing the controls which kept that power in check, and only now had she begun to understand fully what she had done.

She had shattered those controls. The compassion and mercy she'd feared no longer existed, only the red, ravening hunger. Yet terrible as that might be, there was worse. She had found the hole Alicia had gnawed through the wall about her inner rage, and she could not close it. Somehow, without even realizing it was possible, Alicia had reached beyond herself. She'd followed Tisiphone's connection to the Fury's own rage, her own destruction, and made that incalculable power hers as well.

For the first time in millennia, Tisiphone faced another as powerful as herself, a mortal mind which had stolen the power of the Furies themselves, and that power had driven it mad.

Vice Admiral Rebecca Horth sat silently, lips pressed firmly together, as the renegade alpha synth evaded her SLAMs. More forts were firing now, and some of them, at least, were coming closer . . . but not close enough.

She checked the converging vectors again and frowned. The dispatch boat would pass within a few thousand kilometers of Soissons on its course to meet the alpha synth, but if the alpha synth maintained its present deceleration, it would pass well behind the planet when it crossed Soissons's orbit. Which made no sense, unless . . .

She stiffened in her chair and started punching new

numbers into Tracking's extrapolations, and her face paled.

Ben Belkassem stood silent, chewing the inside of his lip raw, and smelled the tension about him. The dispatch boat's velocity was down to seventy-two percent of light-speed, but Alicia's more powerful drive had *Megarea* down to barely .88 C despite her far shorter deceleration period.

No one spoke, and he wondered if Keita suspected what he did. Probably. Did Tannis? He glanced at the major's white, strained features and looked away. She might not admit it to herself, but she must be beginning to.

He returned his gaze to the plot. Thank God he'd left Megarea the O Branch codes. At least they could talk to each other without Defense Command—and Treadwell—listening in.

"What the—?" Lieutenant Anders twitched in surprise and looked up at his supervisor. "Sir, Bogey Two's just made a second turnover! She's stopped decelerating and started accelerating again." Emotionless computers considered the changed data, and Anders gasped. "Oh my God—she's on a collision course for Orbit One!"

Tannis groaned as *Megarea* turned end-for-end and aligned her Fasset drive on the point in space Orbit One would reach in forty-two minutes and sixteen seconds. It turned the drive into a shield against the heavier fire of the inner fortress ring—and at the moment she reached Orbit One, the alpha synth would have regained virtually all the velocity she'd lost. Alicia would be moving at .985 C when she rammed.

Fifty-seven minutes after it had been sent, Keita's desperate message converged with *Megarea*'s receivers.

Alicia looked up incuriously as a com screen blinked to life. She recognized the face, but the person who had known and respected—even loved—that man was dead, and the powerful voice meant less than the brutal vibration lashing *Megarea*'s over-stressed hull.

"Alley, I know what you're doing," the voice said, "but you don't have to. We have independent confirmation, Alley; we know who you're after, and I swear we'll get him. You've done enough—now you have to break off." Sir Arthur Keita's eyes pled with her from the screen and his voice was raw with pain yet soft. "*Please*, Alley. Break off. You don't have to kill nine thousand people. Don't turn yourself into the very thing you hate."

<Alley?> It was Megarea's pleading mental voice. *<Alley, they know about Treadwell. You don't have to—>*

"It doesn't matter! They knew about Watts and let the bastard live!"

<But Uncle Arthur's given you his word! Please, *Alley! Don't make me help you kill yourself!>*

Alicia only snarled in response. She turned her eyes from the screen where Keita's face still begged her to relent. She closed her ears to his voice, and deep at her very core, where even she could no longer hear it, a lost soul sobbed in torment. She locked her attention on Orbit One, ignoring the SLAMs still flashing towards her. All that mattered was that distant sphere of battle steel. Her smoking bloodlust craved the destruction to come—and the last, dying fragment of the person she once had been embraced it as her only escape from what she had become.

"She's not breaking off," Tannis whispered, and Keita nodded. Ten minutes had passed since Alicia must have received their message, and *Megarea* held her course unflinchingly. He glanced at the plot. The dispatch boat had crossed Soisson's orbit eleven minutes ago, and the range to *Megarea* had fallen to thirty light-minutes. The handful of warships in the system were converging on the alpha synth, but none of them could reach her in time.

He closed his eyes, then turned to the dispatch boat's commander.

"I need two volunteers. One in the engine room and one on the helm. Put the rest of your people into your shuttle and get out of here."

The lieutenant looked up in confusion, but Ben Belkassem understood.

"I'm a pretty fair helmsman, Sir Arthur," he said.

"What—?" Tannis broke off, eyes widening, and stared mutely at Keita. The brigadier gazed back, sad eyes unflinching, and she bit her lip.

"Go with them, Tannis," he said gently.

"No. Let *me* talk to her! I can stop her—I know I can!"

"There's no time . . . and there's only one shuttle. If you don't leave now, you can't leave at all."

"I know," she said, and he started to make it an order, then sighed.

"Admiral, that dispatch boat's shuttle just separated."

Admiral Horth tore herself away from the intensifying fire ripping ineffectually towards the alpha synth and checked her plot as the shuttle arced away from the dispatch boat's base course. It was fourteen light-minutes from Soissons, still streaking for the far side of nowhere at sixty-five percent of light-speed, and no shuttle could kill that kind of velocity. Which meant its crew must be counting on someone else's picking them up . . . and must have a very urgent reason for abandoning ship.

The dispatch boat's vector curved very slightly, and Horth swallowed in sudden understanding. Its course had been roughly convergent with the alpha synth's from the start; now the match was perfect, and the dispatch boat was no longer decelerating.

A blue dot swelled ahead of *Megarea* on Alicia's mental plot, far larger and more powerful than any SLAM. Her nostrils flared and she bared her teeth as hate boiled within her. She knew what it had to be—and that, unlike a SLAM, it possessed onboard seeking capability.

She hunched down in her command chair, eyes bloodshot and wild, but her course never deviated. She would reach Treadwell or die trying, and dying would be a triumph in itself.

Sir Arthur Keita glanced at the chronometer. Ben Belkassem had the helm. The dispatch boat's skipper had taken over Engineering, and Tannis manned the communications console. No one else was aboard, and they had eight-point-nine minutes—under seven, given relativity's dictates—to live. It seemed unfair, somehow, to be robbed of those few, precious seconds by Einstein's ancient equations, but he pushed the thought aside.

"Talk to her, Tannis," he said softly.

"Alley—it's Tannis, Alley."

Alicia's eyes jerked back to the com, and her wrath faltered. A strange sound hung in the air, and she realized it was herself, the unbroken, animal snarl of her rage. She sucked in breath, frowning in slow, painful confusion as she peered at the screen. Tannis? What was Tannis doing here?

"I'm on the dispatch boat ahead of you, Alley," Tannis said, and Alicia's heart spasmed. Tears gleamed on Tannis's face and hung in her soft voice, and a tattered fragment of the old Alicia writhed under them. "Uncle Arthur's with me, Sarge—and Ben Belkassem. We . . . can't let you do this."

Alicia tried to speak, tried to scream at Tannis to get out of her path, to let her by to rend and destroy, to run for her own life, but nothing came out, and Tannis went on speaking as the hurtling vessels raced together at a closing speed one and a half times that of light.

"Please, Alley," Tannis begged. "We know the truth. Uncle Arthur knows. We've brought the warrants with us. We'll get him, Alley—I swear we will. Don't do this. Don't make us kill you."

Agony stabbed Alicia. She wanted to tell Tannis it was all right, that she *had* to be killed. Death didn't twist her with anguish and startle tears back into her glaring eyes at last. It was Tannis's voice, Tannis's sorrow, and knowing the only way that unarmed dispatch boat could kill her.

"Please," she whispered to the bulkheads. "Oh, *please*, Tannis. Not you, too." But her transmitter was dead; only Megarea and Tisiphone heard her anguish, and Tannis drew a deep breath on her com screen.

"All right, Alley," she whispered. "At least it won't be a stranger."

Alicia DeVries staggered up out of her command chair and pounded the com with her bare fists. Shattered plastic slashed her hands bloody, and her animal shriek of loss drowned even the howl of *Megarea*'s tortured drive. She ripped the unit from the console and hurled it to the deck, but she couldn't kill the memory, couldn't stop it, couldn't stop knowing who she was about to kill, and hatred and loss and grief were an agony not even death could quench.

"She's not going to break off," Keita whispered through bloodless lips, and Tannis sobbed silently in agreement.

Ben Belkassem only nodded and adjusted his course slightly.

The being called Tisiphone had no eyes. She had never wept, for she had never known sorrow, or compassion, or love. Those things were alien to her, no part of the thing she had been created to be.

Until now.

She felt Megarea's frantic grief beyond the barrier she held between Alicia's madness and the AI, felt it like a pale, anemic shadow of Alicia's agony. The agony *she* had created. The torment she had inflicted upon an innocent. Only the tiniest shadow of Alicia DeVries survived, and the fault was hers. She had reduced the greatest warrior she had ever known to a hate-maddened animal who could be stopped only by death, and—far, far worse than that—Alicia knew what had happened. Somewhere deep inside, she stared in horror at the thing she had become and begged to die.

Tisiphone looked upon the work of her hands and recoiled in horror. She'd been corrupted, she realized. She'd broken Alicia DeVries, shattered her concepts of justice and mercy, of compassion and honor, and even as she stripped them from her victim, they had infected her. She'd seen herself in Alicia from the outset; now she had perfected the Fury in Alicia, but *she* had become something else, and what she saw appalled her.

She fought against the paralysis of her own self-disgust. Alicia's bottomless hate and hunger hissed and crackled before her, and she feared them. She, who had never known fear, knew terror as she confronted her equal. It would be so easy to hold her hand, to wait out the last fleeting minutes and let death separate her from that seething well of power, for Alicia DeVries *was* a Fury, fit to destroy even an immortal.

But Tisiphone had learned too much, changed too fundamentally. It was her fault, she'd told Alicia, and hers the price to pay.

She paused for one blazing second, drawing in her power, and attacked.

Alicia DeVries howled and lurched to her feet, pounding her head with clenched, bloody fists. She staggered, writhing in her agony, and rebounded from the uncaring battle steel of a bulkhead. She went back to her knees, beating her face against the padded deck sole in a blind, demented frenzy, and chaos raged behind her eyes.

The blood-red ferocity of her madness shuddered as Tisiphone drove into it, and thunderbolts of raw, unfocused power flayed the Fury with spikes of agony she had never been meant to know. Fury opposed Fury, clawing and gouging, and there was no mercy in Alicia. She lashed out, frantic to kill, to destroy, to avenge all her loss and torment and suffering even if she must drown a universe in blood, and Tisiphone screamed in soundless pain under the avalanche of hate.

She could not reply in kind—she *would* not! She had said she was more skilled to wound than heal, and it was true, but this time she would heal or perish herself. She refused to strike back. She absorbed the killing blows without riposte, and drove a tortured sliver of her being towards the wound in Alicia's mind—the bleeding hole to Hell that filled Alicia with madness.

She touched it, only for an instant, and staggered as she was hurled away. Bits and pieces of her own being were ripped from her, added to the holocaust reaching to consume her, and she clawed her way back into its teeth. Somewhere behind it she heard the sobbing of a little girl—a mortal girl alone and terrified in hellspawned darkness—and groped blindly for her hand.

Tannis Cateau sat silent at the com station, face bloodless. Sir Arthur Keita stood beside her, one arm around her shoulders, and a display at Ben Belkassem's elbow raced downward, counting off the moments left to live.

Ninety seconds. Eighty. Seventy-five. Seventy. Sixty-five. Sixty. Fifty-five. Fifty—

And then the oncoming Fasset drive swung aside, clawing away from its deathride with frantic power, and Ben Belkassem wrenched his own course to the side while Sir Arthur Keita leapt for the com and began bellowing orders for Vice Admiral Horth to cease fire.

Epilogue

The elevator door opened, and Ferhat Ben Belkassem stepped onto the flight deck of the refurbished starship *Megarea*. Alicia DeVries unfolded herself from the command chair, immaculate as of yore in midnight-blue and silver. Her hair was its natural color once more, spilling over her shoulders in a tide of sunrise, and Ben Belkassem decided it went even better with the uniform than her black hair had. He held out his hand.

"Ferhat." She took his hand in both of hers, squeezing firmly, and he marveled again at the way her smile got inside a person. The fanaticism and hatred were gone, yet they'd left their mark. There was a new depth in her cool, jade eyes, a softness. Not a weakness, but a new strength, perhaps. The strength of someone who understands how utterly any human, however remarkable, can be reduced.

"Alicia." He looked around with a smile of his own. "How was the shakedown cruise?"

"Why not ask someone who knows?" a voice said from a speaker, and his smile turned into a grin. "As a matter of fact," Megarea continued, "it went even better than the original builders' trials." The speaker sniffed. "I *told* them we could increase the drive mass."

"Must have been a shock for the yard to have the ship talking back."

"It was good for them," Megarea insisted.

"Probably." His eye fell on the chair still sitting beside Alicia's, and he settled into it with a little sigh. "Never thought I'd sit here again," he said softly, rubbing the armrests gently.

"You almost didn't get to," Alicia agreed. She could talk about it now with only the faintest twinge. She remembered every horrifying moment, yet the memories held no terror. They were only memories—and warnings.

"How's Tisiphone?" Ben Belkassem asked after a moment, and Alicia smiled wryly, stroking her temple unconsciously.

"Still here—though I'm not too sure Tannis and Uncle Arthur *really* believe in her even now."

"Ha! They believe. The Emperor doesn't hand out citations—not even secret ones—to figments of the imagination. They may not agree on *what* she is, but they know she's there." He cocked his head and eyed her curiously. "Speaking of whom, I sort of had the impression she'd be . . . Well, moving on once the job was over."

<*So did I,*> a voice said wryly in Alicia's mind.

<*Should I tell him?*>

<*You may as well, Little One. I would prefer not to keep secrets from him—nor am I any too sure we could if we tried!*>

"I'm afraid she can't 'move on,'" Alicia said to Ben Belkassem. The inspector raised his eyebrows, and she sighed. "Something happened there at the last. I don't understand it—I'm not even sure Tisiphone does, really—but we both came so close to, well—" She paused and cleared her throat, and Ben Belkassem nodded.

"She stopped me somehow," Alicia continued softly. "There was a . . . a *hole* inside me. I'm not sure I can explain it, but—"

<*I believe I can, Little One. With your permission?*>

Alicia blinked in surprise, then nodded and sat back to listen to her own voice.

"At first, I did not understand what Alicia had done, Inspector," the Fury said through Alicia's mouth, and to his credit, he didn't even flinch. "I had sealed a portion of her mind—a mistake which almost destroyed her, for she is not a person to submit to transgressions tamely."

Ben Belkassem nodded, watching with fascination as Alicia turned pink.

"She attacked the barrier I had built and breached it, and in the process she accomplished still more. I was made three in one, Inspector. There were . . . connections between my selves, but I lost them when I lost my sisters. Or so I thought, for in truth, they exist still. One set I extended without even realizing to Megarea, and so we were able to accomplish much, yet I was in control of that linkage, however little I recognized it.

"But I was not prepared when Alicia forced open the other. Sir Arthur, as you know, once speculated that I was some manner of secondary personality, created when Alicia awakened inherent psionic capabilities of her own. He was wrong, but not entirely. She *did* possess such talents, latent and undeveloped but powerful, and I did not recognize them. I am inclined, as you may have observed, to arrogance. I do not apologize. It is my nature, yet because of my arrogance, I had always scorned human minds.

"That," Alicia heard "her" voice turn wry, "is no longer the case. Alicia has cured me. My presence awoke that capability to reach in through the unused link I had forgotten, and through it she tapped my basic structure. Even the best of human minds—even Alicia's—is not equal to that. I have learned much from Alicia, yet I remain what I am, and it drove her mad."

There was a moment of silence before Tisiphone resumed.

"The only way in which I might cure her madness and restore what I had stolen from her was to close the link, yet she had grown too powerful. I would have failed and been destroyed had not a tiny core of her still stood and fought at my side. Between us, we sealed the wound, but our power, our natures, were interwoven in the sealing. In short, I am bound to Alicia now. I cannot leave her, cannot long exist if I separate myself from her."

"Do you mean to say you're *mortal* now?" Ben Belkassem asked carefully.

"I do not know," Tisiphone said calmly. "With good fortune, I shall not know for many years, for I intend to take very good care of my sister Alicia."

"But . . . but doesn't it bother you?"

"An impertinent question, Ferhat Ben Belkassem," Tisiphone observed, and Alicia smiled around the words at the inspector's expression, "and the answer—like so many others, I fear—is that I do not truly know. My sister selves are long since gone. Without Alicia and Megarea, I would be alone once more, and loneliness is not pleasant. I will remain with my friends and face what comes when it comes."

"I see." Ben Balkassem shook his head, then cleared his throat. "Well, that seems like a perfect opening for what brings me here."

He laid his briefcase in his lap, opened it, and sorted through the old-fashioned parchment documents it contained.

"Let me see. . . . First, your official pardon, Alicia." He extended the document with a flourish. "Sorry it took so long. I understand there were some wrung hands back in Old Earth—especially when you kept the *Bengal*; I think they figured you could at least give *it* back. But when the Emperor awards a second Banner of Terra for services rendered, it would be downright tacky to send the recipient to prison for grand theft, however grand it was.

"Second, a legal opinion I think you'll all be glad to have." He looked at the wall speaker. "This one's for you, actually, Megarea. As you know, imperial law has always held that artificial intelligences are not persons in a legal sense because of the demonstrable fact that AIs are not only artificial and unstable but simply don't have a true sense of personality. You, however, are a special case, and the judiciary, at the Emperor's strong urging, has determined that you are, in fact, a person. As such, you cannot be considered property without violation of the constitutional prohibition of slavery."

"Sounds like a mouthful of lawyer's double-talk to me," the speaker said suspiciously. "And anybody who thinks *I'm* a slave is gonna get a Hauptman coil where he lives!"

"A possibility which, I feel sure, did not escape the judiciary's attention," Ben Belkassem said wryly. "The point, Megarea, is that Fleet is now required to officially renounce all claim of ownership. Not, I suspect, without some sense of relief. You own yourself, dear—and I brought a voter registration form with me if you're interested." He smiled beatifically. "I expect the court hadn't considered that aspect of the matter."

"Hey, that's great!" Megarea exclaimed, then paused. "Whoa! Does this mean I have to pay taxes?"

"All the rights—and duties—of citizenship are yours, dear Megarea," he said sweetly, and a disgusted sound came from the speaker.

"And third," Ben Belkassem dived back into his briefcase for a small leather wallet, "and perhaps most importantly, I come bearing an invitation."

"Invitation?" Alicia asked, and he sobered.

"Yes. I know the whole Colonel Watts affair left a bitter taste in your mouth, Alicia, but I hope some of that bitterness has eased now."

He held her eyes and she nodded slowly. Treadwell and Brinkman had already been sentenced to death, and a relentless Ministry of Justice was bringing down an amazing number of multi-millionaires and even billionaires, as well. The money that had backed Treadwell in the name of profit was no protection now.

"Good, because in light of what the three of you achieved entirely on your own, I've been empowered to offer you this." He opened the wallet, and Alicia's eyes widened as she saw the archaic, glittering badge. It was an inspector's badge—an *O Branch* inspector's badge, with her name engraved upon it. "As a free and independent subject of the Emperor," Ben Belkassem went on,

"Megarea is entitled to a badge of her own—a sergeant's, in her case—assuming you accept. Under the circumstances, I thought it might be best not to ask for one for Tisiphone."

He held out the badge and Alicia reached for it in shock, then snatched her hand back as if it had burned her.

"You can't be serious!" she blurted. "*Me* work for O Branch? What about my reserve Cadre commission?"

"I discussed it with Sir Arthur. He sees no difficulty with retaining you on active duty for indefinite assignment to O Branch. We've worked well with the Cadre in the past; there's no reason we shouldn't in the future."

"But—"

"Before you turn me down, let me point out some of the advantages. First, there's the matter of your logistics. Megarea is a free person, and the starship *Megarea*, as her 'body,' belongs to her, but operating and maintaining an alpha synth is expensive—as much as five million a year even without combat. You'd be hard pressed to show that much profit as a merchant ship, but if you join O Branch, the Ministry will cover your operating costs."

Alicia nodded but had to lower her eyes to hide the laughter in them as she wondered how Ben Belkassem's superiors would react to her bank account on Thaarvhld. Megarea had been conservative in her estimate, and three hundred forty million credits, at twelve percent compound interest, would have covered their costs quite nicely.

"But that's only one reason," Ben Belkassem resumed more seriously, leaning forward in his chair. "You believe in justice, Alicia, and you've proved how much you can accomplish."

She eyed him doubtfully, and he shrugged.

"Think about it. We need you. My God, what the three of you could achieve with O Branch backing! An alpha synth with a mind-reader for a pilot? Alley, my director would paint himself purple and dance naked on the palace lawn at high noon for a combination like that! He's even let me pick your Ministry code name." He grinned again as she raised an eyebrow. "I thought 'Fury' would be fitting."

Alicia sat back in her chair, watching his smiling face, and temptation stirred.

<*Megarea?*> she asked.

<*Count me in, Alley. You* know *it's only a matter of time before the do-gooder in you gets us back into trouble anyway, and it'd be kind of nice not to have the good guys shooting at us for a change when it does.*>

Alicia's lips twitched, and she turned to the Fury.

<*Tisiphone?*>

<*I cast my vote with Megarea. You are what you are, Little One, as I am. I feel the pull yet. After five thousand years, it is difficult to see evil and know it may go unpunished, yet I have learned to respect this concept of justice. It is far more satisfying than meting out punishment on the whim of some irritated deity!*>

Alicia nodded slowly and cocked her head to give Ben Belkassem a long, measuring look.

"I'm tempted—we all are," she said finally, "but there's one little point that bothers me. Once I start working with other people, they're going to figure out I'm talking to someone they can't see. Aren't they likely to think I'm just a teeny bit crazy when I do?"

"Well, of course they are!" Ben Belkassem looked at her in such obvious surprise she blinked. "Surely you didn't think that would be a problem?" Alicia simply stared at him, and he shook his head. "Alley, *everyone* in O Branch is crazy, or we wouldn't be here."

He grinned and extended the badge once more.

This time she took it.

continued ☛

DAVID WEBER

The Honor Harrington series: *(cont.)*

Flag in Exile

Hounded into retirement and disgrace by political enemies, Honor Harrington has retreated to planet Grayson, where powerful men plot to reverse the changes she has brought to their world. And for their plans to succeed, Honor Harrington must die!

Honor Among Enemies

Offered a chance to end her exile and again command a ship, Honor Harrington must use a crew drawn from the dregs of the service to stop pirates who are plundering commerce. Her enemies have chosen the mission carefully, thinking that either she will stop the raiders or they will kill her . . . and either way, her enemies will win. . . .

In Enemy Hands

After being ambushed, Honor finds herself aboard an enemy cruiser, bound for her scheduled execution. But one lesson Honor has never learned is how to give up!

Echoes of Honor

"Brilliant! Brilliant! Brilliant!"—*Anne McCaffrey*

Ashes of Victory

Honor has escaped from the prison planet called Hell and returned to the Manticoran Alliance, to the heart of a furnace of new weapons, new strategies, new tactics, spies, diplomacy, and assassination.

continued ☛